Maya Blake's hopes of becoming a writer were born when she picked up her first romance at thirteen. Little did she know her dream would come true! Does she still pinch herself every now and then to make sure it's not a dream? Yes, she does! Feel free to pinch her, too, via Twitter, Facebook or Goodreads! Happy reading!

Kelly Hunter has always had a weakness for fairy tales, fantasy worlds and losing herself in a good book. She has two children, avoids cooking and cleaning and, despite the best efforts of her family, is no sports fan. Kelly is, however, a keen gardener and has a fondness for roses. Kelly was born in Australia and has travelled extensively. Although she enjoys living and working in different parts of the world, she still calls Australia home.

HIS MISTRESS
BY BLACKMAIL

MAYA BLAKE

CONVENIENT BRIDE
FOR THE KING

KELLY HUNTER

MILLS & BOON

First Published in Great Britain 2018
by Mills & Boon, an imprint of HarperCollins*Publishers*
1 London Bridge Street, London, SE1 9GF

His Mistress by Blackmail © 2018 by Maya Blake

Convenient Bride for the King © 2018 by Kelly Hunter

ISBN: 978-0-263-93524-0

MIX
Paper from
responsible sources
FSC® C007454

Printed and bound in Spain
by CPI, Barcelona

HIS MISTRESS
BY BLACKMAIL

MAYA BLAKE

CHAPTER ONE

ALEXANDROS CHRISTOFIDES STOOD staring at the space where his prized possession used to sit. *Should've* been sitting. He blinked once. Twice. The tattered brown velvet box didn't magically appear, as he'd half hoped.

Somehow, despite the painstaking measures he'd put into place, the box wasn't there. There were other items missing, too. Stacks of pristine hundred-dollar bills, expensive trinkets from his personal jeweller that he'd found over the years quickly healed even the most heartbroken of female hearts when the time came for the inevitable, infamous 'Xandro Christofides' exit speech. But it was the absence of the brown velvet box that held his complete attention. The loss was so visceral he carried on staring at the empty oblong-shaped space, disbelief and icy fury building in his veins.

The only other time the box had been out of his possession was when he'd been forced to let it go in order to make the changes he needed to turn his life around. As defining moments went, that had been one of his most memorable.

It had been that or accept that the road he was taking would inevitably lead to his early and most likely senseless demise. The necklace that had dictated his family's history had formed the cornerstone of his own life. It was and for ever would be more than a piece of jewellery to him. The need to part with it the first time had made him feel just as bereft then as it did now. And it hadn't only been him. He'd felt his mother's pain then too, and felt it echo through him now.

This time, however, the loss wasn't voluntary. Or temporary. Yes, it had taken three long years to get it back the first time, but he'd known where the ruby necklace was every single hour of every day. The deal he'd struck with the pawnshop owner all those years ago had included weekly visual evidence that the necklace was still in his possession. That it was still safe and waiting to be reclaimed the second Xandro was in a strong enough financial position to do so. Sure, it had cost him an extra five per cent interest in the crippling loan he'd taken out but that hadn't mattered. Whereas the necklace had represented dishonour and disgrace for as long as he could remember, he'd fully intended it to represent something else to him. He'd made that promise with his blood and sweat and his mother's heartbroken tears. And he'd needed that visual proof that he was on the right track almost as much as he'd needed oxygen in his lungs.

He'd achieved what he initially set out to do, which was to dig himself out of an unpalatable future, and his mother out of drudgery. He'd reacquired the necklace at the very first opportunity, and while he would never be able to look at it without remembering why it was in his possession in the first place, over the years it'd come to represent so much more to him.

Every time he bested an opponent or he won a supposedly unwinnable deal, he knew he owed that success partly to the unquenchable fighting spirit of that first fierce need to succeed in order not to lose the necklace.

Except now it was gone.

A thief had taken his property from him. Someone he trusted had walked into his office and helped themselves to what belonged to him.

Since attaining the kind of power and success most men only dreamed about, Xandro had gone for a very long time without such a daring personal challenge. These days the only challenges he received, and relished, were those thrown down by his opponents in the boardroom. So he had to admit to having a hard time believing the theft had actually happened. But the empty space he was staring at was its own glaring confirmation.

As much as he hated to admit it, because to do so would be to admit weakness he abhorred, he felt as if a part of himself was missing. Not a vital part—he would never allow anything or anyone such power over him. Certainly nothing akin to the emotional distress his mother had exhibited time and again over the necklace. Or the cloak of terror that he himself had lived with for those three years, knowing one wrong move was all it would take for those with a target on his back to crucify him.

He'd crawled out from underneath that terror of being in a gang leader's crosshairs, and he'd taken his mother away from a life of danger and drudgery.

Those hard years of his youth had left scars, he knew. He'd been accused of being ruthless. Merciless. He'd been labelled cold-hearted by the lovers who were swiftly shown the door after claiming they were absolutely fine with a no-strings relationship only to attempt to tie him down after a few rounds in his bed.

Xandro never intended to forget his past, nor would he ever pine for love the way his mother had.

Nevertheless, he admitted to himself that the absence of the box was...affecting him.

He was so intent on dissecting and attempting to subjugate that unwanted emotion that he barely heard the knock on his office door.

A heavy tread of footsteps halted somewhere near the desk in his vast office. Xandro didn't turn around. He already suspected what was coming.

'He's gone, sir.' The news was weighted with wary apprehension.

Despite the neon lights of the Las Vegas Strip flashing outside his fiftieth floor window, his world turned a very dark and stormy grey.

The heart most people questioned whether he possessed

clenched, almost defiantly questioning whether he deserved it to beat again after taking his eye off his prize.

Truth be told, he'd rarely looked at the necklace lately. The legacy of hardship and heartbreak it'd brought his mother was imprinted on his heart for ever, just like the backbreaking grind he'd endured to drag himself from the clutches of the gang was stamped within his psyche.

Nevertheless, the ruby necklace was part of his DNA. Which made its loss unacceptable.

Fists clenched, he whirled around. 'Who is *he* and where has he gone?' The words felt like crushed glass scraping his throat raw.

'A senior security guard, sir. Benjamin Woods. He passed all the security tests for senior staff and, as per the company policy, we supplied him with a pass to this floor.'

'When did you grant him a pass?'

'A month ago, sir,' Archie Preston, his security chief, confirmed.

Xandro's nails bit into his palms. 'So he's had a month to plan this?'

'Yes,' came the hesitant answer.

'How did he do it?'

'The cameras show him escorting the last VIP guest to their suite at four a.m. Then he took the elevator to this floor. He was seen leaving your office fifteen minutes later with a rucksack. He walked straight out of the hotel, and took one of the taxis out front.'

Xandro forced himself to exhale. And to wait. There was more.

'We tracked down the taxi driver,' Archie continued. 'Woods only went three blocks before he asked to be dropped off. The driver says he took off down one of the side streets.'

'He knew we would track the cab so he used it long enough to throw us off his scent?'

Preston nodded. 'We're monitoring the airports and bus terminals—'

'Enlighten me as to how that will help in any way, Mr Preston, when he's already had a thirteen-hour head start?' he snapped.

'I can only offer my profuse apologies, Mr Christofides. And my promise that wherever he's disappeared to, my men and I will find him.'

Xandro forced his fingers to unclench. He had to or risk smashing his fist into something unyielding. Like the nearest wall. The need to check the safe again one last time pulled at him. But his need not to feel that gut-wrenching loss again was even greater.

It was gone. But he wasn't going to rest until he had it back in his possession.

'I don't doubt that you will. We know how he gained access to my office but not how he knew the code to my safe. However, the most important question now is: how do we find him before he gets round to hawking my property?'

Archie frowned, and scratched his nape.

'If you give me the green light, I'll hire a dozen PIs tonight to start a manhunt—'

'You can do that. Or you can find me everything you can on Benjamin Woods, and every member of his family.'

'I…if you don't mind my asking, what good will that do?' Archie asked cautiously.

Xandro afforded himself a mirthless smile. 'Because family will always remain a man's weakness—especially a broken one.' The threat to his own mother had nearly brought him to his knees once upon a time. It'd been the wake-up call he'd needed to turn his life around, to protect the one person most important to him. He'd never needed to use a man's family as leverage against him the way it was done to him, but then no one had dared to take something this precious from him either.

Xandro intended Benjamin Woods to pay for his crime

and he'd use whatever means necessary. Family was as effective a tool as they came. 'A family that breeds a thief is sure to be a damaged one. So point me in the direction of Benjamin Woods's family. I'll take it from there.'

Archie retreated after more solemn assurances, and Xandro strolled to the window of the office, housed in the most successful hotel and casino chain in the world. He flexed his fingers as his gaze tracked the many neon lights and excess-seeking humanity spread at his feet.

He hadn't come this far, clawed himself out of danger and poverty and distanced himself from his family's disgrace, only to lose the one thing that had helped fuel his ambition and success.

He knew it didn't take much for a family to fracture and break. He intended to exploit his thief's every weakness until he had the necklace back where it belonged.

CHAPTER TWO

THE RHYTHMIC SLAP of feet on the floor was in perfect time with the music. Well…almost perfect. Few people would've caught the lag, but Xandro heard it after a handful of seconds.

He'd had pathetically little as a boy—a legacy of disgrace and debt, and a life spent clawing his way out of that hell-hole had seen to that—but he'd always had music.

When his grandmother had succumbed to her weak heart in their sorry excuse for a hovel in the Bronx, his mother had taken up the tradition. His day had started with his mother's renditions of her favourite singer, Maria Callas, and ended with haunting operettas of long-dead composers. Xandro knew every great tenor and soprano, dead or alive.

He'd grown up watching endless black and white opera films borrowed from the library, and the amateur ballet footage of his own mother that his grandparents had managed to pack in their suitcase before they'd boarded the boat to New York with their pregnant eighteen-year-old daughter: the daughter with the beautiful voice and dreams of ballet that had been ruthlessly crushed by those who'd wielded more power and ambition than she had.

That bittersweet memory was the reason Xandro knew the performer was a millisecond behind the beat of the music.

But music or dance wasn't the reason he was here in Washington, DC.

The room was in semi-darkness, the only beam of illumination centred on the dancer on the stage. The auditorium was large, but only a handful of people occupied the chairs. He tracked them one by one, his mood plummeting when each one failed to reveal his quarry.

He'd flown thousands of miles to find Sage Woods, sister of the thief who'd stolen his most prized possession. Archie hadn't had time to furnish him with an up-to-date picture of her. The only one in Xandro's possession had been taken over ten years ago when the girl was a mere fourteen years old.

But even then her flawless face and vibrant red hair had been arresting enough to make her stand out in any crowd. So, unless she'd changed drastically, she should be easy to spot.

He ignored the few searching looks as he stepped to one side, waiting for the room to empty of both dancer and patrons before reaching into his jacket for his phone.

Archie had redeemed himself by locating Sage Woods in Washington, DC, in record time. But Xandro wasn't in a particularly forgiving mood.

More than what the necklace represented to him, he was reminded of what it'd also meant to his mother, and the joy on her face whenever she'd worn it—on his graduation; on the night he'd taken her to dinner when he'd signed the papers on his first hotel.

Bright moments in an otherwise dismal past that weren't unwelcome, but nevertheless deepened his sense of loss.

On top of the memories he was grappling with, the current deal he was working on had stalled suddenly. Had he been superstitious, he would've attributed it to the theft of the necklace...

It didn't help that Archie had confessed that Woods had gained the code to Xandro's safe by hacking the security chief's computer.

Xandro had bypassed Woods's parents in Virginia in favour of flying straight to DC from Las Vegas. Besides his instincts telling him he would get more traction with the sister than with the parents, the work colleagues Archie had interviewed had reported he frequently mentioned his sister, the dancer.

About to press the phone to his ear to double check Sage Woods's whereabouts from Archie, he paused as a figure clad in a black leotard and matching tights emerged from the wings and walked onto the stage.

Her flame-red hair gave her away immediately, despite it being piled on top of her head in a messy knot. But the slim figure in the picture on his phone had undergone a girl-to-woman transformation destined to stop most red-blooded males in their tracks.

Xandro froze in place, his breath trapped in his lungs as he got a first real-life view of Sage Woods.

Her long, elegant neck tapered to shoulders that were slim but perfectly sculpted. Sleek, well-toned arms swung gracefully as she walked with light, measured steps.

Her posture was exquisite, her spine straight as she moved to the centre of the stage. The moment she turned to fully face the empty seats, Xandro felt a powerful, primitive tug to his groin. He was too busy taking in her remaining features to shove the unwanted sensation aside. His phone forgotten, he continued to stare at the statuesque beauty, absently wondering when he'd last stopped long enough to appreciate such an exquisite creature.

The world he lived in provided him with an endless array of both natural and artificial beauty. But most of it came primped, polished and packaged for maximum attention-seeking effect. The woman standing before him, believing herself to be alone, wore not a single scrap of make-up, jewellery or even shoes. And yet he couldn't take his eyes off her. He let his gaze drop to her trim waist, the feline, feminine flare of her hips, the strong, toned thighs and the long, shapely legs and delicate ankles.

As he watched, she pulled a tiny MP4 player out of her waistband. Head lowered, her forehead was caught in a tiny frown as she unwound the string of the earbuds and placed one in each ear.

Xandro slowly folded his arms as she secured the gadget to her arm. He frowned with displeasure and wondered whether it was because her means of supplying the music was impractical or because he felt robbed of the ability to hear it.

Neither was enough to distract him from observing her though. Witnessing the moment she went from completely still to an explosion of movement so captivating, his arms dropped and his breath stalled in his lungs.

Xandro stood, entranced by the power and control of her motions that could only be achieved by years of dedicated training.

He wasn't aware of how much time passed as he watched her, wasn't aware of the sensation flooding his mouth until he was forced to swallow before doing something unseemly, like drool.

When his lungs screamed with the need for oxygen he finally took a heavy breath. Shook his head to clear the haze threatening to take it over.

He hadn't reached the level of astronomic success he'd never even dared to dream of without paying attention to the minutiae. With his focus on finding her and extracting the whereabouts of her brother, he'd only cursorily paid attention to the form of dance Benjamin Woods's sister specialised in. Now it came to him in a flash. She was a contemporary dancer with a ballet background.

Some of her movements reminded him of his mother's dancing. The rare times Xandro had managed to convince her to give in to the music she loved, she'd exhibited a talent that had taken his breath away.

Of course, those moments had been very few and far between, the reality of their harsh existence a dark, oppressive presence. It was why he'd treasured those moments.

The unique combination of both forms of art manifested

in incredible movement as Sage danced to the music only she could hear. Music he himself yearned to hear. If only to judge for himself that it matched her rhythm.

Nothing else.

Because he couldn't possibly wonder what sort of music was making her move so beautifully, so sensuously. Whether his mother would've liked it—

'Excuse me? Can I help you?'

He stiffened, more than a little irritated that he'd been so absorbed in his thoughts that he'd hadn't realised she'd stopped. That *he* had moved from the shadows of the doorway to the dimly lit front row and even now stood staring up at her.

Irritation grew to annoyance. He was here for one reason only, and it wasn't to be spellbound by a stranger's performance.

'Are you Sage Woods?' He heard the snap in his voice and felt zero remorse for it.

He was close enough to see her tense, to catch her eyes flick over him as she pulled the earbuds from her ears, draping them around her neck as she made up her mind whether he was friend or foe.

'That depends,' she answered eventually in a firm, husky voice.

'On what?'

'On who's asking. And on you telling me what you're doing here,' she replied.

He pushed away the stirring effect of her voice on his irritated senses. 'This is a dance company, not a secret government facility. I don't require special permission to be here.'

Full lips pursed. 'This is a private session, booked and paid for by me. There's a sign above the door that says "No audience allowed".'

He shrugged. 'Your security must be lax then, since here I am.'

Her tension mounted. Her gaze moved from him to the

door and back again. 'You're wearing a three-piece suit and a frown that says someone's kicked mud onto your favourite shoes. So unless you're here to audition for grumpy CEO in a Broadway show, you're in the wrong place. And before you get any ideas about making something up, trust me, I know all the auditions taking place in the school for the next three months. You don't belong here. Leave before I call Security.'

In another circumstances he would've admired her spunk. 'Are you always this suspicious of strangers?'

'Yes.'

'And why is that, Miss Woods?'

Eyes he wasn't sure were green or grey flicked over him once again before she raised her chin. 'Aren't you being a little presumptuous? I haven't said I am who you think I am.'

'Deny that you are and I'll leave,' Xandro challenged.

'We both know that's not true.'

'Do we?'

Her eyes narrowed slightly. 'You don't seem to be the kind of person to take no for an answer since you're still here, eating into my training time.'

'How very…astute of you. Are we ready to stop playing games now?'

'I wasn't playing,' she replied stiffly.

He strolled to the edge of where the auditorium floor met the elevated stage, and felt almost gratified when she took a wary step back. 'Good. Neither was I. My name is Xandro Christofides. Give me the answers I need and I'll let you carry on with your training.'

'*Let* me?'

'Yes, I'll *let* you.' Perhaps it was being caught off guard that hardened his tone even further. Or the unsettling knowledge that Sage Woods would have something in common with his mother mixed in with the absurd ache inside him that, forty-eight hours after the theft, seemed to show no signs of abating.

Either way, he intended to conclude this matter swiftly and return the events of the past where they belonged, locked in an emotionless safe, where his possession should've been. 'Or we can go for the less satisfactory option of you attempting to evade my answers and wasting my time, and what I'll decide to do about it down the line.'

She inhaled sharply, outrage flushing her cheeks with colour. '*I'm* wasting your—who the hell do you think you are?'

'I believe I've already introduced myself. Now it's your turn.'

'I…what do you want with…with Sage?'

'That is a confidential conversation she wouldn't wish me to have with anyone else, I'm certain of it. Unless she wants her dirty laundry aired for everyone to inspect?' he taunted.

There was no immediate comeback this time. Eyes he could now see were a dark, vibrant green inspected him with an extra layer of wariness. Her breathing was measured, but he could see the pulse leaping at her throat, the minuscule nervous twitch of her fingers.

'Fine. I'm Sage Woods. Now would you care to tell me what this is about?' she demanded.

Xandro opened his mouth to do just that. To demand to know the whereabouts of her brother. He wasn't sure what made him pause. Or what made him leap up onto the stage in a single bound to tower over her. Perhaps he wanted to look into the whites of her eyes and judge for himself whether she was as duplicitous as her brother. She was certainly daring enough.

But his actions certainly hadn't been because of the invisible pull tugging at him or the need to find out whether the creamy perfection of her skin was real or just the play of the stage lights.

This time she stumbled back several steps, her eyes widening so the green stood out in vivid, shockingly vibrant colour. Colour he couldn't immediately look away from.

'What…what are you doing? I've told you who I am.

Tell me why you're here right now or I'll—' She stopped abruptly and balled her fists.

Xandro wondered again why he was prolonging this exchange. Surely it wasn't because the woman in front of him held the thinnest fascination for him. 'You'll…what?' he invited.

'I'm not into telegraphing my intentions in advance. Take another step towards me and you'll find out.'

For some absurd reason, despite the churning inside him, he wanted to laugh. His buzzing phone reminded him that outside of this auditorium, outside of this time and place, there was a thief in possession of something vitally important to him.

And the key to finding him was standing in front of him, preparing to defend herself with a martial arts move she was telegraphing loud and clear, despite her assertion otherwise.

'Until forty-eight hours ago, your brother, Benjamin, was employed as a senior security guard in charge of elite clients at my VIP casino in Vegas. For reasons I'm yet to discover, he decided to help himself to money and property that didn't belong to him, after which he disappeared. My sources tell me you're in touch with your brother. You will tell me when you last spoke to him, and where I can find him.'

He knew his instincts to get closer to her had been right when he caught the faint snag in her breathing. No matter what came next, he now had the advantage of knowing she cared about her brother. Just as he knew that even though she tried to hide it by clearing her throat, whatever she was about to say wouldn't be welcome.

'I'm sorry, Mr…?' She raised a neatly sculpted eyebrow. 'Sorry, I've forgotten your name—'

'Xandro Christofides,' he supplied, his gaze trained on her face, reading her every micro-expression. 'Your brother worked his way up from croupier to VIP security in the last eighteen months at the Las Vegas branch of Xei Hotels and Casinos. But I'm sure you know all of this.'

Her gaze swept over his shoulder for a second before reconnecting with his. 'You're wrong. I have no idea where Ben is, Mr Christofides.' She kept her gaze on his for another bold second after her blatant lie, then stepped back. Xandro watched her walk towards the stage door, bend to pick up a small backpack before she looked over her shoulder. 'And even if I did I wouldn't tell you.'

CHAPTER THREE

SHE SHOULDN'T HAVE said that.

It had been unnecessary. And stupidly provocative. An emotional response when she should've given a calm, clinical dismissal. Just like she'd trained herself to. Bullies fed on emotional reactions. Hadn't she learned that the long, hard way as a teenager?

So why did she say that? Why had she provoked him?

Probably because she'd wanted to annoy the overbearing man the same way he'd annoyed her by interrupting her training session. The session she'd paid hard-earned money for. The *private* session she used to settle herself and regain her peace of mind. Sage wasn't ashamed to admit she needed these sessions like she needed oxygen. A successful audition was her ultimate goal, of course, but to her dancing would always be more than a career. She'd sacrificed so much to even get here.

She'd had more right to be on that stage than he had. So why had she walked away like that?

Because those silver-grey eyes and all that leashed animal power had threatened to knock every piece of common sense out of her head the moment he'd prowled to the edge of the stage and stared up at her from a position that should've been inferior, but had somehow made *her* feel small and vulnerable. Singled out. In a way that awakened disturbing memories. And yet it'd been a little different...

Or perhaps it'd been the moment he'd leaped oh-so-gracefully onto the stage and prowled towards her like a marauding predator intent on prying the information he needed from her.

Regardless of that, she should've stepped up to him and

just coolly dismissed the man. But no. Once again, she'd let her control slip, lashed out in response to Xandro Christofides's deliberate baiting.

She'd threatened him with bodily harm, for goodness' sake, when she of all people knew how destructive that was!

Sage suppressed a shiver at the unwanted memories, and hurried along the back corridor that led to the locker rooms of the Washington Performance School.

Her skin still tingled from the charged almost-contact with Xandro Christofides. She could hear his deep, rumbling voice in her ear, feel the electricity sparking from him sizzling along her nerve endings.

'You will tell me when you last spoke to him, and where I can find him.'

No please or thank you from the infuriating man. She was certain he was like that all the time, tossing orders around like confetti at a wedding and expecting people to jump.

Except she'd stopped jumping at orders, had drawn a very painful, but definitive line at being controlled. She was no longer willing to be anyone's puppet, to have her strings pulled this way or that to suit what her parents deemed her destiny. It had come at a huge cost—one she was still paying.

She wasn't about to let the enigmatic stranger add to her woes.

Good heavens, he'd been too much. Too handsome, too incisive, too...*everything*! And he'd probably seen through her half-truth.

It was true she had no idea where Ben was. They weren't scheduled to make their pledged once-a-month call for another two weeks, and the last she'd heard from him he'd still been in Las Vegas.

Dear God, Ben, what have you done?

Her brother had grown increasingly bitter over the last year, his side of their conversations turning rant-filled with constant laments on his favourite subject lately—the financial disparity between the classes.

He shouldn't have been in a place like Vegas in the first place. Not when it'd become heartbreakingly clear he was developing a gambling problem six months ago. She'd urged him to seek help. He'd vehemently denied the existence of the problem but he'd made a reluctant promise to call and check in once a month so she wouldn't worry.

She only had Xandro Christofides's word that her brother had stolen from him but Sage knew in her bones that it was highly likely to be true.

So should she have stayed to talk to Christofides? Pleaded on her brother's behalf even before she knew for sure he'd done anything wrong?

No. She owed Xandro Christofides nothing, and her instincts warned her he was the type to take a mile when given an inch. She didn't have an inch to give. Not when each day that passed was a reminder that her every inch she'd given had got her nowhere. When it'd come right down to it she'd been left on her own. Her parents had chosen their business, their precious way of life, over her.

Only Ben had been there for her. Only he had believed her.

Her loyalty was to her brother, not the boss who looked as if he chewed rocks for breakfast. Sage slammed the locker shut and hitched her backpack over her shoulder. In return for what Ben had done for her, she was prepared to stand up to a hundred Xandro Christofideses.

Except only one of them stood tall and proud and immovable before her when she stepped out of the side entrance onto the quiet side street in Washington, DC.

If she'd thought he looked intimidating in the low lights of the auditorium, the man in front of her looked downright terrifying despite the civilised bespoke clothing he wore.

Her hand tightened around the strap of the backpack as she fought a wave of panic.

Walk away. Just keep walking.

'I guess I was right in thinking you're not great at taking no for an answer. What are you going to do this time, kidnap me?' Damn. She really needed to find a way to get her tongue to obey her brain.

Brooding eyes rested on her. 'I wish you no harm. And while it's rare, Miss Woods, I've been known to accept no on occasion. What I find unacceptable, however, are lies. I know you're lying about your knowledge of your brother's whereabouts.' The words were clipped, coated in cold steel.

Icy fingers whispered down her spine, but Sage forced herself not to react with another outburst. 'And you intend to prove that how, exactly?' she asked coolly.

His jaw flexed and he seemed to grow larger before her even though he didn't move an inch. 'Word to the wise: don't toy with me. I have very little patience for this exercise. Your brother has taken something very valuable to me. The quicker you work with me to ensure its safe return, the more…lenient I'm prepared to be.'

Her mouth dried. Then she caught the tail end of his words. 'Are you saying you haven't reported him yet?' There was more than a little hope in her voice. And he heard it.

Heard it and was less than thrilled about it, if the harsh twist of his lips was anything to go by.

'No such luck, Miss Woods. The authorities in Vegas have been informed of the theft and your brother will face the consequences of his actions when I find him, but you can help mitigate the extent of his punishment by telling me where he is now.'

Her breath snagged in her lungs. 'You want me to help you put my own brother behind bars?' she whispered in a voice that felt as weak as her legs.

'He's committed a crime. Are you naive enough to think he can walk away from it scot-free?' the powerful man in front of her demanded.

She swallowed. 'I have nothing else to say to you so if that's all you're here for—'

'Are you sure you wish to make an enemy of me?'

'What I wish is to be left alone, Mr Christofides. So far all I have is your word that Ben has done anything wrong. Do you even have any proof that he stole…whatever it is you say he stole?'

'One hundred thousand dollars in cash and four pieces of jewellery totalling another hundred thousand dollars. And a priceless family heirloom.'

That last one. Sage heard the peculiar note in his voice and knew it was the last item that had brought Xandro Christofides across the country to her doorstep. She wanted to ask what it was, why it was so important to him. But to do so would mean remaining in his presence, under his control, attempting to withstand those intense magnetic waves lashing at her. It would also give him the impression that she believed him.

'I'm sorry you've lost your belongings. But I can't help you.'

Sage intended to walk away after that final statement. Head down the side street, turn left and walk to the subway station that would take her home to the townhouse she shared with six other dancers in Georgetown.

But for some reason she couldn't move. The look in his piercing, narrowed eyes wouldn't let her. The chilling message in them told her to rethink her course of action. For one blind moment, she wanted to confess that she believed him. That she knew her brother was capable of everything Xandro Christofides was accusing him of. That she would help him find Ben if he promised the leniency he'd hinted at.

The faint pain in her right wrist, the result of a fracture that had never quite healed properly, dragged her back to reality. She tightened her hand on her backpack, silently centring herself on what was important.

Ben deserved her loyalty. Always.

'Goodbye, Mr Christofides.'

For a taut few seconds he didn't answer. Then, 'Goodnight, Miss Woods.'

There was no inflexion in his response, no indication that they would ever meet again. But as she walked away Sage couldn't stop the tingling at her nape or the premonition that the billionaire hotelier boss her brother had griped about for several months was far from done with her.

It was that premonition that kept her awake long into the following six nights, even though she continued to reassure herself he had no power over her. She'd refused his demands and walked away. End of story.

Except she'd spent long hours frantically calling her brother's phone with frustrated tears brimming her eyes when her messages filled his inbox and she finally had to give up. Sleep was a snatched few hours before she had to be up and ready to head to her day job as a barista in the coffee shop attached to the Hunter Dance Company.

Sage had been lucky to land the job after another dancer had won a coveted full-time job as one of the Hunter Dance Company's performers, although it was a bittersweet one since her ultimate ambition was to win that same place as a Hunter contemporary dancer.

She didn't make the cut at the last auditions but since then she'd put in an extra five hours of training per week. She would be ready for the auditions next month. She had to be. Her meagre savings had dwindled to almost nothing, with everything she made from working in the coffee shop going to pay for food and her exorbitant rent. She needed to land a proper full-time job soon.

Because the alternative didn't bear thinking about. She had to succeed because going back home wasn't an option. She'd closed that door. Until her parents accepted her it would stay shut. After three years the painful memories remained as sharp as ever. But to stay in Virginia, waiting to take over the reins of the generations-old hotel and B & B business they ran, would've been to give in and then suffer a slow withering of her spirit.

Thoughts of her parents threatened to induce the despair she'd fought so hard to suppress. So instead she turned her thoughts to her brother.

And again her heart dipped with alarm. Thankfully, Xandro Christofides hadn't made a return visit to the Performance School. Although that had surprised her a little, her paramount emotion was relief.

Now all she needed was to hear from Ben and get his side of the story. Hopefully he'd have an acceptable explanation so they could put this incident behind them.

'Morning, sunshine—uh, scratch that. I feel like that should be *Morning, rain clouds.* Everything okay?' Michael, her co-worker and a fellow dancer, stepped behind the counter and stared at her with a frown.

Sage slipped her phone into her apron pocket and summoned a smile. 'I'm fine. Thanks,' she tagged on when he continued to stare at her sceptically.

'I'm not sure I totally believe that, but anyway, what I'm about to tell you will put some happy in your step. Guaranteed!'

'Okay, I'm all ears,' she responded, simply because she needed something to take her mind off worrying about Ben, and whether the enigmatic Greek tycoon she'd wasted time Internet-searching had found her brother yet.

'You know we were told there were only three places for the audition spots next month?'

Her heart dipped and she clenched her belly in preparation for bad news. 'Yes?'

'Well, I hear there are six spots now!'

Sage gasped. 'Really? How come?'

'Because we have a new patron.'

She refused to let hope soar. Not when this might be second or even third-hand gossip. 'Are you sure?'

Michael shrugged. 'It's all hush-hush, but the director's been locked in meetings off-site for the last two days. I hear she's contorting herself into the godmother of pretzel positions to accommodate this new patron.'

Sage frowned, the hope she didn't want to entertain, dimming a little. 'How could you possibly know that?'

Michael looked a little hurt. 'Because I trust my source. If they say Hunter has a new patron waiting in the wings, then I believe them.'

She sighed under her breath. 'I'm not doubting you, Michael. It's just that we've been down this road before and—'

'Yes, I know. Sure, last time my intel that we had a new patron turned out to be false. But this came straight from the top.'

Sage nodded but kept her scepticism to herself. Even with six spots instead of three the odds were tough, considering there were twenty dancers vying for the positions.

If Michael was right, they'd find out soon enough.

At the Washington Performance School after her shift, she practised and tweaked her seven-minute routine for three hours before she took her first break.

When the faint tingling in her wrist started again, she suppressed the familiar unease that came with it.

'If you can't stand a little schoolyard competition, how will you make it on the big stage you so selfishly crave?'

She pushed her father's heavy, condemning voice away and reminded herself how far she'd come. She *was* good enough. Her wrist was strong enough. Ultimately, she had Ben to thank for her healing too, because he was the only one who'd believed her.

A little desperate to hear his voice, she sent him another frantic message. Then, with an hour to burn until she was allotted another training slot, she found herself returning to the Internet search for Xandro Christofides.

The man was richer than Croesus, with a touch more potent than Midas if the financial media was to be believed.

Coupled with dark, brooding, drop-dead gorgeous looks, it was no wonder there were reams of articles written about him. Except most of them only went back to his early twenties, when he'd graduated from Harvard with a business degree in finance and hotel management and a business plan that had seen him become a multimillionaire within two years.

Now thirty-three, Xandro Christofides had taken that same plan and turned himself into a casino and hotel magnate, providing first-class luxury and decadence to the richest of the rich.

Before twenty-one, nothing could be found on the man, save for the rumour that he'd grown up in the roughest suburbs of New York. That explained the layer of hard ruthlessness that clung to him despite his designer clothes and feline grace.

A layer that attracted beautiful women to the enigmatic man. Picture after picture showed him with dazzling females smiling up at him, clinging to his arm, their possessiveness blatant. All while he stared stony-faced into the camera.

Xandro Christofides was a stranger to the art of smiling. Sure, their encounter so far hadn't lent itself towards affable banter, but she doubted he smiled at any other time. He didn't seem the type. In fact, he seemed impervious to anything besides making money and dating beautiful women.

A quick look through his company history also showed he was one hundred per cent owner of every venture, with no collaborations or business partners. He'd even stated as much during an interview.

'I prefer complete control. I don't like to share. What is mine belongs only to me.'

Apprehension danced down her spine. The man was addicted to control. It spoke volumes that he had travelled from the West Coast in search of Ben when he could've let the authorities or the many minions in his employ deal with it.

So why had he just given up?

Sage noticed she'd been staring at his image for five minutes and grimaced. Resolutely, she cancelled the search then returned to her training.

Four hours later, exhausted, she let herself into the townhouse where she lived. At almost ten o'clock on a Friday night the house was thankfully empty, the other dancers having hit the town. In the kitchen, she fixed herself a quick sandwich, then dug through her rucksack for the five-pound dumbbell she always carried with her. She was halfway through her wrist-strengthening routine when her phone blared to life.

She stared at the number on her screen for a startled second before she slid her thumb across the screen. 'Hello?'

'Miss Woods?' a no-nonsense female voice enquired.

'Yes?'

'This is Melissa Hunter, director of the Hunter Dance Company.'

'Uh…hi.'

'My apologies for calling you so late,' the director said.

'That's okay.' Sage stopped and cleared her throat, setting her dumbbell down to grip the edge of the kitchen counter. 'How can I help you?' she asked cautiously.

'I have news on the next set of auditions.'

Sage's grip tightened, her heart diving into her stomach. 'Okay…'

'The company's circumstances have changed a little and we've decided to bring the auditions forward. Next Tuesday, to be precise. Successful applicants will be given a place in the next Hunter Dance Company production slated for September. I know this is short notice, but if you still wish to be a part of it I need a *yes* tonight.'

Sage stared blindly into space for a shocked three seconds before her brain kicked into gear. 'I…of course. My answer is yes. To all of it!'

'Great. My assistant will be in touch in the morning with further details.'

'Thank you, Miss Hunter.'

'You're welcome. Oh, before I go, you should know that these auditions are going to be held off-site.'

'That won't be a problem,' Sage hurriedly reassured.

'Good. My assistant will require your travel documents when she calls. Be sure to have them ready. We're very pressed for time.'

'Thank you,' she murmured again. 'I appreciate it.'

'I have other dancers to contact, Miss Woods. Expect my assistant's call.' She hung up abruptly, leaving Sage staring at the dead phone in her hand.

A full minute later, the enormity of the call sank in but the smile that broke over her face dimmed all too soon when she realised she had no one to celebrate her news with.

Calling her parents was out of the question. They would have no interest in her news. Not when they'd dismissed her passion and chosen career as callously as they'd dismissed what the bullies at her high school had put her through.

'Havenwoods is your legacy. That's all that matters.'

Unwilling to succumb to the quiet despair threatening to mar her happiness, she picked up the dumbbell and finished her routine. Now, more than ever, she couldn't afford for her body to let her down. Or for any self-doubt to seep through the brick wall she'd erected around the one thing that mattered most to her.

Nothing could go wrong with her audition. Not even worry about Ben and the possibility that he could end up in jail in the very near future if the ruthless Xandro Christofides had anything to do with it.

When she woke up a little bleary-eyed the next morning Sage told herself it was thoughts of Ben's whereabouts that had made her dream so vividly about the silver-eyed magnate.

She was still trying to convince herself of that when her

phone rang. Sage pounced on it, hoping it was Ben. It wasn't. But the friendlier tone of Melissa Hunter's assistant was equally welcome. Until Sage absorbed what she was saying.

'Excuse me—could you repeat that, please?' she asked.

'I said you need to pack enough clothes for a week, maybe more. And also pack for the warm weather. Bring lots of sunscreen too. It's only early May but I understand the temperatures can get quite high on the island.'

Sage blinked. 'What island?' she blurted.

'I'm sorry, Miss Woods, but the exact destination is being kept confidential for now for publicity purposes. All you need to know is that you and the other dancers fly out of Dulles Airport on Monday afternoon. Everything else, including all your expenses, is taken care of.'

She suddenly felt a little uneasy. 'Does this have anything to do with the new patron of the company?'

A few seconds of silence greeted her question, then the assistant giggled. 'I guess the cat's out of the bag, huh? Oh, what the heck. Yes, it is,' she gushed. 'You didn't hear this from me, but the patron is investing in five years' worth of productions, three productions a year, minimum! Isn't it amazing? And if I'd known trips like this would come as part of the perks I'd have trained as a dancer myself, not be sitting here, eight months pregnant and barely able to waddle!'

Sage laughed, breathing a little easier now one question had been answered. 'Good luck with the baby. And thanks for letting me know.'

'No problem. Remember, the car service will arrive to pick you up at one o'clock sharp. Make sure you're ready. And enjoy your adventure!'

CHAPTER FOUR

ENJOY YOUR ADVENTURE.

Three days later, as she stood frozen, her mind spinning, Sage wanted to curse the effervescent assistant for jinxing what should've been the perfect culmination of her hard work.

The wobbles of the first audition had calmed by the second, the bone-deep knowledge that this was what she was born for slicing away the ever-present self-doubt. Her third audition had ended twenty minutes ago and had gone even better. She'd known it even before receiving encouraging praise from the two Broadway choreographers who'd accompanied Melissa Hunter to the Greek island in the middle of the Aegean.

As for the island itself...

The ballroom she stood in was only a fraction less enthralling when compared to the jaw-dropping beauty of the island. At first, when she and her nineteen fellow dancers had arrived, she'd thought she was severely jet-lagged and dreaming the stunning beauty of Ianthe Island.

Every room, nook and cranny of the endlessly sprawling villa revealed a stunning blend of classic Greek architecture and modern style she'd only ever seen in glossy magazines. Marble sculptures of Greek gods vied with contemporary art. Breathtaking sunsets competed with stunning lighting that threw the whole island into a place of wonder come nightfall.

The guest room she'd been shown into by an impeccably dressed housekeeper was so gorgeous she'd been almost too afraid to sleep on the four-poster bed for fear she'd ruin the pristine Egyptian cotton sheets.

None of that beauty registered now, as her frantic gaze settled on the man who'd been absent for the three auditions but had now materialised out of nowhere, her heart dropping because she knew exactly what he was doing here.

She and her fellow dancers had stood at the window an hour ago and watched the sleek helicopter fly over the villa to land on an out-of-view helipad at the back of the property. Agog, they'd all speculated as to who was on board and how it impacted their presence here.

Now she had her evidence.

Her gaze raked him from head to toe, praying he would disappear in a burst of smoke. Or fire. Or a damn blizzard. Anything.

Her fervent wishes didn't materialise. She wasn't jet-lagged and she wasn't dreaming.

Xandro Christofides was really sitting in the throne-like chair in front of her as though he were master of all he surveyed, his gaze conducting a thorough scrutiny of his own over her body, making her wish she'd thrown a sweatshirt over her leotard and leggings.

Her hackles rose higher as the unease she'd felt in DC came roaring back with a vengeance. Timings and too-good-to-be-true coincidences tumbled through her mind, and dread that she'd been manipulated grew too large to dismiss.

She tried to caution herself not to jump to conclusions about the Greek magnate's presence here until she had all the facts. But the blaring of her instincts was all too familiar.

And everything pointed to the fact that Xandro Christofides's presence here, in this place, wasn't by accident.

Sage wrestled down rising panic and looked properly at the man.

With one leg crossed indolently over the other, he stared back at her, a mocking gleam in his eyes telling her he knew the exact effect his presence was having on her. He had her exactly where he wanted her. And he was enjoying the hell out of it.

'What are you doing here?' she blurted when it all got too much and she had no choice but to take the bull by the horns or scream her frustration.

Melissa Hunter jerked up from her seat, her impeccably made-up face tightening with displeasure. 'Miss Woods, I'm going to assume the acoustics in the room just played tricks on me and you didn't demand to know what Mr Christofides is doing here!'

Sage pursed her lips hard to keep from snapping out the other dozen questions burning on her tongue. 'I'm... I'm...'

'Apology accepted,' Xandro Christofides drawled lazily, the gleam in his eyes growing by the second.

She lowered her gaze to hide her blazing need to glare, and took a deep sustaining breath.

'From the ominous rumble of thunder I'm hearing, I assume you two know each other?' Leonard Smith, the well-known Broadway choreographer, asked after a minute of awkward silence.

'Yes, you could say we're...acquainted,' Xandro offered.

The other three judges exchanged looks. When Melissa's eyes narrowed ominously, Sage's already plummeting heart dropped a little bit more.

She didn't want to think the whiff of cloak-and-dagger surrounding their travel from Washington, DC, to Greece had all been because of this.

Xandro Christofides was an indecently wealthy man with time to plot something like this just to teach her a lesson because she'd refused to answer his questions about Ben. Or had he drawn a blank in his search for her brother?

She searched his granite-hard, utterly breathtaking face for answers. All she got back was a cocked eyebrow and inscrutable silver-grey eyes that told her he'd divulge his intentions only when he was well and truly ready.

The sense of déjà vu that assailed her tightened her chest. Once again someone was attempting to control her, threatening the one thing she treasured most in order to bring her to heel for their own purposes. The bitter taste in her mouth was hard to swallow, as was the notion that she'd been foolish enough to think Xandro Christofides had given up and walked away. Even from wherever he'd retreated to after that night in Washington, he'd been pulling her strings.

Melissa Hunter cleared her throat, redirecting Sage's attention back to her. 'Since it seems you already know Hunter Dance Company's latest patron, I won't bother with introductions—'

'We will say, however,' Leonard said in a droll voice, completely unapologetic about interrupting Melissa, 'that your last audition was as impressive as the other two. So good, in fact, that I'm almost tempted to give you a role in my next—'

'Let's not lose sight of why Miss Woods is here, shall we?' Xandro interjected with a soft but deadly bite to his voice that stopped Leonard's words cold. 'She's here under the auspices of Hunter Dance Company. Any deviation from that role will result in an immediate end to her auditions. Isn't that right, Melissa?' he asked without taking his eyes off Sage.

Melissa, lips pursed, glared at Leonard. 'Yes. So try not to dangle your questionable carrots in front of my dancers before this process is over, would you, Leo?'

'Gosh, everyone's so touchy,' Leonard mumbled, but Sage caught a cheeky smirk as he winked at her.

'As I was saying,' Melissa continued, 'we wanted to let everyone know that Mr Christofides isn't just our latest patron, he's also, as of this morning, the majority shareholding member of the board of directors of Hunter Dance Company. Which means, were you to become a member of this company, you'll be answerable to him as well as to me.'

Whatever lingering hope she'd clung onto that this was all a nightmare she would wake up from any second promptly evaporated. Had her feet not stopped working in that moment, Sage would've walked away.

After years of blatant disbelief from her parents about her being bullied, followed by subtle hints that their support would only come if she gave up her dancing, she'd finally drawn a very painful line in the sand. A line they'd repeatedly attempted to persuade her to remove, until three years ago when she'd promised herself never to fall victim to mind games again.

She'd walked away. She'd chosen herself. She'd chosen the one thing that made her feel alive and gave her purpose.

Her dancing was the reason she woke up in the morning. She wasn't going to let Xandro Christofides mess with it. Even if it meant walking away. For now.

She sucked in another breath and addressed Melissa. 'Thanks for giving me the chance. I really appreciate it. Have a good day.' With a nod at the choreographers, she turned to leave the ballroom.

'Miss Woods?' Melissa called out sharply.

Sage gritted her teeth and turned. 'Yes?'

'I wasn't quite finished. Mr Christofides and I will be reviewing the audition tapes this afternoon and we will be announcing the twelve finalists at dinner tonight.'

What's the point of telling me? she wanted to scream.

She bared her teeth at him in a false smile. 'Great. I hope you find what you're looking for.'

'Thank you. I have no doubt that I will,' he replied. It might have sounded like a coolly cordial response, but his eyes told a very different story.

Xandro Christofides was far from done with her.

To achieve that, though, he would need her cooperation on some level. And she wasn't about to give him that. She was done with being manipulated.

She muttered a half-hearted response and quickly left the room. The nineteen other dancers gathered in the large reception room next to the ballroom would be expecting her to return and report on what had transpired next door. That was the frenzied nature of auditions. Michael especially, who'd also made the trip to the island, would be dying to dissect every word a thousand different ways.

Sage couldn't face it. Not when she knew in her bones that her brother's boss had staged every second of her auditions.

Once in the dressing room of her bedroom suite, she gathered her belongings. She was stuffing them into her small case when she heard a knock. She grimaced and held her breath, hoping whoever it was would give up and go away.

After a minute, the knock came again, firmer this time.

She dragged her suitcase into the bedroom and tossed it on the bed. 'Come in,' she called out half-heartedly.

She was reaching up to untie the knot she'd put her hair into for her audition when the door opened and her breath was knocked out of her lungs.

The man filling the doorway with his broad shoulders and overpowering personality was the last person she wanted to see.

Her hand dropped like a stone to her side as Xandro Christofides sauntered into the room, one side of his sensual, mocking mouth lifting in a parody of a smile at what must have been a comical expression on her face.

She unfroze when he was halfway across the room. 'What are you doing here?' she blurted, as she'd done downstairs.

'You don't recall inviting me in a second ago?' he drawled.

'You know what I mean!'

'Do I?' He shrugged. 'I think I know what you mean, but I also know that specificity when it comes to important matters is paramount. So let me try to answer your question as broadly as I can. I'm in this room because you invited me in. I'm in this villa because I own it. I'm on this island because I own that too.'

'Believe it or not, I had worked that out for myself. I

meant: what do you want with me, here, right now? We covered everything we needed to cover downstairs.'

'I'm sorry to disappoint you, but we didn't even come close.'

'Right, you need more time to gloat? Well, get it out of your system quickly. I won't be gracing you with my presence for much longer.'

She had to accept, no matter how painfully, that Hunter was off her list. But there were other dance companies out there. Several in New York that she could audition for. She'd been through worse setbacks. Her high school torturers had literally tried to break her. Her parents' lack of support had nearly broken her spirit. Sage knew she hadn't come out completely unscathed—the occasional pain in her wrist and the bruise she carried in her soul would always be a reminder of what she'd sacrificed for her dancing.

But she wasn't going to give up.

For a tall and impressively built man, Xandro Christofides could freeze in place with the stillness that a performer like her could envy. If she wasn't busy shoving the last of her belongings in her bag and wishing him to hell at the same time.

'Are you going somewhere?' he asked with a definite chill in his voice.

She gave a small bark of laughter. 'Of course I am. Isn't it obvious?' She stopped for a few seconds, the anguish of dreams dashed momentarily lancing her hard enough to rob her of breath. She fought to regroup and tugged one strap of her rucksack over her shoulder. 'Congratulations, though. I guessed something was up, but I didn't quite see this coming.'

'By *this* you mean…?'

She let loose the glare she'd withheld downstairs. 'Oh, don't play the innocent with me. Are you going to deny that you manipulated me into coming here? That it wasn't your intention all along to dangle the promise of a position at

Hunter's in front of me, watch me kill myself to get it, and laugh yourself silly before yanking it away from me? Well, I'm not going to stay here and give you the sordid pleasure. I hate being controlled, Mr Christofides, so yes, I'm leaving. Right now.'

He barely flinched at her accusation. 'You haven't got the position yet. But if you insist on leaving before the auditions are over, then so be it. I look forward to receiving your cheque before you leave.'

Her grip tightened convulsively on her suitcase. 'My cheque? What cheque?'

'Along with the confidentiality papers you signed, you also agreed that if you chose to end this process early you would bear the cost of your travel and accommodation. I can have my accountants work out the cost of first class travel from the States and your food and board on a private island for the last three days for you if you wish? I pay them enough to ensure they'll have the information for me within the hour.'

Shock tightened her insides. 'You are not serious!'

'I never joke about the small print, Miss Woods. Trust me on that.'

He never joked about anything. Wasn't that the conclusion she'd arrived at soon after meeting him?

'I didn't mean you were joking about the small print. I mean you're not serious about demanding all of that from me…' Oh, but he was. His intent was written clear on his face. 'I can't pay you back…not that sort of money,' she muttered, and had the strongest suspicion that he knew that, too.

'Then perhaps you should rethink any hasty decisions you intend to make in the name of standing your ground, hmm?' He held out his hand for her suitcase.

She gripped it tighter. 'All this, so you can what? Toy with me for a little longer? Show me who's in charge? Or is this where you apply a little more pressure on me to tell you where Ben is?'

His hand dropped. 'This is where you stop throwing a tantrum, return your suitcase to your dressing room and go downstairs to await your fate, just like all the other dancers.'

'But we both know I'm nothing like them,' she replied. He'd cornered her. And where her parents had tried to break her with their indifference, disbelief and eventual estrangement, he was threatening her with financial ruin. The ashen taste in her mouth intensified.

His gaze went to the top of her head, a peculiar fire lighting the piercing depths as he took his time to trace her face, her body down to her toes and back up again. 'No, I dare say you're not. But then every performer has the right to believe they're a special snowflake, don't they?'

Somewhere along that disturbing scrutiny, her breath had strangled in her throat. Now the subtle dig struck a little too close to home. Similar taunts had been the start of endless years of torture she'd received from mean girls because her talent had been noticed and nurtured by her high school drama teacher.

Distress at the recurring memories gave way to a spark of anger. 'I don't think I'm a special snowflake, but I am enlightened enough to question your motives where I'm concerned. Can you look me in the eyes and tell me our meeting two weeks ago has nothing to do with my presence here?'

'Of course it does. Our meeting led directly to an investment in Hunter's that I'm hoping will bear fruit for years to come.'

Sage hid her surprise that he was freely admitting to it. 'And this investment fell into your lap, just like that?' she challenged.

His jaw clenched for a long moment, and she got the distinct impression he was recalling a very private memory. 'No, Miss Woods. Nothing worthwhile comes about *just like that*. But I wouldn't be good at what I do if I didn't spot an opportunity when I come across it. Hunter Dance Company has the potential, with the right guidance, to become a great investment. I would've been remiss not to seize it.'

'So this has nothing to do with me?' she pressed, wanting a reassurance she knew would be false.

'I'm not in the habit of investing several million dollars in a company on a whim. Make of that what you will.' He strode to the door. With one hand on the handle, he turned. 'If you still intend to leave today, let my housekeeper know within the hour. It'll give me time to draw up a bill of costs before you go.'

He exited the room, sucking out all the oxygen with him.

She had no idea how much a first-class ticket from DC to Greece cost, nor did she have the first clue how much it cost to stay on a private island with a dozen staff waiting hand and foot on guests. What she did know was that, with less than a thousand dollars in her bank account, she could ill afford it.

That was most likely what Xandro had counted on. Their encounters to date might have been relatively short and sour, but it was clear he calculated his moves a dozen steps ahead before he played a single hand. He'd controlled every single move, right down to his appearance here this morning.

Almost on automatic, she returned her suitcase to the dressing room, emptied its contents back onto the shelf and stashed the case in the provided cubbyhole.

She was still perched on her bed a long while later, contemplating ways to evade the unbreakable net she could feel closing in on her, when the housekeeper came to announce that a buffet lunch was served on the terrace outside.

As Sage trudged downstairs, she realised that at no point had Xandro Christofides revealed to her just what he intended her fate to be. Just as he'd refrained from pointing out why he'd come to her bedroom in the first place.

She found out several hours later that he intended to carry on with his mind games when, with a few simply uttered words, Melissa held out a tantalising glimpse of

Sage's dream, now just one seven-minute audition away from coming true.

'You've made it through to the final twelve, Miss Woods. One more step and you could be part of the Hunter Dance Company. Congratulations,' the director announced with a toast of champagne once their dinner plates had been cleared away.

She forced herself to respond to the felicitations. To nod and smile and agree that yes, it was awesome and everything she'd worked so hard to achieve.

But Sage couldn't stop the premonition blooming that she'd just been handed her worst nightmare. And that Xandro was still very much in control of it.

CHAPTER FIVE

SHE WAS A good actress. He had to give her that.

Her smiles and laughter as she accepted the good wishes from her colleagues seemed genuine. But Xandro spotted the apprehension that crossed her face when her place among the finalists was announced. He'd also caught the brief glimpse of sadness in her eyes. As if the announcement had come with unwanted news that her favourite puppy had suddenly died. More likely it was because someone she'd wanted to celebrate with was absent. He didn't have to think very hard to know who was missing. Her brother.

He knew the feeling. He'd celebrated every successful achievement with his mother. Each time he'd taken her to her favourite restaurant. Each time she'd worn her favourite necklace. The first time he'd celebrated a success after her death, he'd sat in the restaurant on his own, attempting to hold his grief at bay. It was then he'd vowed to cherish the necklace he'd once hated so much.

The necklace now in Benjamin Woods's possession.

He should've felt satisfaction that Sage's celebration had been marred in some way. Perhaps deep down he did, but that emotion was overridden by the fury and hollow sensation that continued to hold him prisoner.

He'd thought making meticulous plans to ensure her compliance would diminish his sense of loss. Instead it'd only intensified it.

It didn't help that Benjamin Woods had proven an elusive and wily thief, continuing to evade his every attempt to locate him. If he weren't growing increasingly incandescent, he would be grudgingly impressed at the man's abilities.

But he didn't intend that state of play to continue. He had Sage Woods exactly where he wanted her.

She was fiercely ambitious, even more than he'd initially predicted. By all accounts, she'd dedicated the last three years of her life pursuing one thing only—to become a dancer with Hunter Dance Company instead of learning the ropes to become a hotelier like her parents. And, as with most people with such a single-minded focus, that was both a strength and a weakness.

Xandro took a sip of the full-bodied Merlot, meeting her furtive gaze where she stood halfway down the long banquet table in his formal dining room, and almost smiled to himself. He was marginally satisfied that she wasn't completely oblivious to his intentions. He was tired of keeping his emotions under wraps. And while he admitted that bringing his emotions into play wasn't the best decision here, he couldn't help himself.

Apart from the inconvenience of chasing his necklace, his latest negotiations with the Macau-based hotel magnate were suffering, and that displeased him greatly. If directing that displeasure at the woman dressed in a dark green dress that showed off her toned shoulders, arms and disturbingly shapely legs brought him a little relief then he would take it, he decided.

He watched her congratulate her colleagues who had also made the cut. Xandro silently observed one of them grab her in a bear hug, watching her throw her head back in laughter before punching him on the shoulder.

Momentarily absorbed by the dining room chandelier lights playing on her fiery red hair, he didn't notice the familiarity between the two until the guy slid one arm around her shoulders and pulled her to his side while reaching for a bottle of champagne in a nearby bucket with the other.

'Your next auditions are early in the morning, are they

not?' Xandro tried very hard to remove his gaze from the male hand dangling irritatingly close to Sage's left breast.

Heads turned his way. The table grew a little quieter. 'Yes. We start at eight,' a young woman at the far end of the table responded.

Xandro's gaze stayed on Sage and the man who continued to hold her to his side. 'Then perhaps you should indulge a little less, no?' he suggested. 'It's also a little ungracious, don't you think, to be celebrating in front of your colleagues who weren't lucky enough to progress to the last stage?'

Silence descended on the table. A few throats cleared. A trace of guilt crossed Sage's face. Mark or Matt, or whatever the hell the male dancer's name was, slowly placed the champagne back on the table.

'At Hunter's we celebrate our victories and commiserate on our losses together,' Melissa said. 'I'm sure you'll agree that in this business, as with any other, developing a thick skin is vital. Delicate egos and spirits that are easily crushed have no business here.'

Xandro noticed Sage's tiny flinch and tucked that morsel away. 'I agree. But there's a quiet dignity in knowing you're victorious without the need to rub it in others' faces, is there not?'

Sage's gaze returned to his, staying for a moment this time, as she tried to read beneath his words. Xandro lifted an eyebrow at her but her expression was shuttered.

'Quite right.' The British choreographer whose name Xandro couldn't quite remember downed his whisky and stood. 'On that sound note, I'm calling it a night. Congratulations again, my dear,' he said, stepping up to Sage to kiss her on the cheeks.

While the move dislodged the male dancer's arm from around her shoulders—easing the band of irritation around Xandro's chest—he found himself frowning.

The choreographer's exit triggered a hurried exodus by the dancers who'd lost out.

'I'm going to bed, too. Goodnight,' Sage said, turning towards the door.

Xandro had every intention of remaining in his seat. Melissa wanted a word with him after dinner. She clearly had more than that on her mind, but he wasn't interested in anything other than a business discussion.

But a minute after Sage's departure, and seconds after the male dancer had also exited, taking the champagne bottle with him, Xandro was striding out of the dining room. His curt, 'Goodnight,' left a very disappointed and disgruntled Melissa staring after him.

He reached the bottom of the stairs and stood there, a little perturbed at his own intentions. Why had he come out here? The next phase of his plan was already in place. He just needed to sit back and let it play out.

Except the thought of sitting back, like everything that had taken place since the theft, just escalated his foul mood and the sensation that the ground was shifting beneath his feet.

He started up the stairs, then paused when he heard light footsteps approaching from the direction of his east wing hallway. He changed course and a second later the elusive perfume he'd caught this morning when he was in Sage's room whispered through the air, almost pulling him towards her.

He found her coming out of the kitchen, a bottle of water in her hand. The hallway wasn't dark or remotely dangerous, but the way she froze, wary and wide-eyed, they might as well have been in one of the dark alleys in the Bronx where he'd been forced to fight for his survival as a young rebel. It'd been one of those skirmishes in a dark alley that had seen him end up in juvenile detention. He'd thought then that things couldn't get any bleaker. He'd been wrong.

Xandro exhaled abruptly, noting that the satisfaction he'd felt earlier, observing her discomfort, no longer lingered. In fact he was growing increasingly irritated by her skittishness around him, and by the fact that every time he was around her he recalled the darker circumstances of a past he'd rather keep under lock and key.

These days he used his intellect for mastering his opponents in the boardroom but there'd been times when he'd let his height and fists do the talking. He'd had very little choice then, after letting anger and frustration pull him down the wrong path. He'd learned very quickly that the streets were no place for complacency or soft-heartedness. He liked to think that each encounter while he'd been in the gang had been a necessity that prolonged his life, but the memory lived like a burr under his skin now, fused into who he was for ever.

The charity he'd set up—to build youth centres in his mother's name to help disadvantaged families in rundown neighbourhoods like the one he'd grown up in—was thriving. He could never wash away the dirty stain of being a gang member, or the knowledge that he'd caused fear and intimidation just by proclaiming himself as a thug, but at least his charity was helping kids like he'd once been.

And the one small satisfaction he could find in all the past mess was that he'd never stooped to stealing from anyone. Witnessing his family's pain and disgrace on that front had imprinted on him a vow never to take what was not his. There were many sins he detested but could forgive. Stealing and everything it entailed struck too close to home to forgive.

'You obviously came looking for me. Again. So are you going to say something or is this a staring contest?' Sage demanded, dragging his attention back to the present.

He shoved his hands into his pockets to keep from shoving them through his hair in frustration, and gritted his teeth. 'Has no one taught you how to tame that tongue?'

A shadow crossed her face, but she raised her chin. 'No one's found fault with it. Until now.'

He strolled towards her, noting her scent became a little

more alluring the closer he got. He inhaled again and drew in a mix of lilac and roses. Xandro found his gaze tracing her slender neck, the valley between her breasts, her wrists, wondering on which pulse points she'd dabbed the scent. When his imagination conjured up a picture of her doing all of the above he gave an inward curse. 'I find that hard to believe.'

Her gaze flicked past him for a moment before it returned to his. Xandro got the feeling he'd hit a touchy subject.

'What you choose to believe is up to you. May I go now?' she asked.

'No, you may not. Tell me where your brother is.'

Her head jerked back a little at his abrupt reply, bringing his attention up to her flaming hair. Yet again. It was coiled in its customary knot on top of her head. As he stared, Xandro was assailed with a driving need to free it, see for himself how long it was. Whether it was as silky as it looked.

'I told you, I don't know. And no amount of manipulation on your part is going to get you a different answer.'

He took another step closer. In all their previous meetings she'd either been barefoot or wearing her dancer's flats. Tonight her heels brought her a little closer to his height although she still had to tilt her head to meet his gaze. As he looked into clear green eyes, he experienced the barest rumble of the earth beneath his feet. Ruthlessly, he pushed the sensation away.

'I don't believe you,' he replied. 'If I recall, you said you wouldn't tell me even if you knew.'

Her gaze remained squarely on his—something most people wouldn't attempt when it came to face to face confrontations with him. A tiny bit of that grudging respect threatened to surface. 'That was… I was annoyed with you.'

'Really? Why?'

'You know why. You were overbearing. Same way you're being now.'

'By all means, don't hold back.'

She pursed her lips. 'Do you enjoy making people feel uncomfortable, Mr Christofides?' she asked.

'I enjoy stating, and receiving, the truth. Do I make you uncomfortable?'

Her lips might have flattened but they still drew his attention to their plump, sensual curve, and the mounting need to test if they were as soft as they looked. 'Not at all. I can't say the same for everyone in the dining room ten minutes ago, though.'

'You find what I said objectionable?'

She blinked, and her gaze dropped. 'Not exactly. I just think you could've been a little less preachy about it. You made one half of the room self-conscious about losing and the other half guilty for winning.'

'I speak my mind without seeing the value of couching it in soft words. Which brings me to my next question. Are you sleeping with him?'

Her eyes widened. 'With who?'

He waved a dismissive hand. 'Matt. Mark. That male dancer.'

Delicately winged eyebrows rose. 'Michael?'

'Whatever. Are you?' he pressed, telling himself he needed an outlet for his rumbling emotions, and perhaps changing the subject was the best way to achieve that.

She inhaled sharply. 'What business is it of yours?'

'A sexual relationship has the potential to disrupt the dynamics of the dance company, so that makes it very much my business. Answer the question, Miss Woods.'

'Or what?'

'Or I'll get the answers I seek from Maxwell.'

'Michael.'

He waited, noting that knot of irritation, far from dissipating, was tightening.

'No, I'm not sleeping with him. He's just a friend.'

His teeth ground together for a bare moment. 'And you

allow all your friends to touch you like that? Or merely those who believe themselves to be potential lovers?'

Her eyebrows pleated. 'I'm not sure exactly what you're implying and frankly this whole conversation is pointless and absurd. Who I let touch me and when really is none of your business. If you're truly worried about your company's dynamics, let me assure you that when it's required of me I'll show up and deliver one hundred per cent.'

'That's commendable, but a relationship involves two people. Should you choose to get involved with another member of the company, how would you propose to prevent an adverse fallout when the relationship ends? Dancers aren't exactly known for their level-headed temperament, are they?'

'What do you want? For me to tell you I have no intention of taking a lover who's a dancer or involved in my profession on some level for the foreseeable future?'

Xandro stared at her for a moment until, burning with the need to demand just that from her, he found himself shrugging.

Her mouth dropped open for a moment before she collected herself. 'Are you actually serious?'

'If you're picked to be part of the company, it will be a sacrifice you'll have to consider making.' Perhaps he needed to instruct Melissa to add that clause to the contract.

She shook her head. 'I can't believe I'm having this conversation with you. I'm not even a member of Hunter's yet. And we both know that if you get your way I won't be, so what do you care one way or the other who I get involved with?'

'You're wrong. The selection process isn't up to me. Melissa has total control over who makes the final cut. Your fate is entirely in her hands.'

Heavy scepticism blazed in her eyes. 'Oh, come on. You acquired a majority stake in the dance company just to sit back and take the hands-off approach? When, according to you, you believe in complete autonomy when it comes to your companies. I believe your exact words when you were interviewed were, "I prefer complete control. I don't like to share."'

He was unprepared for the very male gratification that lanced him at the thought that she'd taken enough of an interest in him to do some research.

Her self-conscious flush at his raised eyebrow almost amused him. Except her words were having a less bemused and more carnal effect on him. 'You've been checking up on me?' he asked.

Her colour deepened. 'I was doing my homework on the off-chance you wouldn't heed my request to leave me alone.'

'Good for you. Well, now you know my stance when it comes to the things I consider mine. And, to answer your question, my success comes from knowing when to allow those with requisite experience to take control. Whether you're successful this time or not, the company will give me the returns I want. It's nothing personal.'

'Now it's my turn to call bull, Mr Christofides.'

'You misunderstand. Until you cooperate with me to find your brother, my interest in you will continue to be personal. And I intend to use every tool at my disposal to achieve that aim.'

He caught the tiny shiver that raked her body at his words. Her gaze searched his for a long moment before she stepped back. 'So what you're saying is that you're coming after me whether I become a member of the Hunter Dance Company or not?'

He allowed himself a small smile. 'Precisely. You can see, therefore, why telling me what I want to know saves us both a huge amount of time and effort.' He paused when he noticed that she was rubbing her wrist. 'What's wrong? Are you in pain?'

She stiffened and looked down, almost in surprise.

Quickly, she stopped the left hand she'd been using to massage her wrist. 'There's nothing wrong. Absolutely nothing.'

The firm denial only prompted him to believe the opposite. Before Xandro could question her further she was speaking again.

'Are we done here? Can I go now?'

'Where is your brother, Miss Woods?'

Her fingers tightened around the bottle until her knuckles showed white. When her chin lifted and her gaze met his again, he knew what was coming. 'For the last time, I don't know where he is. I've tried to contact him but he hasn't returned any of my calls. His message box is full. Or his phone's disconnected.'

Since his own investigation had reached the same conclusion, he tried another avenue. 'But you must have some idea where his usual haunts are. The likely places where he could be hiding.'

'No, I don't. I have nothing else to add to what I've already told you. Goodnight.'

She stepped around him, keeping a few feet between them. He allowed her to walk a few steps before he spoke. 'Every day that goes by without my property back in my possession is another day when my patience dwindles, Miss Woods.' The good, the bad, the ugly. All wrapped up in a few precious gemstones. It was nowhere near the most expensive thing he owned, but it was priceless. 'Think on that while you sleep.'

Her back stiffened but her stride didn't break, nor did she acknowledge his warning.

He watched her walk away until she was out of sight, with a deep, dark knowledge that he hadn't admitted the whole truth to himself or to her. His interest in her was personal, as he'd stated. But it was also morphing into something else—something sexual.

For reasons he didn't want to probe too deeply—because

a part of him didn't want to find anything in common with her—he was attracted to Sage Woods. Considering he abhorred liars almost as much as he detested thieves, that was insanity. Lies and treachery had led to his family's downfall, the worst of all perpetrated by the man whose blood ran through Xandro's veins. The man he'd never once called *Father* and never intended to.

Xandro might be called ruthless, arrogant and power-hungry in the boardrooms of the most notable companies in the world, but he never misled and he never lied. His own conception had been based on lies. That was more than enough for him to have to live with.

He refused to make room for any more so, for the life of him, he couldn't understand why the woman who was blatantly keeping secrets from him affected him with such visceral hunger. Hell, he'd even found himself wondering, as he'd reviewed her audition tapes this afternoon, whether his mother would've been as enthralled with her dancing as he was. Whether she would've seen the pure exquisiteness that seeped from Sage's very soul the moment the music started. It was as if she lived and breathed dance.

All the reasons he'd stated for pursuing Hunter's were technically sound. The dance company would reap good dividends in the coming years. And yet he knew deep down that Sage was the reason for the unquenchable flame burning inside him. She'd sparked the fire the moment he'd stepped up onto that stage three weeks ago. A fire that, like a moth to a flame, he couldn't completely resist.

So what if it'd just taken this long to finally admit it to himself?

So what if it wasn't an admission he welcomed?

Xandro shook his head as he retraced his steps to his study and walked across the large room to the French windows overlooking the pool and well-lit garden.

Focused on dissecting his unwanted reaction to her, he thought for a moment that his imagination was playing tricks on him until movement from the corner of his eye caught his attention.

She was tugging off her shoes as she uncapped the bottle of water. After kicking them away, she took a long drink, set the bottle on a nearby table before taking a few steps to the swimming pool.

His breath snagged somewhere in his chest as she extended one foot and delicately dipped her toes in the water. Xandro exhaled in a mixture of gruff irritation and swelling arousal as the sight of her arched foot caused a hot little tug in his groin.

Thee mou, what the hell was wrong with him? Of all the women he could have at his disposal, he had to be hooked on this one.

He needed to turn away right now, dismiss her from his mind until the next stage of his plan demanded their interaction.

And yet he couldn't move from the window. He watched as, satisfied with the temperature, she took two steps down until her legs were submerged to mid-calves. Then slowly she hitched up her dress.

Xandro's hands balled in his pockets, the heat in his groin intensifying. He growled under his breath, thoroughly perplexed and a little disgusted with himself.

He'd dated many beautiful women, both before and after he'd made his first million dollars. A few of them even had more spectacular legs than Sage Woods. But still he stood there, shamelessly voyeuristic in his scrutiny, unable to summon up even a single image of what those other women looked like.

He rolled restless shoulders, and told himself there was a reason watching her was beneficial. After all, if she was standing in his pool, drifting her fingers seductively through the water as if she were stroking her lover's skin, then she wasn't upstairs, sharing that bottle of champagne with the friend who blatantly wanted to be so much more.

He was looking after his investment: keeping an eye on his enemy's proxy.

Xandro snorted at his self-deception. The only way he could see to nip all this nonsense in the bud was for Sage to confess what she knew about her brother's whereabouts so he could be done with her.

Which meant it was time to bring the next stage of his plan into play.

CHAPTER SIX

SAGE TRIED TO drown out the memory of Xandro's deep, disturbingly sexy voice as she went through her stretching routine before her last audition. The butterflies in her belly from knowing she needed to nail this final performance were enough to deal with.

But that voice…and those eyes had followed her into her sleep and now dogged her waking hours.

My interest in you will continue to be personal.

She knew what those words truly meant, and yet each time she recalled them the icy foreboding she anticipated had been replaced by a sizzle in her belly that was slowly driving her nuts. It was that initial unsettling burn that had driven her to the pool last night instead of going to her bedroom when she'd walked away from Xandro. That and the fact he'd caught her nursing her wrist—a telling habit she'd practised hard to overcome. Until very recently. Until Xandro Christofides had entered her life.

The door opened behind her and Ashley, a fellow dancer, entered. She looked on the verge of tears. 'Heads up—Melissa has had a personality transplant overnight. And it's not made her a better version of her original diabolical self,' she snapped, then burst into tears.

Consoling the distraught girl momentarily put a lid on her own nerves and on the late-night conversation with Xandro that she couldn't get out of her head. More than anything, she was grateful she didn't have to dwell on her body's reaction to Xandro's proximity or the evocative images that her suddenly rampant imagination had conjured up when he'd spoken of lovers and liaisons.

After her single, disappointing foray into a relationship

three years ago when she'd first arrived in Washington, DC, she'd swiftly concluded she was better off pursuing the thing she loved most to the exclusion of all else. Dating, casually or otherwise, had been placed on a back burner that hadn't been lit since.

But last night, with a few words spoken in his deep, faintly accented voice, Xandro had sparked something inside her. Something unsettling enough to disrupt her sleep. Disturbing enough to have made her wonder, for a single insane moment, what it would've been like not to cut herself off so completely from any deeper interaction with the opposite sex. Perhaps even get involved with a man like Xandro?

No. Never him.

He was manipulative and controlling. And she'd gone to great lengths to distance herself from those who wanted to clip her wings. It didn't take a genius to work out that Xandro was growing more impatient and ruthless the longer Ben remained elusive. The fact he hadn't stopped at buying an interest in Hunter's but had gone for a *controlling* interest spoke volumes about his need to control everything and everyone around him.

Even if there weren't battle lines drawn between them, she'd sought this position at Hunter's long before Xandro Christofides had come along. She'd woken up this morning determined to fight for what she wanted. If the final outcome was truly up to Melissa, then Sage wasn't going to let Xandro drive her away. Nor did she intend to lose her focus for the sake of giving in to the extra curious butterflies running wild in her belly.

She'd barely managed to calm Ashley down before another dancer entered the room and signalled to her. 'You're up, Sage.'

A deep breath and a 'break a leg' from Michael, and she was entering the ballroom where the choreographers were waiting.

She noticed his absence immediately.

The tight knot gripping her belly unfurled. But only for a moment because Melissa's narrowed eyes were trained on her, her mouth pinched in a displeased line. Whatever had put the ex-dancer in a filthy mood was still very much present. Sage was wondering whether the enigmatic Greek magnate had anything to do with it, and berating herself yet again for thinking about the man, when Melissa spoke sharply.

'Miss Woods, I'm changing things up a little. This morning we'll be testing your improvisation skills. Some routines have been lengthened, others have been shortened. Your seven minutes have been reduced to four and a half. Use that time wisely.'

Despite her nerves, Sage suppressed a smile. At least something was going her way. The churning inside her subsided as she flicked through her music selection, and set her MP4 player in the provided dock. A slow steady breath filled her lungs with not just oxygen but serenity.

Thoughts of Xandro receded.

Thoughts of her parents and their callous indifference to her bullying retreated to a small space at the back of her mind.

Even the faint ache in her wrist that she'd woken up with faded away as she immersed herself in the one place that she would give her heart and soul to for ever.

The strains of Vivaldi's operetta filtered through the room, mercifully blanking her mind of everything else but the one thing that had made perfect sense to her the moment she'd stepped into Mrs Krasinky's drama class in high school.

Her parents had accused her of being melodramatic when she'd told them dancing was the only reason she got out of bed in the morning. The alternative had been to give up and let her torturers win. She'd tried and lasted for a day. The ache of not dancing had driven her back to Mrs K's class the next day. Before she was done with practice, she'd known it was her life and her lifeline.

Ben had supported that belief. Encouraged her to nurture her talent while placing himself as a solid wall between her and their parents' escalating pressure. Even then, more than a few barbs had slipped through.

'Dancers are born, not made. If you were any good you wouldn't need to practise fourteen hours a day.'

'One day, when this frivolous whim is over, you'll regret that you didn't honour your responsibilities to this family. Don't expect us to welcome you back with open arms.'

Accepting that years of devoting her life to dancing was still seen as just a passing fancy had hurt like hell. Their actions when she'd needed them most had caused even more anguish because it'd forced her to make a painful decision. To walk away.

But she'd done so believing it was a better option than staying in Virginia to be consumed by bitterness.

At least when she was dancing the pain wasn't so bad. And she even managed to forgive them a little bit more for not being there for her. For not believing in her.

A light sheen of sweat had coated her skin and she was fighting for breath by the time she'd finished, but the joy and freedom she found in her dancing was worth every second. As was the affirmation that she was doing the right thing, no matter what her parents thought.

'Bravo, Sage. On the off-chance Melissa is crazy enough to let you go, remember my job offer still stands.'

'Leonard, you really are testing my last nerve,' Melissa snapped.

He waved her away and smiled at Sage. Although Sage smiled back, she cautioned herself not to count her chickens. She'd been down this road before, where half-baked promises were made and offers were hinted at, only to fall through in the end.

'You may leave, Miss Woods.'

'And we promise not to keep you in suspense for much longer,' the English choreographer said, earning himself a dark look from Melissa.

Sage re-joined the rest of the group on the terrace, where breakfast was laid out. She was polishing off her scrambled eggs on toast when a member of staff informed them that Melissa wished to see them again. Varying expressions of hope and fear greeted the summons.

Appetites lost, they hurried back into the ballroom, lining up as the three judges conferred for another minute.

Finally, Melissa leaned forward, her gaze slashing over the crowd before she cleared her throat. 'We've made a decision on the final six.' And, with perfectly manicured fingers steepled before her, she reeled off the names.

And, just like the night before, the news that she had made the cut, that she was finally a member of Hunter Dance Company, hit Sage with a mixture of elation, shock and dread.

She'd done it.

The single ambition she'd pushed herself to the limit of her endurance to achieve for the past three years had come to fruition. And yet the heavy stone wouldn't move from her belly.

The reason for that dread walked into the room one minute later.

'Oh, hell. Here comes Mr Storm Cloud,' Michael muttered with a grimace. 'I don't think he likes me very much.'

'I think you're overreacting,' she offered feebly.

'Really? Then why is he glaring at me right now?'

She glanced at Xandro and, sure enough, his eyes were narrowed on Michael. Sage remained silent, her focus almost magnetically drawn to the tall, lithe figure striding to the only remaining seat in the room.

Xandro was dressed less formally this morning. But although the dark cargo pants and white open-necked linen shirt were a contrast to the bespoke suit and tie he'd worn to dinner last night, the package was no less intimidating. No less visually captivating.

With his broad shoulders, rugged looks and an almost regal profile, the man carried himself like one of the many gods his homeland was famous for.

Inwardly grimacing at herself for her runaway thoughts, she dragged her gaze to Melissa—who was smiling at Xandro as he took a seat next to her and leaned over to catch whatever she was saying to him.

Sage was sure the sour taste in her mouth was due to the shock and nerves strangling her insides and not the mild jealousy the voice in her head suggested.

'Allow me to officially add my congratulations and welcome you to Hunter Dance Company.' His gaze travelled over the group, skated right over her as if she didn't exist, as if their charged conversation last night hadn't taken place, before he continued. 'I have other business matters to attend to this morning but now you're under the broader umbrella of my company, it's right that we celebrate properly. Melissa will give you further details. I'll demand your one hundred per cent commitment to future projects and you have my word that you will be well-rewarded in return.' With a flicked glance at Melissa, who preened under the attention, he stood up again. 'I look forward to seeing you all again very soon.'

Sage was trying very hard to dig out the traps behind his words as he walked out, again without acknowledging her.

Melissa sat back, toying with the ends of her teased blonde hair. 'Before your curiosity eats you alive, the celebrations Xand… Mr Christofides referred to will take place at his hotel in Las Vegas in three weeks' time. He's throwing a party for the whole dance company and you're all expected to attend. Full rehearsals won't start for another month, but until then, you'll be given routines to rehearse on your own. And that's it. Pack your bags; we leave for the airport after lunch.'

With the adrenaline high of their good news settling in, the noise levels rose. Sage forced herself to join in. She must have done a moderate job because she didn't attract any puzzled glances. In fact she made it to her room in one piece, with a promise to join everyone for lunch.

But as she undressed and headed for the shower, the smile she'd pinned on her face dissolved, leaving her eyes prickling with tears.

Her greatest achievement. And she had no one to share it with because the only person who'd ever truly believed in her was still maintaining radio silence. With his mail-box still full, she couldn't even leave Ben a message with her good news.

Hot, bitter tears fell as the jets pummelled her body. She allowed them for a minute, before she furiously scrubbed them away. She'd drawn the line at having the rest of her life controlled.

As much as it hurt to be alone right now, she wasn't about to back down from following her dream.

Helena, the affable and efficient housekeeper, was the first person she met when she went downstairs for lunch. She smiled, then eyed the case Sage had brought down with her before she indicated for Sage to follow her to the dining room.

Sage frowned, wondering why she wasn't heading for the terrace, where their lunch was normally served. She found out why when she walked in to find Xandro seated at the head of the table.

A table set for two.

He stood and muttered an instruction in Greek to his staff. The young man she'd seen around the villa approached and held out his hand to her. 'Stavros will take your suit-case,' Xandro said.

'Why?' she asked suspiciously.

'So you can sit down and have lunch. Unless you intend to eat with one hand?' he mocked.

Sage pursed her lips but, short of snapping out another fiery response, she had no choice but to hand it over. Stannis left the room, shutting the door after him.

She faced the man who, unlike this morning, was fully focused on her in a way that made those damned butterflies in her belly take wild flight again. 'Why aren't I eating out on the terrace with the others?' Already she was beginning to feel isolated, singled out with a ruthless efficiency she'd known he was capable of.

'Because I require privacy for our conversation. And also because your group left the island ten minutes ago to catch their plane back to the States.'

About to sit down, she jumped back up. 'What? No!' She rushed to the nearest window. But of course the speedboat she'd heard from her room was nowhere in sight. Even from here she could see the jetty was empty. She whirled back to face him. 'That's unacceptable. You can't do this.'

His shrug was entirely self-assured. Utterly unapologetic. 'And yet it's done.'

'Well, undo it. Call the captain. Tell him to come back. I want to leave this island. Right now.' She was aware her voice held a sickening tremble, but the connotations of what he'd expertly orchestrated had left her feeling decidedly shaky. That silken net felt even tighter.

'You will in good time, as soon as we've talked.'

She paced back to the table, her insides congealing with dread she'd managed to hold at bay so far. But alongside it came anger fuelled by the unwillingness to play his game. 'I've told you before: I don't know where my brother is.'

He watched her for a beat before he nodded. 'I accept that you don't. I'm not going to grill you further about his whereabouts,' he stated.

Her heart lurched. 'Why not? Have you found him?'

'No, I haven't. Sit down, Sage.'

Whether it was the sound of her name on his lips, or the notion that this game was about to take yet another twisted turn, she didn't know. She took the chair he'd pulled out for her and accepted the glass of water he poured into her glass.

He'd knocked her feet from under her by stranding her with him on the island, and he knew it.

'What's going on?' she asked after he'd taken his own seat. She struggled but succeeded in keeping her voice steady despite the shakiness she felt.

'We picked up your brother's trail briefly, when he bought a first-class ticket to Singapore,' he replied.

She frowned. Watching his face, it occurred to her that something wasn't quite right still. 'Singapore? He doesn't know anyone there.'

His shrug was relaxed but the look on his face was scarily rigid. It was almost as if he was barely holding himself together. 'Whether he does or not doesn't matter now. My men lost his trail again.'

Her stomach hollowed. 'Why are you telling me this? And why are you keeping me here? I can't tell you what his next move will be because I don't know.'

He didn't answer immediately. Probably because he was still caught up in whatever Machiavellian thought process he'd designed to get his own back. But then Helena walked in bearing a large bowl of salad and a platter of meze dishes. Xandro sat back in his chair, sipping the white wine he'd poured as his housekeeper dished out the food onto their plates.

Sage was biting her lip to keep from blurting her impatience when Helena finally smiled and left the room.

'Eat, Sage,' Xandro instructed, his voice a deep rumble that drew an unwanted shiver deep in her belly.

She looked down at the plate of food she would've taken pleasure in devouring had a stone of dread not wedged itself in her stomach. 'You think I have an appetite after what you've just done?' she demanded.

'All I've done is delay your departure from the island.'

'You did it without telling me. I hate being manipulated, Mr Christofides.'

He took another sip of his wine. 'Yes, you said that before.'

'Well, perhaps you should heed it because any cooperation I would've considered giving you is now gone for good.'

'Are you sure?'

Her hand curled into a fist. 'You may find that perfectly acceptable in your world, but I won't jump through any more of your hoops. Especially when you've trapped me here, knowing very well I don't have the first idea how to get off your damn island unless I swim—what—ten miles?'

'Fifteen,' he supplied smoothly. 'But it won't come to that unless you remain stubborn. And you forget that I warned you I would make use of any tool at my disposal. This is merely one of them. Now, it would please me if you ate something. Only then will we have a civilised conversation.'

'Are you serious?' This time her voice was a shaky mess of anger and hopeless frustration, the knowledge that she was right where she hated most, in someone else's overbearing control, raking raw fingers through her.

'Extremely. You have a few demanding weeks ahead of you.'

Sage couldn't tell whether he was referring to her professional or personal life. She told herself it was the need to curtail her temper and keep her wits about her that was preventing her from exploding. If she'd learned anything about Xandro Christofides, it was that even though he had a burning need to be reunited with his possession, which was evident every time he spoke of it, he was also infuriatingly patient in playing the long game.

Right now he was tucking into his meal, helping himself to shrimp *saganaki* with rice, followed by lamb and herb meatballs, as if he had all the time in the world.

There was nothing to be achieved by ranting and raving. Not when he was her only means of getting off the island.

So she forced herself to take a few bites of food, washed down with water after she'd refused wine.

When her plate was half-cleared she set down her cutlery. 'Explain to me what's going on.' Her voice emerged firmer this time, much to her relief.

He twirled his wineglass, looking down into the golden depths for several seconds before he directed his gaze to her.

'I kept you here because your phone records show that he's due to get in touch with you soon. When he does I need you to talk to him. Convince him that he's better off coming back to the States to deal with me.' Again she heard that hint of the unknown in his voice.

'You've already tried to talk to him, haven't you?'

He didn't deny it. 'Like you, I've attempted to reach him since he stole from me. He didn't contact me directly. He left a message with my security chief.'

'To say what?'

He gave a grim smile. 'It's best not repeated, but suffice it to say it's clear he has no intention of returning with my possession soon. I'm hoping you'll be more successful in getting through to him.'

'Or what?'

'Or the next step will be facing the authorities whenever he resurfaces. And, contrary to what he may think, he can't hide for ever.'

Her nape tingled with foreboding. Everything Xandro had said cemented Ben's guilt. So she forced the words that needed to be said to end this. 'So what do you want with me?'

'What I've wanted from the beginning. For you to convince him to return what's mine. I'm the big bad wealthy bastard he sees as the source of his problems. But he cares about you.'

'And so you intend to use me as a pawn?' she surmised.

'If it'll make him come to his senses, yes.'

Ice crawled over her skin as the question she'd asked

her own parents three years ago reluctantly formed on her tongue. 'What if I refuse?'

'My offer hasn't changed. The more time I waste on him, the less lenient I'll be when I eventually catch up with him.'

She balled her fists. 'He hasn't answered any of my messages or emails. What makes you think he'll take my call?'

His gaze swept down for a moment before he rose. 'Because, as of this morning, I've issued a press release stating my new venture with Hunter's. I've also revealed to a few sources who the new members of the dance company are. Your brother takes a keen interest in your career, does he not?'

She nodded because it was no use denying it. Xandro knew enough about her to know she and Ben were close. That was why he'd come after her in the first place.

'I like my privacy. So when I have news to share the media tend to take notice,' Xandro said coolly.

'So you've told the whole world that you've bought a dance company and I'm somewhere on the list of your new members.'

'You're right at the top of the list. With a few careful embellishments that will draw his attention.'

'What embellishments?'

Xandro shrugged. 'Let's just say that if he hates me as much as I think he does, the idea of you being mine will not go down well.'

She gasped. 'The idea of being *yours*? What on earth are you talking about?'

'He will know you're the primary reason I bought the company. He'll know that I attended your auditions and that you're currently here alone on this island with me. I'm letting his imagination fill in the remaining gaps.'

'Which are what, exactly?' she demanded, although a part of her didn't want to know.

'You know him better than I do. How well do you think

he'll take the idea that you and I are involved, that I intend to make you mine, if I haven't done so already?'

It wasn't difficult to imagine Ben's reaction to news like that. Her overprotective brother would hate the idea. Xandro epitomised everything Ben was struggling with. 'This was what you wanted all along, wasn't it? To use me to push his buttons?' she declared with bitterness she'd hoped never to experience again.

'It was a contingency plan, yes. Do you agree?'

Refusal was immediate. 'No, of course I don't. I won't be bullied into giving you what you want.'

He stood and walked to the window and stood there with his back to her. One minute passed, then two. The throbbing silence jangled her nerves, forcing her to her feet.

'Did you hear me?' she prompted when he made no move to reply.

Slowly, he turned to face her. The flint-hard, ruthless expression on his face sent a chill down her spine. 'I did. And here's where I too play dirty, Sage. I know you haven't been in touch with your parents for a while. Allow me to update you on what they've been up to this past year. They've made some...unfortunate business and personal decisions that aren't turning out so great for them. Put simply, they're in dire straits and the loan shark they've gotten into bed with has reached the end of his patience.

'By this time tomorrow their debts will be mine to enforce or renegotiate. How it goes depends entirely on you. Unless you agree to help me, not only will your brother end up in jail whenever he eventually turns up, your parents will also lose their precious lifestyle and their status in that charming little town they love so much, as they'll be forced into bankruptcy. So what's it to be?'

CHAPTER SEVEN

SAGE WASN'T SURE how she managed to withstand the series of emotions charging through her. Disbelief. Shock. Anger. Back to disbelief.

A thousand questions crowded the back of her throat, but she couldn't immediately form the words to challenge everything he'd said.

Her parents lived and breathed Havenwoods, the grand hotel situated in its namesake town in the middle of rural Virginia that had been in her father's family for generations. For as long as Sage could remember, it was the one thing her parents cared about. There'd been times during her darker moments of despair when she'd wondered if they'd even notice if she disappeared from their lives. She knew Ben had felt the same. It was partly why he'd enlisted at twenty-one. And again, her parents had thought it was a whim Ben would grow out of. When he'd made his intention clear by re-enlisting for a second tour in the Middle East they'd issued him with the same ultimatum: *Come home or be cut off.* He'd chosen to be cut off.

That was when they'd turned their full focus on getting her to bow to their will.

That and the fact that ten years ago they'd added four Bed and Breakfast establishments to the hotel with a long-term business plan that included her role as eventual manager of the portfolio. Their single-mindedness hadn't allowed them to entertain the possibility that she wouldn't be in a position to fulfil that obligation. That the sustained barrage on her spirit and self-esteem by her bullies, the same bullies they were refusing to acknowledge, would draw her deeper into her dancing, her only solace in a dark landscape.

But, despite their blindness where their children's needs were concerned, Sage doubted her parents would've been blindsided when it came to their ambition to put Havenwoods on the boutique hotels map, never mind fall prey to the clutches of a loan shark in so doing.

That bitter certainty made her laugh. 'You're wrong. My parents wouldn't allow a loan shark within ten miles of Havenwoods.'

'I assure you I've done my homework. They took on a business partner eighteen months ago. A maverick who convinced them to spend money they could ill afford, considering the business was already struggling.'

It was only because everything he'd told her so far had turned out to be true that her conviction wavered. That and the glaring, painful fact that, not having spoken to her parents in years, she had no clue what was going on in their lives. 'But…why…how…?'

'Total renovation of Havenwoods and the smaller establishments with material more suited to a six-star global chain than a boutique hotel. Extensive advertising to drum up business. The usual pitfalls that overextending can create if undertaken too quickly. They probably could've achieved all that if they hadn't tried to do it in months rather than years. In the last three months they've been forced to take out another mortgage on their home just to keep afloat. If you don't believe me feel free to call and ask them.'

They wouldn't tell her even if she did. As far as they were concerned, she owed them the apology for letting them down, not the other way around.

Still, it took every ounce of strength not to crumple into the chair she'd vacated minutes ago. 'You've done all of this…dug up all this dirt on my family…for what, exactly? What did Ben take from you that's so important you had to do this? And don't say it's the money. You brushed that off the first time we met.'

His face tightened even further as he prowled towards

her, deadly intent stamped on his face. 'What my possession means to me is not your concern. What should concern you is how precarious your family's position is. It's time to wake up, Sage. Your ambition seems to have blinded you to what's happening with your family. You have a chance to stop things from getting worse for them. Do you really want your brother to end up in jail? Or your parents to lose everything?'

Bitterness dredged through her at the thought that she was being asked to become the saviour of her parents when they'd closed their hearts and minds to her when she'd needed them. But the feeling was not enough to overcome the pain his words caused. Regardless of their indifference, she wouldn't be able to abide it if the legacy they'd worked so hard to preserve crumbled to nothing. She might not have wanted it for herself, but Havenwoods was still their home.

As for Ben, the thought of him in jail was unimaginable. Her brother needed counselling for his gambling problem. Possible psychiatric assistance after experiencing the trauma of war, not the cold harshness of imprisonment. 'He can't go to jail,' she muttered, almost to herself.

But he heard her. Heard and pounced on it. 'That is entirely in your power now.'

She opened her mouth, not entirely sure what she was going to say. The insistent trill of a phone in the charged atmosphere made her jump. It took a moment to realise the sound was coming from her handbag.

'I'm guessing that's your brother now, checking to see if there's any truth behind the rumours,' Xandro murmured into the silence.

The uncanny way everything Xandro had predicted was playing out kept her frozen for a moment.

'Answer the phone, Sage.' He plucked her handbag off the floor and held it out to her. His implacable expression told her he would accept nothing but her compliance.

With shaking fingers, she took it.

He didn't move away, completely disregarding her personal space. The harsh gleam in his eyes warned her of the consequences of her next move. On the fourth ring, she took the phone out of her bag.

Could she do it? Could she blatantly mislead her brother? She shook her head.

'You're doing it for his own good. Let that be your reassurance,' Xandro rasped, as if he'd read her thoughts.

'I hate you for this.'

A look passed through his eyes. One that almost hinted at regret. Then his face hardened again. 'I only want back what's mine.'

In that moment, she knew he would go to the ends of the earth itself for it.

Knowing her every choice was gone, she swiped her finger across the screen. 'Ben?'

'Sage?'

'Ben, where are you—?'

'Is it true?' His voice was gruff with barely held-in anger. 'Are you in Greece with that bastard?'

A furtive glance showed Xandro had heard the slur. His jaw tightened but he didn't move.

'Did you take his money?'

A terse silence greeted the question that even now, with the evidence mounted against him, she hoped he would deny.

'What if I did? It's nothing more than a man like him deserves. He struts around like he owns the whole world. Outsmarting him like I did was just the reality check he needed.'

Sage closed her eyes, bitterness and disappointment fighting for supremacy inside her. With no ground to stand on in his defence, her vocal cords stopped working. For a moment, she toyed with the idea of hanging up, burying her head in the sand and pretending none of this was happening.

'Sage,' Xandro rasped warningly, again proving he had a disturbing insight into her thoughts.

Ben inhaled sharply. 'Is that him? What the press are saying is true, isn't it? He bought Hunter's and he's there with you?'

'Yes.'

Her brother cursed viciously. 'Guys like him treat women like dirt. He's not worthy of breathing the same air as you. You need to get away from him, Sage.'

Xandro's gaze trapped hers, forcing her to make the only response available to her. 'I...can't—'

'Of course you can. Call the police. Tell them he's kidnapped you. Let them haul *him* to jail! Give him a taste of what the real world feels like.'

'He didn't kidnap me, Ben. I came here of my own free will.'

'But he tricked you, didn't he?' Ben insisted. 'He bought the dance company and tricked you into going to his damn island. How else did you end up there?'

Her hand tightened on the phone. 'Ben, why are you doing this? All he wants is his stuff back. You need to—'

'That's not all he wants. Anyway, he's not going to get it back! I don't know what the big deal is anyway. What I took is peanuts to him. He's worth billions.'

'You took something that's important to him,' she said. Again she saw the look that passed through Xandro's eyes at her words.

'What? The trinkets he gives to his women when he's done with them to shut them up? He orders them by the dozen from the jeweller in his casino. Did he tell you that?' he snarled. 'I bet he didn't.'

Sage wasn't sure why her stomach dipped at that piece of news. But at least it helped her drag her gaze from the man standing statue-still before her. 'This is still wrong.'

She heard the clink of ice against glass in the background, and her heart sank further. If Ben was drinking, then the likelihood of him listening to reason was diminishing even further.

'It's sweet that you see the world in black and white, baby sister. It's not.'

'Then tell me what you're trying to prove,' she challenged with more than a hint of anger.

'I'm causing him more than a moment of discomfort. I worked my ass off for him, and he didn't even know I existed. Maybe now that he knows what it feels like, guys like him will stop looking down their noses at people like me.'

The snippet she'd read online about Xandro's beginnings in the rougher parts of New York rose in her mind, dragging with it speculation as to whether the piece of property he was pursuing was connected with his past. A look in his eyes told her she wasn't about to find out right now.

'Ben, tell me where you are.'

'Sorry, Sage, but no.'

She closed her eyes, her insides trembling at the resolution in his voice. 'Please—'

'No. He's not going to win. I'm sorry I'm not around for you, but promise me the first chance you get you'll contact the cops—'

The phone left her fingers, the rest of Ben's words fading as Xandro took it from her. 'She will do no such thing. Neither will I where you're concerned. For the time being. But you've had your fun, Woods. Take things a step further at your peril.'

She caught Ben's snort. 'Your threats aren't going to work on me.'

Xandro's jaw clenched for a single moment. 'Very well. Don't say I didn't warn you.' He hung up, and calmly offered her phone back to her.

'Why did you do that?'

'The conversation was going nowhere,' he responded brusquely.

She looked down at her phone, torn between calling Ben back and leaving things be. She raised her head as she heard Xandro's footsteps.

'Wait!'

He turned and raised an eyebrow at her.

'What happens now?'

He shrugged. 'Nothing. He's had confirmation that you're with me. He knows I'm not bluffing. Let him stew over his new reality.'

Another odd sensation dragged through her belly. 'You're not going to let me go, are you?'

His mouth lifted in a facsimile of a smile. 'No. He's been radio silent for three weeks. But he's just shown his hand by reaching out to make sure you're all right. You're his weakness.'

'But you heard what he said. He's not going to return your things.'

'That would be a shame,' he replied. He turned towards the door again.

'So, you're just going to leave me here?'

'Of course not. Until I get my property back, where I go, you go. That is *your* reality from now on.'

Her mouth was still parted in an undignified O when he walked out and shut the door decisively behind him.

She could've gone after him to demand a definitive explanation of what he meant. But Sage desperately needed to regroup.

When her parents had thrown down the gauntlet—compliance or disinheritance—she'd painfully taken the latter option. This time, Xandro had ensured she had no option that she could in good conscience live with except the one he wanted. Had she been watching this drama unfold in someone else's life she would've been marginally impressed by his machinations.

But this was her life. A life she'd scrambled together with Ben's unwavering support in the face of her parents' indifference and callous ultimatum. Now Xandro Christofides was issuing an even more impossible choice: save Ben or lie to him.

She was still staring out of the window when Stavros returned to clear the lunch table. Unable to stand still a moment longer, she walked through the French windows.

The head-clearing she needed finally came with the acceptance that, for now, Xandro had all the power. She'd said that she hated him for what he'd done. She did. But, with a little space, she was grudgingly aware that he'd been willing to give Ben another chance after his outburst. How much longer his patience would hold was another thing entirely.

She got her wish to leave the island two hours later. But it wasn't by boat.

Sage eyed the gleaming black helicopter sitting on its designated platform with unease as she walked beside Xandro.

'Something wrong?'

She looked around. 'I can't see a pilot.'

'That's because I'm flying it,' he replied tersely.

'I'm not in the habit of getting into menacing-looking machines with strangers.'

His mouth flattened. 'That's good to know. But let's be realistic for a minute. You're effectively cut off from civilisation unless I choose to take you off my island. If I wished you harm, wouldn't this be the perfect place to keep you and have my way with you?'

Her heart performed another shaky somersault. 'Well, when you put it that way...' Still, she couldn't keep the nerves down. Probably because he'd yet to expand on this new *reality* she was supposed to be getting used to.

'I have a decent amount of flying hours under my belt, and I'm not interested in crashing any more than you are.' He caught her elbow in his hand when she continued to hesitate, and urged her with firm pressure towards the helicopter. 'Relax. You might even enjoy it.'

It looked even more intimidating up close. 'I seriously doubt that.'

He shrugged, completely unaffected by her tight voice. 'Then think of it this way—you don't have a choice. Where I go, you go, remember?'

Her chest tightened. 'I haven't forgotten. But I didn't agree to it,' she threw in, her last attempt to rebel against a situation that she could no longer control.

He stopped and looked down at her, his eyes gleaming with silver fire. 'And yet here you are. Is it a family trait to be objectionable about everything?' he enquired with a definite bite in his tone.

'I'm not a fan of the ask-how-high-when-you-say-jump club.' She'd had more than enough of that growing up.

He didn't immediately reply. Instead he opened the door and held out his hand. Warily, she placed hers in it, studiously ignoring the zing of electricity when he helped her up onto the wide leather seat. 'I look forward to discovering which clubs you're a fan of.'

He shut the door before she could respond. Which left her to watch him walk round to take his own seat, unable to stop herself from reluctantly appreciating the grace and power with which he moved. The whipcord strength ingrained with each step and the purposeful set of his face as he donned his headset and took control of the helicopter.

Lift-off was smooth enough for her not to notice until they were several feet off the ground.

'Relax. You might even enjoy it.'

She wanted to silently deny that statement, except she found out that the experience wasn't so bad. Even the slight dip in her stomach as the helicopter banked and swung away from the villa was secretly thrilling.

In fact, in other circumstances she might have called it enjoyable. For starters, the view from above was breathtaking, the receding island even more magical from several hundred feet above. But she kept all of that to herself as they flew over several more islands and a beautiful sparkling ocean towards their unknown destination.

'Where are we going?' she asked, dragging her gaze from the strong hands controlling the cyclic stick.

'To Athens. I have meetings there tonight and tomorrow.'

'And I'm supposed to do what—sit around twiddling my thumbs?'

'You can take the afternoon off. You've earned it.'

'I'd much rather be on an airplane going back home.'

He took his eyes off the horizon to stare at her. 'The next time Ben calls, convince him that you and I are an item and, I assure you, your wish will be realised sooner.'

'You're so certain he'll call again?'

His smile was cynical in the extreme. 'He thinks he knows me. Believe me, if I had a sister I wouldn't want him to date the kind of man your brother thinks I am either.'

'Is that your roundabout way of saying he's got you wrong?'

He moved the cyclic stick over to the right, banking the helicopter, before he answered. 'I'm not concerned about your brother's opinion of me.'

She absorbed that for a moment. 'What did he mean by saying that he worked hard for you without you knowing he existed?'

His jaw tightened for a long moment. 'I found out that he applied to be my personal bodyguard three times in the last year. My chief of security turned him down each time. He...took offence.'

Her stomach dipped. She looked out of the window, biting her tongue against the question hovering there. It jumped out anyway. 'Is it true about those thanks-for-the-good-times pieces of jewellery he mentioned?'

He slanted her a narrow-eyed glance. 'It's not your concern.'

She wasn't aware she was holding her breath for an explanation until he deprived her of one. 'I prefer to think I'm embroiled in this for something more worthwhile than your next lover's goodbye present,' she bit out, the knowledge that she'd been so certain that what Ben had taken was worth more than that to Xandro mocking her.

He didn't deign to answer. Instead he flew the helicopter for a couple of miles before he looked over at her. 'Why didn't you tell him about the situation with your parents?'

'And get him to go even further off the deep end?'

He studied her for a long speculative moment. 'You're worried about him.'

She frowned. 'Of course I am. Isn't that what you were counting on?'

His mouth firmed. 'Then the earlier we sort this out, the sooner you can get him the help he needs.'

The tightening in her stomach eased a touch. Which was peculiar because every ruthless act Xandro had perpetrated so far dictated that she'd be foolish not to be extremely wary of him. *'Where I go, you go* is a gross generalisation. I'd like to know more about what you meant by that.'

'Before we get to that, do I have your word that you'll do whatever's necessary to ensure my possession is returned to me?' he bit out.

When she'd believed that whatever Ben had taken held more than a fleeting sentimental value she'd been more apprehensive about the wrongs her brother had perpetrated. She still was, but the knowledge that Xandro was going to such extreme lengths to gain back jewellery he would use to appease his next few lovers opened a vein of mild repugnance.

She didn't agree with Ben's assertion that Xandro could afford it and should therefore let it go. There was no excuse for stealing. Nevertheless a tiny part of her was disappointed with the truth behind Xandro's demands.

'Is there a reason why you're reluctant to give your consent?' he demanded after a minute had passed.

She wanted to scoff and challenge his integrity. That

he'd bought into a dance company and incurred a bill for tens of thousands of dollars to fly a whole dance group first class to his island for the sake of a handful of gems irritated her.

But she bit her tongue. Her parents' livelihood was hanging in the balance. Staying in the toxic environment of their cold indifference to her despair would've killed her spirit. Nevertheless, that wasn't a reason to throw them to the wolves. Or one wolf in particular, whose vicious teeth could prove sharp and deadly should he not reap the results he wanted.

'I need to know that you won't go after my parents, regardless of how things turn out with Ben.'

He remained silent. Long enough for her to hope he was considering her request. 'No.'

Her breath caught. 'What?'

'I won't give any further reassurances. The terms of the deal have been laid out. Make your brother believe you're mine so he comes out of hiding or I go after your parents with every weapon in my arsenal.'

'Blackmail? Is that how you made your billions?'

A grim shadow crossed his face, right before his jaw clenched tight. 'No. I made my fortune through honest hard work,' he replied stiffly. 'But that's not to say I'm unfamiliar with using alternative tactics to get what I want. Remember that for the future,' he warned.

She looked away from the eyes boring into her. But his chilling words continued to ring in her ears. Her gaze settled on the fast-approaching horizon and the landscape she recognised as Athens.

Surrounded by everything that epitomised this powerful, ruthless man, helplessness assailed Sage, making her want to lash out against the stifling ties binding her.

When she glanced over at him, she found his gaze still pinned on her, the hand controlling the helicopter an almost negligent extension of the sheer magnificence and autocracy of the man. Piercing grey eyes commanded her to answer.

So she responded. 'Yes, you have my word.'

He continued to watch her for a moment before his gaze returned to the landscape ahead of them. 'Good. Your brother believes I intend to seduce you. I propose we take it a step further. Convince him that you are I are already lovers.'

CHAPTER EIGHT

XANDRO WATCHED A series of expressions flicker across her face. The emotion he recognised as bewilderment resonated faintly through him.

Blackmail? He had first-hand knowledge of how close it could drive a man to the edge.

And yet the moment he'd issued the ultimatum, he knew it was the perfect means to bring all this to a hasty conclusion. Besides, unlike when it'd been directed at him by his gang leader as a teenager, there were no sinister intentions behind his command to Sage.

All she needed to do was remain by his side until her brother came to heel.

Already it was working perfectly. Woods was riled enough to poke his head out of wherever he was hiding. Xandro's only regret was that he hadn't had the means to trace the call and pinpoint his exact location.

Sage's expression settled into stubborn acceptance. Had he not found this situation intensely unsatisfactory, he would've found it amusing. He didn't want to acknowledge the part of him that was curiously offended that she clearly felt mild abhorrence at his suggestion that they pretend to be lovers.

Without conceit, he knew countless women who would've expressed delight at being given the role of playing his lover. Many more who would yearn for that role to be real. And yes, it stuck in his craw that the woman whose integrity he'd questioned only last night seemed to have a problem with him in return.

He refocused on the horizon, specifically the sprawling magnificence of the Acropolis, and beyond that to the

Xei Athens Hotel rooftop, where his helipad waited. The Vegas hotel and casino were his crowning glory, but coming back to the country where his family had experienced such hardship that they'd been forced to flee and stamping his authority beneath one of its most revered monuments had been extremely satisfying.

These days the Christofides name was no longer spoken of with contempt but with the respect he'd clawed from blood and dirt, from literally fighting his way out of a vicious gang that would've sent him down a path of chaos. He'd taken on the system that could so easily have chewed him up and spat him out, and beaten it. He'd seized his second chance because of a piece of jewellery, and he'd won.

Every member of his family had paid dearly, bearing the stigma of being labelled a thief. Until he'd redeemed the Christofides name.

He smothered the churning memories.

Beside him, Sage was rubbing her wrist. He frowned. He opened his mouth to question her, then closed it again. He didn't want to know about her vulnerabilities or her strengths. She was just a means to an end. Even though her continued silence threatened to escalate his irritation.

Conversely, the slightly agitated sounds of her breathing coming through the headset started a small blaze inside him. His hand tightened on the stick, her effect on his libido startling him as much now as it had last night. Except this time it was more potent. More visceral.

He didn't speak until he'd set the chopper down and powered off the instruments.

'You have a problem with my plan?' he demanded as he removed his headset.

She followed suit, avoiding his gaze as she handed the headset over. 'How long will I have to pretend I'm your lover? I have to practise my routines.'

'You need to work it into your schedule or you won't have a schedule at all.' At her soft gasp, he gritted his teeth, dimly aware that he was growing increasingly annoyed with her resistance. Dammit, he was fed up to the back teeth of pussyfooting around her.

'So we've progressed to outright threats?' she asked, one eyebrow lifted at him.

He sighed. 'I've laid everything out for you and yet you seem to want to keep pushing my buttons.'

'You're a master manipulator—and no, that's not a compliment—so pardon me if I want things laid out in the open and less…nebulous.'

A reluctant smile tugged at his mouth. He killed it dead, unwilling to add amusement to the unsettling mix of arousal and frustration churning through him. 'We're only here for tonight. After my meeting in the morning, we'll leave for the States. You can return to your routine within the next twenty-four hours, with a few adjustments, of course.'

Relief tinged her features. Again he experienced a bite of irritation. He was the wronged party here and yet she made him feel as if she was with him under sufferance. Which, he told himself, she was. He needed to stop being irrational!

By the time he walked round to her side, she was halfway out of the chopper. He caught her hand and helped her the rest of the way, acutely aware of the blaze inside him intensifying at her touch. He also became aware a moment later that he didn't want to let her go. But he forced himself to release her when she tugged at his hand.

In the late afternoon sunlight, her hair gleamed with the fire of a Greek sunset. When Xandro found himself wondering, yet again, how long the silky tresses were, he scowled and strode across the roof towards the lift.

She didn't speak until they were cocooned in the small space, on their way down to his suite. A ride that was long enough for him to inhale her heady perfume, but too short to count the freckles on her pert nose. 'What adjustments?'

It took a precious few seconds for him to recall what he'd

said to her. He exited the lift and took his time to find the key card to his suite as he regrouped.

'Geographical adjustments,' he answered, holding the door open for her.

Curious eyes met his as she slid past him into the suite. 'You're going to relocate to DC?'

Xandro gave a stiff smile as he nudged the door shut with his foot. 'No, Sage. You're going to relocate to Vegas.'

Green eyes widened. 'What? No, that's impossible.'

'You packed a bag and got on a plane to Greece with very little notice. The process is even easier to repeat the second time around.'

Her lips pursed. 'I know how air travel works. I meant I can't uproot my whole life for the sake of this charade. I thought that we would just—'

'Go for coffee a couple of times, maybe a stroll in the park while holding hands? You really think that will convince your brother?'

A small frown gathered between her brows. 'Well, I'm not as well-versed in the act of subterfuge as you seem to be so, by all means, enlighten me.'

He realised he was moving towards her when she began to back away. 'For starters, you need to not shrink away when I come near you.'

She stopped immediately, her chin rising in challenge as she attempted to stare him down. 'I don't like my personal space invaded.'

'Brace yourself then, *glikia mou*, because I intend to do more than just invade your personal space.' Deliberately, he took another step closer. She exhaled in a little rush but, to her credit, she stood her ground.

Xandro wasn't sure the need to get closer to her was a completely sound one, especially when her alluring scent wrapped itself around him again.

He breathed her in, noting with each second that passed he wanted more. He wanted to press his nose to that sweet curve where her shoulder met her neck. He wanted to trail his fingers over that pulse racing at her throat, feel for himself whether her skin was as silky and warm as it looked.

She took another heavier breath, drawing his gaze to the full curves of her breasts. The insistent yearning grew, the blaze gathering strength as it built.

Her hold tightened on her purse. 'Could you…not look at me like that?' she demanded in a low, fierce voice.

Xandro noted the wash of pink in her cheeks. His fingers tingled with the need to touch the colour. 'Like what?'

A faint fluttering of her nostrils as she inhaled. 'So… intensely.'

'Like a lover would look at the woman he can't wait to be alone with?' he asked provocatively.

He'd meant to mock her out of her prudishness. Instead his words backfired by conjuring up images his overeager libido latched onto with alarming eagerness. 'I'm a red-blooded male, *glikia mou*. When I hold your hand in public there will be no doubt that I've known what it feels like to have it on my body. When I stroke your skin like this—' he gave in and trailed the back of his hand across her cheek and, *thee mou*, it was as smooth as he'd imagined '—it'll be clear that I do it with the familiarity of having known every inch of it.'

'Even if you don't?' Her breathlessness only fed the hunger inside him. So did the faint quivering of her skin beneath his touch.

He told himself he was merely demonstrating the importance of her role. It was why he slid his hand slowly up her arm, over the silken landscape of her bare shoulder, to rest his fingers against her pulse. 'Now I know how your skin feels,' he murmured, then, because he simply couldn't resist, he trailed his forefinger up her throat to caress her jawline. 'And I know how fast your pulse races when I touch you.'

She made the faintest sound as a tremble rippled through her body. But she didn't step away, and he didn't withdraw.

They remained like that, caught in a moment Xandro didn't want to admit was perplexing the hell out of him. Her lips parted on another unsteady breath. And, with a magnetic pull he couldn't resist, his eyes dropped to her plump lips. Her tongue darted out to wet her lips and arousal punched him hard in the gut.

And then, because his hunger in that moment overruled everything else in his life, he speared his fingers into her hair and slanted his mouth over hers.

Her lips remained closed against his for challenging seconds, but Xandro didn't care. He was busy sampling the velvety smoothness of her bottom lip, following the sensual curve with his tongue over and over before nipping it with his teeth.

Her tiny jerk was a clarion call to his groin, the puff of breath that washed over his cheek an invitation to repeat the little act. He nipped again, firmer, and earned a gasp that parted her lips perfectly for the insistent slide of his tongue. Angling her head, he breached the sweet barrier of her lips, felt her tongue dart out against his. There was an innocence in the act that, cultivated or not, intensified his hunger. He chased after more of it, flicked his tongue against hers and felt another shiver move through her.

Thee mou, she tasted unbelievable. He'd meant this to be a lesson, but it was fast turning into something else. Something like a mini feast that promised a banquet, the likes of which he'd never known.

He'd made his point. He needed to stop. But…not yet. Just a little more. He pressed his mouth harder over hers, gliding his tongue across her bottom lip again. A tiny groan escaped her.

And then she froze. A second later she was pushing at him, attempting to place distance between them. His fingers convulsed in her hair for a charged second. Then he stepped back.

'Point made, I think.' He sounded as if he'd swallowed a

shovelful of gravel. And the pressure behind his fly wasn't lessened when she raised her hand and pressed her fingers against the mouth he'd just tasted. Again there was an innocence in the gesture that threatened to flay him. Especially when he got the impression she wasn't even aware of what she was doing.

'What point?' she muttered. 'And…how would Ben even know any of this?'

He allowed himself a tense smile. 'He'll know.'

Her head tilted and she dropped her hand. 'Let me guess—another of your contingencies?' she whispered.

He told himself he needed to get on with more important things. And yet he couldn't move. 'It's best if you don't know every small detail.'

'Why not?'

'Because I want your reactions to be natural, organic. Anything less than that and he'll guess it's a ruse.'

She stepped to the side, removing herself from his reach. Xandro balled his hands to stop himself from seizing her once more. She walked further into the living room and dropped her purse on the nearest sofa. 'This is insane.'

He held up his hand to pre-empt her. 'No. This is the most time-efficient way to bring things to a satisfactory end for both of us.'

'Surely you can't expect me to…*perform* at the drop of a hat?'

His gaze rested on her mouth. Her slightly swollen, infinitely kissable mouth. 'I've just kissed you and your response was…acceptable. Besides, isn't playacting what you do when you dance?'

Her tongue darted over her lower lip and he suppressed a groan. 'That's different.'

He turned away before the urge to touch her again grew too hard to handle. 'I'm confident you'll adapt. I have to go out now. There's a private butler who services my suite.

He'll be here in a minute to show you to your room. If you need anything after that, his number is on the phone.'

She blinked then looked around her, as if noticing for the first time exactly where she was.

Since this penthouse suite was his own space, he'd added paintings and art from his private collection, one of which was a Cycladic tapestry sourced from a small village artist in Skiathos. It depicted a red-haired female form reclining on a sandy beach, her gaze riveted on an orange sunset. He had priceless pieces in his homes and hotels all around the world, but this was one of his favourites.

Which was probably why he paused to watch her inspect the painting instead of heading downstairs to the meeting he risked being late for.

'Oh...that's beautiful,' she murmured.

Xandro didn't know he was holding his breath until he exhaled. He needed to leave rather than stand there, comparing her russet hair to the woman's in the painting, and suddenly finding the painting wanting. He needed to go before the urge to taste her again grew too much to resist.

After several moments her gaze, like that of most people who found themselves with this aerial view of the city, turned towards the imposing beauty of the Acropolis. Again she gasped, her feet moving towards the floor-to-ceiling windows that took up an entire wall.

He took a beat to see it through her eyes, and felt a wonder and pride in his motherland. But on its heels the bitterness that was never far away when he returned to Greece rose to poison the waters of his pride. Somewhere in this city was the man whose blood ran through his veins. The father whose actions could've easily ensured Xandro had never been born.

The reminder that he had enemies in this world and that Sage, through her brother, was one of them, eroded a little of the carnal edge gripping him.

'I'll return in a few hours. Be ready to go out to dinner tonight.'

She looked over her shoulder. Whatever response she'd been about to give dried up because, he suspected, of the grim look on his face.

'Okay,' was all she said.

And as he walked away Xandro prayed, for her sake, that it was the beginning of the end of her resistance.

The little black dress she'd thrown into her suitcase at the last minute didn't need ironing. It was one of the many small things Sage was thankful for when she emerged from the most spectacular bathroom she'd ever seen, mainly because every single brain cell seemed to be hooked on the kiss she'd shared with Xandro.

Although *shared* was probably not an accurate description.

He'd conquered her lips. Branded every inch inside and out and left her with a hunger that even now, four hours later, was as acute as ever. Many times after he'd walked away, she'd found her fingers tracing her mouth, a little stunned at the tingling that still lingered.

She knew that he'd picked her as a pawn against her brother. And yet she'd fallen into his kiss at the first opportunity, despite every precaution she'd taken.

But…dear heaven, that kiss had been something else.

His touch had been electric. His eyes had sparked with a hunger that had resonated in her belly. Afterwards she'd hated herself for the weakness but, so far, she'd been unable to stop the sizzling in her bloodstream.

She shook herself free of the unsettling sensation, reminding herself that her focus was on keeping Ben and her parents out of Xandro's retributive clutches. There was no way she would allow it to go further than that.

It was almost seven. Xandro hadn't given her a specific

time but, since this dinner was happening, she would be better off ready and waiting so she could get it over with.

Her freshly washed hair was blow-dried. The sumptuous robe hugging her from neck to ankle came off. As she slipped on the dress, she couldn't stop a momentary pang of disquiet. Everything in Xandro's world was super-luxurious and in a class available to a select few. She fingered her dress, staring critically at its simple off-the-shoulder design. Then her shoes, three-inch black slingbacks from a cheap chain store. Both were nothing special. As for accessories, besides the silver earrings her grandmother had given her for her sixteenth birthday, she had no other jewellery.

Jewellery.

The reminder of why all of this was happening dimmed her spirits further. Her life was in turmoil because Xandro was chasing trinkets for his lovers. Although…the last time she'd asked him, his expression had once again hinted at something more. Something deeper. Or maybe it was just her imagination.

With a twist of her lips, she tugged the dress over her head and briskly attended to her light make-up. She hadn't asked for any of this. So if Xandro didn't care for what she wearing, too bad.

She was standing at the living room window, her gaze and senses once again captivated by the ancient monument on the horizon, when she sensed him behind her.

The fact that she couldn't stop herself from turning around, the view no longer the primary demand on her focus, unsettled her further.

He was dressed differently. He'd showered too if the damp strands curling over his forehead were any indication. Dressed entirely in black, he resembled the formidable, powerful mogul he was, despite the lack of a tie and the buttons left undone at his throat.

The sight of his olive-skinned throat and the hint of chest hair she glimpsed sent a pulse of wild heat low in her belly.

A reaction she tried to studiously ignore when he raised his head from the phone in his hand and speared her with his silver-grey gaze.

'Are you ready?' His eyes conducted a slow scrutiny. One that had a hot little breath catching in her throat.

Her nod brought his gaze up to her face, then higher to her hair. 'Do you ever wear your hair down?' The question was clipped, as if he was displeased.

She frowned, wondering why his displeasure made her stomach roil. 'Yes,' she snapped back. She'd intended to wear it down this evening. Until she'd reminded herself that this wasn't a date. Or even a platonic social outing. She was being blackmailed to bring her brother to heel.

She started towards him, then noticed his gaze still riveted on her hair. Her step slowed, and she found her fingers creeping up her nape to touch the knot. She hastily dropped her hand. 'Is something wrong?'

'Other than your tongue being sharper than a wasp's sting, and your hair the exact shade of an Ayia Hera sunset, no,' he delivered, then frowned. Balled hands shoved into his pockets and he turned on his heel.

Sage got the distinct feeling he'd let something slip he hadn't meant to. But what was the big deal about mentioning a place in his native country? Unless, like her, he'd remembered that this wasn't a date. She mentally shrugged, following him to the door he held open for her.

Their journey down in the executive lift was conducted in silence. Sage tried to take small breaths to avoid inhaling too much of the citrus-layered aftershave blended with his unique masculine scent. But doing so only starved her of oxygen and made her heart pump faster.

It was a relief to escape the charged atmosphere five storeys later, when the lift opened straight onto a marble-floored foyer that led into the chic Michelin-starred restaurant she'd read about in the coffee table book in her room.

She was taking it all in when she felt his breath on her neck.

'I'm going to put my hand on you now. Be an angel and don't jump,' he rasped against her ear.

'I wasn't going to,' she returned in a thankfully firm voice, but nothing could guard her against the electricity that zinged through her system when his hand touched her waist a second later.

'Glad to hear it. That smile wouldn't go amiss now, though,' he added as the maître d' hurried towards them.

'You can't just command me to smile. That's like me commanding you to make me laugh.'

'Sorry, *pedhaki mou*, I'm fresh out of knock-knock jokes. But you can do something about that rabbit-caught-in-head-lights look you're sporting right now.'

She was caught between wondering what *pedhaki mou* meant and snapping at him for his continued commands when his hand tightened on her waist and he pulled her closer to his body. Every thought flew out of her head as the hard contours of his body met hers. Heart rate spiking even more, she gripped her clutch tighter, hoping the discomfort shooting through her fingers would ground her.

She smiled at the maître d' simply because he was charming but felt a little nervous when his gaze flicked to his ultimate employer. He showed them to their table in the middle of the room and was about to pull out her chair when Xandro muttered a few words in his mother tongue.

The maître d' stepped back hastily, leaving Xandro to seat her. More murmured words and the man filled their water glasses and hurried away to fetch menus.

'So, did I pass the test?' she asked for want of something to disrupt the fraught silence that had descended over the table. She'd expected him to take his seat opposite her. Instead, he threw her for a loop by taking the seat to her left. This close, she couldn't avoid his scent suffusing her senses. Within a minute she was back to shallow breathing and wishing herself far, far away from here.

His eyes met hers, but his features remained neutral even though she sensed an undercurrent. 'You would have, had you not missed the point entirely and smiled at another man instead of the one you're with.'

She stopped the urge to roll her eyes when she noted the interest coming their way from other diners. 'We're being watched.'

'And? That shouldn't be a new phenomenon for you.'

'I'm used to an audience when I dance. This is different.' Her fingers found the stem of her water glass. 'Is that why you brought me here—because you knew your adoring acolytes would be ready to document your illustrious presence in their midst?'

One corner of his mouth lifted. 'Of course. Why else?' he demanded imperiously.

Sage was struck with the sudden urge to see that smile grow with a genuine amusement that wasn't at her expense.

She was sure the absurd compulsion was why she hastened into more conversation. 'That place you mentioned. Ayia…?'

He stiffened slightly, his gaze growing hooded. 'Ayia Hera.'

She nodded. 'Is that where you're from originally?'

A terse silence greeted her question, then he spoke. 'It's where my family emigrated from. I was born and raised in New York. The slums of the Bronx, to be exact.'

'Do you have any family back in Ayia Hera?'

His jaw tightened for a moment. 'No. I don't.'

The answer was curt. A warning not to probe further. 'What about New York? Do you have family—?'

Her words were cut off when he slid his hand over her nape, pulled her close and sealed his mouth over hers. The move was silky-smooth, executed with a predatory precision that would've stopped her breath, had the sensation of his warm, demanding mouth on hers not done that already. Just like this afternoon, the feeling was almost otherworldly in its devastating effect on her.

Shock held her still long enough for Xandro to press his mouth firmer against hers, for him to relearn the contours of her lips and then to sweep his tongue over her lower lip in an act so carnal heat shot straight between her legs.

The sensation was so unnervingly visceral, she jerked in her seat. In direct contrast to when his grip had tightened earlier, his fingers drifted over her neck, eliciting an intoxicating swell of pleasure that paralysed her. The fire spread, singeing her in places she'd never imagined a kiss could touch her before today.

When his thumb slid slowly along her jaw, she gasped. The act granted him entry. Xandro deepened the kiss, taking his time to explore her mouth before, just as abruptly as he'd taken hold of her, he released her.

CHAPTER NINE

HE CASUALLY SAT BACK, lifting one hand to beckon the hovering *sommelier*. Stunned and frozen in her chair, Sage tried in vain to calm her runaway pulse. The tingling that hadn't quite abated from this afternoon now almost burned her mouth, and her stomach felt as if the bottom had dropped out of it.

The energetic buzz and the rise in conversation around them justified the creeping mortification of knowing their kiss had been witnessed and they were being gossiped about. Heat of a different kind surged up her neck and scorched her cheeks. She lifted her hand to her face. Or at least she tried to.

Xandro captured it in one of his, thwarting her by diverting it to his mouth. His lips brushed her knuckles, further sending her senses into free fall. When she attempted to use her other hand, he trapped that one too.

Grey eyes gone dark with hunger and whatever evil schemes he was concocting issued a warning at her as their wine was poured. Her whole body was on fire, and she couldn't stop her brain from shrieking in shock.

He'd kissed her again. Without warning. As if he had every right. As if he *owned* her.

He'd done it to shut her up, she knew deep down. But the effect was the same. She felt...invaded. Thrillingly, decadently invaded. Unable to speak with their *sommelier* still pouring their chilled white wine, Sage swallowed, and subtly attempted to disengage her fingers from Xandro's hold. He ignored her, holding on as he nodded to something the man said. She sat through the production of an ice bucket being set up next to Xandro and the arrival of their waiter to take their order.

'Do you prefer the seafood or the salad starter, *pethi mou*?' Xandro enquired in a low, deep voice. 'Have the seafood.'

It took monumental effort to force her brain back on track. 'I'll have the salad,' she told the waiter. She drew the line at having what she ate controlled by Xandro.

His eyes gleamed but he didn't comment. She barely heard him dismiss their server, her every sense focused on the hand linked tightly with hers.

The moment they were alone she exhaled the pent-up angst roiling inside her. Then jumped when his lips grazed over her knuckles once again. 'Stop. You... I...you can't do that!'

She was shaking, she realised. He noticed too. Noticed and folded his hands over both of hers in a gesture that would've seemed warming or comforting to their avid audience. She watched, wide-eyed, as his thumb slowly caressed back and forth over her knuckles. 'Pull yourself together, Sage. Our audience has grown.'

'And whose fault is that?' she hissed. 'God, I can't believe you—'

'Believe it. Or I will kiss you again and keep kissing you until you do.'

The flame that chased through her veins was a little too giddy for her liking. 'Why? If you didn't want me to ask questions, why didn't you just say so?'

'Would you have listened? You don't have a history of doing what I say.'

'And that warrants you assaulting me?'

He took his time to answer, his gaze drifting over her face before rising to meet hers. 'Your pulse is racing, sure. But you hardly look traumatised. And the way you're licking your lips right now makes me think you want more where that came from.'

She immediately firmed her traitorous lips. 'I'd prefer it if you kept your hands and your mouth to yourself. Let me go.'

This time he released her, sat back and calmly picked up his wine. But he didn't immediately drink. 'Within the next hour, news of my mysterious new lover will hit social media. This may not have been how I planned it, but there's an upside to it.'

'You mean I can start counting down my fifteen minutes of unwanted fame?' she asked hopefully.

'However long we spend together depends entirely on you acing your performance. Try the wine, Sage. It's very good,' he drawled.

She wanted to refuse. But a sudden urge to prove that she wasn't always as disagreeable as he claimed nudged her hard. Plus, although she rarely drank, tonight she needed the fortification of alcohol to stop her from doing something stupid. Like running her tongue over her still tingling lips to see if the lingering taste of his kiss was as potent as her senses proclaimed. With hands that hadn't quite regained their steadiness, she picked up her glass and took a sip.

She had no idea of the vintage of the wine, but the gorgeous bouquet exploding on her taste buds was enough to invite another sip. And another.

His gaze cut into her. 'Easy, *pethi mou*. You barely touched your lunch and according to the butler you didn't have anything to eat in my absence. I'd rather not have you tipsy before the first course arrives.'

She raised an eyebrow. 'Why, because you're scared I'll misbehave?' she challenged.

'I think I've already found a curative measure for any misbehaviour on your part. I was thinking more along the lines of answering a few of your questions.'

A little surprised, she set her glass down and toyed with the stem. 'If you were going to answer them anyway, then why did you...?'

'*Kiss* you? You can say it, Sage. It's not a bad word.'

Tell that to my body. 'Fine, why did you kiss me?'

He shrugged. 'I wasn't sure whether I wanted my life pried into just yet.'

'And now?'

'For the sake of authenticity, I've decided it wouldn't hurt for us to know a thing or two about each other. So, to answer your earlier question, no, I don't have family remaining. Anywhere.'

Something about the way he said that made her heart lurch a little.

She might be estranged from her parents but she couldn't imagine them not being there. She couldn't imagine being alone in the world, even though for the most part of the last three years it'd felt as if she was. She glanced at Xandro, further questions burning on her tongue. 'You said your family emigrated but…?' She paused, unwilling to agitate the waters further.

'What?' he demanded.

'Correct me if I'm wrong, but you used the word for want of a better one?'

His jaw flexed for a moment and he took a large sip of wine before he shrugged. 'Perhaps because *emigrated* sounds more civilised than *cast out.*'

Shock spiked through her. 'What?'

'You heard me. My grandparents and my mother were cast out of their home and the only life they'd known. They had little choice but to board the boat that took them to New York. The rest is history.'

His words were casual, offhand even. Except she knew there was a lifetime's consequence of that history bubbling beneath the surface. As she watched his harshly beautiful face, she couldn't help but wonder if he'd been entirely shaped by whatever had happened to his family. Or whether the harshness had come afterwards.

Before she could probe further, two waiters approached and set their first course in front of them. Her wild mushroom salad with truffle oil was delicious but Xandro's sea-food platter looked mouthwatering.

Her delicately growling stomach prompted her to suppress the question darting around her mind and pick up her cutlery. They ate in silence for a brief spell. Until he speared a fat shrimp with his fork and offered it to her. 'Here, try this.'

The intimacy of the action forced her to shake her head immediately. 'No, thanks. I don't—'

'You're in one of the most spectacular cities of the world. Your lover is offering you a morsel from his plate. Are you really going to refuse me? Especially when you've been eyeing my plate since our food arrived. Denying yourself for the sake of your principles is only admirable up to a point. Then it becomes tedious. Not to mention I'm in fear of the double blow to my ego of having my gesture refused in front of our audience.'

She glanced from his face to the delectable morsel poised an inch from her mouth, then to the diners surrounding them, who seemed absolutely absorbed in what was happening at their table.

The smoky aroma of the grilled shrimp coupled with a hint of lemon hit her nostrils, mercilessly teasing her taste buds. Before she could think of another reason to refuse, she parted her lips and accepted the offering. And barely managed to stop herself from moaning at the exquisite flavours that suffused her senses.

'Not so bad, was it?' Xandro asked.

She chewed. Swallowed. Then picked up her glass of wine and sipped. 'No. It was delicious.'

A slight hitch of his brow said her easy agreement had surprised him.

She licked the lingering trace of wine and grilled shrimp from her bottom lip, and saw his eyes darken as he followed the action. An increasingly familiar little charge of electricity descended on the table again as she finished her meal.

When the waiter came to clear their plates, Xandro again made a recommendation for their main course. This time she nodded her agreement. When she refused a refill of her wine, he set the bottle back in the bucket.

They didn't exchange conversation and, for the first time since Xandro had walked into her life, the atmosphere between them didn't crackle with animosity and suspicion. In fact, she'd managed to take the first full breath in his presence when he once again directed those incisive eyes on her.

'Why are you estranged from your parents?'

The easiness evaporated. Her stomach tightened, armouring itself against the pain the question brought. Besides Ben, Xandro was the only one who had an inkling of what had driven her from home three years ago. She didn't want to discuss it with the formidable man seated next to her. But he'd answered her questions, despite his clear reluctance. And, as absurd as it sounded—or perhaps it was the wine talking—that brief insight into his past had lifted a veil of mystery from him, making him seem, if not accessible, less daunting.

When the refusal that rose on her lips withered and died, Sage told herself he already knew almost everything about her parents. Elaborating on why wouldn't give him any more ammunition against her. Not everything though. The parts that hurt the most she intended to keep to herself.

'Havenwoods has been in my father's family for generations, and it's been run by my ancestors since it was built. My parents planned Ben's and my life around managing it when we were still kids. When I turned thirteen I told them I had no intention of following the family tradition. At first they didn't believe I was serious. When they realised that my dancing wasn't just an extra-curricular way to pass the time they weren't happy but they still thought it was a phase I would grow out of.' Her shrug felt painful, but she'd started the story so she pushed on. 'Things came to a head a few years ago. I told them I was moving to DC to try out for the Hunter Dance Company programme. They told me if I left I would be disinherited and never welcomed back.'

His eyes narrowed a little but his attention didn't waver from her face. 'They tried to use your family legacy to control you?'

'You mean—did they blackmail me like you're doing?' she bit out, a little of her pain spilling over onto him.

His head went back as if her words had physically struck him. His gaze swept down and fixed on his wineglass, but he didn't respond.

She took a moment to breathe through the anguish twisting like a live wire inside her. To get her runaway emotions under control. 'My father flew out to see me a few months later to tell me that he and my mother were willing to take me back if I'd come to my senses. That was three years ago.'

He raised his gaze, and his expression was neutral. 'You haven't spoken to them since?'

She couldn't quite pull off another shrug. 'I'm still a dancer. I have no intention of changing that to a pencil skirt and silk blouse, and riding a desk any time soon.'

A hint of a smile played around his lips. 'Unless your role calls for it, when I'm sure you'll rise to the occasion.'

The words weren't charged in any way, except maybe in her overactive imagination. But the silence that followed changed from a somewhat stilted sharing of information into something else. Something that made his eyes gleam and her heart rate pick up an uncomfortable speed once more. The sizzle in her belly sparked to life and Sage couldn't quite catch her breath as his gaze continued to hold hers.

'Have they ever seen you dance?' he asked after a minute had passed.

'One amateur production years ago. They asked me what I wanted for my birthday. I asked them to come and see me. They turned up for the last half hour of the show.'

He drained the last of his wine, a look of distaste filling

his eyes. 'They've deliberately blinded themselves to your talent. It's their loss.'

'I wish it wasn't,' she said before she could stop herself.

'The only way to make your reality different is to change it. Wishing is a waste of time.' The words were spoken with harsh, unshakable determination that spoke of personal experience.

'Is that what you did? Changed your reality?' She pounced on the statement, eager to sidestep the more painful subject of her estrangement with her parents.

His lips firmed. Then he gave her a tight smile. 'Perhaps this isn't the right time to play the get-to-know-one-another game, after all.'

Disappointment spiked her. 'It was your idea. It's fine if you've changed your mind.'

Silver eyes narrowed faintly. 'Are you attempting to reverse psyche me, Sage?'

She shook her head slowly. 'No. Delving into the past isn't always easy. Especially…' She stopped, certain the wine was having way too much effect on her runaway tongue.

But he wasn't ready to let it go. 'Especially?'

This time her shrug was easier. 'I read the history of your hotels in the suite. It hinted at your…darker past. I understand if you don't want to talk about it.'

Again he didn't immediately respond. He drained his glass and set it down. Shook his head at the waiter when he approached. And when he spoke it was almost reluctant. 'In my case changing reality didn't stem from a wish to be different. It stemmed from necessity.'

'What does that mean?'

'It means I was confronted with two paths in a difficult road. The easier path was to perform an act of betrayal that would've earned me the role of second lieutenant in a street gang—and it would also have ensured a very limited life expectancy.'

Her heart dropped at the calm way he spoke of such a volatile past. But, looking into his face, she glimpsed a savage expression that told her Xandro didn't view the subject as lightly as his tone suggested. 'And the other path?' she asked, although she suspected she knew.

'Clawing my way out of a dark hole with no flashlight while the same gang who wanted me now had a price on my head.'

Dear God. 'The journey may have been difficult but surely the destination made it worth it? Most people can only dream of the success you've achieved.'

His mouth twisted with very little humour. 'And some who grow tired of dreaming attempt to take advantage of it instead.'

And, just like that, the atmosphere shifted. Sage didn't know whether he was deliberately stopping her from probing further into his past or whether he wanted to remind her why she was here.

She dropped her napkin on the table. 'You don't need to remind me why I'm here.'

He looked a touch puzzled for an instant before his face stiffened. 'I'm glad to hear it.' He followed suit and placed his napkin beside hers. Then he rose. 'Since we seem to have used up our quota of exchanging life histories, we'll take our nightcap on the terrace.'

He reached for the back of her chair, his tall imposing body bending towards hers. 'I was thinking of going to bed,' she hurriedly replied.

Only to receive a firm shake of his head. 'Not yet. This restaurant isn't renowned just for its great food. The management will be offended if we don't take advantage of its other asset.'

She lifted a sceptical eyebrow. 'The *management*? You mean you?'

'Precisely. Come.'

A firm hand at her elbow accompanied the imperious

command. Sage told herself she complied because it was the fastest route to getting what she wanted, which was away from him at the earliest possible opportunity. The evening hadn't turned out at all how she'd expected, starting with that kiss and ending with Xandro Christofides revealing a fragment of a past she was sure no newspaper or magazine knew about. Because if they did it would already be widespread news.

Another reason for allowing him to take her arm and lead her towards a set of French windows was that she'd grown thoroughly tired of being the cynosure of all eyes.

She was thankful that she managed to remain composed as she walked beside Xandro. Onto the most beautiful terrace she'd ever seen, with potted palms and a view so spectacular her jaw dropped.

She'd thought the Acropolis by day was a sight to behold. But by night, thrown into beautiful relief by giant coloured spotlights, it was simply breathtaking. From this height, it looked close enough to touch. She leaned forward on the balcony, unable to take her eyes off the sight. 'Oh. Wow. Xandro, that's incredible.'

Then she gasped when she realised her mistake. She had no right to such familiarity. Nor could she let down her guard. She was here because he was blackmailing her. Sage started to turn around, away from the seductive view and from the broad-shouldered, powerfully built man behind her.

Her attempt to retreat was immediately thwarted when his arms braced either side of her, trapping her against the balcony. A moment later, he leaned close and whispered in her ear, 'I like the way you say my name.'

Sage cursed the weakness that invaded her body, and pulled back abruptly. *God, what was wrong with her?* 'What are you doing? You've made your point. Two dozen cameras have already recorded our…moment.'

'A moment I would very much like to relive,' he stated blatantly.

When her mouth dropped open in shock, his gaze latched onto her lips. Grey eyes grew turbulent and left her a little more breathless.

Get a grip!

She shook her head, even though her senses leaped wildly at the thought of kissing Xandro again. 'Unless you're trying to win a prize for overkill, I think we should leave well enough alone.'

'On the contrary, I don't think a thirty-second kiss was nearly long enough.'

Thirty seconds? It'd felt as if she'd been trapped in that sexually charged vortex for an eternity.

'Let's try for a full minute this time.'

Before she could respond, he'd captured her mouth in a hot, dominating kiss that left very little brain power to aid her. Just like before, everything else ceased to exist save for the sheer intoxication of what he was doing to her. He explored her mouth with effortless decadence. As if sampling the finest wine, drawing his tongue across her mouth with a lazy swipe before seeking entry. Entry she granted because she just couldn't help herself. The secret place between her thighs plumped and tingled, a hunger taking root deep inside that had her clinging to him by the time he lifted his head.

'I hate to stop, but our nightcap is here,' he murmured against her mouth.

Sage quickly dropped her hands from where they'd clutched his neck. Xandro sent her a wicked look but didn't comment as he turned away. It was only when he dropped one hand that she noticed the waiter setting a tray down on the bar table nearby and pouring the coffee. He then proceeded to lace an amber-coloured liqueur into the beverage.

Sage struggled to get herself back under control as Xandro nodded a dismissal at the waiter and picked up a cup.

'What is that?' she asked, simply in an attempt to dilute the sexually tense atmosphere.

God, what on earth had she been thinking?

'Greek coffee with a lace of Metaxa. Try it.' As he had at dinner, he held the cup to her lips.

Still on automaton mode because her senses were scattered to the wind, she met his dark, fierce gaze then took a sip of the drink.

Like everything she'd tasted this evening, it was a singularly thrilling experience. Which she needed to put an end to if she wanted to survive this minefield Xandro had dropped her into.

When he went to offer her another sip, she shook her head. 'It's great, but coffee makes me hyperactive so I think I'll pass.'

He didn't push. He knocked back the potent drink in one go and replaced the cup down in its saucer. He was about to step up to her again when his phone buzzed from his jacket pocket.

His gaze remained on her face, his eyes scrutinising her for goodness knew what. For a moment she thought he wasn't going to answer it.

Then, eyes still fixed on her face, he reached into his jacket, took out his phone and swiped one long finger across the screen. Only then did he look at the sleek gadget in his hand.

The flare of his nostrils was the first sign that whatever news he'd received was far from pleasing. The second was the flexing of his jaw as he continued to scroll through the message.

Tense seconds ticked by.

Her nerves screeched until she couldn't take it any more. 'What's going on?' she asked.

He continued to stare at the screen. 'It looks like our little PDA exercise has made it online,' he relayed in a tight, grim voice.

'That was the aim, wasn't it?' she asked, then chilled at the deeper meaning. 'Is it Ben?'

'Yes,' he replied.

Her stomach dropped but she forced herself to speak. 'Tell me.'

'He dropped twenty thousand dollars at a Macau casino this evening,' he explained in a voice rusty with anger.

Her chest tightened. 'So he's not reacting as you said he would.'

One finger powered off the phone and he slid it back in his pocket. 'Wrong. The hotel and casino he went to is one I'm in the process of acquiring. It's not a secret that the final stages of negotiations have been delicate lately. The financial media has been running the story for almost two weeks now. Your brother was heard making derogatory comments about me. He was loud and brash enough to get the attention of the management. And he made the point of asking for me by name even though he knows I'm not there. So I'd say he's letting me know he's unhappy about our involvement.'

Sage was not sure which emotion reigned supreme—pain, anger or sadness. 'Is he still there?'

He shook his head. 'He wrong-footed my men. They thought he'd be heading to Hong Kong so they concentrated their efforts there,' he said through gritted teeth. 'They reached Macau three hours ago but haven't found him.'

'Are you…going to lose your deal?' She didn't want to contemplate yet another problem.

Xandro's jaw tightened. 'Ruffled feathers will need to be smoothed over, but I've dealt with more challenging obstacles in a business deal.'

She stared at his resolute expression. After the brief glimpse into his past, a stinging premonition curled over her nape. 'What Ben took from you…it isn't just a meaningless piece of jewellery, is it?'

His eyes locked on hers. Direct. Searing. 'No, it's not.'

He didn't elaborate. She didn't push. In just a handful of hours, she'd learned that his past was an integral part of the man he'd become. And if what Ben had taken was a part of that history, then Xandro wasn't going to rest until he had it back. Which meant his presence in her life, depending on her brother's actions, could get even more overwhelming. She couldn't contain a shiver at the thought.

'Tell me what you're thinking,' he demanded a moment later.

Twin streaks of betrayal and anxiety warred inside her. But in the end she answered. 'I love him. He's been my champion and my strength for a…long time. But sometimes I wish…' She shook her head.

His lips firmed. 'You're wishing again. Let's focus more on getting him to do what we want.'

A pulse of irrational anger charged through her. 'How, exactly? With another fumble at the dinner table?'

If she'd expected a mocking denial, she was about to be sorely disappointed.

'Indeed. Or, better still, a more…demonstrative show.'

Her heart lurched but the free fall wasn't one born of fear but an emotion she didn't want to identify too closely. 'Demonstrative in what way?'

'You, fully ensconced in my life in a way that leaves no room for doubt as to what is between us. You wish to return to the suite to get some sleep? I think it's a good idea. We'll fly out to Vegas first thing in the morning.'

CHAPTER TEN

THE RIDE IN Xandro's helicopter had introduced her to a short but stomach-dipping bout of excitement. His private jet, almost as large as the commercial jet she'd flown to Greece in, introduced her to yet another dimension of his wealth and power that would've made her wonder why he was chasing her brother for a relatively insignificant sum, had she not discovered the truth last night.

One hour after take-off in his private jet, Xandro joined her for lunch. Their meal was served in china she was almost scared to touch. And when she retreated to the back of the plane to wash, the stunning master bedroom suite left her speechless for a long moment. Until she realised she was staring at the bed Xandro slept in when he was flying and her cheeks flamed.

When she returned to the sitting area his gaze rested on her for a long moment, one eyebrow lifted mockingly, as if he'd read her thoughts, before he excused himself to return to the business area.

For the rest of the long flight he left her mostly alone, joining her for another meal when they stopped to refuel in New York.

The straggle of paparazzi at Athens International Airport on their departure was disturbing enough. The flash of cameras when she strode beside Xandro at McCarran Airport in Las Vegas was an experience she never wanted to relive.

As for the questions they'd flung her way—*'Who are you? How long have you been dating Xandro? Is it serious? Are you living together?'*

'It's not always like this for you, surely?' she asked once

they were in the limo, a little bewildered by the invasive questions and the fact that with the partition between them and the driver closed she was cocooned in low-lit privacy with Xandro.

He shrugged, his focus on his phone. 'They take an interest whenever I start dating someone new.'

'And how often is that?' she asked before she could think better of it.

That got his attention although with his eyes shielded by a pair of aviator shades, she couldn't read his expression. 'Are you prying into my sex life, Sage?' he murmured.

'I just want to know how long I have to suffer their interest before I become old news to them.'

'The first few encounters can be a nuisance, but they'll grow tired and move onto the next victim. In your case, however...' He paused, a curious smile playing at his lips.

She waited. 'In my case, what?' she snapped when it became clear he intended to leave her hanging.

'I dare say their interest will last a while longer.'

'That's not funny.'

He removed his shades, then reached across without warning to pluck hers off her nose.

'What are you doing?' she demanded.

'I like to see your eyes when I'm talking to you,' he rasped, his gaze locking on hers with the precision and sizzling effect of a laser beam.

Except now he'd taken her glasses off he just seemed content to stare at her. When his gaze dropped to her mouth a moment later, Sage dragged in a strangled breath. 'You were saying...?'

'Don't count on their interest waning any time soon. There's an innocence about you that draws tabloid hacks like vultures to a fresh carcass.'

'I don't find that reassuring in the least. And I'm not innocent,' she tagged on.

'Are you not? When did you last have a lover?'

She couldn't stop the heat that invaded her cheeks. 'That's none of your business.'

'They're going to eat you up if you blush at questions like that.'

'Well, they're welcome to try. I am not answering you and I certainly won't be answering them!'

The car turned a sharp corner, throwing her across the bench seat towards him. He dropped her sunglasses and caught her by the arms. Between one breath and the next they were inches apart, with his breath washing over her lips as he spoke. 'Who was he, Sage?' he demanded in a low, deep voice. 'Was he your first?'

'Xandro—'

He made a rough sound under his breath. 'Scratch that. I don't think I want to know.'

She was attempting to decipher why his voice rumbled with dark irritation when he dragged her the rest of the way and slanted his mouth over hers, staking a claim she seemed helpless to deny.

The moment she parted her lips he went in deep, stroking her tongue with his in a move so blatantly erotic her breath caught and a moan erupted from her diaphragm before she could stop it.

It seemed the most natural thing in the world to grip his forearms to steady herself against the torrent of sensations buffeting her.

Strong muscles bunched at her touch, an intimation of the leashed power in his body. His tongue stroked hers with increasing insistence, his invasion deepening until she felt as if he meant to devour her.

She'd been kissed before. By the same lover Xandro didn't want to know about. He'd been her first and last experience. One born out of loneliness and curiosity more than anything else. A fellow dancer who'd come to DC at the same time as her and stayed for a short time in the Georgetown townhouse, they'd fallen into a casual friendship, shared the same concerns about being in a strange city and had eventually drifted apart by mutual consent.

She didn't regret giving Paul her virginity. He'd been a gentle, considerate lover. But at the time she'd secretly wondered why the earth hadn't moved for her, or why she hadn't been in a hurry to repeat the experience after the first time. Now she knew it was because he hadn't set her world on fire.

Not like Xandro Christofides was doing now with a mere kiss.

Except it wasn't a mere kiss. It was a blistering lesson in eroticism that singed her to her very toes. The relentless onslaught robbed her of breath and thought, of everything except the need to experience more of the same. Even though she knew she shouldn't.

One hand caressed up her arm and shoulder to rest against her neck, his fingers stroking the runaway pulse beating at her throat. '*Thee mou,*' he muttered gruffly against her stinging lips.

Before good sense could return, he dived in for a longer, even deeper kiss, his groan matching hers as his other hand trailed down her back to the curve of her buttock. He gripped her, kneaded her flesh once, twice, before using his grip to tug her closer.

The shameless evidence of his arousal branded her hip, throwing another log onto the bonfire of her senses. Even through his pants, his girth and power was difficult to dismiss. When her thoughts strayed to what it would feel like to have all that power against her, *inside* her, Sage knew she was in deep trouble.

But, for the life of her, she couldn't pull back, couldn't stop her lips from following where he led, a slave to the pleasure invading her bloodstream. It was why she shockingly heard herself whimper when he lifted his head an age later.

Eyes dark with turbulent hunger raked her face, the tips of his fingers brushing back and forth over her jawline as he sucked in a deep breath.

'We really need to work on our timing.'

'I…what?' she murmured, dazed.

'Much as I'd like to continue this, *pethi mou*, we need to stop. We've arrived.'

It took a long, embarrassing minute for his meaning to sink in. A look out of the window showed the driver waiting for the signal to open the door. Beyond him, the iconic curved skyscraper that was Xandro's flagship hotel and casino soared into the sky in a powerful statement of lights, glass and steel.

Feeling another blast of heat flame up her face, she scrambled away from him. Sage wasn't sure whether he let her go because he also needed to get himself under control.

Just as she wasn't sure why her gaze dropped to his lap at that moment. Sure enough, the erection she'd felt was a bold statement. She quickly averted her eyes, but not before he caught her looking. A breath punched out of him and his jaw gritted for a control-gathering moment before he rapped on the glass window.

He didn't exit immediately, probably because of the surge of paparazzi that surrounded the car.

The bodyguards who'd travelled in a separate car held back the throng as Xandro stepped out and held out his hand to her.

More flashbulbs erupted, the questions coming thick and fast as he helped her out. His sunglasses were back in place. While she was left feeling raw and naked.

'Can I have my glasses back, please?' She silently cringed at the husky, breathless quality of her voice.

He didn't hand them to her. Instead he took his time to tuck a lock of hair behind her ear before he unfolded the glasses, his gaze fixed on her face as he placed them on her nose. Then his fingers drifted down her cheek to brush the corner of her mouth.

If he'd wished to confirm their involvement without saying a word, Xandro achieved it in that single, carefully choreographed moment. The media frenzy erupted around them.

Through it all, he remained calm and supremely collected as he placed his hand in the small of her back and escorted her into his hotel.

She was still shaking, partly with shame, partly with the sinking feeling that he'd manipulated her yet again, as the private lift raced them towards another penthouse suite.

Words churned through her mind. She wanted to accuse, to challenge, to blast him for the rioting emotions coursing through her body. But she was just as responsible. She'd let this wild hunger that he stoked in her take over her senses. She could blame him all she wanted for taking advantage of it, but she'd handed herself over to him on a platter.

Perhaps he was satisfied with the events of the last ten minutes, or he had already moved on from it. Either way, he was back to scrolling through his phone, the very epitome of arrogant control as he strode out of the lift.

The penthouse they entered was twice as large as the one in Athens. 'Do you only live in hotels?' Her voice was sharper than she'd intended.

He stilled, his gaze snapping up from the phone to track her as she paced. 'No. I have several properties around the world,' he drawled.

'Properties, not homes?'

Grey eyes narrowed. 'Do you have a point you wish to make?'

Did she? 'It just seems like a cold existence, that's all.'

He folded his arms and it took a lot of effort not to stare at the flexed power of his biceps. 'You're sure that's all? You want to tell me what's really bothering you?'

She snatched in a breath. 'That was all orchestrated downstairs, wasn't it?'

'Not initially, no. The need to kiss you in the car stemmed from the simple fact that you're exceptionally beautiful and extremely desirable,' he stated baldly.

Her mouth dropped open.

His lips twitched. 'I've succeeded in robbing you of speech.'

It took a minute for her to regroup. 'But again you took advantage of the situation?'

'Every success in life comes from the right advantage being taken at the right time.'

She swung away, unable to look at his breathtaking face and lithe body without recalling how she'd felt plastered to him. But she silently thanked him for reminding her exactly who he was. A manipulator and control freak who used every single situation to his advantage.

Suitably re-armed, she started to walk away, then stopped when she was confronted with a trio of hallways. 'Can you tell me which one is my bedroom? I'm tired.' It was a half-lie. Travelling in private luxury had taken away a huge amount of discomfort, but her senses felt battered. The need to retreat and regroup was paramount.

He studied her for a beat before he started towards her. She tensed, but he walked past her with a curt, 'Come with me.'

She followed, past two doors to the last door on the right. The suite was as plush as the rest of the penthouse, the furnishings elegant and classy. In the small adjoining living room a wide sofa with a dozen cushions beckoned relaxation, as did the impressive drinks cabinet and entertainment centre.

She spotted a door at the far side of the living room. 'Where does that go?'

'A corridor and stairs to the floor upstairs.'

'What's upstairs?'

'My bedroom.'

'Wow. You had secret stairs put in for your lovers? A little archaic, don't you think?' Heavens, what was wrong with her?

He laughed.

And everything inside her stilled at the deep, hypnotic sound. With his head thrown back in amusement, he was almost too much to behold. 'If you ever wish to rethink your career, try your hand at scriptwriting period drama. You have a flair for it.'

She flushed, then pursed her lips, annoyed with herself for continuing to allow him to get under her skin.

'The corridor also leads to my private pool,' he elaborated. 'Use it if you wish. Relax, have something to eat. I have a few things to catch up on so I'm sure you'll be happy to be free of me for a while.'

She didn't answer, simply because a slight hollow feeling yawned inside her with the news of his absence.

His phone buzzed again. With one last look at her, Xandro walked out.

She tried to ignore the bereft feeling that assailed her as he left. She clearly needed something to do.

Decision made, she grabbed her swimsuit, took the door and stairs Xandro had indicated and arrived at a stunning, partially covered swimming pool. Tiled with dark green marble, the waters sparkled with a tropical exoticism that invited her to indulge.

Diving into the pool, she powered through the water, hoping the exertion would clear her mind. She emerged after twenty laps to see the butler approaching with a tray. She devoured the club sandwich and cool drink before returning to her suite.

It was late afternoon but her body clock was wired to Greek time, which was somewhere in the middle of the night.

She lay on the sofa in her favourite T-shirt, grabbed the remote and channel-hopped, with every intention of staying awake because now her mind was a little clearer, she remembered she'd intended to talk to Xandro about where she could practise. The added thought that she had no means of reaching him also began to irk her. Did he work in the hotel? Or did he have offices elsewhere? And, considering he was single with no family, why did he need a penthouse with enough rooms to house a large family?

And how exactly had he managed to evade the gang that had put a price on his head in New York all those years ago?

Questions pelted her mind. Each time she tried to push one away, another rose, more persistent. And then came one that made her chest tighten in disquiet.

She'd stepped into her unwilling role without asking Xandro if he was involved with another woman. Considering the number of pictures she'd seen of him with different women on his arm, it wasn't as if he lacked female attention. When he'd said he had a few things to catch up on, she'd assumed he meant work.

But now she couldn't help but wonder if he'd meant something else. *Someone* else. Regardless of the fact that she was here because he was using her to bring her brother to heel, Sage despised the thought that she might unwittingly be sharing him with another woman.

Except *sharing* meant he was hers. And he wasn't.

Her lips pursed. Nevertheless, it needed to be addressed. Irritated that something so vital had slipped her guard, she turned over, plumped the sofa cushion and turned up the volume on the music station she'd located to drown out the voice mocking her stupidity.

When she opened her eyes again it was to a different view. In the moments it took for her to recall her whereabouts, she stretched her arms above her head, luxuriating in the warm, comfortable sheets.

Then she jack-knifed upright. She was in the bedroom. And the clock on the bedside table showed it was four a.m. She'd slept for almost ten hours. And somewhere during that time she'd been moved from the sofa. The bolt of shock threatened to morph into something else.

She pushed away the covers and stood, looking around

for goodness knew what. Evidence of Xandro's presence? A sign that she might have sleepwalked?

She knew it wasn't the latter. Which made the thought that she'd been in his arms without knowing it all the more unnerving.

Wide-awake and too restless to get back into bed and lie there with her roiling thoughts, she left the room.

The hallway and living room were softly lit. She stood for a moment, listening for signs of occupation. Then, convinced the coffee she smelled was from a timed percolator, she followed the scent to the kitchen.

Xandro stood with his back to her, pouring black coffee into a mug. The temptation to flee warred with the need to stay put, stare at the muscular V-shaped back displayed in all its naked glory above the dark, low-riding sweatpants he wore.

Sage wasn't sure whether she made a sound or whether the predatory instinct she sensed in him alerted him to her presence. He looked over his shoulder, spotted her and swivelled on his heel with a grace that wouldn't have gone amiss in a male dancer. The low buzzing in her ears that had started at the sight of his bare back intensified when she was confronted with his chiselled, silky-haired chest.

'We're both paying the price of jet lag, I see. Coffee?' He lifted his cup.

She wavered.

'Come here, Sage, I'm not going to bite,' he drawled.

It would be childish to retreat now, she told herself. 'Did you move me from the sofa to the bedroom?'

He poured the coffee, added cream and the exact amount of sugar he somehow knew she liked, and strolled over to where she stood. 'Yes.' He held out the cup to her, his gaze moving from the top of her head to her face, then down her body and back again.

She accepted the coffee, making sure to keep her fingers

away from his. Already his scrutiny was messing with her breathing. 'Why?'

'You didn't look comfortable. You were in danger of waking with a sore neck. I tried to wake you but you were dead to the world.'

Somehow that didn't make her feel better. Her every sense warned her that any vulnerability revealed to this man was a bad idea. 'You should've tried harder. Or left me alone.'

'And ignore the rare opportunity to flex my Good Samaritan wings? I don't think so.' His words suggested amusement, but there was a hard look in his eyes that was at variance with his words.

She eyed him warily. 'Are you annoyed about something?'

'Only at the thought that you nearly cost James his job.'

Confused, she stared at him. 'What are you talking about?'

His jaw gritted as his eyes conducted another sweep of her body in the skimpy T-shirt. 'My butler. You're lucky I gave him the night off. Are you in the habit of walking around half naked?'

She frowned. 'I...what?'

'I would've had to fire him if he'd seen you like this,' he rasped.

Her eyes widened. '*You've* seen me like this. Do us both a favour and fire yourself.'

His teeth bared in a grin. Again, she found herself unable to look away. 'Perhaps we should start again. Blame our irrationality on jet lag.'

'That might be wise, although you're winning the irrationality stakes right now.'

'I'm extremely possessive, Sage. Even, I'm discovering, within the boundary of a fake relationship.'

She had no adequate words to counter that. Probably because her brain was still malfunctioning, and his huskily spoken words had started a keen fire in her belly.

She took the safest option and kept her mouth shut and her eyes averted from his breathtaking body.

They sipped their coffee in silence, with him leaning a slim hip on the centre island counter, unapologetically staring at her, and she fighting not to react to his blatant scrutiny. When the tension got too much, she spoke.

'Why were you in my room in the first place?' The thought that she'd been so out of it she hadn't sensed his presence still disturbed her.

He reached into his pocket and brought out her phone. 'You left your purse in the living room. It rang several times after the latest pictures of us hit social media,' he said gravely.

Her gut clenched. 'Ben?'

Xandro gave a curt nod.

'Did you talk to him?'

'Eventually.'

'What did he say?' she demanded.

One corner of his mouth lifted in that half smile she found so intriguing. 'He confirmed he was no longer in Macau, refused to tell me where he was, then threatened murder and mayhem again if I laid another finger on you.'

She lurched forward, reaching for the phone. He raised it out of reach. 'What are you doing? Give me the phone.'

He slipped it back into his pocket. 'Not yet.'

'Xandro—'

His eyes gleamed at her use of his name. But he still shook his head. 'You're feeling emotional. You need to calm down a little before you speak to him.'

Her grip tightened on the cup. 'Don't tell me how to feel.'

'Tell me you're not going to placate him the moment he answers—if he deigns to answer—and I'll give your phone back.'

'Isn't that what you want? For me to speak to him and try to find out where he is?'

He remained silent for a long stretch. Then he shook his head. 'We're past the cat and mouse game of *Guess Where Ben Is*. I made it clear that the only way he'll escape my full wrath is if he comes to me. There's no going back from there. As for you, your hero worship needs to stop.'

She gasped. 'How dare you?'

He didn't so much as blink in the face of her anger. 'I don't need three guesses to know what's got you rattled. We kissed. You enjoyed it. Then you felt guilty afterwards. You're not great at hiding your emotions. Some of it was captured on camera. Now you want to ensure your brother isn't troubled by it. Sorry, *pethi mou*. I can't risk you attempting to alleviate that guilt by confessing our agreement to your brother.'

That the thought had crossed her mind was neither here nor there. But the razor-sharp look he sent her told her he'd guessed her reactions correctly.

'You may be great at ruses like this, but I detest lying.'

'Well, then, enjoy your coffee and allow me to save you from yourself.'

'Xandro...'

His breath expelled a little harsher this time. 'You say my name like that and all I want to do is kiss you.'

'Do you ever not say what you're thinking?' she demanded, partly in exasperation, partly because her body, like the slave it'd clearly become, was already reacting to his words.

'Where's the fun in that?'

She firmed her lips. 'Having a conversation with you is like trying to stop a freight train with a leaf.'

His grin returned. 'I'm touched you find me so formidable.'

'It wasn't a compliment. I meant it was a useless exercise I should think about avoiding altogether,' she said, although she had the most absurd urge to smile back at him.

He shrugged, seemingly unaffected by her glare. After another moment, he straightened. 'Come with me.'

'Why would I do that?'

'Because we've had our first fight of the day and it's not even five a.m. We have a long day ahead of us, so let's counter it with a bit of pleasure, too. Unless you have something against pleasure?' he asked with a wicked glint in his eyes.

She wanted to refuse but curiosity won out. She followed him across the vast double-ceilinged living room to the east corner, where two large windows met. Beneath them the lights of The Strip continued to dance and sparkle in the approaching dawn. But that wasn't where Xandro's attention was centred.

He pointed to a spot on the east horizon between two sprawling luxury hotels. 'Watch,' he murmured.

For several seconds all she saw was grey gloom. Then the purest pulse of yellow burst from behind a mountain. Her breath caught, the sight of the sunrise so pure and gorgeous she gasped. 'Beautiful,' she whispered.

His gaze shifted a fraction and caught hers in the window's reflection. It stayed on her for a moment before he murmured, 'Yes.'

Sage couldn't explain the shiver that charged through her. Her senses had been jumping all over the place since she'd woken up. Xandro's hot and cold play wasn't helping. His smile scrambled her senses. But he didn't attempt to hide his ruthless streak.

She wanted to say something. Thank him for showing her the spectacular sunrise. But she couldn't find words that wouldn't be flippant or reveal the emotions running riot through her. Nor could she dismiss the effect his half naked body was having on her.

'You're fidgeting,' he observed after five minutes. The

sun was now a whole dazzling vision in the sky, anointing the sleepless city with a new day.

'I'm…' She stopped, then broached the only subject she could without confronting her confounding feelings. 'What if Ben never returns?'

All traces of mirth left his face. Once again, he became Xandro Christofides, ruthless and controlling mogul in pursuit of a vital piece of his past. 'Then you'll find out the hard way that you're not as important to him as you think. And I'll devote even more of my considerable resources into getting back what's mine.'

A moment ago she'd been alarmed that she couldn't figure him out. The simple truth was he was a merciless strategist who would chew her up and spit her out at the first sign of vulnerability if it served his purpose.

CHAPTER ELEVEN

THAT OBSERVATION AND acceptance settled a few things for her.

Suddenly chilled, she turned her back on the sunrise, shivering despite the warmth in the room.

Xandro stepped in front of her, piercing eyes narrowing on her. 'Do you think me cold?' he observed clinically.

'What I think of you doesn't matter any more, does it? I'm just a pawn in your battle with Ben.'

His lips thinned. 'Sage—'

She shook her head. 'That's fine; I get it. But there is one thing I'd like, though. Now that you've succeeded in setting your little fire under him, can this ruse be over already? I'll stay here, of course, but no more PDAs, if you don't mind.'

'I do mind,' he returned implacably. 'Our agreement stays in place until I have my possession back.'

She took a deep breath, realising she was partly to blame for her current situation. When she'd first agreed to act as the lure for her brother, she'd been far away from here in a foreign land, removed from the possible consequences such a visible association with Xandro would bring.

Greece was his home, despite whatever had happened to rip his family apart. He was revered there and, according to what she'd read about him, his clout and image extended through the halls of government. But Vegas was his stomping ground and, as she'd witnessed yesterday, the media on this side of the world clamoured for all things Xandro Christofides. She couldn't hide from confronting what that could mean for her. Extended exposure to his world would damage hers in the long run.

'I haven't worked this hard to have people think I got this position by sleeping with you,' she forced out.

'And you care that much about what other people think?' he countered.

'When it can impact on my career long after I'm smoke in your rear-view mirror? Absolutely.'

He raised an eyebrow. 'For all you know, this association will benefit you.'

'I make assumptions based on the evidence I have. Isn't it true that you don't date anyone for longer than a few months?'

His jaw gritted for a moment, then he shrugged. 'Regardless of that fact, I assure you that the impact—'

'I don't want you to impact on me in any way.'

'Don't be naive.'

She inhaled sharply. 'Excuse me?'

'You live in a city where networking literally rules the world. Whatever happens between us, you can take comfort in the fact that it won't adversely affect your career.'

'Sorry, I *don't* want to take comfort in that. I need to be able to go to bed at night knowing I don't owe my success to anyone but myself.'

'And I want to take you to bed at night, period,' he gritted out roughly.

Her mouth gaped, momentarily silenced by the ragged hunger etched in his face. They stared at each other for an age.

Then he gave her a mocking smile. 'Now that I have you adequately speechless, I'll add this. Your brother is in a spiral. This thing will be over by the time the production starts. Whatever rumours arise from our association will eventually die. In the meantime, I intend to explore wherever our attraction takes us.'

'Nowhere. It'll take us nowhere,' she stressed firmly. For his sake and definitely for hers.

He shrugged. 'We'll see. And now I think I'll draw a line under this discussion and get on with my day.'

He started to walk away.

'What about your…whoever warms your bed these days? Won't she object to you carrying on this charade with another woman?'

He glanced over his shoulder, one eyebrow quirked. 'Are you asking me if I have a lover stashed away, Sage? One who is open-minded enough not to object when I kiss another woman in public?'

She shrugged. 'I know exclusivity is optional among some couples these days.'

His face hardened. 'It's not optional for me. I don't have a lover. And if you had a lover, I would object. Very strongly. Have you forgotten that *I don't share*?'

The pulse of anger and possessiveness in his voice made something tighten inside her. She pushed it away. She couldn't afford to be waylaid by superfluous emotions right now. Especially when another important thought impinged.

He gave an exasperated sigh. 'Something else on your mind?'

'Yes. I've spent the better part of two days without rehearsing. I'd like to find a dance studio somewhere in the city and practise my routines.'

He remained silent for a second. 'There's no need to leave the penthouse to do that,' he said.

Surprise widened her eyes. 'What?'

'The big bad ogre has thought of everything. Come.'

The command, like before, was domineering, demanding her immediate obedience. Her curiosity was stronger this time, so she followed.

He took her down the same corridor that led to her bedroom but stopped at the first door and threw it open.

The space was as big as her bedroom suite, but this room was bare, with polished wood floors. It faced the east, and sunlight slanted through the windows, bathing the room in brilliant light.

In one corner a state-of-the-art music system had been set up on a steel pedestal. Next to it was a sofa, a coffee table and a pile of magazines. Everything she needed to keep her training on schedule was right here.

She watched, a little stunned, as Xandro walked to the music station, picked up a remote and hit a button. Familiar music by the artist she used to practise and perform her auditions with filtered into the room. Sage wasn't sure why the discovery that he knew her preferred music should cause her heartbeat to accelerate, but it did.

Accepting in that moment that Xandro Christofides was the most mercurial and dynamic man she'd ever met, she watched him prowl, shirtless and magnificent and totally dangerous to her senses, back to her.

'Now I won't worry that you'll attempt to strangle yourself with the wire from your headphones while you dance,' he drawled. 'Will that be all?'

It was barely six a.m. but she supposed powerful, drop dead gorgeous tyrants, like sharks, needed to keep moving, seeking out their next target.

She nodded, unable to get her vocal cords to work in that moment. He stared down at her for a beat before he nodded and left the room. She looked around, still unable to take in what he'd done for her. Like sharing the sunrise with her, this gift seemed at variance with the ruthless persona Xandro exhibited.

More than a little confused, Sage gave up trying to decrypt this new facet of Xandro, and went to her room to change before returning to the music room. She practised until she heard a knock on the door. 'Come in.'

James entered with a silver breakfast trolley piled with domed dishes. 'Good morning, miss. Mr Christofides asked me to bring you breakfast at nine.'

He lifted the dishes to reveal bacon, eggs, bagels and a

selection of muesli and fruit. He waited for her to serve her-self and sit on the sofa, then set a sterling silver tray on her lap. He returned her smile of thanks with one of his own.

'Mr Christofides asked me inform you that you'll be dining out tonight. And he's also arranged for a stylist to deliver a few items of clothing for you.'

'Um…what?'

James opened his mouth. Sage shook her head. 'Sorry, I heard you. I just…' She stopped. 'It's fine. I'll talk to…' She stopped again, realising that she had no means of reach-ing Xandro. And that even if she did, he'd never returned her phone!

'Can I contact him?' she asked.

'No, I believe he's in meetings for most of the day.'

The distinct feeling that Xandro had done that delib-erately stayed with her, right up until James knocked on the door again after lunch to inform her the clothes had arrived. Except *a few items* turned out to be three clothes racks packed with at least three dozen outfits and countless boxes of shoes and accessories.

'I can't accept all this!'

The butler and maid both stilled. 'Um…would you like me to send them back, miss?' James asked.

She took a deep breath. 'No. I'll take care of it.'

'Very well, miss. Nina will put them in your dressing room for the time being. Lunch will be served in fifteen minutes.' With that, he left the makeshift studio.

Only to return at six to inform her that Xandro was run-ning late. 'He would like you to meet him downstairs in half an hour.'

Gritting her teeth, she barely stopped herself from slam-ming the bedroom door. With more than a little aggres-sion, she tore off the bathrobe she'd shrugged into after her shower. Her irritation not only stemmed from the fact that Xandro was manipulating her—*again*—but she'd also discovered that he'd effectively stopped any mutiny on her part by having the clothes she'd used in Greece removed from her wardrobe.

A slightly concerned-looking Nina had confirmed that Mr Christofides had indeed left instructions for Sage's clothes to be dry-cleaned, and no, she had no idea when they would be returned. So, short of wearing her yoga pants and leotard to dinner, Sage was forced to comb through her spanking-new wardrobe.

She plucked a white silk dress from the rack because it looked the most uncomplicated. The single across-the-shoulder strap design was elegant enough to pass any class test. She also scraped her hair into a neat bun at the top of her head because, with her half-hour notice, it was the most expedient.

Black platform shoes and a black designer clutch finished the outfit. Simple gold hoop earrings, a touch of make-up and perfume, and she was ready. She bit her tongue when James informed her he was to escort her downstairs.

They emerged from the lift into a busy foyer. But still she saw Xandro immediately. He was on the phone, one hand in his pocket as he paced beneath a giant spotlit window with lithe, predatory grace, drawing an indecent number of gazes, mostly female.

He reached the end of the space he'd created for himself, turned and saw her. A deathly stillness froze his body as his eyes locked on her. The wild zap of electricity that charged between them nearly caused her to stumble. Fingers clenched tight around her clutch, she snatched in an agitated little breath, lifted her chin and carried on walking.

Xandro murmured into his phone and hung up without taking his eyes off her. When she was within six feet of him, his eyes shifted to James. The butler stopped abruptly, wished her good evening and quietly retreated.

She reached Xandro, opened her mouth, only to have him shake his head at her. 'Remember, we have an audience.'

She bit back her words, and told herself she should at least be thankful he hadn't ordered her to smile. With a casual wave of his hand, he indicated for her to precede him.

Bodyguards held the door open for them as the paparazzi once again descended the moment they stepped outside. She tried not to outwardly react when she felt Xandro's hand on her hip but, inside, her belly clenched against the branding heat of his touch as he guided her to where his limo idled.

'You took my phone,' she accused the moment the door shut, sealing them in the car. 'And my clothes.'

Eyes gleaming with blatant hunger rose from perusing her body to meet hers. 'Yes. And good evening to you too, *pethi mou*. You look exquisite.'

She brushed away the drawled compliment. 'Smudging the lines between right and wrong isn't a huge problem for you at all, is it?'

His expression momentarily tightened, but his voice was smooth when he answered. 'It was more efficient to provide you with new clothes than to have your things packed and shipped across the country.'

She didn't think so somehow. She'd seen the labels on the new clothes. 'Xandro—'

A breath hissed out and he squeezed the bridge of his nose with two fingers. 'If we're going to fight again, can I at least get a stiff drink first?' He reached for the crystal decanter. He poured a shot of amber liquor and downed it in one go.

She frowned. 'What's wrong? Has something happened? Ben—'

'Not everything is about your brother!'

Her relief was eroded a moment later by a concern she didn't want to feel. 'Okay. Then what's bothering you?'

He laughed as he set the glass in its receptacle. 'Will you give me a chance to count?'

'Are you mocking me?'

He sat back and pinned her to the seat with his gaze. 'You

want to know what's wrong? You, wearing that dress that makes your legs look a mile long and drawing the eyes of every man in the room. You, sitting there, giving me lip for doing something nice for you, while my imagination runs wild with this insane hunger for you, and you glare at me with your gorgeous green eyes. That's what's bothering me,' he finished with a snap.

For the first time in her life Sage wanted to do the unthinkable. She wanted to run from a fight. She wanted this overbearing man to win. Because the charged words he spoke were doing something alarming and infinitely dangerous to her.

'You...you can't say things like that to me.' Her voice shook and there was nothing she could do to stop it.

His sensual mouth twisted. 'I speak what's on my mind. You know this about me.'

'But... I thought what we're doing...'

His hand slashed through the air. 'That's just the problem, *glikia mou*. We're not even doing anything and I'm already aggravated beyond all reason. So let's call a truce on the bickering and just keep *doing nothing*, yes?'

Unable to find a response for that, she nodded.

It set the routine for the next two weeks.

She rose early, drank her cup of restorative coffee while standing at the window watching the sunrise. After that, she practised for three hours before breakfast. The times when Xandro joined her at the window, they stood in quiet, charged silence.

In the evenings, she dressed in another exquisite creation, met him downstairs, and off they went to dinner. Afterwards they would either go to a bar for a nightcap, or a nightclub where he would pull her close, swaying with her on the dance floor while he trailed kisses over her face and suggestive touches along her body.

The moment he was sure their antics had been captured on camera, he would place his hand on her back and guide her to the car. Back in the penthouse, he would bid her a stiff goodnight and retreat to his study.

Although she got her phone back, Ben never called. Her suspicion that his number was being blocked to her phone received a curt, 'Leave it alone,' when she broached the subject with Xandro.

And with Ben's trail having gone ice-cold, they'd arrived at a standoff.

Xandro, for his part, worked punishing hours. Either that or he was actively avoiding the penthouse.

So when a knock came on the studio door late afternoon two Sundays later, she stopped mid-practise and called out a response.

Xandro entered holding two bottles of mineral water. He wore a black T-shirt and his favourite sweatpants, but his feet were bare. It took a lot of effort not to stare at them.

'James tells me you've been in here since dawn.'

She shrugged, warily accepting the drink from him when she noticed the other item in his hand. The dumbbell she'd requested from James earlier. 'I'm not really keeping track of time.'

'At the risk of getting my head bitten off, you'll wear yourself out if you don't slow down.'

Self-conscious of the mild sheen of sweat filming her body, she retreated to grab her towel and dabbed at her face and neck. 'I was just about to do a last set before I call it a day.'

'But you asked for this.' He held up the dumbbell and his gaze dropped to her wrist. 'What's wrong with your wrist? And don't say nothing. I've seen you favouring it more than once.'

'It doesn't affect my work,' she said hastily. A little too hastily if his shrewd gaze was any indication. Sage flinched inwardly.

'I didn't suggest otherwise. But I still want to know,' Xandro said.

'Why?' she asked suspiciously.

He sighed. 'I'm aware I'm still the big, bad ogre in your eyes, Sage, but let's not turn every conversation into a battle, hmm?'

Maybe she was tired from the long day. Or maybe she didn't want the shaky truce they'd struck over the last two weeks ending just yet. Either way, she found herself nodding.

Xandro set the dumbbell on the small table before he straightened and faced her. Bracing herself for sharp questions, she was stunned when he took her hand and slid his thumb over her throbbing wrist.

'Were you injured?'

The spark ignited by his touch slowly began to build. 'Yes.'

'How did it happen?' he asked quietly.

Her mouth twisted. 'For some strange reason I attracted the attention of the most popular girls at school. Except they weren't just popular, they were nasty with it.'

His fingers drifted over her wrist again. The touch was light but she felt it all the way inside. 'It's not strange at all. Talent and beauty is often resented.'

She grimaced. 'I wasn't beautiful. I was all arms and legs and very clumsy inelegance.'

'Your aggressors saw your potential and were envious. Talent like yours is in your DNA.'

The laughter that emerged was raw with pain and bitterness. 'That's not what my parents said. Getting embroiled in the issues at school and getting injured only strengthened their belief that my dancing was just a burden to them.'

His eyes narrowed. 'This is the real reason you're estranged from your parents, isn't it? Not your disagreement over the hotel?'

Her bruised heart lurched. The heavy stone that had lodged itself in her belly for far longer than she wanted to admit jumped into her throat, blocking her answer.

'Sage?'

'Yes,' she murmured. 'That's how it started. They didn't believe me when I told them I was being bullied. Every school day for three years I had to face those girls and their vicious taunts. It worsened when I joined the drama class. Then it grew…physical.'

Xandro's jaw tightened. 'What did they do?'

'It was mostly silly things at the start. A foot tripping me up. A shove here and there.' She stopped and took a shaky breath. 'Then I was picked to be Odette in the school's *Swan Lake* production.'

'What happened?' he pressed.

'The leader of the group, Darcy, wanted the part. She and her gang confronted me in the bathroom. We…fought. She broke my wrist.'

He swore under his breath. 'You told your parents this too?'

It hurt to nod. She wondered why she was baring herself to him. But the time to bolt the door had gone. She'd already spilled her deepest anguish. Whether it would come back to bite her wasn't something she wanted to consider now. 'They thought I was making it all up.'

Xandro's gaze dropped to the wrist he now cradled in both hands. His fingers traced the delicate veins beneath her skin, sparking hotter flames. 'But they took you to get your injury seen to, right?'

Tears clogged at the back of her throat. She swallowed hard to keep them from breaking free as she shook her head. 'No. They kept putting it off. It was Ben who took me to the ER three days later. The X-ray showed my wrist was fractured in three places.'

His fingers tightened momentarily, then he exhaled harshly. 'And your parents still didn't come around?'

'My mother said she was sorry that I was in pain. But she wasn't sorry enough to make the three meetings the principal tried to get her to attend to address the bullying problem. I was almost out of high school anyway so I guess she didn't see what the fuss was all about.' Sage heard the bleakness echoing in her voice and pursed her lips. 'Anyway, that's behind me now. I didn't mean to unload on you like this. Just that…'

'I was relentless and overbearing.'

Her sadness wouldn't allow a smile to slip through. 'Yes.'

Xandro remained silent after her response. For a long time he just caressed her wrist, his gaze riveted on it. 'Did it leave lasting damage?'

'No…it's just…every now and then I think I feel the pain.'

He nodded. 'Phantom pain. When you're overworked or distressed,' he surmised.

'Yes. The doctor said it was all in my mind.'

'And using the dumbbell?'

'It helps me feel strong. Whole.'

His head snapped up, and he stared at her with piercing eyes. 'You *are* whole. You powered through your adversity. If nothing else, you can take comfort in that.'

'And finding out my parents turned away the talent scout who wanted me to join his company in New York when I was eighteen? How do I power through that?' she questioned bitterly. Then immediately shook her head. 'Don't answer that. I'm not even sure why I'm telling you all this.'

'Because you're still upset by it. Dismissing your ambition was one thing. Deliberately setting out to sabotage your chosen career was quite another. They broke your trust.'

She suppressed a sad smile. They'd broken more than her trust. They'd broken her heart.

'Not many people can turn their backs on everything they treasure to make a success of their lives. Don't undervalue what you've achieved. Besides, that scout's loss is my gain.'

His voice had dropped lower, and the fingers moving

over her skin were creating even more potent magic on her senses. 'Xandro—'

The fierce light in his eyes intensified. 'What piece were you working on?'

She struggled to recall. Melissa had sent three choreographed routines the week before. The one she was working on was the final one. 'It's called Resistance.'

He nodded. Looked around. Then back at her. 'May I stay?' he asked. The request was unexpected, as was the plea in it.

Her already feeble resolve weakened further. 'Okay, if you want to.'

'I want to. Very much.'

The way he said the words heightened the voltage of awareness inside her. It grew steadily as he dropped her wrist, picked up his water and walked backwards, away from her, to lean against the wall.

Watching. Waiting.

She dragged her gaze from his hypnotic one and picked up the remote.

The first strains of her favourite music filled the room. She discarded the towel and water, fighting the nerves swarming inside her.

Without taking his eyes off her, he took a drink from his own bottle then slid down the glass wall onto the floor.

'You may begin.'

Self-consciousness while dancing had never been an issue. Until now. Perhaps it was the discussion of her injury, and the knowledge that she'd almost given up after that low point in her life, that made her feel raw now. Or the desire to prove to him, and to herself, that her passion burned brighter than ever.

Whatever the reason, Sage wanted to give the best performance of her life.

She spread her arms wide, feeling the power and joy

tingle up from her toes, taking over the pain in her heart to settle deep in her soul.

The travelling pirouettes took her from one end of the room to the other. By the time she reversed position and executed the first arabesque, the nerves had dispersed.

Instinct and hours of practice made the movement flow from her core, the joy she'd felt from the first time she'd danced fizzing through her blood. As she twisted, leapt and turned, the tricky part of the routine she'd been practising all day grew closer. She hadn't perfected it yet, so she almost bypassed it to finish with a move she knew by heart. At the last moment, she decided to go for it. The slow back bend was melting and effortless, and holding herself up on her fingers and toes made her feel as if she were floating on air. But it was the power she needed to snap her lower body into an upside down split that gave her a moment's pause.

With a deep breath, she planted her hands on the floor and drove up with everything she had.

Xandro's stunned hiss was even sweeter music to her ears than the triumph of executing the move. She never looked his way though, never stopped until the routine was done.

She straightened from her crouched position, flushed, infinitely thrilled, and watched him slowly rise from the floor. Chest rising and falling, he came towards her, a predator fixated on her.

His jaw was set and a ferocious light blazed in his eyes that reached out and singed her. 'I'm glad you're not running a hotel in rural Virginia, Sage, because you are a truly exceptional dancer.' His voice was gravel-rough, terse with an emotion she couldn't decipher. 'I can't take my eyes off you.'

'Th…thank you.'

He stepped closer, remorselessly invading her space. But this time she didn't move or demand he step away. They were caught in the grip of a fever she wasn't sure she wanted to escape.

'We're not in public so I won't attempt to instigate an-

other publicity-seeking stunt. But I would very much like
to taste you again.'

'Xandro... I don't think it's—'

He stepped closer still, until his mouth was a hair's
breadth from hers. 'Don't think. Follow through on this
raw, beautiful emotion and just kiss me, Sage,' he muttered roughly.

Something snapped inside her. She complied because it
felt as if she'd waited a lifetime to kiss him since the last
time. As if her very soul would wither and die if she didn't
succumb to his demand. Her arms were sliding around his
neck before she'd given herself full permission to assuage
her terrible hunger.

A second later it was too late to change her mind. But
that was fine. This was just a kiss. Like the ones before, it
would have a beginning, a middle and end, which would
probably lead to another fight and them both going their
separate ways.

So when his strong hands gripped her waist, captured
and lifted her high as their lips met, fused, then parted in a
breathless dance as old as time, Sage went with it.

Because it felt good. But it would end in a moment.

CHAPTER TWELVE

XANDRO SPEARED URGENT fingers through her hair, glorying in the silky weight as he angled her head for a better, deeper taste of her. *Thee mou*, but she tasted like nothing he'd ever experienced. Just as watching her dance with such glorious abandonment was like nothing he'd ever seen. Knowing she'd carved this beautiful niche for herself in the face of cruel adversity almost threatened to shake his soul. Their paths through life had been vastly different, and yet he felt a kinship that pulled even harder at the connection he hadn't been able to deny since that first moment he'd seen her dance.

Despite the hunger building within him, he pulled away a fraction because he couldn't continue without telling her.

'Do you know how beautiful you looked when you finished dancing, framed against the window with joy on your face and the sunlight in your hair? Do you know how much I wanted you, watching you dance like that?' he breathed against her mouth.

Her breath caught, and the sound transmitted straight through him.

'I...'

He pressed his mouth to hers again. 'I want you, Sage, so much,' he repeated, unwilling to accept that hesitation on her face.

Her breathing fractured. It was all he could do not to drag her out of the room and upstairs, claim her immediately, and to hell with niceties. But that innocence he'd caught glimpses of right from the beginning stayed his hand.

He pulled his fingers from her hair. 'Do you want me?' he demanded when she remained silent.

Her stunning eyes darkened, attempted to shift from his. He tracked her gaze, refusing her the option of denying what she felt. 'Tell me,' he insisted.

'I…can't. This isn't a good idea.'

The thought of rejection, of what was standing in his way, tightened his gut. 'Because your brother disapproves of us?'

She frowned. 'No…'

'Are you going to allow him to dictate your life?'

'That's not what I'm doing. I'm saying no because—'

'You like to cut your nose off to spite your face? Are you really going to deny that you are as hungry for me as I am for you?' His gaze dropped to her ripe mouth, damp with his kiss, then lower to the chest that rose and fell sharply with each breath she took. 'You want me almost as much as I want you. Continuing to deny it is frustrating the hell out of both of us. So let's be adult about this, shall we?'

'And just scratch this momentary itch and to hell with everything else that's important? I don't just give in to my base instincts because the need is there. We don't even like each other. You're an overbearing control freak.'

'And you're too blindly loyal for your own good.' He wanted to close the gap between them because even that tiny distance was driving him nuts. 'We each have our flaws, but I'm willing to overlook them for a chance to experience this insane fire between us. Maybe you should too. Maybe just this once take what you want for yourself and—yes, to hell with everyone else. Are you brave enough to do that?'

The look she gave him was alarmingly resolute. 'You can't dare me into sleeping with you.'

In that moment it felt as if he'd never negotiated so hard for anything. 'I'm daring you to give yourself permission to find pleasure in something you desire. Like you do with your dancing.'

She started to shake her head.

He brushed a kiss across her mouth, mercilessly tempting her. 'Touch me,' he pleaded.

Her fingers fluttered beside her thighs. The need to feel those fingers against his skin grew into an unbearable ache inside him. 'Now, Sage.'

Her chin rose in that damned but adorable challenge that made his blood stir. 'You can't make me.'

With a smile that felt decidedly feral, he breached that last gap between them. Taking care not to touch her, he planted his hands on the glass either side of her head and pulled back until their lips were a scant inch apart. 'I am staying right here, Sage. You can touch me. You can kiss me. Or you can leave. Your choice.'

She made a tiny sound, one he wanted to believe was a sign of her impending surrender. 'You don't play fair.'

Had he not been caught in the grip of the strongest craving in his life he would've smiled. 'No, I don't. But, if it helps, know that I've never wanted anything more than I want you right now.' The words echoed through him, startling him for a moment with their stunning truth.

Along with it came the realisation that the unsettling void that had existed inside him since the loss of the necklace had abated without him being aware of its absence.

Xandro didn't want to think it was her doing. Or even attribute it to the need to keep the truce he'd struck between them, although he was enjoying the peace. So much so, he hadn't read Archie Preston's last three reports on the possible whereabouts of Ben Woods and where he might surface next. Nor had Xandro granted his security chief's request for a meeting. There would be time for all of that later.

For now, he concentrated on the woman before him, saw the effect of his words in the quickening of the pulse hammering at her throat.

He wanted to taste that agitation. But he locked his knees and hung onto his control. Time dragged. The minute that passed was an eternity. Their frantic breaths mingled, the turbulence of their emotions twisting in the air around them.

Her hand coming up to rest on his chest felt like the greatest benediction. And yet it triggered an even deeper hunger. Immediately he wanted more. Her hands, her mouth, her legs wrapped tight around him. He stayed put, staring into her stormy eyes, willing her to take him. Her other hand joined the first, the tentative exploration of his chest causing his stomach to clench tight.

A rough sound exploded from his throat. She inhaled sharply, but whatever she read in his face spurred her on. She trailed her fingers over his shoulders, then wrapped them around his neck.

'Yes.' An encouragement he couldn't hold back.

She blinked, and her gaze dropped to where she was caressing him. He watched, curious and turned on and insanely absorbed by her courage and innocence. He wasn't prepared for her to lean forward and press her lips against the pulse at his neck, the exact same way he had been dying to kiss hers a moment ago.

His knees threatened to buckle, the hands planted on the glass curling into tight fists. 'You're driving me insane, Sage.'

She made that inciting little sound again. Then repeated her campaign to annihilate him by nipping at the skin below his jaw with her teeth. His guttural groan brought a saucy smile to her face. His eyes narrowed. 'Are you enjoying your power?'

Her answer was a shaky inhalation before one hand curled over his nape and fisted his hair. He met her kiss because he couldn't not. Because his hunger had reached breaking point.

Their lips met in a crash of fire and desire. She opened for him and he ruthlessly claimed. The first touch of her tongue against his threatened to wipe him out. Unable and unwilling to resist touching her any more, he wrapped his hands around her waist, pinned her against the glass and gorged on her. They kissed like ravenous animals until the barest edge had been satisfied.

He traced her delicious frame, relearning curves he had explored many times in his imagination. He cupped her full breasts, his thumbs sweeping over her tight nipples. She jerked against him, a sweet groan squeezing through their lips to softly echo around the room. And because he craved it again, he repeated the action.

'Oh.' She sighed against his mouth.

'God, you're so responsive.'

'Xandro…'

He dropped his forehead against hers. 'Why does the way you say my name turn me on so much?'

Her eyes widened, a blush staining her cheeks at his charged words. He laughed under his breath. 'Did I shock you?'

'I'm not going to give you the satisfaction of an answer. You know exactly what you do.'

He laughed again then leaned down to taste her lips. And, just like that, desire erupted again, volcanic in its power and might. Satisfaction punched through him when she immediately wrapped her arms around his neck and opened up to him. Banding his arms around her, he lifted her off her feet.

'Wrap your legs around me,' he commanded.

The journey to his bedroom took longer than anticipated, on account of needing to stop and kiss and caress her in an attempt to satisfy the hunger coursing through him. By the time he kicked the door shut behind them, he was poised on the edge of madness. It was why he tumbled them onto the bed, and reached up to tug the elastic band from her hair.

Thick, lustrous curls spilled in fiery waves onto his pillow. He slid his fingers through the vibrant strands, the act of finally exploring that part of her she'd kept restrained shockingly easing an ache he wasn't even aware resided in him until that moment.

'I've pictured you like this, your flaming hair spread over my white sheets, your beautiful body beneath mine.

And now here you are.' Fingers locked in her hair, he kissed her again.

With her legs still wrapped around him, he only needed to lower himself a fraction to settle his hardness between her thighs.

Despite the layers of clothing between them, her heat surrounded him, driving him another desperate inch to the edge of his endurance. With control fast waning, he tore himself away from her, sitting back on his heels. 'I want you naked.'

Her breath stilled, the beginnings of apprehension flitting over her face. He captured her hands, kissing her knuckles before resting them on his thighs. 'Nothing is going to happen here that you don't want, *pethi mou*. But I fully intend to make you mine.' He was aware that his voice contained an implacability that risked a resurgence of her stubbornness. But he also knew he would use every weapon in his arsenal to keep her exactly where she was.

He was so intent on plotting that he didn't hear her response. The look on her face, however, indicated that his diabolical scheming might be unnecessary.

'Say that again,' he slurred thickly.

'I want you, too.'

Simple words. And yet so powerful, so debilitating to his control that he froze for a stunned second before the promise of pleasure triggered frantic movement. He pulled his T-shirt over his head then disposed of hers. The blush staining her cheeks travelled lower with his avid scrutiny of her sun-kissed skin. Words of praise, unfamiliar words, far removed from those he normally bestowed on a lover, crowded his tongue.

He wasn't sure why he withheld them. Perhaps he already felt too exposed now he'd realised that his reason for having Sage in his life in the first place, had shifted into something else. That the clanging need to retrieve the necklace no longer burned as fiercely.

He still wanted his ruby necklace back but, through Sage,

he'd revived old memories of his mother and her love of music and dancing that had allayed his immediate anxiety over the missing jewellery.

That knowledge, along with the unfamiliar sensation of being on the edge of his self-control, had him more than rattled. So in silence he hooked his fingers into the waist-band of her yoga pants and drew them down with less finesse than he usually employed. But when she lay almost bare before him, her sensational body framed against his sheets, he couldn't hold back his words any longer. 'You are breathtaking,' he extolled in a voice he barely recognised as his own.

She shifted, a mixture of innocence and confidence in her womanhood that tossed another layer of arousal over him. Knowing he wouldn't be able to sustain this level of temptation for much longer, he reached behind her and un-hooked her simple satin bra. Full, beautiful breasts spilled free, and he fell on them with a decidedly unsophisticated eagerness. He laved the sweet tight peaks, shamelessly feed-ing on her tortured groans as her back arched off the bed and her nails dug into his skin.

'Xandro,' she gasped, her movements growing more frantic with each caress of his tongue. He closed his eyes, losing himself in her sounds and scent. Releasing one breast, he trailed his hand over her silky-smooth midriff, then lower until he reached the edge of her panties. He delved beneath, eagerly searching for that tight bundle of nerves and her feminine core beneath. The moment he touched her there, she bucked wildly beneath him. Craving more of that un-fettered response, he circled her faster, firmer, while trail-ing his mouth across her belly.

'Come for me, *pethi mou*,' he growled against her skin.

Sage couldn't believe it was possible to experience so much pleasure for this long without erupting in a ball of flames.

Dear God, she couldn't believe she was here in his bed, shamelessly aroused sounds spilling from her throat.

It was supposed to be just a kiss.

But the magic he'd woven from the moment he'd stepped into the room and asked to stay was always going to lead to this. She wasn't so far gone as to believe what was happening was written in the stars, but there had been an inevitability powered by the chemistry between them. This might be a mistake she'd regret in the morning. Their worlds were too different for anything more than a brief collision of lust to be sustained. But in this moment nothing had felt so good.

She cried out as his fingers increased their decadent pressure. Driven out of her mind with desire, she sank her nails into the only solid thing she could find. Xandro's shoulders. He groaned and muttered something indecipherable. A moment later her panties were tugged from her body. And then his mouth replaced his fingers.

Shock threatened to supersede pleasure. Her head jerked off the pillow, her face flaming. 'No... I...'

Turbulent grey eyes locked on hers, daring her to deny the act he was determined to deliver. 'Come for me,' he insisted again, and then pressed his mouth against her needy core in a bold, possessive kiss.

Her unravelling was wild, unfettered and immediate. Sensation piled upon sensation as he stroked her with his tongue. Minutes passed. The burst of light across her vision slowly faded and her shameless pants reduced to heavy breaths. Then a different sensation suffused her as he kissed his way up her body.

'Incredible,' he murmured against the corner of her mouth.

Sage was certain the tail end of her climax was drawn out just by his deep voice alone. Another shiver rippled through her when she heard him rip the condom open. She opened her eyes to the sight of a gloriously naked and magnificent Xandro crouched above her.

He really was the perfect male specimen. Big and un-apologetically male, the fierce intent blazing in his eyes snatched her newly regained breath away. One hand fisted her hair, the other clamped on her hip. Eyes locked on hers, Xandro thrust steady and deep inside her.

Her hoarse cry tangled with his gravel-rough groan. When he was buried to the hilt inside her, they both stilled, the earthshaking moment of their union demanding a little time to assimilate. And then he was moving, stretching her, filling her again.

The sensation was unlike anything she'd ever experienced.

Again Xandro muttered something in Greek, hot and heavy against her neck, as he penetrated her. Increasing the rhythm, he set them both on a journey that left her clinging to him, her heart threatening to beat itself out of her chest. Just when she thought it couldn't get any better, he slid his hand beneath her, angling her hips to meet his thrusts.

'I love the way you tremble against me like this. Mine. All mine,' he rasped in her ear.

Sage would never know if it was that possessive throb in his voice that sent her over the edge. She had a feeling it was everything about him. His magnificent body, the raging fire in his eyes, the words she couldn't understand, the sheer animalistic power of his thrusts.

She fell off the edge of the world with a searing scream that triggered his own release. Convulsions rippled through them in endless waves of bliss. And when he collapsed against her, sweat from his body mingled with her own, sealing them even tighter together.

They stayed locked like that, catching their breath.

Inevitably, of course, reality crept close. The moment he left the bed to head to the bathroom, unwanted thoughts began to crowd in.

What had she done?

With the itch scratched, would they return to being

strangers who snapped at each other when they were in the same room? Or would that be too much to even bother with—?

'*Thee mou*, we've barely finished making love and already I can hear you thinking loud enough to wake the dead,' he rasped as he slid back into bed and tugged her close.

She bit her lip. 'I can't help it.'

He propped himself on one elbow and stared down at her with eyes that were still stormy from their sexual high. 'Maybe I should dedicate all my time to keeping you completely distracted then,' he mused.

'How on earth will your empire survive in your absence?'

'I'm ace at multi-tasking.'

She believed him. He'd just proven that he was supremely skilled at everything he undertook. The simple—although in hindsight it was never going to be simple—kiss she'd planned had turned into so much more. Now she was torn between leaving Xandro's bed and begging him to do it to her all over again.

'Don't overthink it, Sage.' His tone was a touch graver. Perhaps in warning?

'That's easy for you to say,' she replied, her mounting agitation hard to contain.

'It isn't,' he said. 'I'm having a hard time understanding why you're like a drug in my blood.'

Any feminine power she could've garnered from that admission was wiped out by the fact that he engendered the same feeling in her. Perhaps more. 'Because I'm not your usual type?' she tossed out.

'Yes,' he admitted without hesitation.

A twinge flared from the vicinity of her heart. 'Is that supposed to make me feel better?'

'It's supposed to tell you that this was as irresistible for me as it was for you and ease whatever anxiety is going on inside you.'

Despite cautioning herself not to overreact, her heart lurched.

'Unless you're regretting it?' he added, his eyes narrowing on her face.

She slowly shook her head. It might have been a temporary aberration but, 'No, I don't regret it.'

Satisfied with that, he rolled over and tugged her close. With her head on his shoulder and her hand on his chest, a little of Sage's anxiety diminished, enough for her to conclude that this after-sex thing wasn't so bad. She'd return to her room eventually, of course, but for now there was nothing wrong with enjoying the moment. The voice that warned her that these excuses were getting easier to accommodate was ruthlessly suppressed as she closed her eyes and basked in the sensation of his hand rubbing her back and hip.

She must have drifted off to sleep because when she opened her eyes again Xandro was leaning over her, toying with her hair.

'Distract me, *pethi mou*. The beast in me that's dying to take you again is in danger of overpowering the part of me that knows you need a little reprieve.'

At her immediate blush, he groaned and buried his face in her neck. 'That blush is most definitely *not* helping.'

Sage wanted to ignore the throb between her thighs and give in to the same mounting need. But at the same time she yearned to delve a little deeper beneath his surface. 'Tell me about Ayia Hera,' she suggested.

His whole body stiffened against hers. 'That wasn't what I meant by distraction,' he said coolly as he flung himself away from her.

Stung, she pulled the sheet over her body. 'I'm fresh out of after-sex banter then.'

Tense silence settled in the room. She was debating whether it was time to beat a hasty retreat when he tugged the sheet out of her grasp. 'Don't hide yourself from me.'

'Don't be an ogre then,' she threw back, but she let him pull her back into his embrace.

He sighed. 'Was it too much to hope you'd forgotten I mentioned it?'

'Your description of the sunsets made an impact.'

'Sunset. One. I was there for twenty-four hours ten years ago.'

She frowned. 'But...isn't that where your family is from?'

'It's where the man who fathered me lives.'

Her frown deepened. 'You said you had no family remaining.'

'I don't. He may have sired me, but he's dead to me,' he said through gritted teeth.

'Then why do you sound upset when you talk about him?'

Narrowed eyes glared at her. 'Stop analysing me.'

Irritation and the sensation that she didn't like him this closed-off made her snap, 'Why? You have no problem pointing out all my faults and prying my secrets from me.'

'I have no problem praising your attributes either. Like the fact that you're an amazing dancer. And an exceptional kisser. Come over here and put those lips on me.'

'Don't change the subject.'

'I never wanted to be on this subject in the first place. Especially as it isn't easy for me to talk about.'

'Mine wasn't easy for me to tell you either.'

'Is this where I give in or risk another battle with you?'

'No. But I still want to know.'

'Kiss me first, Sage.'

'Xandro...'

His jaw clenched and his gaze fixed itself on the high ceiling. 'Fine. For the sake of peace, I'll let you win this round. But I'm making love to you again when I'm done with this wretched story. So prepare yourself for that.'

CHAPTER THIRTEEN

'Before I was born, four generations of my family lived in Ayia Hera. It's a medium-sized village on an island south of Skiathos. Like most of those places, one family tends to own and run things. In my family's case it was the Theakopolous family. They employed ninety per cent of the village and controlled the infrastructure. Turned out that they controlled the authorities, too.'

Sage rested her chin on his chest, anxiety already whipping through her. 'What happened?'

'My grandparents worked directly for them. She was the cook and he was their driver. The Theakopolouses had one child, a son my mother grew up with. No one expected anything to happen between them. As a cook's daughter, she was never going to be good enough for him. Besides, at twenty-one he was engaged to someone else.' His lips twisted. 'But he chose to indulge himself on the side anyway.'

'He…didn't force himself on your mother, did he?' she asked.

He glanced at her for a moment. 'No. As far as I know it was consensual. A one-night thing that could've been brushed under the carpet. Except she got pregnant with me.' Dark clouds shifted through his eyes as exhaled harshly. 'My mother was young, with stars in her eyes. But that changed soon enough. There wasn't to be a sudden declaration of love or even support. Hell, there wasn't even going to be the concession of having her baby in her family home, the way she'd been born. When she plucked up the nerve to reveal her pregnancy, my father denied any involvement.'

Sage's hand stilled on his chest, her instinct warning her that there was more to the story. 'What did he do?'

'His fiancée's parents got wind of the possible scandal and threatened to end the engagement. The potential loss of a dynastic merger couldn't be allowed. The terms of reparation did not go in my family's favour.'

'Xandro…'

When he glanced at her, his eyes were a stormy grey. The deep breath he took did nothing to soften the harsh mask of painful recollection on his face. 'They could've allowed my grandparents to take my mother away, as they wanted to do. But the offer to disappear quietly wasn't enough apparently. For one night's indulgence, they decided that only my family's total disgrace would suffice.' He paused, his mouth flattening in a furious line that whitened the edges. 'Several items of jewellery went missing from the Theakopolous household. Enough to interest the authorities and ensure the culprit would pay a high price. A custodial price.'

'They accused your mother?'

He shook his head. 'They accused my grandparents. A member of the household staff warned them. They had every intention of defending their innocence, until the items were found in their possession.'

'They were framed?'

'Conclusively,' he answered with chilling fury.

'All of that to deny the pregnancy?'

'It was effective. After all, if the parents of the unwed girl suddenly named the village prince as the father of her unborn child but then were branded as thieves, who would've believed them? They also hoped that without her parents' support my mother would be forced to get rid of the baby.'

'Oh, God.'

His jaw clenched tight. 'She was only eighteen years old, with a lifetime of being whispered about in front of her, and parents who would have no means of supporting her had they been in jail.'

'So they left.'

'In the middle of the night, with little more than the clothes on their backs.'

Sage didn't need to hear the rest of the story. Xandro had been born in New York. And that was where his story started. But he wasn't finished.

'I grew up wondering why they didn't just go back after I was old enough, to clear their names. My grandfather forbade me from asking, and my grandmother would weep whenever I asked about Ayia Hera. When I was nine I discovered the box in my mother's belongings.'

Sage tensed. 'The box Ben took?'

He nodded. 'It contains a ruby necklace.'

'She took it?'

'No. Every piece of jewellery was returned. But somehow the necklace found its way back into my grandparents' house.'

'You think your father was trying to make amends for what he did?' Sage asked.

His gaze met hers for a brief moment. 'I asked him that same question when I met him for the first time ten years ago. A part of me was stupid enough to want to believe he had a shred of decency.'

'And?'

'He had no idea what I was talking about.'

She gasped. 'You think it was planted again?'

He shrugged. 'My grandparents never found out who put it in their belongings. Returning it would've incriminated them all over again.'

'So they kept it as a reminder.'

Xandro shifted restlessly beneath her. She caressed his chest and after a moment he stilled. 'I used to hate that necklace. My mother would stare at it for hours, crying over it.

She never told me why. It was my grandmother who eventually told me.'

'But it came to mean something to you, didn't it?' Why else would he have gone to such great lengths to come after it? Come after *her*.

'It wasn't all bad. The necklace also brought her joy. She wore it when she was happy. I was okay with that.' He shrugged, a touch of that arrogance on display. 'And eventually it became my reason to succeed. I wanted to buy more of those things for her. I wanted more happy moments for her.'

'But?'

His face grew bleak. 'It wasn't the right kind of success to start off with.'

Sage's heart lurched, and she pressed her palm against his cheek. He didn't seem to notice her touch, his gaze lost in the middle distance of the past.

'I ran away from home and got involved with the gang when I was sixteen. Things spiralled downward from there until I had a choice—do what needed to be done to elevate myself or take the more difficult road to success.' He exhaled. 'I made the wrong choice and eventually ended up in juvie a year later.'

'Oh, Xandro...'

'She pawned the necklace to bail me out, and spent every night for the next three months crying about it because she missed it. The gang leader found out about the necklace and decided he wanted to use it to expand his drug empire and told me to bring it to him.' He stopped.

'But you didn't, did you?' she pressed gently.

He swallowed. 'No, but I almost did. Instead I went to the pawnshop. The rubies were worth a quarter of a million dollars. I negotiated for a hundred-thousand-dollar advance, used half of it to ensure the gang left my mother and me alone, and enrolled myself in college, got a business degree and discovered that honest work that earned me money wasn't so bad.' His smile was less bitter. 'I wanted more of it. So I worked harder and eventually got the necklace back.'

After a minute, she cleared her throat. 'What about your father?'

He tensed again. 'What about him?'

'You said you went to see him ten years ago.'

'After my mother died, yes. The meeting lasted forty-five minutes. I haven't seen him since, and I don't plan to again.'

'You don't want to have a relationship with him?'

He rose and sat on the edge of the bed. 'I found out after my mother died that she'd written to him about me over the years. He never wrote back. He never attempted to find me. He got her pregnant then abandoned her. I have no intention of interacting with him.'

'But you were in Ayia Hera for twenty-four hours. Why did you stay a whole day?'

His profile held grim satisfaction. 'I discovered that he'd fallen on hard times. The fiancée he'd ruined my family for had left him and cleaned him out. I got my lawyers to buy everything he owned for a pittance, including his precious manor, and turned it into my one and only three-star hotel. It didn't deserve a five-star treatment.'

She gasped, her stomach hollowing at the calculating retribution he'd wrought on his own father.

He threw an unapologetic glance at her. 'You think me callous? *He* was a coward who condemned my mother to a miserable life because he didn't want to suffer a little discomfort. I may have his blood flowing through my veins, but that is all that links us. I've made my peace with that.'

'Okay,' she murmured. After a beat, she added, 'I'm sorry about the necklace. I know it's a symbol of everything you've achieved,' she murmured, the enormity of it settling heavily on her.

He frowned. 'What?'

'Isn't that why you want it back so badly?'

He continued to stare at her as if he was puzzled. Then

he surged to his feet, strode away to the window. She could see the restlessness vibrating off him. She sat up, pulled up the sheets to her breasts and wondered whether she'd pushed him too far as she watched him rake his fingers through his hair.

Finally, he turned to face her. 'I used to think so...' He stopped again, his frown deepening.

Her heart sustained its frantic beat and she had no idea why what he'd left unsaid was so important. 'But?'

His gaze swept away from hers. 'It's not just that. It's the last piece of her that I have.'

The quiet words lashed at her heart. 'I'm sorry,' she said again.

His nostrils flared slightly but his gaze didn't reconnect with hers. The sensation that she was missing something heightened. But then he nodded and she decided not to probe any further.

A minute later the decision became null and void when he walked back towards her.

The revelations of the past hour swirled through the room, ravaged memories unsettled between them. But soon another emotion gained supremacy. By the time he mounted one knee on the bed and prowled over her, their focus had shifted from past to present.

'I want you,' he rasped in a low, charged rumble.

'I want you too,' she whispered, unable to hide her need from him.

He made a very male sound of satisfaction before dropping his head to ravish her mouth. Time ceased to exist as they chased after pleasure that seemed to intensify with each touch and each kiss.

Eventually, it was the need to satisfy other hungers that propelled them out of bed.

They raided the kitchen, feasting on cold cuts and French bread and wine. Xandro tried to tempt her with caviar, then mercilessly mocked her as she gagged on the peculiar taste.

'I'm glad I'm not the only one who detests fish eggs,' he confessed.

'Then why do you keep it?'

He shrugged. But then his eyes slid away from hers.

'Oh.' Her mood dampened by thoughts of previous lovers who had shared similar meals with him in this very kitchen, she started to turn away.

He caught her by the arms and pinned her against the central island. 'Don't turn away from me,' he muttered thickly against her mouth. There was an odd note in his voice that struck something soft inside her. If she didn't know better, she would've imagined he was feeling vulnerable about what he'd shared with her.

Welcome to the club.

In the space of a few hours they'd laid heavy revelations at each other's feet.

'I'm okay. Seriously,' she stressed, more to reassure herself.

'You are not. I wouldn't be either if our roles were reversed.'

What those words did to her heart Sage didn't want to admit, even to herself. Because their effect suggested her emotions weren't as fleeting as she wanted them to be. 'Stop it. You don't need to pretend. I'm aware I don't have any rights here.'

'You have a right to be jealous.' He leaned down and rubbed his nose against hers. 'Call me primitive, but I like it.' He nipped playfully at her mouth, drawing a reluctant smile from her.

'You're a caveman.'

'And immensely proud of it.' He kissed her long and deep, and then left her weak and clinging to the counter as he went to the fridge, rummaged through it and dumped the four tubs of caviar he discovered straight into the trash. Then he brushed his fingers in an overdramatic gesture that made her burst out laughing.

He joined in the laughter as he scooped her up, walked out of the kitchen and back upstairs to his bed. He laid her down and stretched out beside her and, as she tunnelled her fingers through his hair, something snapped and dived inside her. She'd only ever felt something similar through her dancing. A pure strain of emotion that she was almost too scared to name.

The sensation terrified her. Enough for her to pull back sharply from it because she knew without a shadow of a doubt that it was potentially life-changing.

'What is it?' Xandro was frowning down at her.

'Nothing,' she hurriedly answered, then tried to remove the doubt lingering in his eyes by rising on her elbows and kissing him. Whether she succeeded in distracting him or he chose to let it go, she wasn't sure. And then she stopped wondering altogether as he took over, deepened the kiss and blanked her mind to everything else.

Everything except the lingering sensation that chased after her in her dreams, and roused her in the middle of the night.

Cautiously opening her eyes, she stared at Xandro.

He was just as formidable in sleep as he was when awake. But, with his eyes shut and his lips slightly reddened from her kisses, he looked almost as though he could be tamed. The temptation to trace his face with her fingers, commit every beautiful angle and smooth surface to memory, rushed through her. But then that intense sensation of her world shifting beneath her feet raced alongside it. It disturbed her enough for her to carefully shift away from the heavy arm pinning her to the bed. She tensed when he grunted in his sleep. When his breathing levelled out again she got out of bed, threw on her robe and left the bedroom.

The last thing she wanted was to be alone with her thoughts, but she couldn't avoid them as she trudged downstairs and headed to her training room.

Now she understood Xandro's reason for pursuing it, she

knew that nothing but having the ruby necklace back in his possession would satisfy him. Her heart squeezed again as her thoughts turned to her brother.

While she yearned to have him back, she couldn't avoid the alarming, wrenching knowledge that it would be at the cost of never seeing Xandro again. Why that inevitability troubled her so much kept her on the sofa, her thoughts and her heart taking turns to twist and dip until Xandro appeared in the doorway half an hour later.

Unashamedly naked, he leaned in the doorway, spearing her with incisive eyes. 'You're still overthinking it,' he said after a long pause.

Then, in silent command, he held out his hand. And she, knowing she wasn't ready to be free of his superb brand of lovemaking, rose and slid her hand into his.

Just a few more hours, she promised herself.

CHAPTER FOURTEEN

BUT HOURS TURNED into one day. Then two more. Wickedly glorious days when he bossily informed her he'd taken time out of his busy schedule to be with her and cajoled her into doing the same. Where he indulged her in a breathtaking private helicopter trip over the Grand Canyon, and a private jet ride to a candlelit dinner for two at an exclusive vineyard in Napa Valley.

With no paparazzi in sight, the occasions felt different. Almost...special. Enough for the fear that she was getting carried away to recede when, under a canopy of stars and the dance of fireflies, he filled her in on more stories about his past, about his mother and grandparents and their love for music. The discovery that he shared that same passion, that perhaps she'd been wrong in assuming Hunter's had just been a means to an end for him, tugged at something deep and sacred within her.

But it was when she found herself swaying with him among the vines, wishing the night would never end and hoping for more like it, that she realised how far she'd strayed from where this had all started.

He was blackmailing her, keeping her prisoner until her brother came to heel.

But even then, knowing she was just a pawn, she couldn't find the words to take back the control she felt slipping from her.

That disturbed her sleep enough to find her awake and at the living room window come the dawn hours halfway through the next week.

Again, she was there barely half an hour before Xandro tracked her down. 'Once again I wake to find you gone from my bed,' he murmured, his voice sleep-rough and more than a little irritated. And, as she'd begun to notice in the last few days, there was a new watchfulness about him, as if he was probing the heart of the feelings she was desperately keeping under wraps.

Her heart performed a crazy somersault when he reached her, staring down at her for several seconds before turning her around to pull her back into his body. Then, slowly, he undid the ties of her robe.

'Before you assume so, it wasn't a challenge.'

'But it's still an unsatisfactory situation. When I go to sleep with you in my arms, I expect to wake up with you still there,' he replied.

'Xandro…' Whatever she'd been about to say evaporated when he tugged off the robe and dropped it at her feet.

'Yes, *pethi mou*. I want you to say my name like that as I remind you how I like to wake up.'

Before she could respond, he'd thrust his hand in her hair and directed her head back to meet the relentless onslaught of his kiss. Ferocious desire was tinged with an edge of frustration, the demanding eroticism of his tongue in her mouth and his hands moulding her breasts setting off blazes that spread like brush fire through her body. She was breathless and weak-kneed when he lifted his head.

'Put your hands on the glass and don't move.'

She gasped. 'What?'

'Do as I say,' he instructed gruffly, his gaze almost challenging.

Her stomach dipped with wild excitement as she complied.

His hand stayed on her breast, fondling and teasing her nipple as his other traced her body from arm to waist to thigh and back up again.

'Your skin feels like silk,' he murmured, almost in wonder. 'And your hair is like the purest flame.'

Trembling seized her, once again the sensation of plummeting towards an emotionally devastating destination growing inside her as her heart unfurled at his words.

'I want to kiss every inch of you.'

'Xandro...'

'Yes, *pedhaki mou*. I'm going to.'

He put word to deed, starting with her nape and trailing kisses down her spine, all the while caressing her with his expert hands. She pried open eyes she didn't remember shutting when she felt his breath on her sex.

To see such a powerful, dynamic man on his knees before her threatened her very sanity. And then that sanity was lost when he parted her thighs and worshipped her with his mouth.

Bliss pummelled her with the force of a thousand drumbeats, drawing cries and then screams from her as she shattered under his touch. And still he didn't relent.

With one powerful lunge he was back on his feet, positioning himself behind her. She heard the rip of a condom foil and then, a moment later, strong hands gripped her waist.

'I've wanted to take you like this since that first morning we watched the sunrise together,' he rasped in her ear.

Her fierce blush brought a husky laugh. Which abruptly cut off the second he thrust, hot and hard, inside her.

The power of his possession lifted her to her toes. 'Oh!'

With a not quite steady hand, he swept her hair out of the way, planted kisses along her jaw before resting his cheek alongside hers. 'You feel exquisite, Sage *mou*.' His voice was barely coherent.

And she had lost the power of speech. So they stayed like that, cheek to cheek, as he completely took her over, the tempo of his thrusts and the magnificent power of the body curled around hers dragging them towards mind-altering nirvana.

'Xandro!'

'*Ne, glikia mou.* Give it up for me,' he commanded hoarsely.

With another cry, she flung herself over the edge. He followed a minute later, shouting his release as his chest pressed into her back and his arms banded tight around her waist. She was glad he was holding her up because her legs weren't in the mood to heed her brain.

And she had a strong suspicion her heart was headed in a direction of its own too. She was still grappling with that knowledge when she felt the sensation of warmth on her face. She didn't need to open her eyes to know the sun had risen.

'Against your beauty, this view has lost its power,' he murmured between kisses on her shoulder.

The fear that she was falling deeper into the unknown tightened a knot in her belly and made her stiffen.

'What is it?' he demanded immediately.

'I don't need false odes, Xandro.'

He paused for a long, silent minute. Then he pulled away, leaving a chasm deep inside her even as he turned her in his arms.

She kept her gaze down against his intense scrutiny. 'Is there something we need to talk about, Sage?'

Yes! Everything! For a start, they hadn't spoken about Ben in ages. Her queries as to whether he'd found her brother had been met with a curt, '*No,*' before he changed the subject.

Now was the perfect opportunity to ask about the hunt for her brother. But the frighteningly large part of her that didn't want this to be over just yet kept the words from forming, and instead proffered different ones. 'I prefer to leave the hearts and flowers for my performances, that's all.'

His eyes narrowed. Then he gave a brisk nod. 'Understood.' He leaned forward and planted a hard kiss on her lips. 'If it's not too much to ask, will you join me in the shower?'

Say no. Take back the control you're losing.
'Yes.'

One corner of his mouth lifted, then he took her hand and led her from the room. A long leisurely shower and another bout of lovemaking later, Xandro emerged from his dressing room wearing a dark grey suit, pristine white shirt and statement-making tie. Every inch of him screamed powerful tycoon. But she'd seen under the suit. Knew he wasn't all hard edges and ruthless dominance.

But what did that matter? As soon as Ben turned up, she would be history. The knot in her belly replicated around her heart. The heart she suspected was no longer completely hers.

'Sorry...what did you say?'

He straightened to send her a wry look. 'I said I'll see you tonight before the party.'

She tensed. 'What party?'

'The one I promised Hunter Dance Company. Did you forget?'

She had. Completely.

'I have a progress meeting with Melissa at six. Be ready to leave at seven.'

With that he leaned down, kissing her thoroughly before walking out. And leaving her with a new set of uncomfortable problems.

Melissa. The choreographers. Her fellow dancers. They would all know by now that she and Xandro were more than acquaintances. With time and distance she'd put it out of her mind. But she couldn't hide from it, or from her life, for ever.

It was time to take back control before she risked her career, too. She feared her heart was already on the line. It took an hour to summon up the courage to accept her decision. As she rose from the bed, she swayed. The temptation to sink back into bed was huge. She didn't want to confront her feelings.

Sage straightened her spine. She'd let this go too far…
But no more.

She repeated those three words to herself through the morning, and in the afternoon when James informed her that the stylist had arrived with a selection of clothes for the party, as per Mr Christofides's instructions.

No more.

'Tell her thank you, but no thanks,' she replied. And then, because she needed to cement the foundations of her decision, she grabbed her purse, took the lift downstairs and headed for the less expensive boutiques she'd seen on The Strip.

Within half an hour, she had an outfit for the party.

At a quarter to seven she grabbed her new clutch and ran a slightly damp palm down her new sleeveless green sequined cocktail dress before raising her chin in the mirror. The vice around her heart had tightened in gradual increments throughout the day, causing that organ to scream loudly at her decision. But she was doing the right thing.

'James, please tell Mr Christofides when he arrives that I'll see him at the party,' she said when she reached the living room.

He hid his surprise and nodded.

Nerves shredding her, she made her way downstairs to the stunning Sofia Ballroom, where the party was being held.

The quiet entrance she'd hoped for never happened. Michael spotted her immediately and bellowed a welcome, drawing dozens of eyes to her.

Sage kept a smile pinned on her face as he drew her into the group. That smile threatened to waver when she caught two dancers whispering about the fact that she was alone. She heard the speculation repeated several times as she drifted through the party.

But all through catching up with her colleagues and skirting personal questions that came her way, her senses remained attuned to Xandro's arrival.

And when he walked through the doors, with Melissa directly beside him, he brought with him an earth-shattering revelation that froze Sage where she stood.

She was indeed too late.

In direct opposition to the hush that settled over the room, her heart was shrieking its new discovery. She was in love with Xandro Christofides. From the crown of his gleaming hair to the polished black shoes he wore with his superb black tuxedo, every atom of him was what her foolish heart wanted.

What her stupid heart couldn't have.

Her heart and stomach lurched hard, but she was too stunned, too pulverised by what she'd let happen, to look away from where he stood at the top of the stairs.

The champagne glass in her hand wobbled as it struck home that she would never kiss those lips again, never touch that body again. Never feel the power and glory of him inside her.

She watched his gaze sweep the room, piercing silvergrey searching. For her. At the last moment, simply because she couldn't let him see what she'd just discovered, she dropped her own gaze, desperately struggling to compose her face when she felt him pause, stop and probe her with those incisive eyes.

The rise of conversation told her they'd fully entered the room. Thankfully there were many people in the two-hundred-strong gathering who wanted a piece of Xandro and it was easy to keep the width of the room between them.

When it was time for speeches, Melissa gave a lengthy one, managing to mention Xandro's name many times, each with a look at the man himself.

When it was his turn, he gave a shorter one, punctuated with purpose and his vision for the company. Applause was followed by endless champagne toasts. Then the middle of the ballroom was cleared for dancing. The last dance she'd shared with Xandro in Napa Valley rose sharp and piercing in her mind, and relief spiralled through her when she saw that he was nowhere near Melissa. In fact, she'd lost sight of him.

When a firm hand grasped her arm she knew immediately who it was. Heart in her throat, her gaze rose to meet storm-chilled grey ones.

'We can do this here or we can do it over there.' He jerked his head towards the open French windows.

'Or we don't have to do anything at all?' she suggested shakily.

The flattening of his mouth was her answer. 'Choose, Sage.'

She did so only because they were drawing the attention she wanted to avoid. Turning on her heel, she walked through the French windows.

Her newly love-shot heart jumped again as she heard him shut the doors behind them and then turn her to face him.

'Is there a reason you chose to come downstairs without me and have been actively avoiding me?' he bit out.

Because I feared I was falling in love with you. Now I know.

Clawing every ounce of composure she could find, she affected a careless shrug. 'I wanted to avoid the attention you're attracting right now by dragging me out here.'

A trace of bewildered fury pleated his brow. 'You think keeping the width of the room between us will hide the fact that we're lovers?'

'Please keep your voice down,' she hissed.

He stepped closer, his eyes telling her he had no intention of complying. 'Every single one of them knows you're mine, Sage.'

She couldn't stop her shiver of longing, but she had to train her heart to accept what it couldn't have. 'No—'

'Yes, don't insult their intelligence.'

'Okay, maybe they know, but after tonight they'll also know that it's over.'

He stiffened, his lips thinning. 'What are you talking about?'

Her insides shook as she averted her gaze and tried to form the words. 'You know perfectly well. It's time to end this.'

Maybe it was the semi-darkness that made her think he paled a little. Because the next instant his face was rigid and harsh. 'Say that again, and look at me when you do.'

Her throat worked as she forced herself to swallow. To look him in the eyes. 'It's over. I think we both know this shouldn't have started in the first place.'

His eyes darkened. 'Do we? Why not, Sage? And tell me the truth. Tell me why I left you sated and happy in bed this morning but have returned to find...*this*?' he sliced at her.

She shook her head. 'It's very simple. I have a life to get on with. I can't stay here playing your fake lover for ever.'

His expression hardened even more. 'We moved from fake to very real weeks ago. And call me egotistical if you wish but you loved every minute of it,' he claimed arrogantly.

The truth of it was too visceral to deny. 'Be that as it may, it's time for me to face reality. You won't even tell me whether you've located Ben or not—'

'I haven't. And we had an agreement.'

Frustrated anger mingled with despair. 'Our agreement wasn't for me to give up my life for ever. I'm drawing the line here, Xandro.' She had to or risk him witnessing her heartache.

He remained silent for an eternity, his gaze analysing her every micro-expression. 'Are you sure this is how you want to play it?'

She straightened her shoulders. 'I know you can take all sorts of actions against my parents. Against Ben too, when you find him. But yes, I'm done.'

Just like in the alley in Washington, DC, when he'd seemed to loom large and fearful even while he was frozen, Xandro was statue-still. Only his eyes moved, boring into her from head to toe in a merciless scrutiny.

Then he nodded abruptly. 'Very well. I want you gone by morning,' he said icily.

Sage knew that enduring the newfound heartache that had arrived with her admitting her love for Xandro would be hellish. She experienced a whole new level of anguish as she watched him walk away, his tall, powerful body cutting a swathe through the guests. The pain was so acute she wondered how she was able to remain standing when everything inside her wanted to curl into a ball of agonising despair.

'I want you gone by morning.'

The finality of it whipped at her vulnerable heart. Tore it to shreds. It was all she could do to re-enter the ballroom fifteen minutes later, and slowly make her way towards the door without drawing more attention to herself than was necessary.

From the corner of her eye, she caught Melissa leaning up to Xandro, her hand on his arm as they conversed. Sage whipped her gaze away, focused on blinking back shocked tears as she headed for the door.

The hallway leading to the lifts was relatively empty and she made it to the penthouse without succumbing to the threatening tears. In the bedroom, she avoided looking at the bed as she hurriedly gathered her things and threw them into her suitcase. At her insistence, Nina had located her own clothes from where Xandro had had them stashed. She changed into jeans and a T-shirt and was slipping on her ballerina flats when she heard the door open behind her.

She whirled around, her heart banging itself against her ribs as she stared at Xandro.

His hard gaze went from her to the suitcase and back again. 'It's the middle of the night. Are you in that much of a hurry to leave me?' he demanded coldly.

The thought of spending another night under the same roof as him was too much to bear. 'I don't see the point in prolonging this.'

His jaw clenched tight, as if he was stemming his words, before he exhaled. 'Before you do, you might want to hear the latest news on your brother.'

Sage froze. 'You've found him?'

He nodded abruptly. 'Yes. I've just heard he's in a hospital in Nice.'

Ice drenched her body. 'What happened?'

Face set in stone, Xandro walked further into the room. 'Apparently, he got into a brawl in a backroom gambling den last night.'

'Is he all right?'

'Two broken ribs, a possible fractured jaw and a black eye,' he relayed in a clipped voice.

Her fingers tightened around the suitcase handle as a wave of despair washed over her. Through the loud buzzing in her ears she heard Xandro issue terse instructions to someone at the end of the phone.

It triggered her own need to act. Frantically, she dug through her clutch to retrieve her phone. She hit the number for the first travel agent her search threw up.

'What are you doing?' Xandro demanded.

'Booking the first flight out to Nice.'

'Hang up the phone, Sage.'

'What? No, I'm—'

'Perhaps you didn't hear me just now instructing my pilot to ready my plane?'

Her hand dropped. 'You're going to France?'

Cold silver eyes met hers. 'Of course. Why would I not?'

'I... I thought you'd have your security people retrieve your property.'

'You thought wrong.'

She heard the faint voice on the phone and started to raise it to her ear.

Xandro held up a staying hand. 'If you want this business over and done with quickly, hang up the phone,' he instructed tersely.

She pressed the *end* button. 'But...why would you want me to fly with you?' His cold dismissal still rang in her ears, breaking her heart.

His lips flattened. 'I'm not prepared to sit around waiting for you to make your way across the Atlantic in case your brother is intransigent about revealing the whereabouts of the necklace. So we'll fly together. If you can bring yourself to do that?'

She hesitated, probably too long. The icy crevasse between them widened, even as she nodded. 'Thank you.'

When he spoke again, his tone was even more remote and chilling, nothing like the man she'd danced with under the Californian sky. 'We leave in an hour.'

CHAPTER FIFTEEN

HE'D BARED HIS soul to her. Completely and utterly. And now he was totally exposed.

He had no experience in that particular area, which was why he'd been reluctant to go there in the first place. He could claim his brain had been addled by sex. But he knew he could've avoided revealing his soul to her if he'd wanted. She'd asked. And he'd granted her wish.

And now, too late, he was painfully reminded that there was a reason he'd avoided return journeys into his past. With anyone. It was why he'd discouraged it with the women he'd dated before Sage.

But he wasn't dating her. Hell, they didn't even like each other.

Liar. Had he not dragged her out to dinner each night in the weeks before they'd slept together because it'd been the only way he could have her in his arms, even though it'd proven to be more torture than pleasure in the long run? And afterwards, those carefully planned trips so he could avoid the media and have her to himself. Touch her. Engage in a conversation that didn't start and end with an argument.

He'd watched her dance and felt as if he was experiencing something pure and transcendental. Something beautiful and special he didn't want to let go.

Only to have it tossed away at the very first opportunity. To think he'd left her this morning toying with the idea that he would be okay if Ben Woods stayed hidden for a little longer. He'd even considered an offer of rehabilitation when Ben returned if it would…what? Make Sage regard him favourably? Make her want to accommodate him in her life?

Dammit. *Yes.*

He cursed the mocking laughter in his head as he flipped open his seat belt and walked to the front of his plane. They'd been in the air for three hours and for all that time she'd had her nose stuck in a magazine, pretending he didn't exist.

'I have a life to get on with,' she'd said.

A life that didn't feature him at all. Did he need anything more definitive than that?

No. Whatever he'd thought he could find with Sage Woods had only been in his imagination. And, like she said, they'd already spent too long on this exercise. It was time to get back to the real world. It was time to take his life back, too.

So why did the thought of her not standing at the east window, of not hearing strains of music from his guest bedroom or, *thee mou,* the thought of not being able to touch her again, fill his chest with such black dread?

He threw himself into a club chair, clicked the remote and raised the volume of the financial news playing on his flat screen TV. Anything to drown out the thoughts tearing through his mind and the sinking sensation that, in a shockingly short space of time, he'd given the most beautiful woman he'd ever met something much more than he'd ever parted with before. And he had no damn idea how to get back on an even keel.

'What's he saying?' Sage demanded urgently as a man in blue scrubs and white coat tossed out long streams of French.

After a strained flight where she'd vacillated between pretending Xandro wasn't sitting in icy silence across from her and wishing the conversation in the ballroom hadn't happened, they'd landed in Nice and raced to the hospital to find out that Ben wasn't there.

Xandro, who, of course, spoke impeccable French, issued another lightning-fast query at the harried doctor.

'Where's Ben?' she demanded again.

That earned her a chilling look from the man who'd donned his ruthless mogul suit with shocking ease. 'It seems everyone is of the view that he's checked himself out against doctor's orders.'

'They've lost him?' she screeched.

Xandro sent her another censorious look. 'He's a grown man, Sage. They couldn't keep him here if he didn't want to stay.'

She curbed her panic as anxiety surged. 'What about his injuries? Ask him how bad he is? Please.'

His lips compressed. 'Believe it or not, it was the first question I asked. They're not life-threatening. Unless he does something more to aggravate them.'

'Oh, God.'

A slight gentling of his features tugged hard at her. Made her wish for the impossible. 'We will find him.'

She nodded. She could believe that. Xandro was relentless when he wanted something.

He ended the conversation with the doctor and then he took her arm and led her out of the emergency ward. The SUV idling at the kerb had tinted windows and the usual contingent of menacing-looking bodyguards.

She shivered as she slid into the back and the doors shut. 'Where are we going?'

'We tracked his phone to Monaco. I have a few ideas of where he might be headed.'

'Another gambling den?'

'If he's running out of money that narrows his options.'

She leaned back against the headrest. 'But not in a good way, right?'

His cold silence said everything.

The miles rolled by as they travelled along the craggy shoreline. Eventually, signs for the Principality of Monaco appeared and she silently shook her head. She'd once longed to visit this place with the man of her dreams. But never like this. Not with a man she'd fallen in love with while knowing he was merely using her as a means to an end.

Pain wrenched at her then rolled over her in unrelenting waves. She was attempting to breathe through it when Xandro sat forward and peered ahead through the windscreen.

Sage looked out too, noting the seedy street. Her heart sank as they pulled into an alley and stopped in front of an ominous-looking door. Two burly men in dark clothes stood on either side of it, eyeing the SUV.

Xandro turned his attention to her. 'You will stay in the car—'

'No. Please, I need to see Ben.'

His jaw flexed. 'You will when I bring him out. This is non-negotiable.'

He didn't give her a chance to respond. He pushed open his door, nodding to one of the bodyguards. Then, without a word, he disappeared through the black door.

The next twenty minutes was the longest of her life. By the time half an hour had ticked by, her nerves were frayed beyond recognition. She held on for another five minutes, then jumped out.

Xandro's bodyguard immediately stepped in front of her. 'Miss, I can't let you go in.'

'I… I need the bathroom,' she lied.

He shifted uncomfortably. 'I can get the driver to take you to a hotel or a—'

'Not to put it too indelicately, but I won't last that long.'

She caught the tiniest pained grimace before his professionalism slid into place. 'I'll take you in, but please stay close.'

Relief fizzed through her. 'Understood.'

His gaze sharpened and Sage fought to keep her expression neutral.

The stench of stale smoke and cheap liquor hit her the moment she went down the dark carpeted stairs into the poorly lit gambling club. Half a dozen tables were grouped in a large room, all occupied by gamblers hunched over their winnings or desperately hoping to earn back their losses. On either side of the room, four alcoves were partially curtained off but Sage caught glimpses of more of the same going on.

'It's that way.' The bodyguard indicated a sign on the far left of the room.

She nodded, noting that while a few heads swung her way, none of the gamblers paid her close attention as she walked past. Nor were any of them Ben or Xandro.

About to head down the corridor that led to the Ladies', she caught sight of Xandro's profile from behind one of the curtains.

She turned to the bodyguard. 'Could you get me a drink for when I come out? A club soda is fine. As you can see, I'm in no danger. Please?'

He gave a grudging nod. The moment he headed for the bar, she made a beeline for the alcove. About to enter, she paused when she heard Ben's strained voice.

'If I win this hand, I'll give you your necklace back, but in return you agree to stay the hell away from my sister.'

'And if I win?' Xandro demanded with a heavy trace of bitterness. 'What grand prize do I get on top of the pain in the backside you've been to me this last six weeks?'

She held her breath.

'Whatever you want. I can work for you for free for however long you want. But my sister is off the table. Agreed?'

Xandro's harsh laugh ravaged her heart. 'Would you believe me if I told you that you don't have to worry about that any longer?' he said. 'That we can end this right now?'

'End this how?' Ben asked after a moment.

Tense silence reigned, dragging nails over her nerves. 'Things didn't end the way I wanted them to, but I'll still keep my word to you. All I want is the necklace. Return it and you can go free,' Xandro finally said.

'I don't believe you. You're a risk-taker, just like me. We

make the deal my way. That's the only way I can trust you to stand by it. So, are we agreed?'

'Agreed,' Xandro bit out.

Pain slashed across her heart. The bottom that was already dropping out of the precarious world she'd built out of paper dreams gave way and disappeared into nothing. Xandro had never hidden his intentions from her and still she'd fallen in love with him. A man who was, even now, as she parted the curtains and walked into the room, sliding over the cards that would seal her exit from his life.

She wasn't aware she'd made a sound until the men at the table turned towards her. Xandro was the first on his feet.

'Sage, I told you to stay in the car!'

She swayed away from him as he lunged for her.

Ben charged to his feet, too, but his steps were halted by a limp and a groan of pain as he clutched his ribs. Despite his hampered mobility, he managed to plant himself partially between her and Xandro. 'Stay away from her.'

'Keep out of this, Woods,' Xandro snapped without taking his eyes off her.

'Like hell I will. I just won—'

'Stop! Enough, Ben. You know how I feel about gambling. Do you really think this is what I want?'

Ben blinked, probably because she'd never yelled at him before. 'Sage—'

'No, I don't want to hear any more reasons why you think your life is so miserable. Where's the strong brother who helped me deal with the bullies? Who urged me to follow my dreams and stood by my side as we defied Mom and Dad? You were brave enough to fight for your country, but this…what you're doing now? I don't recognise that Ben.'

He tried to shrug it off. 'What does it matter? He can afford a hundred more of those necklaces.'

She exhaled in despair. 'No, he can't. Not that one. And, even if he could, you're not a thief. At least you weren't till recently.'

His gaze dropped from hers, a tinge of red flowing into his unshaven face. After a long moment, he reached behind him and tugged something out of his waistband. It was an oblong-shaped object wrapped in black cloth. He tossed it on the table. 'I don't care what happens to me, but we had an agreement.'

Xandro took a deep, shuddering breath. Reached for the object. Discarding the cloth, he opened the velvet box. The necklace was a simple design. But the three rubies were huge, enough to command much more than the sum Xandro had bargained for all those years ago.

It would've been anticlimactic, had she not witnessed the pain in his face as he stared at the piece of jewellery. Then the emotion was wiped clean from his face as he snapped the box shut and set it back on the table.

'I wish to renegotiate.' He spoke directly to her. 'With this.' He held up the box.

But it was Ben who answered. 'No chance—'

'I can speak for myself, Ben,' Sage interrupted him. 'You do whatever you want, Xandro, but I won't be a part of it.'

Xandro stepped towards her. 'Sage—'

She held up her hand. 'No, this ends now. You have what you want. I'm going home.'

Xandro stepped in front of her. 'I brought you here. I'm taking you back.'

'No, it's over, remember?' The reminder was more for herself.

His eyes darkened to a stormy grey. 'Trust me, I haven't forgotten. But if you think I'm going to leave you in this place, you're sorely mistaken.'

She stayed mutinously silent, afraid that the tears building at the back of her eyes and throat would accompany whatever she attempted to say.

Xandro dragged a hand through his hair. 'Besides, your brother shouldn't be subjected to a long flight. Not until he's been medically cleared.'

She glanced at Ben, saw the pain etched on his face. 'Ben?'

He attempted a shrug that didn't quite come off.

Xandro's lips firmed. 'He needs medical care. I can have him in a private clinic within the hour,' he said, his eyes piercing ferociously into hers.

'I'll pay you back.'

Xandro's jaw gritted. 'If you insist.'

'I do.'

With her heart still reeling, she took Ben's arm, fighting back tears as he leaned heavily on her. She was aware of Xandro following them out but she concentrated on Ben until they were outside and the bodyguards took over.

She was so focused on not breaking down that she didn't notice Ben had been placed in the second SUV until it drove away and Xandro strode towards her.

She rushed after the vehicle. 'Why is he leaving without me?'

Xandro blocked her path. 'You'll be reunited with your brother soon enough. If you get in the car.'

She got in, but kept her gaze fixed straight ahead. Silence reigned. Thicker. More charged. And with each mile they drove higher into the hills of Monaco she fought harder to hold herself together.

She was at her wits' end when they finally drove through a set of high double gates. 'Where are we?'

'We're at one of my properties,' he replied.

'I thought you were taking me to Ben.'

'I will, right after we talk.'

'I really don't see what more we have to say to each other, Xandro.'

He scowled. 'You may not have any more to say, but I do. I have no problem carrying you in if that's what you prefer?' he snapped.

Her senses screamed at her to refuse, to save herself more pain and end this now. But that tiny voice replaying Xandro's words to Ben—*Things didn't end the way I wanted them to*—refused to accept that this was over and compelled her to reach for the door.

She followed him through the double front doors of a magnificent villa and into a wide, welcoming hallway. Up a short flight of stairs into a sumptuous living room that overlooked a sparkling pool and more landscaped gardens.

Before she could take a breath, he whirled to face her. 'Why did you end things with me?' he demanded tightly.

Her heart squeezed painfully but she strove to keep it from showing. 'I told you—'

'I blackmailed you and you, quite rightly, wanted to get back to your life,' he snarled. 'I know. But was that the whole truth? Is there more, Sage?' he demanded.

The need to confess her feelings burned on her tongue. 'Xandro...'

'If it isn't, I need to know.'

'Why?'

'Because I lied too,' he gritted out.

Sage swallowed. 'About what?'

'About wanting you gone by morning. It's the worst, most damning lie I've ever told.'

Her insides shook. 'Why?' Her voice was a thin, reedy whisper.

He laughed, a self-deprecating sound, before he lifted one hand to grip his nape. 'Because it's the furthest thing from what I want most in the world. You, Sage. You are what I want. So damn much it hurts.'

Her lungs refused to work properly. 'Why should I believe you?'

'Because I left you yesterday morning still plotting ways to keep you in Vegas with me. I couldn't imagine watching another sunrise without you by my side. Or not having you there to argue about everything with me. I don't know how or when you crept under my skin, but God, the thought of not having you in my life, of not seeing your beautiful face kills me.'

Tears threatened again. 'Why did you make that deal with Ben then?'

'I wanted to get him out of there. It was the quickest way for me to do that. It's become clear to me that argumentative characters run in your family. I'd already spent the better part of half an hour trying to talk him out of gambling away the remaining money he had. That last hand was to get it over as quickly as possible so I could get him back to you.'

'Hearing you agree to it hurt, Xandro. A lot.'

He closed his eyes for a moment. 'I know. It hurt me to say it. But not as much as you ending things with me.'

Her heart thudded wildly. 'I thought the necklace was all you wanted.'

'I haven't thought about it for weeks, Sage. I was even hoping Ben would stay in hiding for longer, just so I'd have more time with you. And tonight…when I held the necklace again I knew it was time to let it go. I'll always have my mother's memory with me. And it did its duty a long time ago. It showed me who I could be, instead of who I was then. Now all I want is to look to the future. With you, if you'll take me back.'

'And if I won't?'

His face went bleak. Then changed to resolute. 'I'm a very resilient and extraordinarily persuasive man. I won't stop begging you to forgive me and be mine.'

She shook her head. 'The things you say to me.'

'Argue with me. Shout at me. But don't leave me, Sage.'

Her throat burned and her heart tripped over itself with a wild hope. 'I thought I would have to. I thought the necklace was all you cared about while I…'

He stepped closer. 'While you…?'

'While I was falling in love with you.'

He paled. Then a hoarse sound ripped from his throat. 'You love me,' he repeated numbly.

Tears brimmed her eyes. 'I loved you from the moment you kissed me in Athens. I fell deeper when you danced with me in Napa.'

'*Thee mou*. I will buy you the vineyard. We can have a date in that same spot every night if you wish.'

She raised an eyebrow. 'You want to date me?'

He stopped, a mutinous expression crossing his face for a moment before he jerked out a nod. 'If that's what you want. To start with,' he tagged on.

'Exclusively?'

He frowned. 'Of course *exclusively*. You think I'm going to allow you to date other—?'

He spotted the beginning of her smile and sucked in a harsh breath. 'I'm going to punish you for that, *agape mou*.'

Her breath caught. 'I'm pretty sure I know what that means.'

'Do you, my love? Do you have any idea just how much I love you?'

'Oh…oh, Xandro.'

He closed the gap between them and caught her up in his arms. 'I love you, Sage. So much.'

They kissed for a very long time, then parted. 'I'm sorry I blackmailed you,' he murmured against her lips.

Her heart snagged. 'I'm not a huge fan, but this time I'll let it go.'

'While I'm confessing, I'll admit I was a little jealous of how unconditionally you love Ben.'

'You don't need to be jealous. I love you, Xandro,' she murmured.

Stormy grey eyes grew ferocious with wild emotion. 'I don't think a thousand years will be enough to hear you say that to me,' he grated.

'I'll say it every day. I promise. Because getting on the plane with you, knowing I wouldn't see you again once we found Ben, was torture.'

He held her tighter and pressed his lips to hers. Thick Greek words choked out from his throat.

'You'll have to teach me what those mean.'

'*Ne.* Yes.' He kissed her again, speared his fingers into her hair and ravaged her lips until she was too weak with love to stand.

He swept her up into his arms. 'Tell me again,' he demanded as he headed for the stairs.

She caressed his taut cheek. 'I love you. I want you. My heart belongs to you.'

'Mine belongs to you too, Sage *mou*. All of it.'

Words became redundant after that. They used their bodies to express their newfound feelings. Then repeated the process all over again, just to be sure.

Six hours later, she stretched in bed, smiling when Xandro trailed kisses down her back.

Going over the events of the past day, she bit her lip. 'I'm worried about Ben.'

He flipped her over and levered himself on top of her. 'I know, *pethi mou*. We'll get him the help he needs when we return home.'

She slid her arms around his neck. 'I like the sound of that.'

'What?'

'Home. With you. I like this house, too.'

'We can tour my properties after your production ends, and you can choose which one you wish to make our home. Anywhere in the world will be home as long as I'm with you. And you're completely naked.'

'Oh, you say the nicest things.'

'I say what's in my heart. I love you.'

'I love you, too, Xandro. So much.'

His nostrils flared as he took in a shaky breath. Then, as natural as breathing, her alpha lover was back, taking charge of her, worshipping her, loving her long into the night. And for as long as they had on this earth.

EPILOGUE

'YOU HAVE A six-week hiatus between productions. Now that you've chosen where we'll live, I think it's the perfect time to plan a wedding.'

Sage gasped and stared across the breakfast table at the owner of her heart. 'What did you say?'

'I have a wedding planner on standby,' he drawled without taking his eyes off the finance article he was reading. But she sensed a watchful stillness about him. And the fingers holding the newspaper were decidedly white-knuckled and unsteady. 'I think it's time to stop this dating nonsense.'

The love of her life wasn't as calm and collected as he wanted to appear.

She slowly relaxed in her chair, raised her face to the beautifully warm morning sun and the breeze blowing from the beach where they'd just enjoyed a pre-breakfast swim in the Aegean.

At Xandro's urging she'd chosen more than one place for them to live throughout the year. Their summers would be spent here on Ianthe Island, the rest of the time split between New York and Vegas, with long weekends away in the Caribbean. The rest of his extensive private property portfolio had been sold off. 'Well, he or she can remain standing by. I'm not interested.'

The paper hit the floor and then it was his turn to look poleaxed.

'What?' His voice was a shocked husk.

'You heard me.'

'You don't want to get married?' he asked carefully.

'Quite the opposite. I'm dying to get married. Only I

haven't been asked. I've just been informed a wedding planner is standing by.'

He shut his eyes for a tense moment. When he opened them they were stormy. He rose from his seat to crouch in front of her. 'I'm sorry. I'm learning, *agape mou*.'

Her heart melted and she placed her hand on his lean cheek. 'I know. But I reserve the right to yank your chain on your journey up the learning curve,' she replied with a saucy smile.

He nodded solemnly. Then he completely chopped her off at the knees by reaching into his pocket and extracting a very velvet, very suspicious-looking box. He dropped to both knees, his eyes pinned to hers as he slowly pried open the box and offered it to her.

She couldn't look. Not just yet. The look on his face was so much more breathtaking.

'Marry me, Sage *mou*. Make me the luckiest man in the world by giving me permission to call you mine.'

Tears filled her eyes. 'Oh, Xandro. I'm already yours. You know that.'

He nodded. 'I want to make it official. Do you want me to call your father, formally ask his permission?'

A sliver of sadness threatened her happiness. Unknown to her, Xandro had flown to Virginia and had a conversation with her parents about her and about helping Ben. Whatever he'd said to them had brought them to her first performance as a Hunter Dance Company member. Despite the Broadway show's rave reviews, and her performance receiving even more acclaim, they hadn't congratulated her.

They'd had a stilted dinner together, during which she'd bitten her tongue against blurting out that Xandro was the secret investor who'd saved Havenwoods from bankruptcy. Only the warning gleam in his eyes had kept her quiet.

When they'd returned home he'd made slow, poignant love to her and cradled her in his arms afterwards. Her strained relationship with her parents might never be whole again, but she was done being heartbroken over it. Her heart belonged to Xandro Christofides and it chose to live in perpetual joy and happiness.

'You can do that if you want, but I'm marrying you either way.'

'Not to be pedantic, *eros mou*, but is that a yes?'

'It's a definite, try-getting-rid-of-me-now *yes*! I love you.'

'I love you too, *agapita*. Now, take this ring from me before I sprain my wrist. This thing weighs a ton.'

She finally looked at the ring. And gulped at the large, exquisite square diamond set in platinum. The sparkle of the gem alone was enough to blind her. 'What did you do, pick the biggest rock in the shop?'

'Of course. My intention is for every man who gets within five hundred feet of you to know you're mine and to stay the hell clear,' he growled.

'My God, you're a Neanderthal.'

He growled once more against her mouth. '*Ne*. I'm *your* Neanderthal. And I intend to be for ever.'

'I love the sound of that.'

'Then so it shall be.'

* * * * *

CONVENIENT BRIDE
FOR THE KING

KELLY HUNTER

CHAPTER ONE

PRINCESS MORIANA OF ARUN wasn't an unreasonable woman. She had patience aplenty and was willing to give anyone the benefit of the doubt at least once. Maybe even twice. But when she knew for a fact she was being passed around like a Christmas cracker no one wanted to pull, all bets were off.

Her brother Augustus had said he wasn't available to speak with her this morning. People to see, kingdom to rule.

Nothing to do with avoiding her until she regained her equilibrium after yesterday's spectacularly public jilting…the *coward*.

So what if Casimir of Byzenmaach no longer wanted to marry her? It wasn't as if it had ever been Casimir's idea in the first place, and it certainly hadn't been hers. When you were the progeny of kings it was common-place for a politically expedient marriage to be arranged for you. And yet…inexplicably… Casimir's defection after such a long courtship had gutted her. He'd made her feel small and insignificant, unwanted and alone, and, above all, not good enough. All her hard work, the endless social politics, the restraint that guided her every move, had been for what?

Nothing.

Absolutely nothing.

Arun's royal palace was an austere one, mainly because Moriana's forefathers had planned it that way. Stern, grey and never quite warm enough, it invited application to duty over frivolous timewasting. It chose function over beauty, no matter how much beauty she found to hang on its walls. It favoured formal cloistered gardens for tidy minds.

Her brother had taken residence in the southern wing of the palace in the gloomiest rooms of them all, and not for the first time did Moriana wonder why. Her brother's executive secretary—an elderly courtier who'd been in service to the House of Arun since before she was born—looked up as she approached, his expression smooth and unruffled.

'Princess, what a pleasant surprise.'

She figured her appearance was neither pleasant nor a surprise, but she let the man have his social graces. 'Is he in?'

'He's taking an important call.'

'But he is in,' she countered and kept right on walking towards her brother's closed door. 'Wonderful.'

The older man sighed and pressed a button on the intercom as she swept past. He didn't actually *speak* into the intercom, mind. Moriana was pretty sure he had a secret code button set up just for her—doubtless announcing that Moriana the Red was incoming.

Her brother looked up when she walked in, told whoever he had on the phone that he'd call them back, and put the phone down.

Damn but it was cold in here. It didn't help that the spring just past had been a brutal one and summer had been slow to arrive. 'Why is it like an ice box in here?'

she asked. 'Have we no heating you can turn on? No warmer rooms you could rule from?'

'Or you could wear warmer clothes,' her brother suggested, but there was nothing wrong with her attire. Her fine wool dress was boat-necked, long-sleeved and fell to just above her knees. Stockings added another layer to her legs. She was wearing knee-high leather boots. Had she added a coat she'd be ready for a trip to the Antarctic.

'It is a perfectly pleasant day outside,' she countered. 'Why do you choose the coldest rooms we have to call your own?'

'If I had better rooms, more people would be tempted to visit me and I'd never get any work done.' His eyes were almost black and framed by thick black lashes, just like her own. His smile was indulgent as he sat back and steepled his hands—maybe his whole *I'm in charge of the universe* pose worked on some, but she'd grown up with him and knew what Augustus had looked like as a six-year-old with chickenpox and as a teenager with his first hangover. She knew the sound of his laughter and the shape of his sorrows. He could wear his kingly authority in public and she would bow to him but here in private, when it was just the two of them, he was nothing more than a slightly irritating older brother. 'What can I do for you?' he asked.

'Have you seen this?' She held up a thick sheet of cream-coloured vellum.

'Depends,' he said.

She slammed the offending letter down on the ebony desk in front of him. Letters generally didn't slam down on anything but this one had the weight of her hand behind it. 'Theo sent me a proposal.'

'Okay,' he said cautiously, still looking at her rather than the letter.

'A *marriage* proposal.'

Her brother's lips twitched.

'Don't you dare,' she warned.

'Well, it stands to reason he would,' said Augustus. 'You're available, he's under increasing pressure to produce an heir and secure the throne, and politically it's an opportunistic match.'

'We loathe each other. There is no earthly reason why Theo would want to spend an evening with me, let alone eternity.'

'I have a theory about that—'

'Don't start.'

'It goes something like this. He pulled your pigtail when you were children, you gave him a black eye and you've been fierce opponents ever since. If you actually spent some time with the man you'd discover he's not half as bad as you think he is. He's well-travelled, well-read, surprisingly intelligent and a consummate negotiator. All things you admire.'

'A consummate negotiator? Are you serious? Theo's marriage proposal is a *form* letter. He filled my name in at the top and his at the bottom.'

'And he has a sense of humour,' Augustus said.

'Says who?'

'Everyone except for you.'

'Doesn't that tell you something?'

'Yes.'

Oh, it was *on*.

She pulled up a chair, a hard unwelcoming one because that was all there was to be had in this farce of a room. She sat. He sighed. She crossed her legs, etiquette be damned. Two seconds later she uncrossed her legs, rearranged her skirt over her knees and sat ramrod-straight as she stared him down. 'Did you arrange this?' Because she wouldn't put it past him. He and their three neighbouring monarchs were close. They plotted together on a regular basis.

'Me? No.'

'Did Casimir?' He of the broken matrimonial intentions and newly discovered offspring.

'I doubt it. What with burying his father and planning a coronation, the instant fatherhood and his current wooing of the child's mother... I'm pretty sure he has his hands full.'

Moriana drummed her fingers on his ugly wooden desk, partly because it gave her time to digest her brother's words and partly because she knew it annoyed him. 'Then whose mad idea was it?'

He eyed her offending fingers for a moment before casually pulling open his desk drawer and pulling out a long wooden ruler. He held it up, as if gauging its reach, before bringing the tip to rest gently in his palm. 'Stop torturing my desk.'

'Or you'll beat me? Please,' she scoffed. Nonetheless, she stopped with the drumming and brought the offending hand in front of her to examine her nails. No damage at all. Maybe she'd paint her nails black later, to match the desk and her mood. Maybe her rebellion could start small. 'You haven't answered my question. Whose idea was it?'

'I'm assuming it was Theo's.'

She looked up to find Augustus eyeing her steadily, as if he knew something she didn't.

'It's not an insult, Moriana; it's an honour. You were born and raised for the kind of position Theo's offering.

You could make a difference to his leadership and to the stability of the region.'

'No.' She cut him off fast. 'You can't guilt me into this. I am *through* with being the good princess who does what she's told, the one who serves and serves and *serves,* without any thought to my own needs. I'm going to Cannes to party up a scandal. There will be recklessness. Orgies with dissolute film stars.'

'When?' Augustus did not sound alarmed.

'Soon.' He didn't *look* alarmed either, and he should have. 'You don't think I'll do it. You think I'm a humourless prude who wouldn't know fun times if they rained down on me. Well, they're about to. I want the passion of a lover's touch. I want a man to look at me with lust. Dammit, for once in my life I want to do something that pleases *me*!' She'd had enough. 'All those things I've been taught to place value on? My reputation, my sense of duty to king and country, my virginity? I'm getting rid of them.'

'Okay, let's not be hasty.'

'Hasty?' Princesses didn't screech. Moriana dropped her voice an octave and gave it some gravel instead. 'I could have had the stable boy when I was eighteen. He was beautiful, carefree and rode like a demon. At twenty-two I could have had a sheikh worth billions. He only had to look at me to make me melt. A year later I met a musician with hands I could only dream of. I would have gladly taken him to my bed but I *didn't.* Would you like me to continue?'

'*Please* don't.'

'Casimir's not a virgin,' she continued grimly. '*He* got a nineteen-year-old pregnant when he was twenty-three! You know what I was doing at twenty-three? Taking dancing lessons so that I could feel the touch of someone's hand.'

'I thought they were fencing lessons.'

'Same thing. Maybe I wanted to feel a little prick.' All these years she'd denied herself all manner of pleasures others took for granted. 'I have *waited*. No romance, no lovers, no children for Moriana of Arun. Only duty. And for what? So that today I could wake up and be vilified in the press for being too cool, too stern and too focused on fundraising and furthering my education to have time for any man? I mean, no wonder Casimir of Byzenmaach went looking for someone else, right?'

Augustus winced. 'No one's saying that.'

'Have you even read today's newspapers?'

'No one *here* is saying that,' he amended.

'What did I do wrong, Augustus? I was promised to an indifferent boy when I was eight years old. Now I'm getting a form letter marriage proposal from a playboy king whose dislike for me is legendary. And you say I should feel honoured?' Her voice cracked. 'Why do you sell me off so *easily*? Am I really that worthless?'

She straightened her shoulders, smoothed her hands over the skirt of her dress and made sure the hem sat in a straight stern line. She hated losing her composure, hated feeling needy and greedy and hard to love. She was wired to please others. Trained to it since birth.

But this…expecting her to fall all over herself to comply with Theo's request… 'Theo's uncle is making waves again and questioning Theo's fitness to rule. I do read the reports that come in.' She read every last one of them. 'I understand Liesendaach's need for stability and a secure future and that we in Arun would rather deal with Theo than with his uncle. But I am *not* the solution to his need for a quickie marriage.'

'Actually, you're an excellent solution.' Augustus was watching her carefully. 'You've been looking forward to having a family for years. Theo needs an heir. You could be pregnant within a year.'

'Don't.' Yes, she wanted children. She'd foolishly once thought she'd be married with several children by now.

'You and Theo have goals that align. I'm merely stating the obvious.'

Moriana wrapped her arms around her waist and stared at the toes of her boots. The boots were a shade darker than the purple of her dress. The pearls around her neck matched the pearls in her ears. She was a picture-perfect princess who was falling apart inside. 'Maybe I don't want children any more. Maybe keeping royal children safe and happy and feeling loved is an impossible task.'

'Our parents seemed to manage it well enough.'

'Oh, really?' She knew she should hold her tongue. She didn't, and all her years of trying and failing to please people bubbled to the fore. 'Do you think I feel loved? By whom?' She choked on a laugh. 'You, who would just as soon trade me into yet another loveless marriage in return for regional stability? Casimir, who never wanted me in the first place and was simply too gutless to say so? Theo, with his form letter marriage proposal and endless parade of mistresses? Do you really think I've basked in the glow of unconditional parental love and approval for the past twenty-eight years? Heaven help me, Augustus. What *planet* are you living on? Not one of you even remembers I exist unless I can *do* something for you.'

She felt stupid. Stupid for putting her life on hold for a decade and never once calling into question that childhood betrothal. She could have asked for a time frame from Casimir. She could have pressed for a solid commitment. She could have said no to many things and got over trying to please people who didn't give a damn about her. She gestured towards Theo's offending letter. 'He doesn't even *pretend* to offer love or attraction. Not even mild affection.'

'Is that what you want?'

'Yes! I want to be with someone who cares for me. Why is that so hard to understand?'

'Maybe he does.'

'What?'

'Theo. Maybe he cares for you.'

'You don't seriously expect me to believe that.' Moriana looked at him in amazement. 'You do. Oh. You must think I'm really stupid.'

'It's a theory.'

'Would you like me to disprove it for you?' Because she had years and years of dealing with Theo to call on. 'I can count on one hand the times I've felt that man's support. The first was at our mother's funeral when he caught me as I stumbled on the steps of the church. He made me sit before I fell. He brought me water and sat with me in silence and kept his hatred of women wearing black to himself. The second and final time he was supportive of me was at a regional water summit when a drunk delegate put his hand on my backside. Theo told him he'd break it if it wasn't removed.'

'I like it,' said her brother with a faint smile.

'You would.'

'He knows where you are in a room full of people,' Augustus said next. 'He always knows. He can describe whatever it is you're wearing.'

'So he's observant.'

'It's more than that.'

'I disagree. Maybe he's wanted me a time or two,

I'll give him that. But only for sport, and only because he couldn't have me.' She plucked the form letter from the desk and folded it so that the offending words were hidden. 'No, Augustus. It's a smart offer. Theo's a smart man. I can see exactly what kind of political gain is in it for him. But there's nothing in it for me. Nothing I want.'

'I hear you,' Augustus replied quietly.

'Good.' She sent her brother a tight smile. 'Maybe I'll send a form letter refusal. *Dear Applicant, After careful consideration I regret to inform you that your proposal has been unsuccessful. Better luck next time.*'

'That would be inviting him to try again. This is Theo, remember?'

'You're right.' Moriana reconsidered her words. *'Better luck elsewhere?'*

'Yes.' Her brother smiled but his eyes remained clouded with concern. 'Moriana—'

'Don't,' she snapped. 'Don't you try and guilt me into doing this.'

'I'm not. You're free to choose. Free to be. Free to discover who and what makes you happy.'

'Good. Good chat. I should bare my soul to you more often.'

Augustus shuddered.

Moriana rounded her brother's imposing desk and kissed the top of his head, mainly because she knew such a blatant display of affection would irritate him. 'I'm sorry,' she whispered. 'I like what Theo's doing for his country. I applaud the progress and stability he's bringing to the region and I want it to continue. There's plenty to admire about him these days, and if I thought he actually liked me or that there was any chance he could meet my needs I'd marry him and make the most of it. I don't need to be swept off my feet. But this time I *do* want attention and affection and fidelity in return for my service. Love even, heaven forbid. And that's not Theo's wheelhouse.'

Augustus, reigning King of Arun and brother to Moriana the Red, watched as his sister turned on her boot heel and headed for the door.

'Moriana.' It was easier to talk to her retreating form than say it to her face. 'I do love you, you know. I want you to be happy.'

Her step faltered, but she didn't look back as she closed the door behind her.

Augustus, worst brother in the world, put his hands to his face and breathed deeply before reaching for the phone on his desk.

He didn't know, he couldn't be sure if Theo had stayed on the line or not, but still…the option to do so had been there.

Mistake.

He picked up the phone and listened for a moment but there was only silence. 'You still there?' he asked finally.

'Yes.'

Damn. 'I wish you hadn't heard that.'

'She's magnificent.' A thousand miles away, King Theodosius of Liesendaach let out a breath and ran a hand through his short-cropped hair. He had the fair hair and blue-grey eyes of his forefathers, the build of a warrior and no woman had ever refused him. Until now. He didn't know whether to be insulted or to applaud. 'The stable boy? Really?'

'I wish *I* hadn't heard that.' Augustus sounded weary. 'What the hell are you doing, sending her a form letter marriage proposal? I thought you wanted her co-operation.'

'I do want her co-operation. I will confess, I wasn't expecting quite that much *no* in response.'

'You thought she'd fall all over the offer.'

'I thought she'd at least consider it.'

'She did.' Augustus's tone was dry—very dry. 'When's the petition for your removal from the throne being tabled?'

'Week after next, assuming my uncle gets the support he needs. He's close.' The petition was based on a clause in Liesendaach's constitution that enabled a monarch who had no intention of marrying and producing an heir to be removed from the throne. The clause hadn't been enforced in over three hundred years.

'You need a plan B,' said Augustus.

'I have a plan B. It involves talking to your sister in person.'

'You heard her. She's not interested.'

'Stable boy,' Theo grated. 'Dissolute film star. Would you rather she took up with them?'

'Why are you any more worthy? A damn *form letter*, Theo.' Augustus appeared to be working up to a snit of his own. 'Couldn't you have at least shown up? I thought you cared for her. I honestly thought you cared for her more than you ever let on, otherwise I would have never encouraged this.'

'I do care for her.' She was everything a future queen of Liesendaach should be. Poised, competent, politically aware and beautiful. Very, *very* beautiful. He'd dragged his heels for years when it came to providing Liesendaach with a queen.

And now Moriana, Princess of Arun, was free.

Her anger at her current situation had nothing on Theo's when he thought of how much *time* they'd wasted. '*Your sister* put herself on hold for a man who didn't want her, and you—first as her brother, and then as her King—did nothing to either expedite or dissolve that commitment. All those years she spent sidelined and waiting. All her hard-won self-confidence dashed by polite indifference. Do you care for her? Has Casimir *ever* given a damn? Because from where I sit, neither of you could have cared for her any *less*. I may not love her the way she wants to be loved. Frankly, I don't love anyone like that and never have. But at least I notice her *existence*.'

Silence from the King of Árun.

'You miscalculated with the form letter,' Augustus said finally.

'So it would seem,' Theo gritted out.

'I advise you to let her cool down before you initiate any further contact.'

'No. Why do you never let your sister run hot?' Even as a child he'd hated seeing Moriana's fiery spirit squashed beneath the weight of royal expectations. And, later, it was one of the reasons he fought with her so much. Not the only one—sexual frustration had also played its part. But when he and Moriana clashed, her fire stayed lit. He *liked* that.

'I need to see her.' Theo ran a hand through his already untidy hair. 'I'm not asking you to speak with her on my behalf. I've already heard you do exactly that and, by the way, thanks for nothing. What kind of diplomat are you? Yes, I'm being pressured to marry and produce heirs. That's not an argument I would have led with.'

'I didn't lead with it. I mentioned it in passing. I also sang your praises and pushed harder than I should have on your behalf. You're welcome.'

'I can give her what she wants. Affection, attention, even fidelity.'

Not love, but you couldn't have everything.

'That's your assessment. It's not hers.'

'I need to speak with her.'

'No,' said Augustus. 'You need to grovel.'

CHAPTER TWO

PUBLIC FLAYING OR NOT, Moriana's charity commitments continued throughout the day and into the evening. She'd put together a charity antique art auction for the children's hospital months ago and the event was due to start at six p.m. in one of the palace function rooms that had been set up for the occasion. The auctioneers had been in residence all day, setting up the display items. Palace staff were on duty to take care of the catering, security was in place and there was no more work to be done beyond turning up, giving a speech and subtly persuading some of the region's wealthiest inhabitants to part with some of their excess money. Moriana was good at hosting such events. Her mother had taught her well.

Not that Moriana had ever managed to live up to those exacting standards when her mother was alive. It had taken years of dogged, determined practice to even reach her current level of competence.

The principality of Arun wasn't the wealthiest principality in the region. That honour went to Byzenmaach, ruled by Casimir, her former intended. It also wasn't the prettiest. Theo's Liesendaach was far prettier, embellished by centuries of rulers who'd built civic buildings and public spaces beyond compare. No, Arun's claim to fame lay in its healthcare and education systems, and this was due in no small measure to her ceaseless work in those areas, and her mother's and grandmother's attention before that. Rigidly repressed the women of the royal house of Arun might be but they knew how to champion the needs of their people.

Tonight would be an ordeal. The press had not been kind to her today and she'd tried to put that behind her and carry on as usual. The main problem being that *no one else* was carrying on as usual. Even Aury, her unflappable lady-in-waiting, had been casting anxious glances in Moriana's direction all day.

Moriana's favourite treat, lemon tart with a burnt sugar top, had been waiting for her at morning tea, courtesy of the palace kitchens. A vase full of fat pink peonies had been sitting on her sideboard by lunchtime. She'd caught one of her publicity aides mid-rant on the phone—he'd been threatening to revoke someone's palace press pass if they ran a certain headline, and he'd flushed when he'd seen her but he'd kept right on making threats until he'd got his way.

There'd been a certain lack of newspapers in the palace this morning, which meant that Moriana had had to go online to read them.

She should have stayed away.

There was this game she and her lady-in-waiting often made out of the news of the day. While Aury styled Moriana's hair for whatever function was on that evening, they'd shoot headlines back and forth. On a normal day it encouraged analysis and discussion.

On a normal day the headlines wouldn't be proclaiming Moriana the most undesirable princess on the planet.

'Too Cold to Wed,' Moriana said as Aury reached for the pins that would secure Moriana's braid into an elegant roll at the base of her head.

'No,' said Aury, pointing a stern hairbrush in the direction of Moriana's reflection. 'I'm not doing this today and neither are you. I stopped reading them so I wouldn't choke on my breakfast, and you should have stopped reading them too.'

Jilted Ice Princess Contemplates Nunnery,' Moriana continued.

'I'm not coming with you to the nunnery. They don't care what hair looks like there, the heathens,' said Aury, pushing a hairpin into place. 'Okay, no, I will give you a headline. *Byzenmaach Mourns as the Curse Strikes Again.*'

'Curse?' Moriana had missed that one. 'What curse?'

'Apparently you refused to marry King Casimir in an attempt to avoid the same fate as his mother. Namely, being physically, mentally and verbally abused by your husband for years before taking a lover, giving birth to your lover's child, seeing both killed by your husband and then committing suicide.'

'Ouch.' Moriana caught her lady-in-waiting's gaze in the mirror. 'What paper was that?'

'A regional one from Byzenmaach's northern border. The *Mountain Chronicle.*'

'Vultures.' Never mind that she'd accidentally overheard her parents discussing a remarkably similar scenario involving Casimir's parents. She'd never repeated the conversation to anyone but Augustus and she never would. 'Casimir doesn't deserve that one.'

'Byzenmaach Monarch Faces Backlash over Secret Lover and Child,' said Aury next.

'That one I like. Serves him right. Do we have the run sheet for the auction tonight?'

'It's right here. And the guest list.'

Moriana scanned through the paperwork Aury

handed her. 'Augustus is attending now and bringing a guest? He didn't say anything about it to me this morning.'

Not that she'd given him a chance to say anything much. Still.

'Word came through from his office this afternoon. Also, Lord and Lady Curtis send their apologies. Their granddaughter had a baby this afternoon.'

'Have we sent our congratulations?'

'We have.'

'Tell the auctioneer to put my reserve on the baby bear spoon set. They can have it as a gift.' Arun might not be the wealthiest or the prettiest kingdom in the region but its people did not go unattended.

'I put the silver gown out for tonight, along with your grandmother's diamonds. I also took the liberty of laying out the blood-red gown you love but never wear and the pearl choker and earrings from the royal collection. The silver gown is a perfectly appropriate choice, don't get me wrong, but I for one am hoping the Ice Princess might feel like making a statement tonight.'

'And you think a red gown and a to-hell-with-you-all attitude will do this?'

'It beats looking whipped.'

'The red gown it is,' Moriana murmured. The Ice Princess was overdue for a thaw. 'Now all I need is a wholly inappropriate date to go with it.' She took a deep breath and let it out slowly. 'Actually, no. I'm not so merciless as to drag anyone else into this mess. I'll go alone.'

'You'll not be alone for long,' Aury predicted. 'Opportunists will flock to you.'

'It's already started.'

'Anyone you like?'

'No.' Moriana ignored the sudden image of a harshly

hewn face and glittering grey eyes. 'Well, Theo. Who I've never actually tried to like. It never seemed worth the effort.'

Aury stopped fussing with Moriana's hair in favour of looking stunned. 'Theodosius of Liesendaach is courting you now?'

'I wouldn't call it courting.' Moriana thought back to the form letter and scowled. 'Trust me, neither would anyone else.'

'Yes, but *really*?'

'Aury, your tongue is hanging out.'

'Uh huh. Have you *seen* that man naked?'

'Oh, yes. God bless the paparazzi. *Everyone* has seen that man naked.'

'And what a treat it was.'

Okay, so he was well endowed. And reputedly very skilled in the bedroom. Women did not complain of him. Old lovers stayed disconcertingly friendly with him.

'You'd take me to Liesendaach with you, right?' asked Aury as she started in on Moriana's hair again, securing the roll with pearl-tipped pins and leaving front sections of hair loose to be styled into soft curls. 'I can start packing any time. Say the word. I am there for you. Of course, I am also here for you.' Aury sighed heavily.

'You should have pursued a career in drama,' Moriana said. 'Arun's not so bad. A little austere at times. A little grey around the edges. And at the centre. But there's beauty here too, if you know where to look.'

'I know where to look.' Aury sighed afresh. 'And clearly so does Theodosius of Liesendaach. Be careful with that one.'

'I can handle Theo.'

Aury looked uncommonly troubled, her dark eyes wary and her lips tilted towards a frown. 'He strikes me as a man who gets what he wants. What if he decides he wants you?'

'He doesn't. Theo's been reliably antagonistic towards me since childhood. And when he's not prodding me with a pointy stick he's totally indifferent to my presence. He's just…going through the motions. Being a casual opportunist. If I turn him down he'll go away.'

Aury sighed again and Moriana could feel a lecture coming on. Aury had several years on Moriana, not enough to make her a mother figure, but more than enough to fulfil the role of older, wiser sister. It was a role she took seriously.

'My lady, as one woman to another… Okay, as one slightly more experienced woman to another…please don't be taken in by Theodosius of Liesendaach's apparent indifference to events and people that surround him. That man is like a hawk in a granary. He's watching, he's listening and he knows what he wants from any given situation. More to the point, he knows what *everyone else* wants from any given situation.'

'He doesn't know what I want.'

'Want to bet?' Aury sounded uncommonly serious. 'Yes, he's charming, he's playful, he's extremely good at acting as if he couldn't care less. But what else do we know of him? Think about it. We know that for the first fifteen years of his life he never expected to be King. We know that for ten years after the death of his parents and brother he watched and waited his turn while his uncle bled Liesendaach dry as Regent. *The young Crown Prince is indifferent to our plight*, the people said. *He's bad blood, too busy pleasing himself to care about the rape of our country*, they said. *We can't look to him to save us. He will not bring an end to this.* That's what his uncle thought. It's what everyone thought. It's what he wanted them to think.'

Aury reached for another pin. 'Do you remember the day Theodosius of Liesendaach turned twenty-five and took the throne? I do. Because from that day forward he systematically destroyed his uncle and squashed every last parasite. He targeted their every weakness, he knew exactly where to strike, and he has fought relentlessly to bring his country back to prosperity. That's not indifference. That's patience, planning, ruthless execution and fortitude. He was *never* indifferent to his country's plight. I don't trust that man's *indifference* one little bit.'

'Point taken.'

'I hope so.' Aury finished with Moriana's hair and pulled the make-up trolley closer. She rifled through the lipstick drawer and held up a blood-red semi-gloss for inspection. 'What else are we thinking?'

'I'm thinking smoky eyes and lipstick one shade lighter. It's a charity auction, not a nightclub.'

'Boring,' said Aury.

'Baby steps.' Moriana had already chosen a dress she wasn't entirely comfortable with.

Aury found a lighter shade of lipstick and held it up for inspection. 'What about this one?'

'Yes.' Aury rarely steered her wrong. 'And Aury?'

'Yes, milady?'

'I'll be careful.'

Augustus was a deceitful, manipulative son of Satan, Moriana decided when he stepped into the auction room later that evening with his *guest* in tow. It wasn't a woman. Oh, no. Her brother hadn't done anything so lacklustre as bringing a suitable date with him to the event. Instead, he'd brought a neighbouring monarch

along for the ride. Theo, to be more precise. He of the
hawkish grace, immaculate dinner suit and form letter
marriage proposal.

Theo and Augustus had been thick as thieves as children. They'd grown apart in their teens when Theo had
flung himself headlong into reckless debauchery after
the death of his family. Augustus had only followed him
so far before their father, the then monarch of Arun, had
reined him in. Theo had experienced no such constraints.
Lately though…now that Theo bore the full brunt of the
Liesendaach Crown… Moriana didn't quite know what
kind of relationship Theo and her brother had. They'd
been working together on a regional water plan. They
trusted each other's judgement in such matters. They
still didn't socialise together.

Much.

That they were socialising now, the same day she'd
refused Theo's offer, spoke volumes for Augustus's support of the man.

So much for blood being thicker than brotherhood.

She turned away fast when she caught her brother's
gaze because this betrayal, on top of Casimir's rejection, on top of Theo's demeaning form letter, almost
brought her to her knees. So much for men and all their
fine promises. You couldn't trust any of them.

The chief press advisor for the palace appeared at her
side, his eyes sharp but his smile in place. 'Your Highness, you look pale. May I get you anything?'

'How about a brand-new day?' she suggested quietly.
'This one's rotten, from the core out.'

'Tomorrow will be a better day,' he said.

'Promises.' Her voice was light but her heart was
heavy.

'I promise we're doing our best to shine the brightest light we can on everything you do for us, milady. The entire team is on it. No one dismisses our princess lightly. No one has earned that right.'

'Thank you, Giles.' She blinked back rapid tears and looked away. 'I appreciate your support.'

And then two more people joined them. One was Theo and the other one was Augustus. Years of burying her feelings held her in good stead as she plastered a smile on her face and set about greeting them.

'Your Majesties,' she said, curtseying to them, and something of her hurt must have shown on her face as she rose because Augustus frowned and started to say something. Whatever it was, she didn't want to hear it. 'What a surprise.'

'A pleasant one, I hope,' said Theo as he took her gloved hand and lifted it to his lips.

'Oh, we all live in hope,' she offered. 'I live in hope that one day the people I hold dear will have my back, but that day's not here yet.'

'Yes, it is; you just can't see it,' Theo countered. 'I'm here, welcome or not, with the ulterior motive of being seen with you in public.'

'Indeed, I can see the headlines now. *Ice Princess Falls for Playboy King. Liesendaach Gives It a Week.*'

'Perhaps.' Theo didn't discount it. 'Or I can give your publicity officer here a quote about how much respect I have for you as a person and as a representative of the royal family of Arun. I can mention that it's no hardship whatsoever to continue to offer you my friendship, admiration and support. I can add that I'm not at all dismayed that you're now free of your ridiculous childhood betrothal to the new King of Byzenmaach. And we can see how that goes down.'

The press advisor melted away with a nod in Theo's direction. Theo and her brother stayed put.

'Damage control, Moriana. Look it up,' Theo said curtly.

'Well, I guess you'd know all about that.'

'I do.' But he didn't defend his wild past or the chaos he occasionally still stirred. He never did. Theodosius of Liesendaach didn't answer to anyone.

A small—very tiny—part of her respected that.

'So,' she said. 'Welcome to my annual Children's Hospital Charity Auction. Have you seen the catalogue?'

'I have not.'

'I'll have one sent over.' She nodded towards some nearby display cases. 'By all means, look around. You might see something you like.'

'You won't accompany me?'

'No, I'm working.' He'd dressed immaculately, as usual. No one wore a suit quite the way Theo did. He was broad-shouldered and slim-hipped. Tall enough to look down on almost everyone in the room. His cropped blond hair was nothing remarkable and his face was clean-shaven. It wasn't a pretty face. A little too stern and altogether too craggy. Lips that knifed towards cruel when he was in a bad mood. His eyes were his best feature by far. She might as well give the devil his due. They were icy blue-grey and often coolly amused. They were amused now.

'I have other duties to attend and people to greet,' she continued bluntly. 'How fortunate Augustus is here to take care of you. What a good friend.'

'Indeed he is.' Theo's gaze had yet to leave hers. 'I like it when you wear red. The colour suits you and so do the pearls. My compliments to your wardrobe mistress.'

'I'll be sure to let her know. I mean, it's not as if I

could ever be in charge of my own clothing choices, right? Who knows what I'd come up with?' There was something different about Theo tonight. Something fierce and implacable and hungry. She bared her teeth right back at him. 'Any other underhand compliments you'd like to shower me with before I take my leave?'

Augustus winced. 'Moria—'

'No!' She cut him off. 'You don't get to diminish me either. All your fine talk this morning of supporting my decisions, of letting me be. I believed you. Yet here we are.'

'Your brother's not at fault,' Theo said smoothly. 'Moriana, we need to talk.'

'About your proposal? My reply is in the mail, seeing as that's your preferred method of communication. Seeing as you're here, I dare say I can give you the highlights. I refuse. It's not you, it's me. Or maybe it is you and all those other women I'd have to live up to, I don't know. Either way, my answer's no. I am done listening to the two-faced, self-serving babble of kings. Now, if you'll both excuse me.'

'Go. Greet your guests. We can talk after you're done here. I'll wait,' said Theo the Magnanimous. 'I'm good at waiting.'

Moriana laughed. She couldn't help it. 'Theo, you may have waited for your crown but you've never waited on a woman in your life.'

She was close enough to see his jaw clench. Close enough to see hot temper flare in those eyes that ran more towards grey tonight than blue. 'Oh, Princess. Always so *wrong*.'

It wasn't easy to turn away from the challenge in his gaze but she did it, more mindful than ever of Aury's warning. This wasn't the boy she remembered from

childhood or the teenager who'd poked and prodded at
her until she'd snapped back. This was the man who'd
watched and waited for ten long years before rising and
taking his country back. This was the hawk in the granary.

And maybe, just maybe, she was the mouse.

Fifteen minutes later, after personally greeting all the
guests in attendance and seeing that they were well lu-
bricated, Moriana looked for Theo again. Not that she
had to look hard. She always knew where Theo was in
a room, just as she always tracked where her security
detail was, and where her brother was. It was an awareness that would have made a seasoned soldier proud and
she'd been trained for it since birth.

*Know your exits. Know where your support is. Know
where your loved ones are at any given moment.* Theo
wasn't a loved one but he'd always been included in that
equation for he'd been a treasured child of royalty too.
The last of his line and therefore important.

Casimir, her former intended, had also been the last
of his line and she'd always tracked his whereabouts too,
whenever they'd been at functions together. She'd misplaced Casimir on occasion—no one was perfect. She'd
misplaced him on several occasions.

Many occasions.

Moving on.

Theo didn't look up from the display he was brows-
ing as she made her way to his side. He didn't look up
even as he began to speak. 'You're good at this,' he said.

'Thank you.' She wanted to believe he could pay
her a genuine compliment, not that he ever had before.
'I've been hosting this particular fundraiser for the past
seven years and I have it down to a fine art, pardon the

pun. Collecting the auction items, curating the guest list, knowing what people want and what they'll pay to have it. Knowing who else they might want to see socially. People say I have a knack for fundraising, as if I simply fling things together at the last minute and hope for the best, but I don't. I put a lot of work into making sure these evenings flow like water and do what they're meant to do.'

'I don't doubt it,' he said, finally turning his gaze on her. 'Hence the compliment.' He tilted his head a fraction. 'You're an exceptional ambassador for your people and you'd have been an exceptional asset to Casimir as queen consort. It's Byzenmaach's loss.'

He wasn't the first person to say that to her tonight and he probably wouldn't be the last. 'I doubt Casimir's feeling any loss.' She didn't like how thready she sounded. As if she'd been stretched too thin for far too long.

'He hurt you.' Three simple words that cracked her wide open.

'Don't. Theo, please. Leave it alone. It's done.'

She turned away, suddenly wanting to get away from the sedate auction room and the gossip and the expectations that came with being a Princess of Arun. Perfect composure, always. Unrivalled social graces. A memory trained to remember names and faces. She had a welcome speech to give in fifteen minutes. Who would give it if she walked out?

He stopped her before she'd taken a step. The subtle shift of his body and the force of his silent appraisal blocked her retreat. 'You're not coping,' he said quietly. 'Tell me what you need.'

She didn't know why his softly spoken words hurt so much, but they did. 'Damn you, Theo. Don't do this to me. Don't be attentive all of a sudden because you want something from me. Do what you usually do. Fight. Snarl. Be you. Give me something I know how to respond to.'

He stilled, his face a granite mask, and she had the sudden, inexplicable feeling she'd just dealt him a brutal blow. And then his gaze cut away from her face and he took a deep breath and when he looked at her again he wore a fierce and reckless smile she knew all too well. 'I'll fight you mentally, physically, whatever you need, until we both bleed,' he promised, his voice a vicious caress. 'Just as soon as you stop *breaking* in front of me. I know your family trained you to hide weakness better than this. It's what you do. It's all you do. So do it.'

Yes. This was what she needed from him, and to hell with why. No one said she was the most well-balanced princess in the universe.

Thread by thread she pulled herself together, drawing on the anger she sensed in him to bolster her own. *Build a wall—any wall.* Anger, righteous indignation, icy disdain, attention to duty, whatever it took to keep the volcano of feelings in check.

'Have you seen the Vermeer?' she asked finally, when she had herself mostly back under control. 'I thought of you when it first came in. It would round out Liesend-aach's Dutch collection.'

He studied her for what felt like hours, before nodding, as if she'd do, and then held out his arm for her to claim. 'All right, Princess. Persuade me.'

Moriana carved out the time to show Theo the most interesting pieces in the auction. She made her speech and the auction began. And by the end of the evening a great deal of money had been raised for the new children's hospital wing and Theo had almost purchased the Vermeer for a truly staggering sum. In the end the painting had gone to a gallery and Moriana dearly hoped they needed a tax write-down soon because they clearly hadn't done their sums. That or they *really* wanted to support the children's hospital.

'I thought you'd lost your mind,' she said when only a handful of guests remained and he came to congratulate her on the evening's success. 'Not even you could justify that amount of money for a lesser Vermeer.'

'But for you I tried.'

His smile reminded her of young boys and frog ponds and sultry, still evenings, back when Theo's parents had still been alive. Augustus had always caught his frogs with quick efficiency and, once examined, had let them go. Theo, on the other hand, had revelled in the chase. He'd been far more interested in which way they jumped and where they might try to hide than in actually catching them. To this day, Moriana didn't know what that said about either Theo or her brother.

'Are you ready for that drink yet?' he asked.

'What drink?'

'The one we're going to have tonight, when you graciously reconsider my proposal.'

'Oh, *that* drink. We're not having that drink any time soon. You're getting a form letter rejection in the post, remember?'

'You wouldn't.'

'I did. You'll receive it tomorrow, unless you're still here. I assume Augustus has offered you palace hospitality?'

Theo inclined his head.

Of course. 'Then perhaps you should find him. I'm about to retire for the evening.'

'You said you'd give me five minutes of your time.'

'I said nothing of the sort. And yet here I am. Giving you my time.' If she'd worn a watch she'd have glanced at it.

'I gave you a fight when you needed one earlier.' Since when had his voice been able to lick at her like flames? 'I didn't want to, but I did. Here's what I want in return. One kiss. Here or in private. Put your hands on me, just once. You have my permission. I'll even keep mine to myself. And if you don't like touching and kissing me I'll withdraw my pursuit at once. Does that not sound fair and honest? Am I being unjust?'

Gone was the teasing menace of her childhood and the reckless philanderer of her youth. In their place stood a man in pursuit, confident and dangerous.

He'd been waiting for her when she'd finished her speech, approval in his eyes and a glass of champagne in hand that he handed to *her*. Faultlessly attentive. Silently supportive.

Tell me what you need.

A fight. A snarl. Barbed compliments. His attention. Something other than rejection to focus on.

'One drink. One kiss,' he murmured. 'Do you need to collect a coat of some sort? Because I'm ready to leave.'

'Why would I leave with you? Why would I indulge you in this?'

'Because I have something you want. Several somethings.'

'No, you don't. If you had anything I wanted, I'd be giving your proposal all due consideration.'

'Position.' His eyes never left her face.

'Yawn.' She was Princess of Arun.

'Passion. You've never felt it but you want it, nonetheless.'

'Maybe.' She was honest enough to concede his point. 'But you're not the only man to inspire passion in a woman. Plenty do. I can find passion without you.'

His eyes flashed silver.

'Temper, *temper*,' she said.

'Commitment,' he offered next.

'We all exercise that. I'm already committed to various causes, not to mention my country and my family. Some would say I'm blindly overcommitted to many things and receive little in return, and they're probably right. Commitment is overrated.'

His eyes never left her face. 'Commitment to you.'

CHAPTER THREE

HE WAS GOOD at this. Aury had warned her. He knew exactly what to offer in order to make her heart thump with painful hope and longing.

'Let's talk about this somewhere without the avid audience,' he muttered.

She glanced beyond him discreetly, only to realise he was right. Those who had yet to leave seemed to have no intention of doing so with her and Theo putting on a show right in front of their eyes. Even Augustus was staring at them, his eyes full of clear warning.

Don't make a spectacle of yourself. Remember your place.

Don't embarrass me.

Don't make me regret that we're related.

'Five minutes,' she said to Theo, as she nodded minutely at her brother—*message received*—and headed for the door.

Moriana lived in a wing of the royal palace. She'd furnished it to her taste, raided the palace's art collection until she was satisfied with the result and had purchased whatever pieces she felt were missing. Augustus could complain about her spending—and he did—but her ledger was in the black.

In the space of five years she'd tripled the value of

the royal art collection and outlaid only a fraction of that cost. She wheeled and dealed, had an eye for a bargain and the sensibilities of a curator. And, of course, she had the throne of Arun behind her.

She had dual degrees in politics and fine arts. Connections the world over. She was the ambassador for a dozen different charities and she took those roles seriously. She was educated, accomplished and blessed with favourable looks, or so she'd been told. She was in a position to make a difference.

And nervous. Dear heaven, she was nervous as Theo prowled around her sitting room, staring at her furnishings and possessions as if they held secrets he wanted to know.

'You wanted a drink?' she asked.

'If you're having one.' He put his hands in his trouser pockets and continued to study the sculpture on a small side table. 'It's fake,' he said of the copied Rodin.

'I know. But it's a good copy and it's still very beautiful.' She'd paid a pittance for it. 'How do you know it's a fake?' Not many would. Not without examining it thoroughly, and he hadn't.

'Because my father gifted the real one to my mother on their tenth wedding anniversary.'

Oh, well. There you go. 'I have Scotch.'

'Perfect.'

She poured him a serve and then doubled it because it wouldn't do to have her serve be twice the size of his.

He was standing by the fireplace and she crossed the room with all the grace she could muster and handed him the drink.

'I like this room,' he said. 'It's more comfortable than I thought it would be.'

'I use it,' she said simply, and tried not to look at his

lips but they were impossible to ignore now that he'd put the idea of kissing into her head. 'I like jewel colours and textured fabrics. I like comfortable furniture.'

'Your taste is exquisite.' He sipped his drink. 'Does Augustus know you serve his special Scotch?'

'Does he need to know?' she countered. 'Because, frankly, he's slightly precious about it.' She took a sip of hers. 'You sent me a form letter proposal.'

'I had it specially made just for you.'

'Now you're making fun of me.'

'Not really. The scions of the House of Liesendaach always put their marriage proposals in writing. It's the rule.'

Byzenmaach didn't have such a rule and neither did Arun. Her and Casimir's engagement had been more of a verbal agreement between their parents than anything she'd signed up for. Maybe there was some small merit to Theo's form letter after all.

'A marriage proposal is usually accompanied by a ring,' she said. There'd never been one of those between her and Casimir either.

Theo slipped his hand into his trouser pocket and pulled out a small wooden box.

'Oh, for heaven's sake. I suppose you had that especially made for me too,' she said.

'Yes.'

He was the best liar she knew. And she'd been surrounded by courtiers and politicians since birth.

'What?' He looked anything but innocent. He was inviting her to enjoy the joke, but she couldn't.

She turned away.

'I'm putting it on your mantelpiece so you can think about it.'

'I've thought about it.' She'd thought of little else all

day. 'I've decided I'd rather pursue a different kind of life. I'm going to take half a dozen lovers, one for every day of the week, and I'll rest on Sundays,' she continued. 'I'm going to throw debauched parties and seduce the unwary. I'll use you as my role model.'

'You don't want to do that.'

'Oh, but I do. Purity is a construct of my own inhibitions. It's time to let those inhibitions go.'

He smiled tightly. 'As much as I agree that you should definitely explore your sensual side, I'm not a fan of your proposed method of doing so. May I suggest choosing one person to take you on that journey? More specifically, me. We could aim for one new sensory experience a day. I could teach you everything I know. Assuming you enjoy our kiss and agree to marry me.'

'I've yet to agree to kiss you at all, let alone all the rest. What if I enjoy the kiss and refuse to marry you? What if I ask you to teach me everything you know regardless? Would you do it?'

'No.'

'Why not?'

'Yawn.' He stared into his drink and then drained it in one long swallow before setting the delicately cut crystal tumbler on the mantel next to the ring box. 'It's not what I want and it's definitely not what I need. I meant what I said about commitment. I'm prepared to pay close attention to your wants and needs and see that they're met.'

She wanted to believe him, even if she couldn't quite bring herself to. 'And you expect the same from me.'

'Face it, Moriana, you've spent a lifetime making sure other people's needs are met. It's ingrained in you.'

He made her sound like a particularly comfortable leather chair. 'That's about to change. I'm on a *Moriana First* kick.'

'It's about time.' He smiled faintly. 'I happen to believe a person can be both kind to themselves and committed to the people they care about. But first things first. What is it you think I can't give you?'

Where did she begin? 'You've never been exclusive with a woman before.' Understatement.

'I've never asked one to marry me either, yet here I am.' He met her gaze, and there it was again, something hard and implacable and patient in his eyes. 'I happen to think we'd make a good team. There's fire between us; there always has been. We rub each other the wrong way. We could also rub each other the right way—so much so that there'd be no room for other lovers. That's what I believe. I'm attracted to you. I may have missed that point in the form letter.'

'You did.'

'I'm making it now.'

He was. 'Theo, you're attracted to a lot of people. You've proven that quite spectacularly over the years. Kissing me and enjoying it would prove nothing.'

'You're wrong. A kiss could prove extremely informative for us both.' He smiled that charming smile. 'Come on, Moriana. You have nothing to lose and only experience to gain. Don't you want experience?'

'Yes, but I'd rather have it without strings.'

'No strings.' She'd never seen him so obliging.

'There's an engagement ring on my mantelpiece,' she said drily.

'That's a measure of my sincerity, not a string.'

'We get this wrong, you go away,' she said firmly.

'You have my word.'

It sounded so deliciously reasonable. He was offering up his warm, willing and very attractive body for experimentation and, for all her fine talk of acquiring a legion of lovers, she didn't have the faintest idea how to actually go about getting even *one* lover in place. Men did not approach her. They never had and she had no idea if they ever would. One kiss. She could probably learn something. 'So…how do you want to do this? The kissing.'

'You tell me. However makes you comfortable.'

He was laughing at her; the little crinkle at the corner of his eyes gave it away.

'Maybe if you sat.' She waved her hand at a number of sofa and armchair options.

He unbuttoned his jacket—nothing a gentleman wouldn't do before being seated. And then he made an utter production of taking it off completely and draping it over the back of a chair. He made an even bigger production of rolling up his sleeves, his blunt nails and long fingers making deft work of it. His royal signet ring stayed on and so did his watch. He'd probably been a stripper in a former life.

'Well?' he said when he'd settled in the middle of a crimson sofa, legs wide and eyes hooded. 'What next?'

'You said I could touch you as well as kiss you.' She didn't stammer, but it was close.

'You can.'

'Right. Good. So.' She didn't move. Instead she sipped at her drink for courage, only she sipped a little too deeply and almost choked on the fire in her throat.

To his credit, he let her flounder for a full minute before breaking the silence. 'Put the drink down and come closer. It's hard to touch and kiss someone from such a distance.'

Distance. Yes. Was she really going to do this?

'What do you have to lose?' he murmured, and the answer was nothing.

Absolutely nothing.

She set her drink next to his little ring box and his empty glass and turned her back on them. She crossed to the sofa he'd claimed as his own and sank to her knees between his wide open legs, pleased when his breath faltered and his lashes fluttered closed. Was he nervous? Why would he be nervous? He wasn't the virgin here and, frankly, she was nervous enough for both of them.

She didn't even know where to look. At his shoes? The subtle sheen of his very expensive suit? His legs to either side of her? Anywhere but the not so subtle bulge in his pants. Then there was the not so small matter of where to put her hands. On his shoulders? His waist? Where? He looked altogether unsettled. 'Is this okay?'

He ran a hand over his face. 'Yes. Continue.'

Yes. Continue. Let's just seduce the playboy king with her untried self because *of course* he'd find her tentative floundering attractive. 'I don't—'

'Touch me.'

'Where?'

'Anywhere.'

'I thought you were supposed to be patient.'

'I am patient. I have the patience of a *saint*.'

'Hardly.' She put her hand on his leg, just above the knee, and felt his muscles shift. Even through the fine fabric of his suit she could feel the warmth of him. Cautiously, she circled her thumb over the inseam and slid her hand an inch or so up his leg. She'd never been this close to a man before. She'd never been invited to touch and explore.

He felt good.

She placed her other hand above his other knee and braced herself as she leaned forward, stopping just before her lips hit the juncture between skin and the snowy white collar of his shirt. She closed her eyes and let her other senses take hold. 'You smell good,' she murmured. 'What is it?'

'Soap,' he rasped, his hands now clawing at the velvet upholstery before he deliberately let out a ragged breath, tilted his head back and closed his eyes.

She drew away slightly to study his face, the frown between his eyes and rigid cord of his neck. 'Did you close your eyes so you can pretend I'm someone else?'

He opened his eyes specifically to glare at her. 'I swear on my mother's grave, Moriana, you're the most infuriating woman I know. I'm thinking of you. Get used to it.'

She could get very used to it. She moved her hands up his thighs until her fingers brushed the crease where hips met legs, her eyes widening as he gave a tiny rolling grind of his hips in response. 'You seem very...ah... responsive.'

'Yes.' A harsh rumble of a word, nothing more.

'Are you always like this?'

He had no answer for her.

She rolled her fingers, he rolled his hips, and that proved a powerful incentive to become even bolder in her exploration. It hadn't escaped her notice that Theo's eyes being closed allowed her to look wherever she wanted to look without being caught. He'd never know. And if he didn't know, how could he possibly reproach her for it?

She looked to his crotch, fascinated by the size and shape of him beneath the fine cloth. She flexed her fingers and dug into firm flesh, just a little, just below where she truly ached to touch, and he sucked in a breath but kept his eyes closed.

'Touch wherever you want,' he whispered harshly. 'I'm not going to judge.'

She traced her hands over his hips to his waist, up and over his powerful chest and the lines of his neck, she looked her fill until she reached his lips. He was biting his lower one and she didn't want that, so she touched her fingers to the spot and smoothed out the crush. His chest heaved and a broken sound escaped his lips as he turned his face towards her touch, eyes still closed, and he was beautiful in his abandon.

Was this sex? This utter acquiescence to someone else's touch?

She cradled his jaw and felt the prickles from invisible whiskers against her palm. She dragged her thumb across the seam of his lips, inordinately pleased when he parted them for her. She wanted to kiss him and keep touching him in equal measure and didn't know if she had the co-ordination for both.

She started with her lips to the underside of his jaw, close to his ear. It seemed safer than starting with a kiss to his lips and if she dragged her lips across his skin it would hardly count as a kiss at all, merely a warm-up.

'That wasn't a kiss,' she murmured against his skin. 'I'm working my way up to your lips.'

His tongue against her thumb was her only reply so she kept right on exploring, opening her own mouth and employing her tongue to learn the taste of his skin and find the pulse point in his neck, there, right there, fast and strong, and she sucked, just a little, and he groaned and the world burned that little bit hotter because of it.

She went up and over the cleft of his jaw, emboldened, but that wasn't her only area of exploration. She was working on two fronts here as she traced the long, thick length of his erection with unsteady, barely-there fingers.

She let her fingertips dance lightly over the crown and finally, finally pressed her lips against his.

One kiss, just one, because this was Theo and she believed him when he said he wouldn't judge her, and that if she didn't like it he would leave. She felt strangely safe with him.

She wanted to make the most of the opportunity he was offering.

His lips were warm and softer than she would have believed possible. He didn't invade; he let her take her time and adjust the pressure to her liking before moving forward. The tiniest tilt of her head allowed for a better fit overall. The lessening of pressure allowed her to tentatively touch her tongue to his upper lip, and the taste, oh, it was deep and dark and hinted of Scotch and flavours she wanted more of. Further exploration with her tongue was followed by the shifting of his body beneath her hand so that she cupped him more firmly, and maybe she was supposed to stroke and kiss and breathe all at once, and she probably could if the heat coursing through her body wasn't quite so overwhelming.

His tongue had come to play with hers, softly teasing, and she couldn't help her whimper or the way she wordlessly begged him to teach her more.

The sweetly subtle grind of his erection into her hand became a demanding roll.

He had no problem whatsoever co-ordinating mouth and body in a clear attempt to drive her out of her mind with lust.

It was one kiss and it blew her mind, and she couldn't breathe and she couldn't stop.

Even as he pulled his lips away from hers she ached for more.

'Breathe,' he whispered and she did, and then dropped

her head to his shoulder to hide the fact that she was already utterly undone.

'Right,' she murmured, more to herself than anyone else. 'One kiss. All done.'

She looked down and there was her hand, still laying claim to his privates. She snatched it away and he huffed out a laugh.

'Right,' he murmured.

'You said I could touch.'

'And I'd never deny it. Pour me another drink before I forget my promise *not* to touch you back.'

She pushed off him and up as gracefully as circumstances would allow. She turned her back and closed her eyes, trying not to imagine exactly how good sitting in his lap and rubbing against him might feel.

She cleared her throat. She poured the Scotch and by the time she turned back around he was standing in front of the fireplace again, his features an impassive mask.

'Did you enjoy the kiss?' he asked.

'Yes.'

'Did you enjoy putting your hands on me?'

She nodded. 'It was extremely educational, thank you.'

He took the drink from her outstretched hand. 'Are you wet for me?'

She sipped her own drink and dropped her gaze. 'Yes.'

'Marry me,' he said next.

Theo watched as Moriana crossed her hands around her tiny waist and turned away from him. Her back was ramrod-straight and her bearing regal. All those dancing or fencing lessons or whatever they were had clearly paid off. She looked at the ring box for a very long time but made no move to touch it. And then she turned back to face him.

He honestly thought she'd say yes. Between persuasive argument, the strength of that kiss and the benefits to both Arun and Liesendaach, he thought he had her.

And then she spoke.

'I'm flattered by your offer.'

It wasn't a yes.

'I'm surprised by your chivalry and more than a little stunned by my response to your...your *that*, although maybe I shouldn't be,' she continued quietly. 'You're clearly very experienced and I'm a dry river bed that's never seen rain. I would soak up as much of *that* as you'd give me. And then you'd grow bored and move on.' She shook her head, her gaze steady and shuttered. 'That wouldn't end well for either of us.'

'Why would I grow bored and move on?'

'You always do.'

'Doesn't mean I always will.'

'And then there's your family history to consider. Your marital role models, so to speak.'

Theo scowled. His parents' marriage had been... complicated. The joint state funerals for his mother, brother and father had been even more complicated. Seven of his father's mistresses had turned up for the show. Three of them had offered to comfort a fifteen-year-old Theo before the night was through. 'My parents are long dead,' he said flatly. 'Let them rest. Leave them out of this.'

'No. Your father wasn't exactly one for marital fidelity. I need to know if you want the same kind of marital relationship for us that your parents had.'

'I am not my father.'

'Nor am I your mother. She was a tolerant, pragmatic

woman who was willing to turn a blind eye to your father's many dalliances in exchange for a title and a great deal of power. I already have titles and enough power to satisfy me and I'm no longer feeling either tolerant or pragmatic. Do you really want to marry a woman who'd rather cut out her husband's eyes than have him look elsewhere for sexual pleasure?'

Bloodthirsty. He liked it. 'I'd rather keep my sight.'

'Pick a different wife and you can keep your mistresses *and* your sight.'

'Or I could be faithful to you. I don't do love, Moriana. You know it and I know it, but if you help me out in this…if you wear my ring I *will* be faithful to you. Think of it as part of our negotiation. You need it and I'm willing to accommodate it in return for your service. This isn't an area of potential conflict. Move on. Say yes.'

But she didn't say yes.

'What now?' he grated. He didn't have time for this.

'That kiss we shared, was it normal?' she asked tentatively.

He didn't know what she meant.

She sent him a look, half-pleading, half-troubled. 'I don't have the experience to know if it was good, bad or mediocre. You do.'

'It was good.' Blindingly good. 'Surely you've kissed Casimir before?'

'Not like that.' She looked away.

'Someone else?'

She shook her head.

'*Anyone* else?'

'No.'

'It was good.' Never had he cursed a woman's inexperience as much as he did in that moment. Her eyes widened as he stalked towards her. 'What would you have me do to convince you? Another kiss, perhaps? A better one?'

She didn't say no.

He wasn't patient with her the way he was before. He didn't bury his desire to touch and to take. Instead he wrapped one hand around her neck, wrapped his other arm around her waist and hauled her against him.

Her sudden rigidity shouldn't have thrilled him the way it did. Her gasp as he plundered her lips shouldn't have made him stake his claim the way he did. She opened for him, melted against him and let him own the kiss in the same way he wanted to own her.

At the age of ten, the betrothal arrangement between Moriana, Princess of Arun, and Casimir, then Crown Prince of Byzenmaach, had been nothing but an amusement to tease them with.

At fourteen, their arrangement had been like a thorn in Theo's paw. He'd known what the stirring in his trousers meant by then. Known full well he wanted her with an intensity that never waned, no matter what he did. *Pick at her, scowl at her, argue with her and, by all that was holy, don't touch her.* That had been his motto for more years than he could count.

At fifteen, his father had seen where Theo's gaze had led and told him in no uncertain terms that Moriana of Arun was off-limits. Liesendaach needed to maintain cordial relationships with bordering kingdoms far more than Theo needed to seduce a pretty princess.

At fifteen, he'd done his father's bidding.

At fifteen, his parents and brother had died and ripped Theo's heart straight out of his chest. There'd been no room for love after that. When he chased women, he'd been chasing only one thing: sweet oblivion. They'd meant nothing to him.

Standing here at thirty, he still chased sweet oblivion. The open, loving part of him had broken long ago, and no one had ever come close to fixing it—least of all him. But he could give the woman in his arms some of the things she wanted. Good things. A good life. All she had to do was let him.

He heard a groan and realised belatedly that it had come from him, but she answered with another and that was all he needed to keep going. She tasted of warm spirits and untrained passion and it shouldn't have lit a fire in him the way it did. The slide of their lips and the tangle of tongues turned to outward stillness as she learned his taste and he learned hers.

She was slender to the touch, long-legged and gently curved, and he pressed her into his hardness because to do otherwise would be sacrilege. She had both hands on his chest and he wanted her to do more. He could teach her everything she wanted to know about passion.

But not until he got what he wanted.

Theo eased out of the kiss and took his sweet time letting her go, making sure his hand stayed on her waist in case she needed steadying. She wasn't the one with a clearly visible erection but she did have a fine flush running from cheek to chest, her lips looked plump and crushed and her eyes were satisfyingly glazed.

She looked…awakened. It was an extremely good look on her.

'Our bed would not be a cold one, Princess.' Theo stepped back and reached for his jacket. 'The weight of the crown is heavy enough without adding infidelity and a spurned queen to the mix. I would not look elsewhere if I had you. We *are* sexually compatible. Save yourself the trouble of years of casual sex and take my word for it.' He let his gaze drift from her face to glance at the little wooden box on the mantelpiece. 'You know what I want.' Time to leave her be before he opted for plan C—which was to take her back into his arms and have her pregnant by morning. 'Think about it.'

CHAPTER FOUR

MORIANA SLEPT BADLY. Maybe it was because Theo's words and his kisses were on a replay loop in her brain. Maybe it was because Theo's marriage proposal was still on the table and his ring box was still unopened on her mantelpiece. Maybe it was because she was so sexually frustrated that nothing was going to fix the ache in her tonight. Whatever the reason, sleep proved elusive and there was no other option but to get out of bed, fix a post-midnight snack of banana, blueberries and unsweetened yoghurt and take it through to her sitting room. The same sitting room she'd entertained Theo in.

The room with the ring in it.

If he had commissioned the ring especially for her—and she didn't believe that for a minute, but if he had—what would he choose? Something traditional like a solitaire diamond? Something ostentatious like a coloured stone surrounded by diamonds and big enough to picnic on? Something square-cut and colourless? She wouldn't put it past him.

And there was the box, sitting oh-so-innocently on the mantel, just waiting for her to open it and find out.

She retrieved it from the ledge and set it on the side table beside her chair. There it sat until she'd finished her snack and then she picked up the box and ran her fingers across its seam. The box was beautiful in its own right—a walnut burl, polished to a dull sheen, with a maker's mark she didn't recognise. A clover leaf or some such. Pretty.

Theo of Liesendaach had offered for her, and it wasn't a joke. He'd promised to be faithful to her. He'd offered kisses that made her melt.

He'd even made her forget the debacle with Casimir and the morning's Ice Princess headlines.

Words of love had been noticeably missing from his offer—at least he'd been honest about that—but he had done something good for her this evening. He'd made her feel wanted.

Oh, she still resented his form letter proposal. She still thought marriage to him would be a volatile, loveless endeavour, but there would be benefits she hadn't previously considered.

Like him. Naked and willing.

Taking a deep breath, she closed her eyes and opened the ring box. On the count of three she opened her eyes and looked.

He'd chosen an oval, brilliant cut diamond, flanked on either side by a triangular cluster of tiny dove-grey pearls. The stones were set in a white-gold filigree almost too delicate to be believed. She'd seen some beautiful diamonds in her time, and this one was flawless. Not too big and unwieldy for her finger, not too small as to be overlooked. The grey pearls reminded her of her homeland, and as for the whimsical, playful design…that element put her in mind of Liesendaach. She slipped it on.

It fitted.

'Bastard,' she murmured with half-fond exasperation,

because it really did seem as if he'd chosen it with her in mind. And then her smile faded as anxiety crept back in.

How—in the space of two kisses—had he managed to make her feel so alive? He'd been so responsive, so free with his body and secure in his sexuality, so *open*. No one had ever given themselves over to her so freely and it had been better than any aphrodisiac.

He'd said it was good and she'd believed him.

There were reasons for this marriage that she could understand. A political merger, yes. Stabilisation for a region. A smart, politically aware queen could lighten her husband's load considerably. It didn't matter how hard Moriana had worked to get there, she *was* a smart and politically aware player these days. An asset to any monarch. She knew this.

She'd been worried about Theo's sexual experience and her lack of it but, after that kiss and Theo's parting words, she wasn't nearly as worried as she had been. Call it attraction, pheromones or alchemy, their kisses had been explosive.

Moriana knew she had self-esteem issues. Her utter fear of never measuring up had turned her from a curious child with a too-hot temper into a humourless, duty-bound over-thinker with an unhealthy attention to detail. A woman who thought of failure first and for whom success had always been hard won.

And then there had been Theo, telling her to touch him and that he wasn't going to judge her curiosity or her inexperience and find her wanting, and hadn't *that* been a revelation. Touching him, wanting him, enjoying him—everything had been so *effortless*.

She smirked, and then snorted inelegantly as she pictured her mother at the dining table, damning Moriana with faint praise for whatever task her daughter had tried and failed to do that day. Disguising her disappointment behind impeccable manners as she told Moriana yet again that one day she would find her true calling, something she would be instinctively good at.

Not fencing or dancing or music or drawing. Not horse riding or shooting or politics or fundraising or running a castle or making a social function an event to be remembered. She'd never been good at any of those to begin with.

But kissing Theo, she'd been good at that.

Moriana ran her hand across the sofa cushion, smoothing the velvet first one way and then digging her nails in to rough it up on the back stroke.

He'd been sitting right where she sat now, taking up more space than any one man had a right to, and she closed her eyes and wondered if she could still scent his arousal in the air. Maybe not. Maybe it was long gone.

Maybe he was right this minute taking care of his needs somewhere in the palace, and he'd damn well better be alone, his legs spread wide and his hand pressing down, just as hers was snaking down towards her panties, pushing aside the layers of silk and cotton, dipping into warmth. Maybe he had no shame whatsoever when it came to pleasing himself while remembering every shudder and every breath he'd given to her this evening.

Why *should* there be shame in this?

Her fingers moved quickly and her body grew taut. She'd always known what her body could do in this regard, how lost she could get. She'd never before thought of her inherent sensuality as a strength, but Theo had it too and tonight he'd shown her how he wielded his, succumbed to it, even as he owned it, until it was more than just a strength.

It was a gift.

* * *

The headlines the following morning were still not kind
to Princess Moriana of Arun. She'd found the newspapers in their usual place in the breakfast room and had
mistakenly thought that their presence heralded other
more appealing news than her love life or lack of it.

Not so.

Out of Her League one paper proclaimed, with a picture of her and Theo from last night beneath the headline. The photographer had caught them as they'd been
discussing the merits of the Vermeer. Theo looked
sharp-eyed and handsome, the edges of his lips tilted
towards a smile but not quite getting there as he studied the painting. She'd been looking at Theo and the
photographer had captured her from behind. There was
something vulnerable about the lines of her shoulders
and neck and the curve of her cheek. From the position
of their bodies, it was obvious her attention had been
on Theo rather than the painting. Her hand had been
resting on his sleeve, and instead of it looking like a
courtesy on his part it looked like a desperate plea for
attention on hers.

Great. Just great. She tossed the paper aside and
picked up the next one.

The Fall and Fall of Arun's Perfect Princess this one
said, and the photo must have been taken when she first
saw Theo and her brother stepping into the auction room
last night because she looked gutted. It was there in her
eyes, in the twist of her lips. One single moment of despair at her brother's betrayal and they'd caught it; of
course they had. Her mother would have been horrified
by such a vulgar display of emotion. Moriana didn't
much care for it herself. Not in public. Masks should

never slip in public. All that ever did was invite predators to circle.

The article went on to criticise her dress, her shoes and her too-slender frame, and suggest she needed professional help in order to cope with her rejection. Arun's relationship with Byzenmaach was now strained, they said. Trust between the two kingdoms had been shattered and she *knew* that wasn't true, only there it was in black and white.

And then Theo walked into the breakfast room and drew her attention away from the hateful words.

He wore his customary dark grey trousers and white dress shirt but he'd done away with the tie and undone the first two buttons on his shirt.

'You're still here,' she said, and he nodded agreeably. 'I still need a wife.'

Half-dressed and unashamedly comfortable in his skin, he leaned over her shoulder and plucked a paper from the pile she'd already looked at before settling into the chair next to hers to read it.

'Two-timing Princess,' he read aloud. 'Go you.'

'Read on,' she muttered. *'You're* a ruthless despoiler of all that is pure and good in this world.'

'Of course I am. How is this even news?' He put that paper down and picked up another and was smirking two minutes later. 'Don't let anyone ever tell you those shoes you wore last night were a bad fashion choice. The shoes were good.'

The shoes had been vintage Jimmy Choo. Damn right they were good. 'You're reading the one about how I was dressed for seduction last night in a desperate attempt to end civilisation as we know it and finally get lucky?'

'I am. You should dress for boar-hunting one evening. Knee-high leather boots, armguards, stiffened leather corset, breeches and a forest-green coat that sweeps the floor and hides your weapons. See what they make of that.'

He was even better than Aury at mocking press articles. He truly didn't seem to give a damn what was printed about them.

'Doesn't it bother you? All these stories?'

'No.' His voice turned hard and implacable. 'And it shouldn't bother you. The only reason the press are on you now is because you've never been at the centre of any scandal before and they're hungry for more. Strangely enough, now is the perfect time to reinvent yourself in the eyes of your public—assuming that's something you want to do. Or you could mock them. Tell them you're pregnant with triplets and don't know who the father is. Make Casimir's day. *Four* royal bastards for the new King of Byzenmaach.'

'Oh, you cruel man.'

'Made you smile though, didn't it?'

She couldn't deny it.

Finally he turned his attention away from the newspapers. She could pinpoint the moment he truly looked at her, because her body lit up like sunrise.

'Good morning,' he murmured. 'Nice dress.'

She'd worn one of her favourite casual dresses from the same section of her wardrobe where the red gown usually hung. It was part of her 'love it but where can I wear it?' collection. It was lemon yellow, strapless, snug around the bodice and flared gently from the waist to finish a couple of inches above her knees. She'd kept her jewellery modest. Two rings for her fingers—neither of them *his* ring—a pair of diamond studs for her ears, and that was it. Her sandals were the easy on and off kind and she'd caught her hair back in a messy ponytail that spoke of lazy weekend sleep-ins.

'Yeah, well. Maybe I'm out to seduce you.'

'A for Effort,' he murmured. 'That dress is a weapon. You need to be photographed in it looking all tumbled and content. With me.' He picked up the pile of still unread papers and dumped them on the ground between their two chairs.

'I hadn't finished with those yet.'

'They were making you unhappy. Why read them?' He reached for a croissant and the blackberry jam. 'I need you to be more resilient in the face of bad press. I honestly thought you were.'

She wasn't. Not at all. 'And it bothers you that I'm not?'

'It bothers me a lot.' For the first time this morning he sounded deadly serious. 'Liesendaach's court can be hard to navigate. My uncle's legacy of corruption still lingers, and every time I think I've stamped it out, it comes back. I don't trust my politicians or my advisors. I barely trust my palace staff. You *will* get bad press if you marry me. You *will* get people trying to befriend you and use you in the hope that you can influence me on their behalf. I can't protect you from either of those things, so I need to know in advance that they won't break you. I need you to know that some days it's going to feel as if the world is out to get you and no one has your back.'

'You're not exactly selling your marriage proposal this morning, are you?'

'Not yet. I'm mainly mentioning the fine print. But I will be selling it. Soon.' He shot her a quick glance. 'Just as soon as I think you're up for an onslaught.'

'Maybe after my next cup of coffee,' she murmured.

He reached for the coffee pot and offered to top her up but she shook her head so he filled his own cup. 'How did you sleep?'

'Poorly. Your ring is lovely, by the way. I lasted until almost two a.m. before looking at it.'

'Well done.' He smiled wryly. 'I notice you don't have it on.'

'Don't push. I'm considering your proposal. Yesterday, I wasn't even doing that.'

'Yesterday, you thought me indifferent to you. Now you know I'm not.'

'Which means you now get a hearing. It doesn't mean we're ready for marriage. Why the rush?'

'Well, we could always wait for old age.' He was annoyed and doing little to hide it.

'There's something you're not telling me.' She'd been around him long enough to know that this relentless pushing wasn't usually his style. 'You're too urgent. You're pushing too hard for this to happen and making mistakes in your approach. It's not like you.'

A muscle flickered in his jaw.

Something was very definitely up. 'Spill,' she murmured. 'I know you're under pressure to marry. Liesendaach wants a queen and you need an heir. But I didn't think you were under this much pressure.'

'My uncle is petitioning for my dismissal,' Theo said finally. 'He can't get me on fiscal incompetence or general negligence. I do my job and I do it well. But there's a loophole that allows a monarch of Liesendaach to be replaced if they haven't married and produced an heir by the time they turn thirty. We didn't even know it was there until my uncle found it and raised it. I turned thirty last month. I can challenge the clause at a judicial level, no problem. Buy myself some time. But the best way to address the petition is for me to secure a fiancée and schedule a wedding as soon as possible. When Casimir let you down I saw a solution I could live with. Meaning you.'

'And here I was beginning to think you had a crush on me all these years and simply couldn't wait to claim me now that I was free.'

'That too. I should have led with that.'

'I wouldn't have believed you.' Moriana definitely needed more coffee this morning.

Theo sighed and started slathering jam on his croissant. 'There's no talking to you this morning, is there?'

'Not before the caffeine hits my bloodstream. So who will you marry if you don't marry me? A Cordova twin?' The Cordova twins had made a splash last year, when they'd taken turns dating him. One twin one week, the other twin the next. It had gone on for months. Theo either hadn't cared or hadn't noticed.

'You're picking a fight that's not there.'

'And here I thought I was identifying an alternative solution to your problem.'

His eyes flashed silver and his lips thinned. 'You're a better one.'

'I know.' There was no point pretending the Cordova women were better options when it came to political connections. 'But you have to look at your offer from my point of view too. For the first time in my life I'm free to do what I please. I want to cut loose and have some fun. I want some romance.' She gave a helpless little shrug. 'I know what your offer means. I know the work involved. There's a lifetime of it, and I'm not sure it's what I want.'

'Yet you were all set to marry Casimir.' His voice had cooled. 'You wanted it once.'

She had. She'd looked forward to it. So what made Theo's offer so disturbingly different?

Breakfast continued in silence until finally she could stand the silence no more. 'I spoke to Casimir this morning.'

Theo looked up from his breakfast but made no comment.

'I'm investigating my flaws. I had ten years in which to kiss him properly and I didn't. Nor did he ever push for more. We spoke about that.'

Theo raised his eyebrow. 'Did he tell you he was celibate? Blind? Hormonally challenged?'

'No, but thank you for the suggestions for my own utter apathy.'

'You weren't apathetic last night.'

Maybe that was what was different about this offer of marriage. Casimir had never really hurt her with his indifference because Moriana had been similarly indifferent right back. But Theo—she wasn't indifferent to him, and never had been. He could wind her up at whim and leave her reeling, without any effort whatsoever. And that was a dangerous position for a queen to be in.

'Casimir mentioned that—for him—chemistry with another person starts well before the kissing,' she began hesitantly. 'He said there's an awareness between two people, a connection that can't be faked. He said that good kisses, spectacular kisses, were as much about letting someone into your head as they were a physical thing. He said kissing random strangers and expecting to see fireworks was a stupid idea.'

'Remind me to send him a fruit basket,' said Theo.

'I told him you'd offered for me. He laughed.'

'A fruit basket minus the strawberries.'

'Why did he laugh?'

'I'm not a mind-reader, Moriana. You'd have to ask him.'

She had.

Casimir had mumbled something about everything falling into place. He'd wished her every happiness, told her she'd be happier with Theo than she ever would have been with him, and she'd cut the call shortly thereafter. It was that or start wailing at her former intended for being an arrogant moron.

'He did give me one nice compliment,' she offered wryly. 'He's going to miss our political conversations. He said I have great depth of knowledge and an impressive ability to influence decisions. His and beyond. I'm a political muse. Go me.'

Theo's gaze grew carefully shuttered. 'The unseen hand.'

'A guiding hand,' she corrected.

'I don't need one.'

'You've never had one.' But she was one, with intimate knowledge of how deals were done across four kingdoms.

Theo said nothing.

'You offer physical intimacy with such a sure hand,' she murmured. 'But would you ever seek my counsel?'

'I'd...think about it,' he said with a twist of his lips that suggested discomfort. 'I find it difficult to trust people. Anyone.'

'And you would include me with the masses? Don't you want to be able to trust your wife?'

'When it comes to trusting people, it's not really about what I want. It's about what I'm prepared to lose.'

'Wow. You really are alone. In your head and in your heart.' She couldn't quite comprehend how a king who trusted no one could function in office. 'Aren't you lonely?'

'No.'

'So *the main duty* of a queen towards her king—that of offering full and frank emotional, political, social

and *well-being* support to the man behind the throne—
you don't want it.'

He said nothing.

Moriana sat back in her chair, still stunned. 'Seriously, Theo, you don't need me. Just pick anyone.'

He didn't like that, she could tell. But she didn't much
care for the position he was offering either.

'I mean it,' she said. 'I am not trained to sit at your
side and do nothing. I need your trust in order to function as your queen. Without it, I'm worse than useless.
And I will *not* be rendered useless this time around.'

'Come to Liesendaach for the week,' he offered
abruptly. 'And I'll try and give you what you want.'

'Not want. Need. This one's a deal-breaker,' she finished quietly.

'Trust takes time,' he snapped, and, yes, she'd give
him that.

'I have time. You might not, but if you want my co-
operation I suggest you make time. I can deal with a
marriage minus the love. I've been prepared for that for
a long time. But I'm telling you plain, I will not become
your queen until I have your absolute trust.'

'Is that your final position?'

She nodded.

'Then I'll try. There can be political discussion and
getting to know each other and a great deal of kissing
and touching and fun. You might like it more than you
think.'

'Perhaps. Okay, here's the deal. I *need* your trust. But
I *want* more sexual expertise. I'd like to prioritise both,
this coming week in Liesendaach. Can we do that?'

It was as if her question flipped a switch in him. His
uncertainty bled away, leaving a confident, sharp-eyed
negotiator in its wake. 'I'll do you a deal,' he murmured.

She stopped ripping her pastry into ever smaller pieces and brushed her fingers against each other to rid them of crumbs before reaching for her napkin and squeezing. 'I'm listening.'

'I'm prepared to offer you a minimum of one new sexual experience each and every day of your stay,' he continued. 'As an offer of good faith I'll even throw in a lesson here and now at the breakfast table. But if at any time during our lessons you climax for me...from that point onwards you wear my ring.'

'No deal.' She didn't trust her body to remain sufficiently restrained during these lessons. He'd have her seeing stars so fast she'd be wearing his ring by lunchtime.

'Okay, I'll do you a new deal. What if you were able to stop me with a word at any point during a lesson? Climax averted, so to speak. Everyone backs off to allow for breathing space. We could even think of it as an exercise in trust-building. No commitment or ring-wearing required. Easy.'

'It doesn't sound that easy.'

His eyes gleamed. 'Some lessons *are* harder than others. You did say you wanted to learn. Also, it'll be fun. You said you wanted that too. I'm merely attempting to provide some for you.'

'Good of you.'

'I know.'

The room temperature jacked up a notch as their gazes clashed and she contemplated just how badly wrong this week could go. 'You're offering me a week full of fun, sex education, political discourse and trust-building exercises? What about romance?' She'd bet he wouldn't offer that.

'The offer includes romance. You'd be a fool not to see if I can deliver.'

Even if he didn't deliver, she'd quite like to see him *try*.

And they said she didn't have a sense of humour.

'Agreed,' she murmured. 'Let's go to Liesendaach for a week.'

He sat back, pushed his meal aside. 'First lesson starts now. You might want to lock the doors.'

Even as she dropped her napkin across her plate and headed for the double doors that would take her from the room, Moriana still didn't know whether she would lock the doors or not.

Theo was playing her, she knew that much.

But maybe, just maybe, she wanted to be played with.

She closed the doors and locked them, and then did the same to the doors on the other side of the room. She stood there, with her eyes closed and her back to him for a moment, trying to find her equilibrium but it was gone.

He thought her innocent, and in a physical sense she was. She'd never been touched, she'd never had sex. But she was twenty-eight years old and there was no cap on her imagination. In her imagination, she'd had any number of sexual experiences. She knew exactly what kind of things he might teach her. She could describe them in great detail.

And, oh, how she wanted to see if the reality lived up to her imagination.

'Come here.' Even his voice could seduce her when he wanted it to.

She took a deep breath, opened her eyes and turned. He was right where she'd left him. She walked towards him, feigning a confidence she didn't have.

He smiled.

He'd pushed away from the table and sat sprawled in his chair and he indicated the cleared space where his meal had once been. 'Sit on the table.'

He could have her for breakfast.

She half leant, half sat, hands curling around the table edge, and all the time he watched her like a hawk. She could feel the weight of his gaze and the assessment behind it as he sized her up and planned his approach.

'Your dress has a zip at the back. Undo it.' The purr was back in his voice and so was the edge of command.

'Why should I?' She was embarrassed to undress for him here in broad daylight. It smacked of her owning her actions when maybe, just maybe, she wanted to be led. 'You have hands.' They were very nice hands. Large and strong-looking, with short nails and an appealing ruggedness about them.

'And I'll use them. Right now I'm more interested in watching you undress for me. You blush so beautifully.'

Well, he would know. He could make her blush with a glance, and if that didn't work all he had to do was use his words. Haltingly, she fumbled behind her back and slid the zip down to her waist. The bodice of her dress had boning and would stay up unless pushed.

He raised an aristocratic eyebrow.

She pushed the top part down and folded her arms around her waist for protection. Moments later she unfolded her arms again, dropped them to her sides and curled her hands over the table edge in a desperate bid to at least *appear* a little more casually confident than she was.

She still had a bra on. It was white, strapless and covered almost as much as the dress had.

His eyes grew intent and he reached out to draw a path from her collarbone to the very top of her bra, tracking the shape of it with his fingertips as it fell away under her arms. 'This too.'

Her nipples pebbled at his words and he rewarded them by stroking his thumb gently across one of them, back and forth, back and forth, causing the tug of want in her belly to pull tight. She reached behind her for the hook and the bra fell away—he helped it fall away.

'Your breasts are perfect.' He sounded almost angry.

They were a little on the small side, as far as she was concerned, and right now they were aching for more than just the flick of his thumb, but the appropriate response to a compliment, sincere or not, had been drummed into her since birth. 'Thank you.'

Heat stole into her cheeks and across her chest and she looked away from his fierce, bright gaze. The wall was right there, suitably dressed with a painting. Nothing abnormal about that wall. The only abnormal thing in this room was her. And maybe Theo. Or maybe sitting half naked atop the breakfast table *was* normal in his world. 'What next?'

He moved, and she closed her eyes and when she felt his lips on her they weren't where she'd expected him to put them. He'd placed them just below her left ear and she shivered when his tongue came out to trace a delicate circle.

'Promises,' she muttered and she could feel his smile on her skin.

'Patience.' He placed his hands either side of hers and continued to kiss a leisurely path across to her lips, where he proceeded to tease and tempt and never give her any actual substance.

'I hate you,' she muttered next.

'You shouldn't. I'm giving you my best.'

He went lower, with his hair brushing her neck as he

kissed her collarbone and the swell of her upper breast, and *now* they were getting somewhere. Her nipples had been tightly furled since she'd unzipped her dress and now they were throbbing and desperate for attention. She pushed up against him, not begging, but hoping, and he responded by drawing that tiny circle with the tip of his tongue again and then pulling back to blow on the skin he'd just licked.

Heat pooled low in her stomach and made her gasp. Dear heaven, he was good at this.

He kissed her some more, lighting a fire beneath her skin, and then finally he closed his mouth around her nipple and sucked.

'Oh.' She kept her legs tightly closed and rode out the thrumming clench of pleasure his actions had caused.

A lick for her other breast now, and then he obliged by closing his mouth over it and suckling hard. There. That. The fierce pull of want and the heady coil of desire. She moaned her pleasure, and he grazed her with his teeth. And then his lips were on hers again only this time he was claiming her, devouring her, and she melted into that too. She went where he led, mindless and willing, and when he pulled back and studied her again with glittering grey eyes she obligingly caught up on her breathing.

'Nice,' she whispered raggedly. 'Good lesson.'

'There's more.'

She wasn't at all sure she was ready for more.

'Raise your skirt,' he ordered gruffly.

'I—' There was a whole world of imagination waiting for her in that region. 'What's the lesson?'

'The lesson is that compliance has its rewards.'

She met his darkly mocking smile with a level stare.

At least she hoped that was what her face was doing. She'd rather *not* look like a startled fawn.

'Of course, if you don't comply you'll never know,' he murmured.

He knew he had her; she could see it in his eyes. He knew exactly how badly she wanted to know. Not just to imagine her sexual encounters but to *know* what one felt like.

With as much shamelessness as she could muster, she put her hands on the skirt of her frock and slid it slowly up her thighs, up and up until he could see her underwear. She'd worn white panties today, with tiny black polka dots, and they were pretty but nothing special. Not skimpy, not lacy, just normal. She wondered whether he would ask her to take them off.

'Good.' She could barely hear his low rumble. 'Now put your hands back on the table and lean back a little.'

The skirt stayed up, her head stayed low and her hands went back on the table as she waited for his next move.

His hands finally settled either side of her thighs, the heat of his body engulfing her as he set his lips to that place where her pulse beat frantically in her neck.

'You drive me mad, Moriana. You always have. You think you're so flawed.'

His next kiss landed on her shoulder and she shuddered her surrender. The kiss after that touched the outer curve of her breast and avoided her nipple, but not for long. He left no part of her breasts and belly uncovered as he worked his way down to her panties, and by the time he got there she was a flushed and writhing mess.

'I tend to think you're rather perfect,' he murmured as his breath ghosted over her underwear. He pushed them aside a little and licked. She'd heard about this.

Hell, she'd *dreamed* of it. But not in the broad light of day, and not in the breakfast room.

Slowly, hesitantly, she slid her hand down over the front of her panties, putting a barrier between herself and him. She didn't know if she wanted him to continue his exploration or not. On the one hand, there was embarrassment. On the other hand, her fingers found the damp, swollen groove, even over her panties, and her eyes closed on an involuntary shudder.

'What are you doing?' he rasped, looking up at her with a glittering warning in his eyes.

'Helping.'

'Hands on the table, Moriana. I don't need any *help*.'

And then his hands were high on her thighs, gently parting her legs. Moments later something soft and warm and moist found her hard little nub through already moist panties, and she thought it was his finger but both his hands were well and truly accounted for, wrapped around her thighs as they were, and his hair was tickling her inner thigh and, yes, indeed, that right there was his tongue.

It was even more spectacular than she'd imagined.

Heat flooded through her and she didn't know whether to scramble away or stay right where she was. There was another option, of course, and that was to give him as much room as possible so he could keep right on doing what he was doing.

Option three won.

'Hold on,' he muttered, and then he was pushing her legs wide apart and her panties aside and then his mouth was on her, kissing and kissing and flicking and sucking and *kissing*. It was too much. It was not enough. Her hand raked its way through his hair before she could even think to hold back, and *there*, right there, as she whimpered and began climbing through clouds.

Not yet.

Not. Yet.

Up and up and up.

'Stop!'

He stopped. He kept his word, his chest rising and his shoulders granite-hard as he pulled back and rested his forehead on her knee, his hands still curved high on each thigh, holding her open, keeping her in place. One more stroke was all it would take to topple her. She closed her eyes and pushed his hands away. Closed her legs and bit down on a whimper, because even the clench of her thighs had almost been enough to send her soaring.

'What do you want?'

He sounded ragged, almost as desperate as she'd been, and she laughed weakly and pressed the heel of her palm down over her centre to try and stave off completion and wasn't that a mistake. She was too close to climax.

'Oh, no...' she whimpered. 'No— Stop...stop... stop...'

He wasn't even touching her and she was toast, soaring, and cursing, and toppling over onto her side on the table as she rode out the waves breaking inside her body.

Control. She didn't have it. Another tremor racked her. 'That was—that.' She was vastly surprised she still had the power of speech. 'Phew! That was *close*.'

He barked out a laugh and she gathered her courage and continued with the deception.

'Yeah.' She pushed her cheek into the cool wooden table and tried not to drool through her smile as she cracked one eye open the better to see his response. 'Really close. You almost had me there.'

'Princess, I *got* you there. You came. I win.'

'No. I didn't come.' Lies, all lies, as another wave rode her hard. She fought the lassitude that followed in its wake by pushing up off the table and into a sitting position, hands either side of her and her legs pressed tightly together. She had a fair idea what she looked like, but she'd see to herself in a minute. She was far more interested in what Theo looked like, and he didn't disappoint. His eyes glittered fiercely and his colour was high, as if he was either mightily aroused or mightily annoyed. It was hard to say which sentiment rode him harder. His lips were moist, his jaw tight. His crotch was…well. It was reassuring to know she hadn't been the only one enjoying the lesson.

'You came.' He sounded so utterly confident.

'No, I *almost* came.' She looked for her bra and found it at the far end of the table. She wrapped it around her and fastened it quickly. The reapplication of her dress took longer, mainly because it was all askew and tangled around her waist. She figured her legs would probably hold her but she kept one hand to the table just in case, as she stood up and tried to get dressed. Panties—they were already on and damper than a wet cloth. Bra—on. Dress—

'Turn around and let me help,' he muttered.

So she turned around and he zipped her up and then smoothed her dress down over her curves. 'You came,' he murmured in her ear. 'You know it. And I'd trust you a whole lot more if you admitted it.'

Damn. She couldn't look at him. She didn't want to uphold her end of the bargain. 'I can't.'

'Hard, isn't it? Knowing when and who to trust,' he offered silkily.

She stepped away to reclaim her shoes. 'Time will tell.'

'I'll give you a pass this time because that's what you seem to need but, I promise you, your body's not that hard to read.' His words licked at her. 'You're headily responsive, Moriana, but I do know what I'm doing. This time I *wanted* you to come for me. Next time I'm going to keep you on the edge of satisfaction until you're begging for release.'

He was better at these games than she was. 'That sounds...'

'Cruel?' he asked. 'Depraved? Torturous?'

'Kind of perfect.' She smoothed back her hair and wondered how she was going to explain her current state of dishevelment to her lady-in-waiting. Maybe she could set Aury to packing for Liesendaach by way of distraction.

'So,' she began, and if she was a little throaty, a little breathless, it couldn't be helped. Having Theo's warmth at her back and his words in her ear did that to her. 'I'm coming to Liesendaach for a week, and at this point I won't be wearing your ring. Any social functions I should know about?'

He hadn't given up when it came to seducing her into marrying him. The glittering promise in his eyes told her he was just getting started. She was flustered, still reeling from the negotiating and the kissing and the not so simple act of resisting him.

The trust issues between them were a little bit heartbreaking.

'One State Dinner on Friday, four luncheons, bring riding gear if riding's something you like to do, and you're going to need at least half a dozen breakfast outfits similar to the one you have on. We'll be breakfasting together every morning. Think of it as lesson time.'

'And in the evening? What do you do of an evening?'

'Usually I work.'

'Oh.' She was ever so slightly disappointed. 'I'll bring some of my work too. You don't mind?'

'I don't mind. Or we could occasionally meet for a nightcap.'

'We could.'

He was laughing at her, not outwardly, but she could still sense his amusement. She was like putty after only one of his lessons. Totally malleable and greedy for more of his attention, never mind that he'd just given her more than she could handle.

'When would you like to leave?' Thankfully she could still manage to ask a sensible question.

'Whenever you're ready.'

Still so *amenable*. She was looking forward to this week. 'I can be ready within the hour if you'd like to leave this morning? My lady-in-waiting can follow later this afternoon with a suitable wardrobe and my work.'

'Let's do that.'

'Theo.' He was a king in need of a queen, a ruler with a genuine predicament and she respected that he was trying to solve his problem. 'I'm not going to meekly say yes to marriage after a week with you on your best behaviour. You might be wasting your time.'

'I'm not wasting my time. I know you'll give me a fair trial, and that you'll be looking at ways to make this work for you and everyone else around you. You won't be able to help yourself.' He held her gaze and she couldn't read the look in his eyes. 'It's what you do.'

CHAPTER FIVE

THE ROYAL PALACE of Liesendaach was exactly as Theo had left it. Grey slate roofs, creamy sandstone walls arranged in a U-shape around a huge central courtyard that could fit a small army. Six hundred and eighty-five white-sashed windows graced the building. The front half of the palace was surrounded by immaculately kept lawns and the back half of the palace grounds was a series of garden rooms, radiating outwards like the spokes of a wheel.

The palace employed fourteen full-time gardeners and many more seasonal workers, and every spring and autumn he opened the gardens to the public and allowed tours and special events to take place there. It was an incredible waste of water, according to some, but Theo's gardeners knew better than to be wasteful with the precious resource. They were forever experimenting with hardy plant varieties and watering regimes. The forest that bordered the gardens on three sides kept the worst of the hot drying winds away in summertime and took the edge off the icy north winds in winter. Theo's ancestors had known what they were doing when they'd kept the forest in place centuries ago. Naysayers could kiss his royal brass before he let anyone dismiss the gardens as frivolous.

They more than paid their way.

Moriana had been to the palace before, but not lately. Theo signalled to the helicopter's pilot to loop around the building to give her a bird's eye view.

The palace of her birth was starkly grey and forbidding, and beautiful in its own way. This place probably looked like a blowsy showgirl in comparison, but he wanted her to like it.

'The beauty here is not just for beauty's sake,' he said, leaning over her shoulder to look out of the window at the orchard. 'A lot of botanical research takes place here, education for schoolchildren, animal husbandry and breeding programmes, patronage of the arts—'

'Theo,' she interrupted gently. 'I know. Liesendaach's royal palace is and should always remain both functional and beautiful. You've no need to defend it. Not to me.'

'Do you have any idea how you might split your allegiance between Liesendaach and Arun?'

She turned to look him in the eye and her smile was bittersweet. 'You need to read the *Princess Handbook*,' she said. 'If I take your name my loyalty will be to Liesendaach.'

'But how would you feel about that?'

'Given the caning I'm getting in Arun's papers at the moment, I'd feel quite vengefully good about it. On a more practical note, it might just give my brother the incentive to take a wife.' She turned back to look out of the helicopter window. 'Your country has been without a queen for almost two decades. For me that means no recent shoes to step into, no impossible expectations. There's just me and what I might make of the role, and that's liberating in a way. I'm not scared.' Her lips twisted. 'I've been well trained. Byzenmaach would have given me that fresh start too.'

He didn't like the reminder of Byzenmaach and her future there up until a few days ago. A couple of kisses and a tiny taste of her and already he was feeling a possessiveness he'd never felt before. 'Byzenmaach's loss.'

'Indeed.'

They landed, both of them well used to getting in and out of helicopters. Theo had been hoping to make a quiet entrance but his Head of Household Staff had other ideas. Samantha Sterne stood waiting for them at the entrance closest to the helipad and one look at her ultra-serene demeanour promised a storm of rare intensity. The calmer she appeared, the worse the problem was.

'Sam,' he said. 'Meet Princess Moriana of Arun, my guest for the week. You got my message about readying the Queen's chambers?'

Moriana might not be wearing his ring but he could make it clear in a multitude of ways that she was no ordinary guest.

'Yes, Your Majesty.' Sam turned and curtseyed to Moriana. 'My apologies, Your Highness. The maids are finishing up now. The suite is clean but hasn't been in use for some time. I wanted it aired, fresh flowers brought in, new linens…'

'And he gave you fifteen minutes' notice?'

Sam smiled slightly at Moriana's dry words. 'Something like that, Your Highness.'

'Sam, is it?'

'Yes, Your Highness. Head of Household Staff.'

'Ma'am is fine.'

'Yes, ma'am.' Sam nodded, but didn't move on. 'Your Majesty.' She turned back towards Theo and there it was, the surface calm that spoke of a major problem. 'Your cousin arrived this morning, requesting an audience with you. When you weren't here he insisted on waiting, no matter how long it took. I put him in his old suite. George is currently seeing to his needs.'

'I'll take care of it.' Cousin Benedict had called the royal palace home during the years his father—Theo's uncle—had been Regent. He'd never shown any outward desire for the throne, preferring a playboy lifestyle to one of service, but he was a troublemaker at heart and a sly one at that. Family on the one hand; one laughing breath away from stabbing Theo in the back on the other. Benedict hadn't actively sought his company in years.

Sam nodded and took her leave, her stiletto heels clicking rapidly across the polished marble floor. Theo turned to see Moriana watch the other woman go, her expression assessing.

'She's very young to be your Head of Staff,' said Moriana finally.

'The old one was loyal to my uncle. This one's not.' That wasn't the line of thought he was expecting. His mind was still on Benedict.

'She's very pretty.'

'She's very competent.'

'I hope so. There are people I'll want to bring with me to Liesendaach if we do go ahead with a union.'

'Your Head of Household Staff?' he asked drily.

'No, Augustus would kill me. I'm merely pointing out that some staffing changes and additions will be inevitable. I like things done a certain way and I'm not shy about making it happen. Don't worry,' she murmured. 'If Samantha Sterne is as competent as she is pretty, she won't be going anywhere. What's up with Benedict?'

'You mean besides the usual? It's hard to say.'

'You were close to him for a while, weren't you?'

'If by *close* you mean that after my parents died he and I set about creating as much havoc as we could, then yes, we were close. I grew up. He grew petulant. And now would be a very good time to slip my ring on your finger if you wanted to. For your protection. Not that I'm harping on, but I don't trust my cousin not to skewer you when you're not looking. It's his specialty.'

'And how exactly is wearing your ring going to protect me from that? Because I would have thought it painted a target on my back. Unless competing with you for something you've laid claim to is something your cousin *never* does.'

He and Benedict had often made a game out of competing for women; he couldn't deny it. 'It'd still make me feel better.'

'Ownership usually does.'

Ouch.

'Ring or no ring, I can handle cousin Benedict,' she said with a smile. 'Shall we see what he wants?'

Benedict could wait. 'Let me show you to your rooms and then *I'll* see what he wants.'

'Of course, Your Majesty.'

He wasn't nervous about showing her his home. He wasn't suddenly sweating, hoping she'd like her quarters, and the artwork, and the gardens, and the people. He wasn't.

It was just warm in here.

Moriana knew Theo's palace was beautiful. She'd been there before, in its ballrooms and Theo's living quarters when he was growing up. But she'd never been in his mother's rooms before and she hadn't quite realised how stunning the incoming light from a wall full of windows would be, or how magnificent the second storey view out over the gardens would be. The floor of the Queen's chambers consisted of polished wooden parquetry in a

floral design and the ceiling was high and domed. Someone, at some point, had fallen in love with chandeliers,
and they caught the sunlight and scattered it.

'There are other suites to choose from.' Theo was
watching her, waiting for her reaction. She walked towards the windows to stare out, not wanting to drool.

'This'll do.'

'I can bring in some grey stone. Make you feel more
at home.'

She turned in a circle, feasting her eyes on absolutely
everything. 'Don't you dare.' Okay, maybe she could be
seen to drool a little bit.

And there was Theo, hands in his trouser pockets
and his back to the wall, standing just inside the door.
Watching her. 'Where are your rooms?'

'The other side of the hall, with windows facing east.
I get the sunrise, you get the sunset.'

'But do you have chandeliers?' she said.

'You want to see my rooms?'

She did.

His suite was situated on the other side of the long
hallway. There were more windows. Lots of tans and
blues, hidden lights rather than chandeliers and the pick
of the artwork. She eyed the Botticelli painting over his
decorative fireplace with frank interest and heard a faint
growl from somewhere behind her.

'You can't have it,' he murmured. 'You want to look
at it, you can come here.'

'But *would* I look at it if I came here? That's the question.' If it came to a competition as to whether she'd be
more likely to study Theo or that painting, Theo would
win. She still hadn't forgotten what he'd taught her this
morning at the breakfast table. She wondered what he

could teach her in a living room with soft surfaces all around them.

'I could be persuaded to have more than one lesson per day,' she said, eyeing the nearby sofa.

'I need to preserve my strength.' He looked darkly amused.

'Ah, well. Tomorrow morning, then.' She didn't linger during her tour of his rooms. It felt a little like trespassing, for all that he seemed to have no problem with her being there. He kept to the corners of his rooms as well, whereas she was currently standing in the middle of a parquetry circle that was itself probably the dead centre of the room. She let him escort her back to her quarters, where he obligingly made way for two chambermaids, one carrying a vase, the other with her arms full of blooming roses that left a fragrant trail in their wake, but he didn't make to follow her inside. 'I'll leave you to settle in,' he said. 'If you want anything changed or moved, call Sam.'

Moriana nodded. 'Give your cousin my regards. Will I see him at dinner?'

'On Friday at the State Dinner, yes. He's on the guest list.'

'So you do still socialise with him on occasion?'

'It's unavoidable.'

'But you won't be inviting him to stay on, now that he's here?' She couldn't fathom Theo's relationship with his cousin.

'No. He won't be staying on.'

'Because I'm here?'

'That's one of the reasons, yes.'

'Benedict has always been courteous to me,' she said.

'I'm sure he has. You are sister to a king. You were betrothed to a crown prince. You outrank him. Besides, why make enemies when you can charm someone instead?'

That was one way of looking at it. 'How come *you* never embraced that philosophy around me?'

'You were annoying.' He smiled as he said it, and for a moment she felt the heat of his laser-like focus. 'If Benedict stays, my attention will be split. I'd rather concentrate on you alone.'

'Very charming,' she murmured. And she quite enjoyed the view as she watched him go.

Theo didn't have to go looking for his cousin. Five minutes after stepping into his office, Benedict found him. Benedict was two years older than Theo, two inches shorter and as vain as any peacock. He appeared in the doorway to Theo's office, wearing a sneer Theo strongly hoped wasn't hereditary. Benedict had introduced a teenage Theo to Europe's fleshpots and vices, and back then Theo had needed no encouragement to make the most of them. Still finding his way after the death of his parents and older brother, he'd found a willing companion in Benedict.

But Benedict, for all his easy grace and charm, had a viciousness and immorality about him that couldn't be ignored. Theo had started pulling back from their exploits. Benedict hadn't liked that.

It had gone steadily downhill from there.

'You could say hello and offer me a drink,' Benedict said.

'I assumed you'd already helped yourself,' Theo replied, turning his attention momentarily from the other man to finish an email response to his secretary. 'What do you want?'

'The palace requested my presence at dinner on Friday so here I am.'

'You're early.'

'Quite. Had I known you were returning with a guest I may not have made myself quite so at home. On the other hand I get to watch you try to impress the lovely Princess of Arun. That could be fun.'

'Benedict, you specifically asked to see me and I was given to understand that you thought the matter important enough to wait for my return. What do you want?'

'A couple of things. First, the petition for you to marry and reproduce or get off the throne is being abandoned. I never supported it, by the way. It would put me in line for the throne and, suffice to say, I have even less desire for a wife and children than you do.' Benedict's smile turned sly. 'Does Moriana know she's the chosen one? Will you promise her your all? Faithful at last? I'd like to see that.'

'Perhaps you will.' Indifference was important when dealing with Benedict. Admitting weakness or desire was tantamount to handing him a sword to skewer you with.

'I'll tell Father you're courting with intent. He'll be thrilled.'

'I'm sure he will. Are you ever going to tell me why you're here? Run out of money? Still can't choose between the Cordova twins and their younger brother?'

'It's almost as if you know me.'

'I have work to do.' Theo reached for a pile of reports and dropped his gaze to the topmost.

'Father's dying.' Benedict's words came tightly furled, like little bullets that Theo hadn't seen coming until they hit. 'He found out two weeks ago that he has cancer and it's too advanced to treat. He's riddled with it. That's why he's dropping the petition—he can't follow through and take the Crown and I have no desire to. He's in hospital in France. I know you're not given to mercy, but he wants to come home.'

Theo sat back in his chair, reports forgotten, and gave Benedict his full attention. 'Your father's exile was self-imposed. He doesn't need my permission to return to Liesendaach.'

'He wants to come here. He wants to die in his childhood home.'

'No. That's not happening.' Dying or not, Constantine of Liesendaach was a dangerous adversary who'd never once stopped looking for ways to tear Theo down.

'It's not as if he wants the royal suite,' snapped Benedict. 'He's barely lucid. I'll provide the medical care and pick up the cost. All he wants is a room.'

'Then take him home with you.' Benedict had a townhouse in the city, provided by and paid for by the Crown. It wasn't a palace but it sure as hell wasn't a hovel.

Theo could see it now—an endless stream of visiting dignitaries and schemers coming to pay their last respects. People who hadn't graced the palace doors for years. Let Benedict deal with them; Theo would have none of it.

'What are you so afraid of?' Benedict taunted. 'You won. He lost. The world turns. So my father wasn't cut out to be King. Few are. He ruined the economy, so say some. He made too many deals in his own interest, so say others, and maybe they're right. He also raised you, fed and clothed you and never limited your education. He didn't *stop* you from doing anything. You wanted him gone; he *went*.'

'That's one version of his Regency,' Theo said acerbically. 'Would you like to hear mine?'

'*Yes*. I would. Because maybe then I could understand why you turned on us like a rabid dog the minute you took the Crown!'

Theo watched as his cousin turned away, his face red and his lips set in an ugly twist.

'I knew this for a fool's errand,' Benedict said into the deepening silence.

'Then why come?'

'Because he's my father. It's his dying wish to return to the place he calls home, and maybe, just maybe, he will find peace here.' Benedict leaned against the door frame, crossed his arms and employed a passable gimlet stare. 'He knows you think he orchestrated your family's death, even if he doesn't know who fed you the idea. He said to tell you that if he had done, you'd have been on that helicopter too.'

'I was supposed to be. Instead, I was skiving off with you. Horse racing, wasn't it? Your sure-fire winner you simply had to see race?'

'Lucky for you. Or would you rather have been on that flight?' Benedict smiled but it didn't reach his eyes. 'We were family once. I cared about you. Looked after you.' *Saved you.*

To this day, Theo still didn't know if Benedict had acted in complete ignorance when he'd prevented Theo from getting on that flight, or whether he'd known what his father was up to and simply hadn't been able to stomach losing Theo. Whatever the reason, Theo had lived. His parents and brother had not.

And Benedict had ceased to be Theo's confidant.

'Leave the numbers for the doctors.'

'And what?' said Benedict. 'You'll monitor the situation? I left those numbers with your secretary two weeks ago, one week ago, and again yesterday. *Three times* I asked you to call me. Good thing I remember where you live.'

'I didn't receive any of those messages.'

'Then fire your secretary.'

'Was there anything else?' He'd had enough of this conversation.

'Yes. I won't be joining you and all the other righteous souls for dinner this week, or any other week in the foreseeable future. I would have let your staff know...if I thought the message would ever reach you. Don't set a place for me. Don't expect me to play the royal prince once my father is gone. I'm done.'

'You'll lose your title and your allowance.'

Benedict spread his arms wide. 'At least I'll be my own man. My position in this family is untenable. I've tried to get through to you. I can't. Nor am I willing to do what my father wants me to do. Time to move on.'

'I'll let my staff know.' Theo didn't want to feel sick to his stomach. There was no use wishing for a different outcome. 'By the way, Moriana knows you're here. She sends her regards.'

Benedict laughed. 'Poor little pedigree princess, always so proper. First Casimir and now you. I feel sorry for her. Maybe I should ask her if she wants to run away with me. She'd probably be better off.'

'I wouldn't advise it.'

'Then tell her I hope she enjoys her stay and regret that I must take my leave before renewing our acquaintance. There. Aren't we all so civil and grown-up?' Benedict bowed, a mocking salute. 'See you at the funeral. *Cousin*.'

He turned and made his exit, his long, angry stride echoing down the corridor.

Theo closed his eyes and banged his head softly against the padded headrest of the chair.

Of all the confrontations he'd ever had, dealing with Benedict had always been the hardest. He *wanted* to trust the man. They'd been close as children. Similar in age, similar in temperament, royals but not the heir apparent. Less had been expected of them and they'd lived up to that expectation and beyond.

Benedict *had* looked after him at times.

And sometimes, when his back was to the wall and the vultures were gathering, Theo still wanted Benedict at his side.

Theo was still sitting in his chair half an hour later. He'd done no work. Hadn't even glanced at the reports on his desk other than to leaf through them in search of a memo saying Benedict had called. If the information was buried in there somewhere, he hadn't yet found it. And then his deputy Head of Security knocked on the door frame. He'd asked the man to monitor Benedict's departure from the palace. Discreetly, of course.

'Has he gone?' he asked, and the older man nodded.

'Not before he found the visiting Princess and had a few words with her.'

'Was he civil?'

'Exceedingly, sire. The Prince told the Princess she was looking divine and said something to the effect that her broken engagement must be agreeing with her. She laughed and asked after his health and they talked a little about a painting they'd both bid for at auction but neither of them had won. He asked how long she was staying and she said a week. He bid her a pleasant stay, told her to make sure she saw the artwork in the southeast drawing room and then left.'

'Did I ask for a rundown on their conversation?'

'No, sire. My recount is probably wholly unimport-ant.'

'Wrong.' The information was extremely important. Benedict hadn't told Moriana about the petition being buried. He hadn't caused trouble. And that was unusual. 'Thank you. It's useful knowledge.'

The man nodded. 'I'm also here because you'd best be telling me what you want done regarding security for the Princess. Because she's just stationed the three men I put on her too far away to be of use and she didn't bring any security personnel of her own.'

'They'll be arriving this afternoon.' Augustus had insisted.

Theo picked up his desk phone and searched his mind for the internal number for the Queen's chambers. He thought it was zero zero two, but he couldn't be sure. It had been so long since he'd used it.

She picked up, and her voice was warm and relaxed as she said, 'Hello.' His Princess was in a far better mood than he was. Hopefully she'd stay that way when he overruled her security arrangements.

'You need to know what is and isn't going to hap-pen, security-wise,' he told her curtly. 'There's a brief-ing in ten minutes. My security team will show you to my office.'

'Actually, I've just ordered tea brought to the most romantic little sitting room I've ever seen,' she said, the laughter in her voice a startling contrast to the encoun-ter he'd recently had with his cousin. 'There's a huge vase of fragrant roses on the table, the sun is streaming in through the open windows and the breeze is sending the gauze curtains flying. I can smell the forest and I've just discovered a pair of armless white leather recliners which are either sunbeds or massage beds. Regardless, I'm currently lying on a cloud and your chances of getting me off it any time soon are…ooh, *nil*. More to the point, if this security discussion is about me and my needs I want it to happen here, in these quarters, so I can see for myself what you're proposing. I want you to walk me through it.'

Her words made sense, more was the pity. 'Be ready in five minutes,' he grated.

'I'll order more tea,' she said smoothly, and hung up on him.

His security deputy stood there, still largely oblivious to the force of nature Theo was about to unleash on their world. 'We're going to her.'

He was a good man, his security guard. Well trained. Because all he did was nod.

Theo's mood did not improve as Moriana negotiated her security requirements. He overrode most of her requests, acceded to two of them, and wore her contemplative stare in silence once the security team was back in place.

'Seems like overkill,' she said.

'My team is experienced. They'll only step in when needed.' He couldn't joke about security measures and he would never, ever downgrade them. 'I don't take risks. I do need to sleep at night, and I won't if I'm worried about the safety of the people under this roof. I can protect you, Moriana. But you need to let me.'

He wasn't negotiating.

Finally, she spread her arms wide. 'Okay.'

But he still didn't relax.

'Bear with me while I try and figure out what pitched your mood blacker than tar,' she said as she headed for the sunroom she seemed to like so much. 'Augustus gets like this. It's not always my doing but I'm not ruling it out. More tea?'

'No, thank you.'

'What did Benedict want?'

'Too much.' The words were out of his mouth before he could call them back. Then again, wasn't he supposed to be sharing his life with her? Trusting her with the complications of his court?

'So either you refused him and you're brooding about it or you agreed to do something you don't want to do,' she said. 'Which is it?'

'Do you think me cold?' he asked instead of answering her question.

'No.'

'Do you think me ruthless? Calculating?'

'Yes. Both. Show me a good ruler who isn't.'

'My uncle's dying,' he said.

Her eyebrows rose.

'He wants to spend his last days here at the palace.'

'Ah,' she murmured. 'And the petition for your removal? What's happening there?'

'Benedict says it's been abandoned.'

'Interesting. Do you believe him?'

Theo couldn't sit still beneath her carefully assessing gaze. He stood and crossed to the window but he could still feel her eyes on him like an itch between his shoulders. 'I don't know.'

'How long does your uncle have left?'

He didn't know that either, but apparently he had the doctor's contact details somewhere to hand. 'Got a phone?'

She disappeared through the doorway and came back moments later and handed it to him. It was gold-plated and disguised as a set of balance scales. He looked at the phone, looked back at her.

'If there's a less absurd phone around here, I've yet to find it,' she said. 'Why do you think I always sound so thoroughly cheerful when I answer it?'

Two minutes later, Theo had the contact details he needed. Two minutes after that he was speaking to his uncle's head physician in France. When he put the phone down ten minutes later he was armed with the knowledge that Benedict hadn't been exaggerating Constantine of Liesendaach's illness. The doctor had given Constantine days to live. Already, he was slipping in and out of consciousness as his body's organs began to fail. Constantine had refused life support assistance and Benedict had told the medical staff to honour the request. Palliative care only for the former Regent.

'We're talking days,' he said. 'Assuming he doesn't die in transit.'

'Okay. Now we know.' Her calm poise steadied him. 'Will you grant him a state funeral?'

'No.' He couldn't stomach giving that honour to a murderer. 'There can still be enough pomp to satisfy the burial of a former Prince Regent without gazetting it as such.'

'Do you seek my opinion on the matter?' she asked.

'Yes.' Why not? There was something grounding about the sheer practicality of her questions so far.

'Okay, here goes. You neutralised the man ten years ago but didn't exile him. Either before he dies or after, you're going to have to bring him home. You're going to have to try and make sense of his life and actions and then you're going to speak in public of human frailty, temptation and forgiveness, whether you mean those words or not. Do it now. Get it done. Show your people—and him—a strong king's mercy.'

She hadn't moved from the sofa but her words drew him away from the window and back around, such was her command of his attention. She sipped her tea, an island of serenity, and it dawned on him that she was extremely good at being someone's muse.

'Your uncle is no threat to you now. Benedict, bless him, is in the same boat as you in that he has no wife or heirs. Benedict won't challenge you. He *can't* challenge you. The throne is yours.'

She was good at this. 'I still need a queen.'

'And now you can take your time and search properly and find one who suits your needs.'

She was *right there in front of him*. How could she be so clear-eyed when it came to dealing with his uncle and cousin and not know she was the perfect candidate?

'How often does Augustus seek your counsel?' he asked.

'Almost daily, why?'

'You're good at it.'

She smiled wryly. 'I grew up listening to my father speak freely of state concerns at dinner each night. Not major concerns, nothing classified to begin with, but even as children we always had one topic of state to discuss, alongside the regular conversation about our days. He'd ask our opinions. Make us defend our positions. Showed us how to respectfully discuss problems and the fixing of them. They were lessons in statecraft.'

'And how old were you when you started this?'

'I hardly recall when it started, only that it was an everyday occurrence. My father always paid attention to my mother's voice. He relied on her for support and to bring fresh perspective to the table. When she died, so too did much of my father's enthusiasm for his role. It's one of the reasons he abdicated early, even if not the only one.'

She put down her teacup. 'I'm scaring you, aren't I? You're not used to dealing with women who expect a great deal of intellectual intimacy from their nearest and dearest.'

He wasn't used to dealing with *anyone* who expected intellectual intimacy from him.

'I did warn you,' she said.

'You did.' And, God, he wanted more of it. He ruled alone; he always had. But this…this effortless back and forward, argument and counterargument, not for argument's sake but with the clear aim of lifting a burden… He would have more of this.

'You're looking a little wild-eyed,' she said.

He'd just realised what he'd been missing all these years.

She rose and came to stand beside him, looking out over the gardens, following his lead and dropping the subject. 'What's that?' she asked, pointing towards a tiny cottage on the edge of the forest.

'It used to be my mother's painting studio. These days the gardeners use it as their headquarters.'

'Will you walk me there? Through the gardens?'

'Now?'

She nodded.

'You'll need a hat. And a shawl for your shoulders. Possibly an umbrella.'

She looked at him as if he amused her.

'What?' he said. 'It's a long way. You're fair-skinned. You'll burn.'

'I have dark hair, dark eyes, olive skin and when I encounter the sun I tan. Also, you're starting to sound like my mother.'

Her mother had been a tyrant.

'You do realise,' he murmured, 'that mothers are, on occasion, right?'

By the time they reached the outer doors of the palace there was a woman's sun hat, an umbrella and a gauzy cotton scarf waiting for them. Moriana sighed. Theo smiled. Heaven knows where his household staff had sourced them from.

First the scarf—Theo draped it around her neck and made a production of rearranging it several times until it completely covered her bare shoulders. Clearly he was more adept at taking a woman's clothes off than helping one put clothes on.

The hat came next. Then he offered her his aviator sunglasses. 'We should take water,' he said.

'It's a walk in the garden, not a mountain trek. Why are you being so...'

'...attentive?' he offered.

'I was going to say *weird*. I've been in gardens with you a dozen times over. Never before have you offered me a hat.'

'It wasn't my place. Ask me how often I wanted to offer you a hat. You wore one once. It was bright green, floppy-brimmed and had a red band with purple polka dots. You had your hair in a long plait that went half-way down your back and your hair ribbon matched your hat band.'

'I remember that hat,' she said. 'I don't remember the day you speak of.'

'Your brother dared you to fetch us some wine from the kitchens but you told him you already had two strikes against you and he'd have to get it himself because three strikes a day was your limit and you still had to get through your dance lesson.'

'Do you remember what my strikes were?'

'Apparently you'd chosen the wrong shoes for the right dress and embarrassed your mother in front of her friends. That was strike one. Strike two happened at lunch because you'd forgotten the name of someone's pet spaniel.'

'Oh.' One of *those* days. 'Good call when it came to me not stealing the wine, I guess.' Moriana drew the scarf more tightly around her shoulders. Criticism had shaped her days as a child. It had been constructive criticism, of course. But it had also been relentless and demoralising, and she'd crawled into bed and cried herself to sleep more nights than she cared to remember, convinced she was an utter failure at life, the universe and everything. 'I used to take criticism too much to heart. I still do.'

'But you're working on it. *Moriana First*, remember?' His smile was warm and his eyes more blue than grey today. 'I'd never seen you looking prettier, that day, mismatched shoes and all. Naturally I had to steal the wine myself and pull your hair when I returned. Heaven forbid you didn't notice my reappearance.'

'I remember now. You then proceeded to ignore me for the rest of your visit.'

'I was fourteen. You were the prettiest thing I'd ever seen. Your hat made me want to sneak beneath it and kiss you and the wine made me almost brave enough to do it. But you were already spoken for and I was still a good boy back then. Kissing you would have sparked an international incident involving parents. My father would have handed me my ass. Naturally, I ignored you for the rest of my visit.'

His words were sweet. His eyes were shielded by long, sweeping lashes several shades darker than his hair.

'And why are you telling me this now?'

'Because confession is good for the soul.' He slid her a smile that held more than a hint of the boy he'd once been. 'I still wish I'd done it.'

And then he ducked his head beneath the brim of her hat and kissed her swiftly on the cheek.

What was that for? She didn't say the words but her eyes must have spoken for her.

'You said you wanted romance,' he said.

'You can stop courting me now. You're free and clear, remember?'

'I know.' He shoved his hands in his pockets and fixed his gaze on the horizon, giving her a clear view of his strongly hewn profile. 'But maybe I want to court you anyway.'

CHAPTER SIX

LIESENDAACH WAS A treasure trove of loveliness, Moriana
decided later that afternoon as she and Aury investigated
the Queen's wardrobe facilities more thoroughly. Theo
had retreated to his office for the afternoon and exploration had beckoned in his absence. Theo's mother's
clothes had been removed, but the three empty rooms
devoted to clothes storage, hat and shoe space and a
cupboard-sized jewellery safe spoke of a woman who'd
loved to dress up and had spared no expense when it
came to indulging that passion.

'If I remember correctly, the late Queen of Liesendaach used to collect clothes,' said Aury. 'Period clothes.
Centuries-old gowns once worn by the aristocracy. Ve-
netian masks, Russian uniforms, everything. Want to
go looking for them?'

One of the two security guards standing just within
her line of sight coughed and Aury rolled her eyes before turning to look at him.

'You wanted to say something?' Aury asked the
guard.

'Yes, ma'am. There's a costume collection on the third
floor, right above us.'

'I didn't know this place had a third floor,' said
Moriana.

'Storage only. There are no windows, Your Highness. But that's where you'll find the costume collection. There's a staircase up to it from the door on your far left. The one that looks like a regular cupboard door.'

'I love secret staircases. Makes me feel right at home,' said Aury, with a flirtatious glance in the guard's direction. 'What's your name, soldier?'

'Aury,' Moriana chided, with a glance that spoke of not seducing Theo's security force within five minutes of their arrival.

'But everything's so *pretty* here,' Aury said with another coquettish glance in the direction of the unwary. Come to think of it, the poor man appeared quite aware and looked to be holding up just fine. And yes. He was very pretty—in a rugged, manly kind of way. Fair-haired and light-eyed, like so many of Liesendaach's people, he was also large of frame and lean when it came to bodyweight.

'What's your name, soldier?' Moriana repeated Aury's question.

'Henry, milady.'

'Good sturdy name,' Aury said. 'We should keep him. He knows where things are.'

'Uh-huh.' Moriana opened the door he'd spoken of. Sure enough, a spiral staircase beckoned, up, up and up towards darkness.

'I'll need to call it in and go on ahead if you want to take a look.' This from Henry again, all security-wise and conscientious.

'Let's do it.'

Two minutes later Henry led the charge up the stairs. Aury let him get all of two steps ahead before she started ogling the man's backside with a pleased little sigh. 'After you,' Moriana told her lady-in-waiting drily.

'*Thank* you, milady.'

'You're incorrigible.' But Aury's obvious enjoyment of her surroundings fuelled her own. Nothing like a fairy tale castle to explore to pass the time.

They eventually reached the third floor. Henry switched on lights as he went and when they reached the top of the stairs he crossed to a bank of old-fashioned switches and flicked them on, one after another. The place lit up, one tennis-court-sized section at a time, to reveal row upon row of gowns and costumes stretching into forever.

'There's a ledger,' Henry said, pointing towards a long side table. 'I believe the costumes are organised by period and then colour.'

'Henry, what's with the superior knowledge of the costumes?' asked Aury.

'My mother was seamstress to the late Queen,' said handsome Henry. 'I spent a lot of days up here as a child.'

'Were you ever a centurion?' Aury wanted to know. 'A Knight Templar?'

Henry smiled but neither denied nor confirmed his tendency towards dress-ups as a child.

'What does your mother do now?' Moriana asked.

'She works as a palace chambermaid, Your Highness.'

Handy. 'I don't suppose she's working *now* and would like to join us up here?'

'Imagine what we could do with these,' said Aury.

'Charity exhibitions, loans to museums...' Moriana was thoroughly on board with investigating ways of making sure these costumes were *seen*.

'Liesendaach's little big book of heavenly dresses,' said Aury. 'For charity, of course.'

Aury flipped open the ledger and started scanning the index. 'Oh, my lord. Royal wedding gowns!'

'We could be here a while.' There wasn't a lot that was going to compete with a collection of royal wedding gowns through the ages.

'Henry, I'm forward. It's a terrible flaw, I know,' Moriana began, and Aury snickered and handsome Henry blushed. 'But I think it's time we met your mother.'

Theo found them two hours later. He'd spent the afternoon on the phone to various medical specialists, including his uncle's physician yet again. He'd organised transport. He'd spoken to Benedict. No way was he bringing his uncle home without Benedict accompanying the man and staying on until Constantine's death.

Benedict probably had whiplash from Theo's change of heart, but he hadn't said no. Instead, he'd offered subdued thanks, asked for the lower west wing to be placed at their disposal, and promised not to linger once his father passed on.

Theo had a knot in his stomach at the prospect of all three of them being under the one roof again, and a burning need for Moriana's company. Not to talk it out, the way he'd done earlier. This time he was looking solely for a distraction.

She didn't disappoint.

There she sat, a tiny general in butter yellow, wholly surrounded by clothes in every colour imaginable, and attended by two chambermaids, her lady-in-waiting, his Head of Household Staff and two royal guards.

'Theo!' Moriana coloured prettily when she saw him. 'How long have we been up here? We were just…er… planning an exhibition for your…er…'

'Consideration,' Sam murmured helpfully.

'Yes, indeed. For your consideration.' Moriana smiled.

'And the benefit to me would be...?'

'Immense,' she said. 'Think of the children.'

'I'd like four,' he said silkily, and watched her expression grow wary. 'Walk with me. Please. There's something I'd like to discuss.'

'Of course,' she murmured and, with a nod for those surrounding her, she followed him along the narrow walkway with costumes on either side.

'What is it?' she asked as they began their descent down the spiral steps towards the second floor.

'The press know you're here.'

'How?'

'How do they know anything? On the one hand, my reputation precedes me. On the other hand, you're you, freshly jilted and vulnerable, and they know I was at your charity auction last night. They can smell a story and they've already been in contact with my press secretary for a statement. I'm willing to let them speculate as to what I'm doing with you. What are you willing to do?'

'No comment?' She nibbled on her lower lip and he was hard pressed not to bend his head and join her. 'I think "no comment". I'm through with thinking the press will treat me well any time soon, and you've never thought of them as allies.'

Worked for him.

'Do you really want four children?' she asked.

'Why not?' The only number he didn't want was two. The heir and the spare.

He'd been the spare, forever in the shadow cast by his brother's bright light, and he'd never liked the dynamic.

'Do you want children?' He remembered her reply to Augustus.

'Would you still offer for me if I didn't?' She slid him a rueful glance. 'Don't answer that. Rhetorical question. I know full well you need heirs.'

'But do you want children?' he pressed.

'Yes,' she said quietly. 'And there's no medical reason why I can't have them. I'm still fertile.'

'Do you remember that conversation? The one at your place when we were younger?' All the children of neighbouring monarchs had been there. All the young crown princes—him, Augustus, Casimir and Valentine—along with Moriana and Valentine's sister. Moriana had been subject to a fertility test in the days beforehand and had ranted long and loud about women's rights and invasion of privacy. And then Valentine and his sister had revealed they too had been tested for fertility and a host of other genetic flaws. Casimir had then bleakly revealed he'd been subject to not one but two DNA paternity tests.

There'd been a question on everyone's lips after that, and it had nothing to do with fertility.

It had been Valentine who'd finally caved and asked if Casimir was his father's son.

The answer had been a sullen, scowling, 'Ycs.'

'I still remember that conversation,' he murmured.

'So do I,' said Moriana. 'Is it wrong for me to breathe a sigh of relief now that Casimir's poisonous father is dead? Is it wrong for me to think that you'll have less to worry about once your uncle has passed, and that I really like the shape of this new world order? Because I do like it. It makes me feel hopeful for the future—and the future of any children I might have.'

'*We* might have.'

'So you're still courting me,' she said. 'I thought now your marriage problem has been solved we might go back to being adversaries.'

'I still need a wife. Liesendaach still needs a Queen and an heir. And I'm doing my very best to be open and trusting with you and, believe me, it doesn't come easy.' Damn right he was still courting her. 'I'm asking questions. I'm sharing my thoughts. I brought a personal problem to you earlier. Marriage may not be something I need quite so urgently, but it's still something I want. See? This is me—sharing and caring.'

'I...see,' she said dubiously. 'Well, then...good job.'

'And there you go again. Lying to me,' he said darkly. 'What *else* can I improve on?'

'I...' She spread her hands somewhat helplessly. 'Theo, I appreciate your efforts and the confidences you've shared with me today. Truly.'

'But you're still not taking my proposal seriously.'

'I am now.'

She looked at him uncertainly and he wished he could rid her of her insecurities.

'I'd even throw in your favourite wedding gown from upstairs.'

'They're all quite exquisite.'

But she didn't say yes.

'I wonder what Casimir's going to do about his daughter,' she said suddenly.

'Where did that come from?' Moriana was hard on his ego at times; he'd give her that. Moments ago he'd been offering up his innards for her perusal. Now she was talking about her former fiancé's daughter.

'I'm thinking about a king's need for an heir—you started it. Then I thought of Casimir. He'll claim his daughter—he told me as much—but she's still illegitimate. She'll never rule.'

'Did he say he was going to marry the mother?'

'No. He spoke of her only briefly, to say that everything was up in the air. But I get the feeling he cares for her more than he's letting on. More than he let on to me, at any rate.'

'You care for him.' Theo had never liked that thought.

'Yes, although perhaps never as romantically as I should have. I feel for Casimir. For over twenty years I thought I was to marry him. He has a six-year-old daughter he never knew he had. He may be considering taking a commoner—a foreigner—for a wife. He's burying his father, who he had a difficult relationship with. And now he's a king. I wouldn't want to be him.'

Moriana was well rid of him. 'His transition to the throne is assured.'

'Do you think he'll have an easier time of taking up the reins than you did?'

'He's older, wiser, and there's no other royal alternative waiting in the wings. The throne is his.'

'Will you help him? Counsel him?'

'If he asks for my counsel, yes.'

'Why did you never ask for help when you first took the throne?'

Always with the difficult questions. 'Help from whom? Byzenmaach? Casimir's father supported my uncle as Regent; there was no help for me there. Thallasia stayed neutral until Valentine took the throne. Only then could I look there for support and by then I was through the worst of it. Your father was the only one to ever offer the hand of friendship and even then I didn't take it because I didn't trust him. I didn't trust anyone.'

'We know. It was one of those round-table conversations we had about you. My father thought you a wastrel, initially. In his defence, you had gone out of your way to give that impression.'

Theo smirked. 'I was hiding in plain sight.'

'But then you neutralised your uncle and began to undo the damage done and within six months my father was your biggest fan.' She slanted him a glance. 'Would it surprise you to know that another reason my brother took the throne early was so that *you* would have a regional ally you might trust?' Theo stopped walking. Moriana continued her stroll along the corridor before finally looking over her shoulder. 'Do keep up.'

He had no words. His day had been full of too many surprises already. 'Who *are* you?'

'I'm Moriana of Arun, sister to a King, daughter to a King, and potentially your future Queen.'

'I need a drink.'

'I concur. How about you walk me to a bar?'

He turned her around and walked her to his rooms instead. They were closer and there was a bar in there. It wasn't fully stocked, but all his favourites were present and hers could be delivered.

'Is now a good time to let you know that if we marry I'll be wanting full access to Liesendaach's education, healthcare and arts portfolios, and I wish to be kept apprised of the regional water resources plans?' she asked.

'Tomorrow would be a better time to hit me with that,' he muttered. 'I'm surprised Augustus is willing to let you go, what with all you do.'

'Needs must.' They'd reached his rooms and he stepped back to let Moriana enter before him. 'Although, in the interest of full disclosure, there is the small matter of my overdrawn bank account,' she said dulcetly. 'He's not particularly happy about that.'

'What did you buy?' Augustus had never mentioned his sister being a frivolous spender. He was more likely to gripe about her inability to stop buying and selling major artworks.

'A tapestry. It was one of ours from long ago. My great-grandfather sold it and seven others like it. Together they told a story of love, war and an abandoned child who grew to be a great warrior and mistakenly fell in love with his mother, at which point he put a sword through her heart and then fell on his own. Sword, that is.'

'Happy. I can see why you had to have it back.'

'Yes, well, unfortunately, the original set was split between several buyers. My grandmother bought the first one back; my mother recovered three more. Augustus found one. I found two more. The last remaining seller knew their tapestry would complete the set and priced accordingly. I paid up and Augustus froze my spending account until June next year.'

She sounded amused rather than put out. 'Quite a good time for me to consider marriage, all things considered. I *will* have a spending account as your Queen, right?'

'Yes, but you'll have to answer for it.'

'I always do.' She crossed the room to look out of his window. 'You keep horses here.'

'We breed horses here. Warhorses for Liesendaach's mounted guard regiment.'

Moriana hummed her approval. '*Very* nice.'

She was biting back a smile and he crossed to her side and looked out. His stable master was supervising the unloading of horses from a livestock transport truck into the courtyard below. Three big greys and a tiny black Shetland stallion were being introduced to several stable hands.

'Is there anything here that's not pretty?' she asked, and he remembered an overheard conversation about stable boys and lustful thoughts.

'You'd best be looking at my horses, Princess, and not my stable hands. And I suggest you avoid entirely the company of royal horsemen stationed here.'

Moriana's smile turned positively beatific. 'You have a company of royal horsemen stationed here? How did I not know this? I need to tell Augustus.'

She wanted to torture Augustus with visions of her sleeping her way through Liesendaach's mounted regiment, most likely. The problem was, Theo couldn't admit to overhearing that conversation between her and her brother because then all hell would break loose. He didn't want all hell to break loose right now. He wanted to relax and regain some small sense of control and maybe, just maybe, get her to look at him the way she'd looked at him last night and then again this morning.

'Have you ever just wanted a day to be over?' he asked.

'You mean how I felt most of yesterday and the day before?'

'Point.'

'Are you thinking about your uncle?'

'And Benedict. And you. And the future and what to make of it.' And trust and how to build it with this woman.

'No wonder you need a drink. Weighty topics all.'

And connected all, for together they did—or would—make up his family unit.

Moriana turned, her back to the window now, as she stood before him. At least her attention was no longer being diverted by his horsemen. 'Of course you don't have mindless sexual conquests to distract yourself with any more. What a shame.'

'Moriana, I'm going to strangle you soon,' he warned.

A mischievous smile lit her face. 'Are you ready to teach lesson two? I'm ready for lesson two.'

'Breath play? I doubt it.'

She blinked.

He smiled. 'Was that not what you meant?'

'I…er…no. Definitely not what I meant. Baby steps, Theo. It's only lesson two.'

'A lesson that isn't scheduled until tomorrow.'

She sighed. 'Guess I'll have to keep looking at all the pretty horses…and their handlers.'

On the other hand, it wasn't as if he had anything better to do. He could use a little distraction. And there was something to be said for physical release as a means of easing tension.

'Would you like to keep looking at my stable hands?' he murmured. 'Because hands on the windowsill if you would.'

'Oh, no. No.' She quickly put distance between her and the window, before turning to keep him in sight. 'I know what "hands on flat surfaces" involves. We covered that lesson this morning, and we are not doing it again in front of a window with your men looking on. That's lesson eight hundred and sixty-five *thousand*. Not to mention a very bad idea.'

'Or you could sit on the bed.'

One moment she was railing at him, eyes wide. The next minute she was perched on the end of his bed, arms crossed in front of her.

'I have a request,' she said.

He expected nothing less.

'I'd like you naked this time,' she said.

'As you wish.' Theo smiled, the focus firmly back on him as he stalked towards the bed. 'Perhaps you could undress me.'

Moriana tucked her hands a little higher beneath her arms. 'I didn't expect these lessons to require quite so much initiation on my part.'

'Live and learn. You could start with my buttons if my belt's too intimidating.'

'I refuse to be intimidated. I can do this. I want to do this.'

'That's the spirit.'

She started with his belt buckle, her touch deft and light. By the time she had his fly undone he was hard beneath the brush of her hands and he was the one unbuttoning his shirt, because bravery should be rewarded.

She leaned in and closed her eyes and set her cheek to the skin just above the low ride of his underwear, and when she turned her head the better to taste skin he clenched his hands into fists instead of sliding them through her hair and guiding her actions. If the last lesson had been about Moriana surrendering control of her body to him, he wanted this lesson to be about her taking control and keeping it, exploring it. And for that he had to ease off on his.

He shouldered his shirt to the floor and she looked up as if he was offering the finest of feasts after a lifetime of starvation. He wished she had more experience but he wasn't ever going to let her get it from anyone else. She'd had her chances and hadn't taken them.

She took her time when it came to getting his trousers off. He took his time laying her on the bed and stretching out beside her. She liked looking at him, when he wasn't distracting her with kisses, deep and drugging. She liked touching him and he encouraged it.

'What's the lesson?' she asked again, so he named one.

'Rubbing,' he whispered. 'Rocking.' Until they drove each other mad. 'No penetration.' He hadn't done this since his teens. 'Easy.'

He wrapped his arm around her waist and hauled her on top of him, knees to either side of his hips, and if that wasn't giving her full control he didn't know what would.

'Should I take my clothes off?'

'Your call.' Her dress was soft and her panties felt like silk against his erection. Hot wet silk.

The panties came off and her dress stayed on as she positioned herself over him again, and slowly settled against him.

'I like feeling you against me,' she murmured against his lips and he closed his eyes and tried to think of anything but the feel of warm wet womanhood against him. Slowly she began to rock against him, her hands either side of his head. 'Like this?'

'Yes.' Sliding his hands beneath her dress, up and over the globes of her buttocks, the better to position her for maximum drag over sensitive areas.

She was slick enough for both of them and for the most part he let her find her way, only sliding his hand around to rest his thumb against her once or twice to begin with until she arched up to a sitting position, grabbed his hand by the wrist and held it there.

She closed her eyes and her trembling increased as he used every trick he'd ever learned to make it good for her.

'Do you close your eyes the better to imagine someone else?' he grated, because he could be cruel and tender in equal measure and because she'd said the same to him.

'Put it in,' she whimpered. 'Theo, please. Fill me. Put it in.'

'Not until we're married.'

'Since when has this been one of your conditions for bedding a woman?' Disbelief coloured her voice but her body still moved and so did his.

'Since you.' He rolled her over and wrapped her legs around him and added his weight and a sinuous roll to the negotiations; it had been years since he'd been this close to coming with such minor stimulation, but this was Moriana and her abandon had always fuelled his. 'I will put my mouth on you and my hands, do this all day long, take you to the edge and make you wait, but you only get me in you when you're mine.' Which begged the question... How long did it really take to arrange a royal wedding? Because the restraint was killing him.

'I hate you.' But her hands were in his hair and she was drawing his head down into a kiss so hot and desperate that the groan he heard was his.

'You want me.'

'Yes,' she sobbed. 'Theo, I'm—'

Coming, and so was he, all over her stomach, messing her up, painting her his.

She was too responsive. 'You came again, I don't care what you say. I win.'

She laughed a little helplessly.

'You know, simultaneous satisfaction is quite a feat. Very rare.'

'Is it? I wouldn't know.'

'It's rare.'

She studied his face, her eyes searching and solemn. 'You're still courting me.'

'Yes, and I fully intend to win you. How much plainer do I have to make it?'

'I have a temper,' she said next.

'Pent-up passion has to go somewhere.'

'I have high standards. I'm hard on myself and on others. I'll be hard on you if you fail me.'

'I'd expect nothing less. If I think you're being too hard on either yourself or others I'll call you on it. We'll argue and your passion will go somewhere.'

'I can be a workaholic.'

'Liesendaach needs a lot of work.'

'You're not the slightest bit self-conscious about lying here naked, are you?'

'Should I be?'

She sighed and shook her head. 'No. Your body is flawless.' She dropped her gaze below his waist. 'And very well proportioned. I never realised that shamelessness could be quite so enticing.'

He was comfortable in his skin. She, on the other hand, still had her dress on. 'I would see you comfortable in your skin before we're through,' he told her. 'Especially in private.'

'More lessons.' The curve of her lips was captivating and always had been.

'Yes, many more lessons, starting now. Take your dress off.'

'But…aren't we done for now?'

'I promised to keep you strung out on the edge of release for hours,' he reminded her silkily. 'I need to keep my word.' She had a very sensitive neck. It responded well to lips and tongue and the faintest graze of his teeth.

'I think you're overestimating my resistance to your touch,' she murmured as she arched beneath him.

Twenty minutes later and after two orgasms, ripped from her body in rapid succession, Princess Moriana of Arun told him to stop.

'Have I persuaded you to marry me yet?'

'Not yet,' she murmured with a thoroughly satisfied smile. 'But full points for trying.'

CHAPTER SEVEN

MORIANA CRACKED ONE eye open to the sound of cutlery landing on a table. She was in Theo's room, in Theo's bed, wholly naked, but the man himself wasn't there. Instead, a chambermaid was busy setting a dinner table in the room next door. Moriana could see bits of her every now and again through the half-closed door and the reflection on the window. It was dark outside and dark in the room she'd been sleeping in. The adjoining room looked as if it was lit by candlelight.

Perhaps it was.

She'd been schooled, she remembered that much. She remembered Theo playing her body the way a master violinist played a foreign instrument. Paying attention, learning what worked and what didn't, down to the tiniest detail, and adjusting his attentions accordingly. He'd played her to perfection. He'd known what she wanted before she did and kept her waiting.

He still hadn't bedded her fully.

And now she was in a strange room with no clothes to wear other than stained ones, and no idea what to do next. The maid finished her preparations and slipped from view and Moriana took the opportunity to escape into the bathroom. A shower later, she entered his dressing room and took one of his shirts from its hanger and put it on. It was of the softest cotton and fell to the tops of her thighs. She found her panties and put them on too.

She tried not to think about what she looked like but there were mirrors on three walls and in the end it was inevitable that she would meet her reflection. Make-up gone and hair untended, she barely recognised herself. In her eyes was an awareness of pleasure. On her skin were faint marks left by the press of strong hands and a hot, sucking mouth. Theo hadn't treated her like a princess. He'd treated her like a woman fully capable of pleasing herself and, in doing so, pleasing him.

She took a blue two-tone tie from his collection and used it as a hairband, and now she looked all carefree and confident.

Looked, not felt. Because she'd never felt quite so laden with doubt.

She'd only ever repressed the more passionate side of her nature and here she was feeding it, and Theo was nothing if not encouraging. With him at her side she was slowly eroding the self-control she'd fought for all her life—the control her family valued above all else.

'You're screwed,' she told the woman in the mirror, and then turned her back on her and there stood Theo. Watching. The hawk in the granary.

'Not yet,' he said, and straightened as she approached. 'What is it you think I can't give you?' His eyes were sharp, more grey than blue in this light.

'There doesn't appear to be anything you can't deliver.'

He was still watching her so she sent him a smile to back up her words.

'Don't do that,' he said.

'Do what?'

'Retreat behind your mask of cool politeness. It

doesn't work when you're wearing nothing but my shirt.' His gaze slid to her face. 'And my favourite tie.'

'Is it really your favourite tie?'

'It is now.' She needed to get used to Theo's lazy compliments and the intensity of his gaze. 'Dinner's ready. It's the romance portion of the evening. I added candles.'

He turned away and she followed him into the adjoining room. 'So I see.' The room was bathed in soft light and shadows and the table was set for two. A nearby balcony door stood open and she could smell the scent of the forest and feel the lingering heat of the day in the air.

'I love it here.' It wasn't like the palace she'd grown up in, heavy on grey stone and small, defensible windows. This palace had been built for openness and sensual delight and showing off its beauty. It made her feel wide open to possibilities in a way that her home palace never had.

Or maybe it was the man currently pulling her dining chair out for her who was doing that.

His loose weave shirt was a dove-grey colour and unstarched. His trousers were khakis and he hadn't got around to putting on shoes.

'I got your meal preferences from the Lady Aury and took the liberty of sending them to my kitchen staff,' he said. 'We have our own regional specialities, of course, and tonight I thought we could try a mix of both your preferences and mine. See how well they mesh. The serving staff will come to the door. We can take it from there.'

A soft ping of a bell prevented her from answering. Theo went to the door and came back with a trolley laden with dome-covered dishes. There were scallops, fish stew or soup of some sort, duck salad with a pome-

granate dressing—one of her favourites—and there was
Mediterranean salad, heavy on the olives—which was
perhaps a favourite of his. There was baked bread and
lots of it.

'Fish stew and sourdough. Messy but worth it,' he
said.

She took the bowl of stew he handed her and passed
him the bread basket in return. 'Do you dine in here
often?' she asked.

'More often than I should,' he answered. 'There's a
family dining room, of course. It hasn't been used for
years. Not since my uncle's rule.'

'Where did your family dine? You know—before.'

Before the helicopter crash that had cost them their
lives. 'My mother used to enjoy dining on the west terrace on warm summer nights. In winter there was a
modest dining room with a large fireplace that we used
a lot. I don't use either any more. Too many ghosts and
there are so many other rooms to choose from.'

'Do you ever get lonely here?'

'There are people everywhere,' he said by way of an
answer and, yes, they were his people but they weren't
family or loved ones; they were employees. He'd lost two
families, she realised. One in a terrible accident and the
other when he'd taken the throne and stripped his uncle
of power. No wonder he kept to himself and found it
hard to contemplate having loved ones he could rely on.

'I took your advice. Benedict and my uncle will be
arriving tomorrow or the next day, depending on my
uncle's condition,' he said. 'It may not be fun. I'm considering sending you home until it's done.'

Moriana put her fork down and her hands in her lap.
Hands were revealing. And she was suddenly nervous.
The food she'd been enjoying suddenly sat heavy in

her stomach. She didn't have the right clothes on for a farewell speech. More to the point, she'd only just got here and didn't want to go. They'd been making progress, of a sort. Working each other out, learning each other's strengths and weaknesses, and she wanted that to continue because it was challenging and fun and the sex was flat-out fantastic, and did he really expect her to get a taste of that and then just *leave*? Because that was inhumane.

'Of course.' She couldn't look at him.

And then she did look at him, and it wasn't just lust she felt. She also had the strong desire to comfort him and be with him so he didn't have to go through this alone. 'Unless, of course, you think I might be of use to you here. I could stay if you thought that. I've been through the death of a family member before. I know how it goes and what to do. Of course, so do you.'

'I'm trying to spare you, not push you away.' His voice was soft and deep and utterly compelling. 'Would you rather stay?'

'If you—'

'No,' he said gently. *'Moriana First*, remember? You're turning over a new leaf. What do *you* want to do?'

'I want to stay and be of use,' she said, and meant it. She wanted to be with him, stand by him.

'And would you like the lessons and the romance and my awkward moments of oversharing to continue?' he asked, and there was no more denying that he was turning her into a believer of all things Theo.

'Yes.' She nodded, and reached for more bread so she wouldn't reach for him. 'Yes, I would.'

Benedict and his father arrived the following morning. They were put in the west wing, out of the way, no visitors allowed, and Moriana stayed out of their way. Benedict did not dine with them—she didn't see him for two days—but on the morning of the third day he ventured into the garden and when he saw her he headed her way.

He looked haggard and sleep-deprived, but the reason for it was obvious. His father was dying. Theo was ignoring him. This family was a fractured one, and she didn't know what to make of it.

'You were right about the artwork here,' she said when he reached her. 'It really is extraordinary.'

'I know. My ancestors have done us proud. This place. These gardens.' He smiled faintly and looked around. 'There's nothing quite like them.'

'How's your father?'

'Asleep. That's the easy word for what he's doing. Better than unconscious or comatose. The journey here knocked him around, but he knew he was home. He recognised it.'

'Does your father ask for anyone?'

'No.'

'Has Theo seen him yet?'

'No.' Benedict smiled grimly. 'I doubt that's going to happen.'

'Have *you* caught up with Theo yet?'

'Briefly.' Benedict shoved his hands in his pockets as they started walking and she fell into step beside him. 'Not that there was a lot of catching up involved. We haven't been close for years.'

'I heard that.'

'Theo wasn't always like he is now,' said Benedict. 'He was more open as a child. More inclined to let people in. Then his family died, and that dimmed him a lot but he was still accessible. Still him. It was a couple of months after his twenty-third birthday that everything changed between him and me—between him and everyone—and it was like a wall went up overnight and it was twenty feet high and made of obsidian and there was no way to scale it.'

Moriana said nothing.

'God knows I'm not without flaws,' Benedict muttered. 'But they'd never bothered him before. These days I like to think I've got a better handle on those flaws.'

'Do you care for him?' she asked quietly.

'I used to. He was like a brother to me. Now he's a stranger and I'm here under sufferance. Once my father is dead and buried I'll choose a new life and walk away from this one. It's time.'

She'd voiced a similar sentiment only days ago. The circumstances were different but the dream to simply walk away from a life of royal duty was a vivid one at times. Hard to say how it would work in reality. No one she knew had ever been bold enough or weary enough to try.

'You're his closest blood relative. Second in line to the throne. He could use your support.'

Benedict snorted softly. 'Theo doesn't want my support. I've already offered it too many times to count. By the way, this State Dinner tomorrow night that I can no longer avoid—I'm bringing a date. One of the Cordova twins.'

She narrowed her gaze and shot him a sideways glance. 'Why would you do that? To make Theo uncomfortable or to make me uncomfortable?'

'Two birds, one stone,' he said, and then shrugged as if in half-hearted apology. 'Would you believe it wasn't my idea? I owe the Cordovas a favour. They called it in.' Benedict held her gaze. 'Don't be jealous, Moriana. Theo's Theo. He has history with half a dozen women who'll be there tomorrow night, none of whom he ever wanted for his Queen. That list only ever had your name on it. You win. You both win.'

'He…had a list?'

'He had a wish. Why is this news to you? My cousin has never been able to take his eyes off you, even as a kid. He's yours. He always has been.'

'But…'

'Let me guess. His marriage proposal was framed as pure politics.'

'His marriage proposal was a form letter with my name filled in at the top and his signature at the bottom.'

Benedict laughed long and hard.

Moriana glared, until a reluctant tug lifted her lips. 'I hate humour. I'm a serious soul and why can't people just *tell me things*?' she muttered, and set Benedict off all over again.

'Seriously, go easy on my date,' Benedict said when finally he caught his breath. 'You're hard to compete with.'

'You mean I'm the perfect Ice Princess? Because, you've probably been too preoccupied to read the papers but that particular image is swiftly becoming tarnished. This morning I'm apparently intent on blackmailing Theo into marrying me by being pregnant with his triplets.'

Benedict's gaze skidded to her flat stomach. 'Congratulations?'

'Oh, shut it. It's pure fabrication.'

'You don't say.' And then he was grinning again. 'Tomorrow you should tell them they're mine.'

'Tomorrow I'll probably be brawling in public with a Cordova twin. I don't share well.' She chewed on her lip. 'You might want to forewarn her that I'm not feeling merciful.'

'If I do that her twin will want to come along as backup. Not to mention their brother.'

'I'll see to it that two more places are set for you and your friends. I may as well deal with them all at once.'

'You're fearless.'

'So I'm told.'

'Also slightly scary.'

'Spread that thought,' she said encouragingly.

They walked some more in companionable silence, and then Benedict spoke again. 'Moriana, a favour, if you please. If you do mean to invite all the Cordovas to dinner, seat Enrique next to me—as my partner. Because he is. In every sense.'

Oh. 'Oh, I see.' No wonder Benedict didn't want the throne. The fight required to accommodate his partner of choice would be enormous. 'Does Theo know?'

'He knows I enjoy both men and women, yes. I doubt he knows that I've finally made my choice. It's been made for years. Hidden for years.'

Oh, again. 'Does your father know?'

'No.'

'And yet you still want the Cordova brother at your side tomorrow night rather than wait until your father's dead? Why?'

'Because I'm burning bridges. I've no wish to be King and this is the strongest message I can send to those who might be inclined to rally around me after my father's death. Because Enrique thinks I'm ashamed of him and I'm sick of being that man. I don't care any more what anyone thinks. I love Enrique. I can't imagine my life without him in it. End of story.'

'Well, in that case, an invitation for Enrique and his

sisters can be with them this afternoon,' she murmured.
'I'm game if you're sure.'

'I'm sure.'

'You realise you should be having this conversation
with Theo rather than me?' she asked him.

'I can't talk to a wall.' He turned on a smile that
nearly blew Moriana away with its wattage. 'I've decided I like you, Princess. You're easy to talk to, you're
smart and I suspect you're very kind. You're also very
beautiful. Theo chose well for Liesendaach.' He stopped
in front of her, heels together, and reached for her hand
before bowing low and brushing her knuckles with his
lips. 'A favour for me; now it's my turn to do a favour
for you. Never forget—no matter who comes at you from
Theo's past and tries to make you doubt him—never forget that he chose you. He even seems willing to change
his ways for you.'

'You don't know that,' she said raggedly, no matter
how much she suddenly longed to believe it. 'You don't
know him any more.'

'I have my sources. Besides, I still have eyes. He still
watches you as if there's no one but you in the room.
He's watching you now.'

She looked around the garden and back towards the
palace, where the guards stood stationed. Theo stood
with them, hands in the pockets of his trousers. 'How
long has he been there?'

'A few minutes, maybe a few more,' Benedict answered obligingly. 'I don't think he likes you walking
with me. Hence the kiss.'

'What are you, five years old? How is annoying him
going to help your cause?'

'It won't. But it does amuse me. Shall I walk you
back to him?'

'Only if you're going to play nice.'

'Ah, well.' Benedict's amusement hadn't dimmed. 'I was heading to the stables anyway. Your Highness.' He bowed again. 'The pleasure was all mine.'

'You're a rogue.'

'Runs in the blood.'

'You realise I'll more than likely relay our conversation to Theo, word for word.'

'I never would have guessed.'

Benedict smiled as he walked away and she knew that look, even if she'd never seen it on this particular face before.

Do try and keep up, Moriana. You're my conduit to my cousin.

That was the point.

'What did he want?' asked Theo when she joined him. His eyes were flinty and his jaw was hard, and if he thought she was going to be their messenger girl he could think again.

'He wanted to talk to you. Apparently I'm the next best thing. The Cordovas are coming to the State Dinner tomorrow night. All of them, and it's going to be interesting.' She snaked her hand around his neck, with every intention of drawing his lips down towards hers. 'Are you angry with him for waylaying me?'

'Yes.'

'Are you angry with me for letting myself be waylaid?'

His lips stopped mere centimetres from her own. 'Yes.'

'Scared I'll like him?'

Theo's lips tightened. 'He can be charming.'

'I like you more.' She closed the distance between

their lips, not caring who saw them. She closed her eyes and stroked the seam of his lips until he opened for her. He was as ravenously hungry for her as she was for him and the thought soothed her soul even as it inflamed her senses. His arm was a steel band around her waist, the hardness between his legs all the encouragement she needed to continue.

And then one of the nearby guards cleared his throat. 'Photographers,' he said, and Theo's palm cupped her face protectively as he eased them out of the inferno of their kiss.

'Sorry,' she whispered, her confidence evaporating as he escorted her inside.

'Don't be. Think of the headlines. There'll be a love triangle. That or Benedict and I will be sharing you. Either way, you can expect a stern talking-to from your brother. So can I, for that matter.'

Moriana sighed. 'Welcome to my world.'

'I like your world, Princess. And I sure as hell like having you in mine. Don't overthink it.'

And he kissed her again to make sure she wouldn't.

The papers the following morning did not disappoint. *Claimed*, one headline ran, with a trio of pictures directly below it. Theo and Moriana just before that kiss, lips close and tension in every line of their bodies. Then the kiss itself, and it made her hot just to look at because it was a kiss better kept for the bedroom. Her family would despair of her. The third picture had Theo in full protective mode, his hand on her face and her head turned towards his shoulder as he glared at whoever had taken the picture. Mine, mine and *mine* that glare said.

That one she liked.

'Oh, message *received*,' Aury said when she saw the

headline and the pictures. 'That man is going to peel the skin off the flesh of anyone who tries to hurt you. It's even better than the picture of him butt naked. Your future king just bared his soul for you, and he did it for all to see.'

'What do you see?' Moriana snatched the paper back from the other woman. 'What soul?'

'It's there in every line of his body. His focus, the *want* in that kiss, the protection. Oh, this one's going on the fridge.'

'What fridge?' Moriana still couldn't see past her own surrender. 'What soul?'

'That man is totally committed. I knew it!' Aury was beaming. 'This isn't *just* the royal wedding of a generation…this is a love match.'

'Wait! What wedding? No! I'm not in love. I barely know the man. This is a…a sex match, if we ever get around to having sex. And it's convenient.'

'To have a husband who is head over heels in love with you, yes, it's very convenient.' Aury was practically dancing around the room. 'Henry, did you see this?'

'Yes, ma'am.'

'Henry, how many times do I have to tell you to call me Aury?'

Henry smiled with his eyes but his face remained impassive. 'Ma'am, I'm on duty. There are protocols.'

'But we *can* still solicit your opinion on the headlines, yes? It's a matter of state and safety and stuff.' Aury waved her hand in the air, possibly to encapsulate all the stuff she wasn't saying.

'The King knows what he's doing, ma'am.'

'See?' Aury whirled back around to face Moriana. 'Henry thinks Theo's in love.'

'That wasn't what he said.' Moriana did a little hand

waving of her own. 'I need new guards. And I definitely need a new lady-in-waiting.'

'You're right. I'm not waiting any more,' Aury declared. 'You're done. Gone. Claimed by a man who will move heaven and earth for you. It's my turn now.' She glanced at Henry from beneath her lashes.

'Henry,' said Moriana. 'Run.'

'Sorry, Your Highness, but I can't.' Henry looked anything but sorry. 'I'm on duty.'

'Do you want her back?' Theo asked Augustus, neighbouring King and brother of one Moriana of Arun. 'Because she's been here four days and I've lost control of my palace staff, my press coverage and the plot,' said Theo into the phone. He was staring down at the paper and wondering if Moriana was going to speak to him any time soon. *Claimed!* was the headline, and then there were pictures. And the pictures were revealing. Theo wanted to find a hole in the ground and bury himself in it.

Some things were meant to be common knowledge. His dangerous growing infatuation with Moriana was not one of them.

'She's a Combat General in a sundress,' he moaned.

'And you've *claimed* her,' Augustus said smugly. 'Enjoy.'

'You're looking at exactly the same paper as I am, aren't you?'

'When can I post the banns?' How could Augustus sound even more smug?

'I'm working on it. She's invited the Cordova twins and their brother to dinner, at Benedict's request. I'm taking it as a declaration of war on my past.'

'Reasonable call.'

'I don't often ask for advice,' Theo began.

'You've never asked for advice,' Augustus said drily.

'What should I do?'

'Why, Theo, you sit back and enjoy the tempest that is Moriana proving a point. You have to remember, *you wanted to let her run hot!*'

'You're saying this is my fault?'

'I'm saying you wanted it; you've got it.'

'She sent my dying uncle a book of prayer and a book about war.'

'Very subtle. You've already neutralised him. She's simply making sure he sees no avenue of counter attack through her. I imagine that's what inviting the Cordovas will be about too. Moriana's not one for extended torture. She'll give them a hearing, try to get them to reveal their hand, and if she doesn't like what's in it she'll cut them off at the wrist. Your role in this endeavour is to watch and learn what it's like to have my sister in your corner when enemies are present. Should you be foolish enough to reminisce with either of the delectable Cordova twins, you will lose your balls.'

Theo snorted.

'This is Moriana unleashed, remember? What could possibly go wrong?' said Augustus, with the blithe disregard of a man who knew he'd be elsewhere that evening. 'By the way, I'll be sending Moriana's dowry to you by the usual method. Meaning three hundred matched black cavalry horses and their riders will escort the dowry from my palace to yours—in full ceremonial garb.'

'I—what dowry?'

'Didn't she mention it? It's quite considerable. Paintings, linens, jewels, a regiment or two. It'll take the cavalry just under a month to get to you and I suspect Moriana will want to ride with them part of the way.

They should aim to reach your palace one week before the wedding, unless the Liesendaach cavalry decides to meet them at your border. You've met us at the border before, by the way, some three hundred years ago when Princess Gerta of Arun married Liesendaach's good King Regulus. If that happens it may take them all a little longer to reach you on account of all the jousting and swordfights that will likely take place along the way. I've been reading up on royal wedding protocol.'

'You're telling me you want *six hundred* steeds and riders prancing through *my* countryside for two weeks. Guarding *linen*?'

'And you thought Arunians were stern and resoundingly frugal.' Augustus was enjoying this. Theo was mildly horrified to find his reckoning of Augustus's character all wrong. 'Theo, I've already had six meetings with my highest advisors on how to honour Moriana properly should she ever decide to marry you. We will be parting with one of our most revered national treasures. If I had elephants I'd be sending them.'

'Elephants?'

'And now you're repeating my words. My work here is done. Good luck at dinner. Remember, do not take your eyes from the prize. Not that you ever do.'

'You're enjoying this too much.'

'I am. And there's more, and it needs to be said. If ever you want my advice regarding your beloved future wife, just call. I have the experience to help you through. Soon-to-be brother, I am here for you.'

Theo hung up on him.

Never again would he call Augustus of Arun for advice. Never, *ever* again.

CHAPTER EIGHT

MORIANA PREPARED FOR Liesendaach's State Dinner with the same kind of care she gave to any new social situation. She dug into the history of those attending, noted their interests and successes and their relationships to each other, memorised names, and dug deeper into anyone she thought might pose a problem. The information file on the people attending this dinner was already three hundred pages long, not including the staff, for she would have her eyes on them too, looking for areas of improvement.

Aury was on deck to guide her clothing choices and so too was the sixty-four-year-old former seamstress to Theo's mother and mother to bodyguard Henry. Of late, Letitia Hale had been a chambermaid and palace function assistant, which was, to Moriana's way of thinking, a regrettable waste of palace resources that she would see rectified. Letitia had a lifetime of service to call on and the inside knowledge Moriana needed when it came to what palace guests would be wearing.

Wise Owl Counsel, Aury called her. 'We need her,' she said, and Moriana agreed.

Henry just called her Mother.

'This evening I need to outshine the Cordova twins

and every other woman Theo has ever bedded,' Moriana told them.

'An admirable goal; I'm all for it,' said Aury. 'But we don't have half your jewellery here. Intimidation by necklace is going to be difficult.'

'Let's start with the gown. What did I bring?'

'Forest-green, floor-length and backless?' Aury disappeared into the dressing room and returned moments later with the garment. It was another one from Moriana's love-it-but-never-wear-it collection.

'Did you bring *anything* I normally wear?'

'Ah…'

'What *did* you bring?'

'The silver gown that makes you look like a fairy tale villain. Your favourite black gown—always a winner. The beaded amber with the ivory chiffon.'

'Can we see that last one?' said Letitia. 'Please?'

Aury brought it forward.

'Yes,' said Letitia. 'That one. The dining room is decorated in ivory with amber and silver accents. The tables are polished walnut, the floors a shade darker; the tableware has blue accents. The gown will play to all of those colours. Plus, the beading on that dress is magnificent.'

It was and there was no denying it. The strapless bodice was beaded, the fall of the chiffon skirt inspired. Back in Arun she'd have felt overdressed but it was the type of gown this palace called for. Elegant yet showy too, no apologies. Moriana had never worn it before, had never had to choose jewellery to match. Aury had not been remiss when it came to packing jewellery to go with the gown. The coffers of Arun didn't *have* any jewellery to match this one.

'The amber beaded gown it is,' she said. 'What jewellery *did* we bring? And if we brought sapphires let's ignore them. I'd rather not match the tableware.'

'Why did we not pack rubies?' said Aury, decidedly upset. 'I don't think we have time to—'

'Aury,' Moriana said gently, 'don't worry about it. We don't have anything that fits this dress. You know it as well as I do. There's no shame in it. Besides, I have it on good authority that I'm intimidating enough, even without the jewels.'

'Well, this is true,' said Aury, slightly mollified.

'Liesendaach has Crown Jewels to match the gown,' said Letitia and promptly blushed. 'It was my job to know what jewels were available to the late Queen. I often designed dresses around them. I wasn't only a seamstress.' The Honourable Letitia looked to Aury. 'What the Lady Aury is to you—that was my role.'

Confidante. Friend. Moriana vowed, then and there, to make this woman an integral part of her world, should she ever reside here permanently. Gifts like Letitia should never be shelved.

'You could always ask His Majesty for access to Liesendaach's jewellery vault,' said Aury boldly. 'Nothing ventured.'

'I could.' Moriana chewed on her lower lip. On the other hand, she'd already been imposing her will all over the place and it seemed somewhat presumptuous to be calling on Liesendaach's treasures. 'Okay, calling for a vote from all present, and no exceptions, Henry, or your mother will find out. Do I ask Theo to let me at Liesendaach's Crown Jewels? If yes, say aye.'

'Aye,' said Aury swiftly, still holding up the amber and ivory beaded gown as her gaze drifted to some point behind Moriana. 'Oh, hello, Your Majesty.'

'Lady Aury,' said a dry voice from the doorway, and

there stood Theo. He wasn't dressed for dinner yet, but he was wearing a suit nonetheless and it fitted him to perfection. 'What do you need?'

'Rubies,' said Aury.

At the same time Letitia said, 'The South Sea Collection.'

'Both,' said Aury, ever the opportunist.

Moriana turned. Theo smiled.

'Your brother is wanting three hundred of my mounted guards to be put at your disposal for a month should you ever decide to marry me, and I said yes,' he said by way of hello. 'Do you seriously think I'll object to you requesting old jewellery that's there for the wearing? One of these actions involves prostrating myself before my cavalry and begging their forgiveness. The other involves walking down to the vault and opening a drawer.'

'I adore pragmatic kings,' said Aury. 'Truly, they're in a league of their own.'

Moriana agreed but she had other angles to pursue. There was a lot to unpack in his offhand comment. 'What do I want three hundred of your mounted guards for?'

'Your wedding procession. Apparently.'

'You've spoken to Augustus?' He must have done. 'Did you know that royal Arunian dowries used to be delivered on the backs of elephants?'

'So I've heard.'

Moriana smiled. Aury looked utterly angelic, as was her wont. Letitia looked vaguely interested, in a serene, grandmotherly fashion that belied her sharp mind, and the guards at the door never moved a muscle—facial muscles included.

'Elephants in procession,' she murmured. 'Think about it. There are lesser evils.'

'Whatever you want from Liesendaach's vaults by way of jewellery you can have,' he countered. 'Anything rubies and the South Sea Collection. What else?'

'That's it.'

Letitia nodded. Aury nodded. Henry observed.

'I'm cultivating a new image that involves less austerity and more...something,' Moriana explained.

'*Something* being a whole lot more in-your-face fairy tale beauty,' added Aury.

'I can't wait.'

Hopefully he could. 'Is there a battle room where we gather beforehand to discuss strategy?'

'Not until now,' Theo murmured. 'But stateroom six should serve the purpose. Anything else you need?'

'The name of every person in attendance tonight that you've ever been intimate with.' The words were out of her mouth before she could call them back.

Theo looked as calm as ever, even if it felt as if everyone else in the room had taken a breath and held it.

'That's not a list you need to worry about,' he said.

His opinion, not hers. Forewarned was forearmed. 'Shall I simply assume everyone between twenty and fifty is a possibility, then?'

'You can assume it won't be a problem.' His voice carried a cool warning. 'Leave us,' he told everyone else in the room, and they left and Moriana held his gaze defiantly. She shouldn't have asked for the list in front of his people or hers. Chances were she shouldn't have asked for it at all, but she wanted to be as prepared as she could for the evening ahead, and that included being prepared for smiling barbs from the women Theo had bedded and then spurned.

He strode lazily over to where she sat at her dressing table and took up the space Aury usually occupied, facing her and a little to the right.

'Want to tell me what's wrong?' he asked quietly.

'Nerves.' Enough to make her hands shake when they weren't folded in her lap. Enough to make her drop her gaze. New court, new people, new...*hope* that this thing between her and Theo was going to work out fine. 'Fear of making mistakes tonight. Fear of letting people down.'

'You won't.'

'I just did, when I asked for the list in front of everyone. But I'm not jealous, not...really. I always do this. I like to be prepared.' She gestured towards the sheaf of papers on the dressing table in front of her. It had the name and head shot of every person attending the dinner on it, along with a brief rundown on their interests, family lives and political affiliations.

He picked it up and scanned the first page and the next.

'I have it almost memorised. A couple more hours should do it.'

'You do this for every event you attend?' His eyes were sharp, his expression non-committal.

'I used to.' Her mother had insisted. 'I don't need to be quite as diligent at home any more. I remember them all. I haven't made a mistake in years. I don't want to make mistakes here either.'

He frowned. 'I don't expect you to remember the name and occupation of everyone at dinner tonight. There will be over two hundred people there. No one expects that of you.'

'Which will make it all the better when I do.'

'Are you having fun?' he asked abruptly.

'What?'

'Is this fun for you?'

Not exactly. She'd woken up feeling anxious, had barely touched her breakfast, been blissfully distracted by Theo's daily lesson, and then had reverted straight back to a state of anxiety the moment he'd left.

She had work to do. She still did. 'I don't understand,' she said, and wanted to squirm beneath his fiercely intent gaze. 'It doesn't have to be fun. This is my job. This is what I do.'

'Not today,' he said. 'I have to look at yearling horses this morning. My horse-breeding specialist has brought them in for selection. You can come too. Help us choose.'

'Theo, I don't have time for this.' She put out her hand and he took it, but only to pull her from the chair and coax her to lean into him.

'Humour me.' He could make her melt when his voice was pitched just so. 'I'll have you back in time to dress.'

Which was how she found herself far from the castle, on the other side of the forest, driving alongside a high stone wall that seemed to stretch for miles. Theo drove them through an elaborate set of wrought iron gates and finally the stables came into view.

It was a huge three-sided structure with an arena in the middle as big as a soccer field. She'd seen similar in Arun—where the mounted regiments were based— but never had she seen climbing roses frame the stable stalls the way they did here.

Theo raised his hand in greeting to a woman on the other side of the arena. The woman lifted her hand in return and started walking towards them, and the closer she got the more familiar she seemed.

She had a perfect face and eyes so deeply violet

they looked painted, and she was dressed for riding. The woman was from Moriana's mother's era, and she greeted Theo like an old beloved friend.

'Belle,' he said, 'this is Moriana. Belle is in charge of the horse breeding programme that supplies Liesend-aach's mounted guard.'

The name clued Moriana in, even though she'd never met Belle in person. This was Theo's father's legendary mistress—the circus performer he'd always kept close, no matter what.

'Ah. You know my name.' Belle's smile turned wry. 'Many don't in this day and age but I had a feeling you might. I like to think I was the late King's favourite mistress, but he never did say and I never did ask. And you, of course, are the Arunian Princess. I remember a very young Theo getting positively indignant about you from time to time. Apparently your mother never taught you how to handle boys of his ilk. Trust me, a smile and a compliment would have made him your slave.'

'I would have liked to know that,' Moriana said.

'It's never too late. Come, let me show you the year-lings before I let them out into the arena. Benedict has already been by to make his choices.'

Theo eyed the older woman sharply. 'They're not his choices to make.'

'And yet I value his opinion and so should you,' Belle admonished. 'No one has a better eye for temperament than your cousin—not even you.'

'So tell me what else you look for in the yearlings you choose?' asked Moriana hurriedly, hoping to pre-vent argument.

'Let me show you instead,' said Belle, gesturing them towards the nearest stall.

It wasn't difficult to feign interest in the horses on

show. They were big grey warmbloods with hundreds of years' worth of breeding behind them, many of them destined to serve in Theo's mounted regiment. There was a gelding with one white leg and Belle hurriedly went on to explain that, aside from colour, the horse had perfect form and his leadership qualities amongst the other yearlings were well established. The horse was unshakeable, Belle said. 'He does everything in his power to compensate for not being the perfect colour.'

'You know we don't take marked horses.'

'Make an exception,' Belle said, but Theo did not reply.

'If you don't keep him, I will,' Belle said next. 'Or Benedict will. He has a soft spot for imperfection, that boy. Here he is now.' She looked beyond them and Moriana turned too, just in time to see Benedict leading a saddled black horse in through the double doors at one end of the stable complex. 'That's Satan,' said Belle. 'I brought his grandsire with me when I left the circus, and he's a menace to ride. Too smart for his own good. Benedict always takes him out when he visits. I get the impression they both enjoy the challenge.'

Benedict had seen them and nodded in their direction. Theo's expression hardened.

'He won't come to you, if that's what you're worried about,' said Belle drily. 'Even as a boy he knew better than to abandon a freshly ridden horse in my stables.'

True enough, Benedict handed the saddle off to a groom and haltered the horse himself before leading it to the wash area. But he looked back at Theo and beckoned him over with the tiniest tilt of his head.

'Have you asked after his father yet today?'

'The physicians keep me updated.'

'Physicians don't know politics,' said Belle. 'Perhaps you should see what he wants.'

'Did he know I was going to be here?'

'He's here every morning, Theodosius, from around five a.m. onwards, and I put him to work. Just like when he was a boy.'

With a curt, 'Excuse me,' Theo headed towards his cousin.

'Shall we continue our rounds?' Belle asked Moriana and, without waiting for a reply, made her way to the next stall. This one was a filly, proud and fully grey.

'I've never seen Theo so easily led,' Moriana said finally, polite conversation be damned. 'How did you do that?'

'It helps that I've known both those boys since their teens. They were inseparable once.'

'Do you know why that changed?'

'I have my suspicions.'

'A woman?'

Belle snorted. 'They never fought over women—there were always so many to choose from—and for Benedict, men and women both. No. I fear the rift was caused by something far less mundane.'

'Can it be mended?'

'I try to help.' Belle smiled. 'Perhaps you will try too. Now, *this* filly has an interesting bloodline…'

Theo didn't wait until Benedict had finished hosing down the horse before speaking. *Get in, get out, keep it short.* Those were his rules when dealing with Benedict. 'You have something to say?'

Benedict nodded, not even sparing him a glance as he turned the hose off and picked up a nearby scraper. 'You're not going to like it.'

No surprises there.

'My father filed the petition for your dismissal early this morning. He says he has the numbers and he doesn't care that I've no intention of challenging you for the position and that there is no other option from our bloodline. He's simply in it for the chaos now. It's his parting gift to you.'

'He has to know I'll fight it.'

'I'm sure he does.'

'And that I'll win.'

'You usually do.' Benedict began stripping water from the horse's back. He rode them hard, as a rule, but never beyond what a horse would willingly take and the care he took of his ride afterwards would have done an Olympic athlete proud. 'You could announce your engagement to Moriana and bury the petition within a day.'

He could. That had been his intention all along and he'd made no secret of it. And yet... *Moriana First.* 'Not happening,' he grated.

'Why not? It's the perfect solution. You've always been hard for her.'

'Because I've already asked and she didn't accept.'

Wicked amusement danced across Benedict's face. '*You* couldn't get the girl? Oh, that's beautiful.'

Never give Benedict ammunition. Why could Theo never remember that? 'If I applied pressure to Moriana now and appealed to her sense of duty and the need for ongoing regional stability, I *would* get the girl. But I'm not going to do it. For the first time in her life Moriana has a chance to make up her own mind about what she wants to do and who she wants to be, going forward. I'm not going to take that away from her.'

'You're getting soft.'

It wasn't a compliment. 'You want to know what Moriana was up in her rooms doing just now? She was memorising tonight's guest list. She has dossiers of information on every guest invited. And she was miserable. Near frantic with worry that she wouldn't perform to expectations. That's not the life I want for her. She deserves more. She has to believe she can find happiness here, and I'll wait on her answer for eternity if I have to. I will not put time pressure on this decision. My court, my people, they can all *wait* on her answer.'

'And if her answer is no?'

Benedict sounded strangely subdued and now Theo was the one who needed to be doing something with his hands. He picked up a towel and began to rub the horse dry. 'If it's no, only then will I consider other options. Because she's it for me.' It was easier to say it to the side of a horse than it was to say it to a person. 'She always has been.'

Voices carried here. Belle had to know it, for she'd shepherded Moriana into a stall to examine a foaling mare. They were out of sight but plenty close enough to overhear the conversation between Theo and Benedict. And now the older woman was leaning against a stable wall, scuffing patterns in the sawdust with her boot, listening, as Moriana was listening, and Theo was putting his crown on the line. Declaring his allegiance not to his country first but to Moriana's happiness.

And then Belle's gaze met hers. 'I've only ever loved one man,' Belle said quietly. 'I gave up my world for him and I loved him as hard as I could—whenever he wanted, wherever he wanted—and he took, and he took, and he *took*. I've always told myself a King can never afford to put a woman first, but he can. And some do.'

And then Belle moved forward and her hand snaked

out to catch a tiny hoof that had appeared beneath the mare's tail. 'Aha. This foal is breech. I thought as much.' She smiled conspiratorially. 'Do you want to see what those two boys can do when they work together?' And in a louder voice that was bound to carry, 'Theo! Benedict! We need a hand. Or two.'

CHAPTER NINE

MORIANA DRESSED FOR the evening with uncommon care. Some of Liesendaach's Crown Jewels had been delivered to her room in her absence, and Aury and Letitia fussed and compared and had a glorious time and Moriana let them. The list of names she hadn't finished memorising sat to one side of her dressing table. A little wooden box sat on the other side, and she knew exactly what was in it, even if Aury didn't. She'd put it there herself as a reminder of a decision that needed to be made. A decision Theo had not asked her to revisit but he *needed* her to revisit it nonetheless.

She thought he might have said something about the petition on their way back from the stables, but he hadn't. He'd talked of the new foal instead—a little colt that he and Benedict had delivered with ease.

When they reached the palace entrance he'd excused himself from her company. He had a little business to attend to before the dinner, he'd said. And kept her clueless as to the nature of it.

The amber gown with the beaded bodice won them all over once she had it on, and the diamonds and pearls of the South Sea Collection complemented it beautifully. First the earrings and then the necklace. There was a bracelet too, but she waved it away. 'I think the white gloves instead,' she said. The ones that went up and over her elbows. She could take them off at some point. And then…

She reached for the little wooden box and snapped it open, her decision made.

And then Theo would have his answer.

She slid it onto her wedding ring finger and Aury gasped. 'Is that…?'

'Yes.'

'Congratulations, Your Highness,' said Letitia.

'When did this *happen*?' asked Aury.

'He asked me before we came here. I've been trying to decide what to do ever since. And now I have.'

'But…are you sure?' Aury's eyes were dark with concern. 'I mean, I know the two of you get on better than you used to, but if you're going to obsess over all of his past conquests, I mean, that's not a habit you want to get into if you want to stay healthy.'

'I know,' she murmured. 'I'm over it.' *She's it for me. She always has been. She has to believe she can find happiness here.*

The sex, the fun, all the attention Theo had paid to her needs these past few days had come together in one blinding moment of clarity. He cared for her. He was willing to put her needs before the needs of the Crown and his own best interests.

Theo might not call that love, but it was close enough.

She wanted this.

She wanted him.

Duty and passion—and a little bit of trust and that thing they weren't calling *love*—had made the decision easy. She *wanted* to stand beside this man, proudly and for ever.

And love him.

'Wish me luck,' she said as she pulled the glove on over the ring and began to work her fingers into it. 'He doesn't know my answer yet.'

Aury snorted. 'You're going to slay him.'

'One can only hope.' She worked the other glove on, took a deep breath and reached for the royal blue sash that proclaimed her a Princess of Arun. Aury helped her slip it on and fastened it with a clasp that proclaimed the highest honours a King could bestow. When she straightened again her posture was perfect.

'You will not fail me,' she told the regal woman staring back at her from the mirror. 'You are a Princess of Arun and a future Queen of Liesendaach. You've got this.'

Aury nodded, her expression grave. The lady-in-waiting had heard it all before, the pep talks that masked Moriana's screaming insecurity every time she had to perform in public.

'Milady, Your Highness—' Letitia looked to the floor, her fingers twisting together with either hesitation or anxiety '—on behalf of myself and…and others—all the people you've taken the time to get to know this week, so many of whose names you already know—we are so very proud to serve you. We are grateful for your care.' She raised her eyes. 'We will not fail you either.'

She never forgot a name. Theo watched in outright awe as Moriana worked the room. He'd seen her in action before but that was on her turf, with dignitaries she'd grown up with. That she could so easily converse here was a testament to ruthless discipline and hours of preparation.

She favoured no one, except perhaps Benedict, who

she'd shared a few words with towards the beginning of the evening.

Theo's uncle was unwell, unable to make the dinner and receiving no visitors. Theo had already uttered that line more times than he cared to remember. He wondered cynically if he hadn't been playing into his uncle's hands by not allowing him visitors. Would so many from his court support the petition to dethrone Theo if they knew Constantine of Liesendaach was dying?

They must know, some of them. And they were behind the petition regardless.

Theo had been in a foul mood ever since his conversation with Benedict and not even saving the little colt had shifted it. Did his court really want him gone or were they simply trying to mobilise him towards marriage? He knew what they wanted.

He'd never thought dragging his feet on the issue could cost him the Crown.

He'd put a security detail on Benedict the minute he'd returned to the palace. He wanted to know who Benedict spoke to, who he phoned, what was said.

Benedict hadn't gone to see his father before dinner. He'd called the Cordova house and spoken to the brother, a curt conversation that hadn't gone well, according to the security team. He'd dressed for dinner. Taken two whiskies and paced his sitting room until it was time to attend.

Theo wished he knew how to trust his cousin the way he'd trusted him as a child.

Had Benedict been complicit in his father's plans?

If only he *knew.*

Theo watched his cousin move assuredly between one group of people and the next, and wondered exactly when the thought had taken hold that Benedict had to have known about his father's plans.

Shortly after Theo had obtained proof of his uncle's actions, he figured grimly. He'd re-examined every move the people around him had ever made, and Benedict hadn't made the cut.

Moriana and her brother had, and so had Casimir. Valentine and his sister—the royal children of Thallasia—had made the grade. No one older had—there'd been too much doubt.

'What's he done?' asked a voice from beside him, and there stood Theo's Head of Household Staff, a picture of elegance and efficiency in black trousers, black shirt and buttoned blazer.

'Who?'

Sam sent him one of those looks that told him she was aware of his avoidance tactic but she didn't call him on it outright.

'Why are you here?' She usually left the running of state dinners to the functions team.

'Her Highness wanted things done a certain way tonight. I'm making sure it happens.' Sam looked unruffled.

Theo eyed her warily. 'Is that a problem?' he asked.

'No problem. Quite frankly, it's an honour. This is me wanting to make a good impression on a woman who can teach me, and possibly everyone else around here, how best to run a royal household.'

He nodded, his attention already returning to his cousin. Moriana was with Benedict again; she'd sought him out and the conversation they were having looked to be a private one, their dark heads bent towards one another, familiar enough to be close in each other's space. Any closer and tomorrow's press would have them eloping.

The press was fascinated by the newly emerging Moriana—the one who'd always moved through the spotlight with seeming effortlessness. Her dress made her look every inch the Princess she was and the Liesendaach jewels had not gone unnoticed. Her long white gloves were driving him mad. All he wanted to do was take her some place private and peel them off, and why stop there?

Theo watched as Benedict smiled unhappily and Moriana touched her hand to his forearm in comfort as she started to speak again.

And then she pulled back and began to peel her gloves off. Why the hell was she doing that? So she could touch Benedict with her bare hands?

Theo's feet were moving before his brain had even made sense of it. All he knew was that the time for watching from afar was over and that Benedict needed to step away from Moriana right about *now*.

They looked up as he approached, Benedict's gaze widening and then turning assessing.

And then Theo looked down at Moriana's bare arms and hands. Only they weren't quite bare because she was wearing his engagement ring.

Happiness licked through him, fierce and complete. Moriana was his. *To have and to hold*, and he'd never wanted anything more than he wanted this. His world narrowed to a point, sharp and bright, as he lifted her hand and put the ring to his lips, and then his lips to hers. 'Are you sure?' he asked, rough and gruff against her lips.

'I'm sure,' she whispered, and put her beringed hand to his cheek. 'I want this.'

'For yourself.' He had to be sure.

'You're very persuasive.'

'Can someone please spare me?' said Benedict. 'I don't want to be sick. The stains, they never come out of the sashes.'

Moriana blushed and dropped her hand. Theo glared at Benedict. 'I'm sorry—are we boring you?'

'Yes,' said Benedict. 'A thousand times *yes*.'

Never give Benedict a tree branch to club you with. Because he would.

'Benedict, there you are!'

Theo turned to scowl at whoever dared interrupt them and there stood Angelique Cordova, wearing a red gown and a serene smile. *Perfect.* That was all they needed. But she was Benedict's date, and Benedict stepped back to allow more room in the circle for her.

'I gather you got Enrique's message?' Angelique said next.

'Yes.' Benedict smiled bleakly, but then he rallied and gave her a kiss on the cheek. 'Thank you for coming.'

'Someone had to support you, darling. We couldn't *all* leave you hanging. We're family.'

'How so?' asked Theo.

'Family of the heart,' she said next. 'Bear with my brother, Benedict. He's frightened for you as well as himself. He thinks now is not the time and I happen to agree with him.' She glanced up, as if only now noticing Moriana, and dropped into an elegant curtsey.

Benedict sighed, and waved his hand in a languid parody of an introduction. 'Your Highness, Princess Moriana of Arun, and so on and so forth, may I present my lovely companion for this evening, the utterly fearless Angelique Cordova, one of the brightest lights of my life. Or, at the very least, a matchstick in the darkness.'

'Pig,' she said and turned towards Moriana and curtseyed again. 'A pleasure to meet you, Your Highness. I've heard so much about you.'

'Tell her you have so much in common,' Benedict prompted his date maliciously.

'Be a boor then,' Angelique replied smoothly. 'I intend to do no such thing.'

'I'm happy to finally meet you, Ms Cordova.' Moriana had rallied in the face of the interruption and was every inch the regal princess. 'I hear we have a lot in common.'

Theo blinked. Benedict crowed a laugh. Angelique looked momentarily startled but recovered quickly.

'Only in that I gave the world countless opportunities to tease Theo for his utter inability to tell two women apart. Of course, that then backfired because men will be men, and I'm now known as a woman not memorable enough to require close attention. I truly wish we'd never pulled that foolish stunt, but the world still turns, no?'

'Indeed it does,' Moriana murmured.

'May I offer my congratulations on your engagement?' the woman said next.

'You're the first to congratulate us,' said Moriana lightly. 'Thank you.'

'Please, let me be the second to offer my congratulations,' said Benedict. 'Assuming, of course, that Theo doesn't mess it up by assuming you don't really mean it.'

'But I do really mean it,' said Moriana.

'Good for you. Tell him often.'

And then Sam was between them, drawing Theo's attention with a glance. 'Your Majesty, my apology for interrupting but your uncle's physicians are requesting a word with both you and Prince Benedict. Now.'

That couldn't be good. 'Where are they?'

'In your uncle's room, Your Majesty.'

'Go,' said Moriana. 'I can hold the fort here until your return. I suspect Ms Cordova and I can amuse ourselves and doubtless find more shared interests in your absence.'

The mind boggled. Theo wanted not to think about it. Ever.

'Yes, that's not going to set tongues wagging at all,' murmured Angelique Cordova, heavy on the caution. 'Are you sure?'

'I don't think tomorrow is going to be a slow news day,' Moriana said and pressed a kiss first to Theo's cheek before turning to Benedict and doing the same. 'Go.'

'Scary woman,' said Benedict when they were halfway along the west wing corridor. There were guards to the rear and more up ahead but otherwise they were alone.

'Which one?'

'Yours. I waver between being totally intimidated by her one minute and wanting to bask in her attention the next.'

'Stay away from her.' Of all the emotions seething inside him, this one was foremost.

Benedict frowned and glanced Theo's way. 'I'm not a threat to you where she's concerned.'

'I know better than to believe you.'

'Then you're a fool.'

Benedict subsided into silence and Theo was glad of it. They walked the rest of the wing in silence until they reached the suite of rooms that currently housed Benedict's father. Two security guards stood sentry; one of them opened the door for them and Theo stood back to let Benedict through first—and that *was* a first. Benedict's startled glance and hesitation in stepping forward confirmed it.

'He's not my dying father,' Theo said and waved his cousin forward. It was a callous move rather than an act of respect and Benedict knew it.

'You're a monster,' Benedict muttered.

An insecure, needy, untrusting one, yes.

Theo let Benedict ask most of the questions as they spoke first to the physicians and then entered the bedroom where Constantine of Liesendaach lay. They'd taken away all life support machinery and the man lay in bed, his eyes closed and the shallow rise and fall of his chest the only indication that he still lived. *Not long now*, the physicians had said. *Tonight*. The shadow of death was in the room.

Benedict sat beside his father and took his hand, but when the old man's eyes slitted open they focused on Theo, not Benedict.

'I knew you'd come,' said Constantine, his voice no more than a rasping protest against a throat too close to seizing. 'You want to confront me before I die.'

'Maybe I do. Maybe it's time.' Theo had kept the knowledge so close that sometimes he'd felt as if it was strangling him. But it was family business and if Constantine wanted to air it, family would bear witness. 'I know you killed my family,' he told the dying man. 'I've had proof of it for years and I don't care for your denial and I sure as hell don't care to hear your confession. You did it. I know it. I know why, and I only have one question left. Did Benedict know of your plans?'

The cadaverous old man wet his shrunken lips with his tongue, tried to speak and then started to laugh before any words formed. 'That keep you awake…at night…boy?'

'Yes.' It was no lie, and there was no ignoring Benedict's pale and frozen face.

'Father, what—?'

Benedict stopped speaking when his father started coughing but it wasn't so much coughing as it was cracked and rattling laughter. 'My weak, pathetic…son. Think I don't know…about your sodomy…or your plans to renounce your family? No loss. No loss.'

Benedict recoiled from that serpent's tongue but Theo moved in; his need to know the truth was riding him hard. 'I'm talking to you, old man. Did Benedict know of your plans?'

'Weak…like his mother. Soft…'

'Answer me!'

His uncle's eyes gleamed with pure malice. 'Don't think I…will.'

But Theo wasn't looking at his uncle any more; his attention was solely for his cousin and the blank, uncomprehending shock in Benedict's eyes as he stared at Theo. Theo pushed away from his chair, toppling it as he stood.

'Did you know? Is that why you saved me?' This time Theo's question was for Benedict.

'Is that what you think? You truly believe me capable of saving you and letting the rest of your family fall? What for, Theo? To what purpose? Because I'm my father's son? Does it sound to you as if I enjoy his approval?' Benedict looked shattered, lost in memories maybe, or mired in his father's cruel contempt. *'This* is what you've been punishing me for all these years?'

Benedict stepped back, and then again, still facing them both. As if he didn't dare turn his back on either of them. And then he drew himself up. 'Father, I've never been the son you wanted. I've always known it. I used to crave your approval, more than anything. I don't any more. I have value—maybe not to you or to the King, but to some, and I am content.' Benedict turned to Theo next. 'I renounce you.' Benedict's voice shook. 'I absolve you of all dealings with me, going forward. We are not kin. I have no King. Now, get out of my sight while my father dies, and then I will get out of yours.'

It was no small matter, renouncing one's family. It was a testament to how badly Theo had handled things here tonight. He'd left cool intellect at the door, already emotionally engaged and disinclined to give Benedict the benefit of the doubt. He'd let the old man get to him while simultaneously trying to analyse Benedict's reaction, and now the old man was laughing, and Benedict was broken and Theo was responsible. 'Do you need— would you like anyone else with you? I can bring Angelique.'

'Unfortunately, she's not the Cordova for me.' Benedict crossed to the sideboard and poured a full tumbler of Scotch.

'Her brother then. I can get him here.'

'Why? So you can display your tolerance for our kind?'

'So you're not alone,' Theo said doggedly.

'Too late.' Benedict scowled. 'He won't come.'

'Then I'll stay.' He held his cousin's bitter gaze.

'You just want to hear your family's murderer draw his last breath.'

'I would see that chapter of my life closed and a new one opened, yes,' Theo admitted. 'Benedict, I'm sorry I ever doubted you.'

'Yeah, well.' Benedict drained his drink in one hit and opted to pour another. 'Your loss.'

Constantine of Liesendaach, former Prince Regent and father to Benedict, died during the main course of Moriana's first State Dinner in Liesendaach. Both Theo and Benedict were absent when the meal was served and rumours had already started to spread as to why. Some said they were in conflict over Moriana's favouring of Benedict earlier in the evening. Others declared Angelique Cordova the bone over which they fought. Moriana withstood the mutterings until the main course had been cleared away and then stood and held up her hand for silence.

Two hundred people quietened and stared at her with varying degrees of tolerance. Her introduction to Liesendaach society wasn't exactly going to plan but there was nothing she could do except stand tall and bear their regard.

She was a Princess of Arun and the future Queen of Liesendaach, assuming Theo didn't want his ring back. And she would damn well command their attention if she wanted it.

'Many of you here tonight have offered congratulations on my engagement to your King, and I welcome it,' she said. 'All of you are no doubt wondering where my fiancé is right now. You might be thinking what could possibly lure him from my side? Is Moriana of Arun being jilted? *Again.*'

A titter of nervous laughter ran the length of the room.

'Exactly,' she said drily, and lowered her hand now that she had their attention. 'Former Prince Regent, Constantine of Liesendaach, died ten minutes ago. Prince Benedict and the King attended him, and won't be returning to dine with you this evening. Dessert will be served directly, after which we'll bring the evening to an early conclusion. I look forward to meeting you all again under easier circumstances and I thank you for your understanding.'

She didn't expect applause and she didn't get it. Her appetite for sweets was non-existent. For the first time in her life, she walked out of a function and didn't care if she was doing right or wrong. She caught the Cordova twin's eye on the way to the door and gestured for her to join her. Benedict had brought her here. Moriana would not abandon her.

'What now?' asked the other woman once they were clear of the dining room. But Moriana's confidence had run out.

'We go and find them.' Although, given the way tonight was running, they'd probably stumble straight into whatever it was that Benedict and Theo needed to sort out between themselves.

'I need to call my brother,' said the other woman. 'He'll want to know.'

'Brothers are like that.' Augustus too could do with an update. 'Do you need privacy? I'm sure there are rooms available.'

'Here is fine, Your Highness.'

She could like Angelique Cordova, given the chance. 'See if you can get your brother here. I'll see to it that he has security clearance.'

'I'll try, Your Highness, but, with all due respect, it may be better if I simply find Benedict and take him home. My brother will be waiting.'

Moriana nodded and turned to walk away.

'Your Highness, thank you for your patronage this evening. It was more than I expected.'

It was more than Moriana had expected to give the Cordova twin, truth be told, but she didn't regret it. 'My mother used to tell me to face my fears rather than let them grow. And I did fear you, just a little, as a woman who might have held Theo's heart.'

Angelique Cordova smiled ruefully. 'I never even came close, and neither did my sister.'

'Tell your sister I'd like to meet her too. Perhaps we could all go riding one day. Tell me, do you ride?'

'Since infancy, Your Highness. My father breeds horses in Spain. They're quite famous.' Angelique Cordova paused. 'But then, you already knew that.'

'I did. Still. There's a forest here I've yet to explore and an entire regiment of mounted guards with nothing to do but tend horses. I'm sure some of them could be persuaded to accompany us.'

'That would definitely be a pretty ride.'

Aury was going to like this woman too.

Angelique Cordova took her leave, pulling a phone from her evening bag and retreating to the far corner of the ballroom foyer for privacy.

As for finding Theo and Benedict, Sam was heading her way and would probably know. 'Where are they?'

'Benedict went to his rooms and the King is in the Lower West Library. Past the Rafael, two doors down on the left. Neither of them are in fine spirits.'

That was hardly a surprise. 'You'll see to it that the guests take their leave?'

'Leave it with us.'

'Thank you, Sam. The meal was delicious and the service was prompt and unobtrusive. Let the kitchen know I'm pleased.'

'Yes, ma'am.'

'And have some food sent to Theo. He hasn't eaten yet.'

'Yes, ma'am. Shall I organise a meal for the Prince as well?'

'No. Just take Angelique Cordova to him once she finishes her call.'

Moriana found Theo in a room that reminded her less of a library and more of her father's den. Dark leather and wood dominated a setting scattered with low reading lamps, deep wingback chairs and a wall full of books with ancient spines. There was a bottle of whisky on the table at Theo's side and one crystal tumbler. He watched her come in but said nothing. He didn't smile.

'I'm guessing it was a rough finish,' she said, approaching cautiously. She didn't know this Theo, the one with the burning eyes and the coiled tension. Her teasing suitor was gone and in his place stood a man with a gleam in his eye that said, *Don't push me—stay back*.

She never had learned how to back away from a situation she didn't know how to deal with. She'd only ever learned how to push on and muddle through.

Theo didn't answer her so she filled his silence with words. 'The dinner is winding up. I announced that your uncle had died and you wouldn't be returning. I hope I didn't overstep.'

'Do you ever? You're the perfect princess. What more could a man want?'

Something else, judging by the sneer on his face, and she should have retreated then and there and left him to his grieving. The ring on her finger had never felt heavier. She hadn't even *warned* him she would be wearing it. 'May I stay and have a drink with you?' she asked.

'Help yourself.'

She did and eyed him pensively while she sipped. 'Did you and Benedict clear up your differences?'

'No.' Theo drained the rest of his drink.

'Is it because Liesendaach's royal family can't accommodate his relationship preferences?'

'Benedict can bed whoever he wants.' Theo's lips curled. 'As long as it's not you.'

'Where did *that* come from? You know I will never encourage Benedict to see me as romantically available. I mean...how can you not know that? I'm wearing your ring. What have I *ever* done to make you or anyone else think I'll not honour my promises?'

'Nothing.' He put his drink down and slumped forward in his chair, elbows to knees and hands clasped loosely together. He fingered the royal signet ring on his middle finger, looking for all the world like a penitent boy. 'I trust you. I do. I was just...jealous earlier, when you put your hand on his arm.'

'It was an act of comfort. His partner refused to attend the dinner. He was upset.'

'He was playing you.'

'No, Theo. He wasn't. Benedict is at his most vicious when he's upset. How can you not know that? It's all he ever is around you. And as for you... You never give him the benefit of the doubt. Why is that? What did he do to you?'

Theo ducked his head and ran his hand through his hair. 'Trust, right? I need to trust you with my secrets and my failings, even the worst of them. Even the ones you'll think less of me for. Especially them. For years I've held Benedict partly responsible for something he knew nothing about. I should have trusted him. I didn't.'

Trust wasn't his strong suit. He knew it. Everyone knew it.

'You could ask for your cousin's forgiveness,' she suggested.

Theo snorted. 'Yeah, that'll fix it.'

'It might.'

'You know *nothing*, Moriana! Why are we even talking about this?'

'Because you're upset and I want to help you!' Her temper rose to match his. 'It may have escaped your notice but it hasn't escaped mine that I still don't know what the hell you're talking about. Why do you limit yourself and not share a problem? Why do you limit *me*?'

'You're not limited!' *Here* was the fiery boy she remembered from childhood. The one who fought and scrapped and roared. 'Whatever you want to do, *you do*. My palace is open to you for reorganisation, my regiments mobilised at your request, education and health reports sit on your desk. Every time you want me to put my hands on you, *I do*. There is nothing I wouldn't do for you!'

'Except confide in me.'

'I do confide in you. I just did! The details are irrelevant. My uncle is dead and I will not grieve for him. Benedict is gone, and I don't blame him and I can't fix it. Enough! I bend for you, I do. Come on, Moriana, *please*. You need to bend too.'

She looked away rather than continuing to burn beneath the fierceness of his gaze. His cousin was gone, his uncle was dead and she was making things worse.

'I'm sorry; you're right. I came in here to see if there was anything you needed me to do. I didn't come here to push or to argue with you, and you never asked for my company in the first place, and I have no experience with grief other than when my mother passed and I remember when you made me sit at her funeral and gave me a glass of water and it was just what I needed and right now I want to give you just what you need and I'm not, and I'm sorry, and I'm babbling and I need to stop right now and leave you be.' She dug her nails into her palm and tried to find her lost composure. It was definitely time for her to leave. 'I apologise. I'll try to do better next time.'

She set her glass down and headed for the door, her back ramrod-straight and her heart thundering. She'd screwed up. Talked too much. Made things worse, not better. *Stop, Moriana. Don't panic. Breathe.*

He hadn't made her take the damn ring off. Not yet, at any rate.

She had her hand on the brass doorknob and another breath of air in her lungs when his palm snaked out to slam against the door and keep it shut. She hadn't heard him move, she'd been too busy berating herself, but she felt his arms come around her and saw his other hand land on the other side of the door, trapping her between his big body and smooth oak.

'Stay.' His breath warmed her cheek. 'Please. I know I'm not good company, just… I don't want to be alone.'

It wasn't the same as *I want you to stay because you're the only one for me* but she stilled her hand on the doorknob nonetheless. *Stay. Concentrate on the request and leave his reasoning the hell alone.*

'Stay,' he said again, and she closed her eyes as he pressed his lips to her neck. 'Sit with me, read with me, curse me. Just don't leave.'

She pressed her forehead to the door and let her body melt into his. 'I don't want to. I'm trying to be what you need.'

She turned and brought her lips to his, to offer comfort and a way for him to forget, and he took to the kiss like a dying man to water. There was no finesse, no les-

son here, only need and heat and Moriana was powerless in the face of it.

He picked her up and carried her to the overstuffed
leather daybed, all without releasing her mouth. She
ended up stretched out beneath him, her fingers at his
collar and tie and then his jacket as she slid it from
his shoulders, but her dress stayed on and her jewellery
stayed on and her hair stayed up.

She raised her hands to one earring and began to
take it off, but he shook his head and clenched his jaw.

'Leave them on.'

'I can't.' She had one earring out before he'd even
sat up. 'The jewellery's too valuable to lie on and the
gown is heavier than it looks. I want them gone.' She
took the other earring out and held them in one hand as
she fumbled with the clasp on the necklace. It was too
complicated, never meant for the wearer alone to take
off, and certainly not in a hurry. 'Please.' She captured
his mouth again with hers, soft and crushed where he
was hard and demanding. Willing. And he was still willing too, was he not? 'I don't want the worry of them.'

She needed him to know that there was a woman beneath the perfect princess image.

'Turn around.'

'One of my favourite phrases. Who knew?' she said
raggedly but she turned around so he could remove the
necklace. The zip was to the side of the gown but he
found it without prompting and she held her breath as he
slid it down her side and over her hip. She let the dress
fall to the floor and there was no bra to bother with,
only panties and high heeled shoes, and she slipped out
of those too, before he could say *leave them on*.

She wanted nakedness and skin on skin and nothing
between them but sweat and sweet promises.

'Still every inch a princess,' he offered when she turned around to face him, but he stepped in closer and slid his hand up and around the nape of her neck. 'It's in the curve of your neck.' His hand slid around to the front and his thumb tilted her head until she raised her eyes to his. 'And the tilt of your jaw. It's in your heart.' Fingertips slid back down her throat and over her curves until he flattened his palm just below her breast. 'My heart now.'

Because it was.

Another kiss. A ragged sigh.

He reached for his cufflinks and then for his belt and shortly thereafter he too stood naked and proud, pinning her with his hungry gaze. She was ready for whatever came next. Mindless pleasure and the losing of self. She could help him there.

He drew her down onto the leather daybed, on his back with her half draped over him. He ran his hand from neck to flank and then urged her leg up and over his exquisitely hard body, opening her up but not boxing her in, pressing against her but not pushing in.

'That's it,' he murmured into her mouth but she was through with being schooled by him.

She dragged her lips from his and started again at his shoulder, tasting his skin until she reached his pebbled nipple. She closed her mouth over him and sucked, darkly pleased when his breath left his body with a whoosh and his head dropped back on the bed.

Moriana rubbed her cheek against his skin as his body bowed towards her, releasing the tight little nub in favour of settling herself across him more fully. He let her wriggle until she'd found the most comfortable place to sit, and it was like the rubbing lesson all over again, with her finding friction against the silken hardness of his erection. She looked down towards where they weren't quite joined as intimately as she wanted them to be and swallowed hard at the sight. There was so *much* of him still visible, and how it was *ever* going to fit was still a mystery to her at this point.

She wasn't scared, but she could admit to being ever so slightly daunted.

He'd been over every inch of her body with lips and hands but he'd always pulled back from truly claiming her. She'd thought he was waiting until after the wedding, part of his royal need for legitimate heirs, but now she wondered if he hadn't simply been letting her get used to the idea of something that size going places no man had ever been.

'Are you sure about this?' There was no judgement in his quiet question.

'I want to. You want to forget, right? This is how you do it.'

'I won't forget this,' he said, his eyes darkening. 'We need to get you ready.'

'I'm ready.'

'Not quite. You're still capable of thought.'

Five minutes later, that was no longer a problem. He'd used his fingers to tease and tempt and stretch and a wave of pleasure hovered just out of reach. Skin on skin, one hand soothing as the other inflamed, he murmured nonsense words of encouragement as she took him in hand and lined him up until she felt the wide, wet press of him against her opening. Her gaze met his and his eyelashes fluttered as she gained an inch. She bit her lip, because there was no way this didn't hurt, but he'd never been wrong about pleasure yet and if she could just get *past* this first bit she'd be fine.

She willed herself to relax and gained another inch

that felt like a mile and lost her breath somewhere along the way. No more, surely, except he was less than half-way in and she was stuck. 'I—help?'

He took control, hands that had been quietly strok-ing and coaxing, turning firm as he cupped her buttocks and slid her off him, not all the way but enough that she could breathe.

'Circle your hips.' Big hands guided her way and slickness returned and this time when she slid back down on him she ventured further. This time he helped by drawing back before she did, his palm coming to cover her belly and his thumb gently pressing down on her sensitive flesh. 'Better?'

They were going to be here all night.

'You're thinking again,' he rumbled.

'Patience isn't one of my gifts.'

His eyes warmed. 'I have enough for both of us.'

He pulled out as he rolled her beneath him and slid down her body, proceeding to turn her into a mind-less, writhing wreck again. This time when he rose back up and entered her it was easier. Slowly, inexorably, he worked his way in and somewhere along the way he stopped being so careful and she stopped worrying about pain versus pleasure, because the pleasure was back and it was constant.

She tilted her hips and he groaned and she thought he might have been seated to the hilt, but then he wrapped his hand beneath one of her knees and brought her leg up and thrust, and *now* he was all the way in and it was tight, and breathtakingly good.

For her, at any rate.

It was more intimate than anything she'd ever experi-enced with him. His previous lessons in sexual exploration had been fun, heady and all too often overwhelming. This was soul-stealing.

She would have more of it.

She drew him closer, sipped delicately at his lips and then licked within. He'd never been more beautiful to her than he was at this moment, his tightly controlled movements bound only by his will.

'Please,' she whispered, because surely he needed more than this. His focus had never wavered from his quest to make this good for her, not once. When did he get to let go and feel? 'I'm really, *really* ready.'

His lips quirked above hers. 'What would you have me do?'

'Move.'

The man could follow direction when he wanted to. He raised himself to his knees, still inside her, one hand to her hip and the other to her nub, and he moved. Every stroke sent a tremor through her, every slide and every breath wound her tighter as he coaxed her to a rhythm she somehow already knew. Sensation piled in on her—it was too much, too good, and she wasn't a quiet lover, she discovered, but neither was Theo. The flush on his cheekbones had spread down his neck and across his chest, a sheen of sweat made his skin glow, and there was nothing she wanted more than to see him come undone.

'Tell me what you need.' His voice was hoarse but his eyes spoke true. He meant it.

'Give me all of you.' They were thoughtless words but true. He stilled above her and then with a groan that choked out like a sob he let go of his restraint.

It took him less than half a dozen savage thrusts before she felt her body clamp around him. She tightened unbearably as the rest of her scattered to the four winds.

There was no thought beyond this, and him, and when he followed moments later she could have sworn she could feel him spilling into her, claiming and being claimed in equal measure.

'This. I need this, whatever this is,' she whispered against his shoulder and his arms tightened around her. 'Let me love you.'

CHAPTER TEN

MORIANA WAS SILENT in the aftermath, but it wasn't the comfortable, sated silence a man could fall asleep in. This silence was prickly, tense, and for the first time in forever Theo wondered if he'd done wrong by a woman sexually. Had he been too reckless, too forceful, too greedy? Or all of those things? Because with Moriana involved all bets were off. Smoothness deserted him and neediness ruled.

Self-control fled when passion crept in.

He could barely believe she was his.

She'd curled into his side, her cheek to his shoulder and her hair a rampant tumble of curls. Her limbs were curled around his and the evidence of their joining lay wet between them both.

'You okay?' he asked gruffly, when what he wanted to ask was, *Was I good enough for you? Do you still want me the way you did before? Have you changed your mind about all this?*

He tightened his arm around her and ran his fingers over the knuckles of the hand she'd placed on his chest, which led him to the ring she wore, the one he'd chosen for his Queen. It was about time he admitted to himself that Moriana had always been there in the back of his mind. Practically perfect. Unobtainable. Already taken.

And claimed now, by him.

He turned, ever so slightly, and pressed a kiss into her hair. 'Have I rendered you speechless?'

'No, just sated. And thinking.'

'Thinking what?'

'That making love to you was more than I ever imagined. And I imagined a lot.'

He could stand to hear a little more. He brushed his fingers over her ring, loving that she'd chosen to wear it. 'When did you decide?'

'Oh.' Her fingers curled into themselves a little but he wasn't having it; he wanted their fingers entwined and now they were. 'Well. Today some time, around about the time you delivered that foal, or a little bit before then. After letting me at the Crown Jewels but before the dinner. And then the petition to remove you because you weren't married got resurrected and I figured—'

'You figured *what*?'

'I figured now would be a good time to tell you I was ready,' she said.

He pulled away. Not hard but enough for him to see her face. Such a beautiful face. The one that now haunted his dreams.

'You knew the petition had landed.'

'I—'

He could see the truth in her eyes.

'I knew,' she said.

'Get up.' True rage had always settled on him cold rather than hot. 'Get dressed. I don't need you to marry me because it's your royal duty to shore up my reign.'

'I'm not.'

'Get up! Get dressed. And *get out*. Do you think I want you to do this because duty compels you to? Moriana the perfect, Moriana the good. For God's sake, for once in your life *do what you want!*'

'I did! I am! And if you can't see that you're blind. I love you, Theo. Wholly and without caveats, but no. You can't have that. I'd get too close.' She picked up his trousers and threw them at him. '*You* get out. You're the one who can't stand being here with me like this. Give you a reason, any reason, to mistrust a person and you're there, filling in the blanks. You did it with Benedict. You're doing it with me. So get out and take your conspiracies with you and leave me alone.'

He got up. He put his trousers on and reached for his shirt. 'Moriana—'

'Get out! You don't *see* what other people want you to see. You couldn't accept love if someone laid it at your feet. Benedict loves you. I love you, but no. You can't see past your own towering mistrust.'

'Moriana, I—'

'Please go.' She picked up her dress. 'I don't want to talk to you right now. Just go. And in the morning I'll go.' He looked at her, just looked at her, and, to his utmost horror, got to see Moriana, perfect Princess of Arun, break wide open.

'For heaven's sake, Theo, get out,' she screamed. *'Can't you see I'm giving you exactly what you want?'*

He got out.

He went back to his rooms and sent Aury to her, and Sam to her, and food to her. Everything he could think of except himself.

And then he too held his head in his hands and broke.

She should have seen it coming. Moriana stood at a window in the Queen's suite and looked out over the grounds below, bathed in soft morning light. She'd showered already this morning, and twice last night, but her body still ached in places it had never ached before, and her feelings kept slipping to the surface, bringing hot tears she couldn't afford to show. She *had* seen this coming— Theo's inability to let her into his life and share his innermost thoughts and feelings. And then she'd gone and fallen deeply in love with him anyway.

She's it for me.

That was the moment she'd lost all caution. But those words weren't the same as *I'll fight my demons for you.* They weren't *I'll never hurt you.* Quite the opposite, in fact.

Moriana stared down at the ring on her finger, tracing it with unsteady fingers, twisting it round and round. She'd take it off soon and leave it sitting on the dresser in its box. Engaged for less than twenty-four hours. A new record for Moriana of Arun. The illustrious members of the press were going to crucify her and she could barely raise the will to care.

Let them.

'Milady, will you be breakfasting with the King this morning or shall I see to it that breakfast is served here?' said a voice from the far corner of the room, and she turned and there stood Aury in the doorway, still sleepy and dressed in her nightgown. Aury, who'd come for Moriana last night and got her back to the Queen's quarters with a minimum amount of fuss, and who'd then firmly shut everyone else out and earned Moriana's undying gratitude.

And then Aury had left too, with a sympathetic smile and eyes sure with the knowledge that some things were best worked through alone.

Breakfast. Right. She'd never felt less hungry but it was the principle of the matter. Hearts got given and sometimes those holding them didn't know how to keep them safe, and the sun still rose.

'I'll be having breakfast here, please, Aury. Just some fruit and coffee.'

'No bacon?' Aury shot her a pleading look. 'Bacon on sourdough, with the heritage tomatoes and mushrooms from the gardens. Not that I'm mourning the impending loss of such bounty. At all.'

'All right, that too. And the yoghurt and the passionfruit and the black sapote.'

'Oh, *yes*,' said Aury. 'And about that outfit you're wearing… It's perfect. Very sensual. Very confident.'

'Good.' Because she wasn't inclined to take it off. The sundress was another from her never-worn-before collection, bright orange and red silks and chiffons, unapologetically fitted to make the most of her curves, and she'd pulled her hair into an untamed ponytail and secured it with a white silk scarf. 'It's the new me.' Moriana liked being confident in her sensuality, a virgin no more. 'I guess I have Theo to thank for that.'

'Or we could call him an emotionally stunted imbecile and not thank him at all,' offered Aury. 'Just a thought.'

But Moriana shook her head and turned back to the view out of the window and the weak sun on her face. 'Let's not. Theo's taught me a lot this week, and a lot of it was good.' He'd encouraged her to think more of herself and she couldn't regret that. He'd shown her how to embrace her sensuality and make a man fall apart in her arms and she'd never regret that. He'd stolen her heart, and that was unfortunate given that he didn't seem to want it, but at least now she knew love in all its passionate, painful brightness.

And she refused to regret that.

Only the wearing of the ring had been a mistake, and that was easily fixed. All she had to do was take it off.

Word came with breakfast that Theo's helicopter would be at her disposal from nine a.m. onwards. Aury received the message in silence and Moriana acknowledged it with a cool nod. Only when Moriana bade the guards to leave the room and shut the door behind them did her brittle façade drop. She'd been hoping Theo would come for her this morning, ask to see her, maybe even be contrite when it came to their harsh words spoken last night. She wanted him to fight for her love. He was a fighter, was he not? A master strategist who knew what everyone else at the table wanted?

She guessed not.

She took the ring off and set it on the table and Aury looked at it and sighed. 'So that's it?'

Moriana nodded, not trusting herself to speak.

'You could talk to him,' Aury suggested carefully.

'I have talked.' And loved, and given him her all and discovered herself stronger for it. 'Marriages are built on trust and Theo trusts no one. I'm worth more than he's offering and I don't want to compromise.'

'Good for you.' But Aury looked as miserable and uncertain as Moriana felt. 'His loss.'

A knock on the door drew their attention—and Moriana's hope—but it was only the newspapers for the day and she sent them away unread.

'I've grown,' she told the uncharacteristically silent Aury.

'I'll say.'

'For the better, I hope.'

'Definitely for the better.' Aury smiled and it was small but genuine. 'So, this foreign palace for a week was adequate but ultimately unsatisfying.' She waved her hand dismissively at the chandeliers and the light streaming in through gauze-curtained windows. 'We can do far better than this. Perhaps somewhere with more sunshine and fewer kings.'

'I think perhaps the south of France.' Moriana could get behind that. 'Sun, fun and healing.'

'Please let there also be retail therapy,' added Aury.

'There can be. I'll sell a painting.'

'We could go there directly.' Aury never complained of rapid changes in plans; she embraced them. 'It would take one phone call to get the villa up and running.'

'Do it.' Maybe there could even be hedonism and debauchery and falling in love all over again with someone new.

Doubtful, but still… Better than thinking she was going there to mourn the loss of a future that would have been a perfect fit.

Had Theo loved her.

'Pack light for us both and have Sam send the rest back to Arun.' There was no point staying where she wasn't wanted. 'We leave at half nine.' Long enough to pen thank you notes for the staff who had attended her so well during her stay. Long enough to draw up a plan for exhibiting those heritage gowns and to hand it over to Letitia, who might see it done.

'Good plan,' said Aury. 'Consider it done. Would you like me to call Arun and let them know?'

'Yes, but I don't want to talk to anyone.' She couldn't deal with speaking to either Augustus or her father right now. She had no strength left for flippant defences or breezy reassurances. 'If Augustus wants to talk, he can call Theo. Tell them I'm busy seducing the unwary and I'll call once we get to France and I have a spare moment.'

'You do realise your brother will have a fit when he learns the engagement is off?' Aury warned.

'His choice.' Moriana tried to shrug off her guilt at disappointing her family and almost succeeded. 'I tried to fit in here and didn't succeed. I hurt, I bleed, I make mistakes and love unwisely. No one's perfect and I'm through with trying to be. I'm me. And they can take me or leave me.'

Theo handed Moriana into the helicopter and tried not to let his terror show. This past week had been more intense than he ever could have imagined. Laughter and luxury, anguish and self-loathing, argument and unbearable intimacy—he'd been bombarded by emotion, and he still hadn't told Moriana how much she meant to him.

Oh, he'd shown it in a thousand wordless ways but Moriana didn't speak the language he'd perfected back when there was no one to talk to and no one he could trust and the only way to show favour was by deed. He could have trusted Benedict, had he known then what he knew now, but he hadn't, and that was a stain on his conscience that was destined to spread. He trusted Moriana more than he'd ever trusted anyone, and he loved her beyond measure, but he couldn't find the words, and here he was putting her into a helicopter similar to the one that had taken his family and all he could think was *Never again*. He couldn't go through that again.

They'd travelled from palace to palace by helicopter to get here but that was different. He'd been going with her then. He wasn't the one on the ground about to look skyward.

'Don't go.'

She either hadn't heard him above the noise of the rotor blades or she didn't understand. He leaned closer, caught her arm and figured he must look like a madman. 'Go by car, by train, by damn horse—anything but this. My family died like this and my uncle arranged it. Don't leave in a helicopter. I can't stand it. I can't lose you too.'

He saw her eyes, dark and startled. And then she was out of the helicopter and tilting forward as she strode towards the castle, turning when within safe distance to draw a line across her throat for anyone watching. *This flight wasn't happening, cut the engine, stand down, at ease.*

He'd never felt less at ease.

He strode from the courtyard, Moriana silent at his side, keeping pace with him but only just. They passed Sam, who stood at the doorway but she chose not to make eye contact and neither did any of his security detail. Good call. What could he tell them that they didn't already know? The Princess wasn't leaving as arranged.

He kept his silence as they walked to his rooms. Moriana kept her confusion to herself, faltering only when they were away from prying ears and eyes and he'd shut the door behind them.

When he turned back around she stood by the fireplace, hands clasped in front of her and her stance so regal and assured that he knew she was quailing inside.

'What was that?'

That was him, trying to make things right with her, only it was entirely possible that he needed to do some more explaining. 'I didn't want you to go. Not like that.'

'Your office organised that flight. *You* authorised it.' Her voice held a hint of disbelief.

'I know. I changed my mind. I had a flashback to the day my family died and... I may have lost faith in helicopter travel. A little.'

There was no objection from her there.

'Your uncle did what?' she asked tentatively.

Theo pocketed his hands and nodded. It was now or never, and never wasn't an option with this woman. 'The day my family died I was meant to be on that helicopter too. The trip had been planned as a family outing, but I was wilder then and not always inclined to obey my parents. Benedict had turned up and talked me into going to the races with him. Fortune had favoured me—that's what they said. I had a bad case of survivor guilt—that's what Benedict said. It wasn't until years later that the information came to light that the helicopter had been tampered with and my uncle was behind it. He wanted the throne. He'd have kept it if not for me.'

'And do you think this helicopter has been tampered with too?'

'No. Nothing like that.' He'd been standing there, watching her leave, and fear had snaked into him and squeezed. 'But all of a sudden I couldn't stand to watch you leave in one. My uncle's gone. Benedict's gone. I've only just claimed you and you were leaving too. I couldn't let you.'

He wanted her to talk now, to gently guide him, to be his muse but she stayed silent.

'I always assumed that Benedict had known of his father's plans and had…saved me…or something. I realised yesterday that Benedict knew nothing. He just wanted someone to go to the races with. When Benedict realised what his father had done, and that I'd thought him complicit, he disavowed us both. Who could blame him? But it made me realise that I should have trusted him. I could have talked to him more, not kept everything to myself. That's not a mistake I want to make with you. I trust you. I need you to know what I think of you.'

'Go on,' she said warily, looking for all the world as

if she expected him to list a dozen faults in minute detail, but that wasn't where he was going with this at all.

'You think I don't know how to love you but I do,' he began. 'You don't know whether I enjoyed this past week or not but it's the best week I've ever had, and as for the sex…the sex is incandescent. I don't get lost in it the way I used to but that's only because there's never a moment when I can't see you and feel you and want you. That connection to you means everything to me. I want you at my side more than ever and I've wanted *that* since I was fourteen years old.' He took a deep breath and ploughed on. 'I love you and never want to lose you the way I've lost so many others, and sometimes that's going to mean that I haul you off a helicopter for no good reason other than I'm scared.'

'You love me?'

'So much. And I would spend my life trying to make you happy and proud of me, and maybe sometimes you'd have to poke and prod before I let you into my thoughts, but I'd do it. For you I'd do it. For us. And I know I've never asked properly, but I'm asking it of you now. Please will you marry me?'

She ventured forward, tentatively at first, but by the time she reached for his tie and wound it around her fist and reeled him in she was smiling. 'I'm going to hold you to the sharing part, and the loving part. And the having fun. And there should definitely be more lessons. Yes, I'll marry you,' she said, and kissed him and it felt like coming home.

'I'll drive you to Arun later,' he promised. 'Or we'll both go by helicopter. Okay?'

'I'm a little busy here.' Unbuttoning his shirt, yes. Why wasn't he *helping* with that? 'We should travel to Arun tomorrow.'

'We *should*.' She'd discovered his belt buckle and his rapidly rising appreciation.

'I have a form letter to write today,' she continued as she took him in hand. '*I, Moriana, the almost Perfect, take you, Theo, the mostly Magnificent*—this is where you write your name—*to have and to hold and never let go. Know that when you place your trust in me I will never let you down or give you cause to doubt my allegiance. You're mine and I'm yours and with you at my side I feel invincible.*' She smiled and he was powerless to stop himself pressing his lips to that generous curve. 'That should worry you.'

'It doesn't,' he murmured, with a kiss for the dimple at the corner of that smile.

'I'll make you proud.'

'You always do.' She didn't know her own worth but he had a lifetime in which to convince her of it. 'You make me strong.'

'You've always been that.'

'Not always.' Sometimes he'd been lost. 'I've never been surer of anyone. I've never been more prepared to make a spectacle of myself in pursuit of you. I love you.'

She lifted her hand to his cheek and brought her forehead to his. 'I love you too.'

CHAPTER ELEVEN

MORIANA LOOKED IN the gilt-edged mirror and a royal bride stared back at her. The gown glowed with a faint ivory sheen, the bodice and waist crafted to fit and the skirt flaring gently to flow like water when she walked. Her tiara glittered with centuries-old Arunian diamonds and her veil was currently pushed back to show her face. Today was the day and although Letitia fussed and Aury sighed, Moriana had never missed her mother more.

It was four weeks to the day since Theo had buried his uncle, with full State Honours. Three weeks and six days since Theo and Benedict had settled their differences by getting royally drunk after the funeral and facing off against each other in the palace vegetable garden, wielding antique swords and shields that neither of them could lift and wearing helmets that rendered them blinder than they already were.

They'd been aided in their reconciliation efforts by their capable and significantly less inebriated seconds, namely one Princess Moriana of Arun, who stood for the King, and commoner Enrique Cordova, who stood for Prince Benedict. Moriana liked Enrique—he balanced Benedict's acerbic wit and volatile disposition with dry good humour and unshakeable calm.

Theo had knighted Enrique just prior to the duel, although to what Order was anyone's guess. No one remembered the finer points.

What Moriana did remember was Benedict and Theo stretched out on the ground staring at the sky and ragged words dredged from somewhere deep within both of them.

Words like, 'I still love him, even though I hate him for what he did.'

Words like, 'You could stay on. You and your Knight.'

By morning Theo had a best man and Benedict had his cousin back. In the past weeks they'd reconnected and Liesendaach had loudly rejoiced that the rift that had come between the two cousins these past years had been mended.

Long live antique swords, alcohol and forgiveness.

If Theo had Benedict at his side today, Moriana had Aury—who would not stop nervously double-guessing the stylists and dressers until forced to desist by the ever-wise Letitia. The older woman took control, and by the time they were ready to leave for the cathedral both bride and bridesmaid looked their absolute best.

The spectacle that greeted them as they stepped from the palace and headed for the closed bridal carriage made the breath catch in her throat. She'd grown used to having a mounted guard these past three weeks as she'd journeyed from Arun's palace to Liesendaach's. She and three hundred of Arun's finest black warhorses had been met at the border of the two countries by three hundred of Liesendaach's matching greys—and then all six hundred mounted guards had accompanied her the rest of the way, with the big greys leading the way and the black steeds protecting the rear.

A circus had nothing on the last three weeks of travel. On the jousting and melee demonstrations the horsemen put on each evening for the gathering crowds. On the way Theo often turned up at the end of the day and rode with her for the last hour so that when they stopped he could help her from her horse and lavish her with a meal provided by a local hotelier or innkeeper.

Today, though, the mounted guards had opted for a different formation. The six steeds pulling the carriage were all black, but the rest of the guards had formed in groups of four. Grey, black, black, grey—two countries entwined and stronger for it.

She had all of this and at the end of the day she would have a man who worshipped her body and kept her warm and looked at her as if she hung the moon.

It was two hours to the cathedral, with the horses moving at a fast walk. They'd debated taking a car instead but Moriana had insisted that tradition be upheld. They had water in the carriage and biscuits that would leave no stain if dropped on clothes. They had a computer and could watch the procession on the news, and wasn't that a surreal experience? Watching an aerial view of the crowds lining the streets, and the horses and her father and brother at the head of the guard coming into view, being talked about in glowing terms, and then seeing the carriage come into view and knowing she was *in* the carriage.

She watched as various guests made their way into the cathedral. Watched as Theo and Benedict arrived by Bentley and smiled and joked as they strode up the steps, only for the cathedral to then swallow them too.

The press were being more than kind to Moriana today—it seemed she could do no wrong. From her choice of wedding gown, courtesy of the coffers of Liesendaach's costume collection, to the clear happiness of King Theodosius—every wedding choice she'd made had been celebrated and embraced.

The old Moriana would have revelled in the honeymoon period with the press. The new Moriana had been too damn *happy* to give it more than a passing thought.

And then it was time to touch up her make-up and bring the veil down over her face, and to take her bouquet of white roses from their storage place and let Aury alight before her to pave the way for Moriana's appearance.

With her father on one side and her brother on the other, she stepped out of the carriage and into first her father's arms and then her brother's.

'Do you feel loved yet?' Augustus asked drily, because as far as he was concerned the past three weeks had been one long, loving, expensive farewell. 'Or would you like even more adulation?'

'You can tell me I'd make our mother proud of me today and that you're going to miss me like crazy,' she suggested, and blinked back sudden tears when her ultra-reserved brother did exactly that.

The veil brushed her face as Aury made last-minute adjustments to its fall. Finally the flowers, veil, the train of her gown, *everything* was perfect as Moriana started up the stairs on her father's arm. They stopped at the cathedral doors and waited for the signal to continue.

Moriana had practised for this moment. In the flesh and in her head, more times than she could count. But nothing had prepared her for the roar of the crowd and the butterflies in her heart as the bishop appeared and beckoned them inside.

'Are you ready?' asked her father quietly.

'I love him.'

'Then you're ready.'

She didn't remember how she walked up that aisle, only that the choir sounded like angels and the ceiling soared and light shone down on everyone from behind stained glass windows and not for a moment did she falter. Theo was waiting for her, Theo was there, in full black military uniform, weighed down with military braid, medals and insignias. He was every inch the royal figurehead, and then he turned to her and smiled and it was wicked and ever so slightly sweet, and *there* was the man she wanted to spend the rest of her life with.

She remembered very little of kneeling and taking her vows. She did remember the ring sliding onto her finger and sliding a similar ring onto Theo's finger and she definitely remembered the lifting of her veil and the wonder in Theo's eyes as he kissed her.

'You're mine now.' His hands trembled in hers and she was grateful for that tiny show of frailty, just for her. It matched her own.

'I really am. For the rest of our lives.'

'I love you,' he whispered as they turned to face the congregation and beyond. 'And I'm yours.'

* * * * *

MILLS & BOON

Coming next month

IMPRISONED BY THE
GREEK'S RING
Caitlin Crews

Atlas was a primitive man, when all was said and done. And whatever else happened in this dirty game, Lexi was his.

Entirely his, to do with as he wished.

He kissed her and he kissed her. He indulged himself. He toyed with her. He tasted her. He was unapologetic and thorough at once.

And with every taste, every indulgence, Atlas felt.

He felt.

He, who hadn't felt a damned thing in years. He, who had walled himself off to survive. He had become stone. Fury in human form.

But Lexi tasted like hope.

"This doesn't feel like revenge," she whispered in his ear, and she sounded drugged.

"I'm delighted you think so," he replied.

And then he set his mouth to hers again, because it was easier. Or better. Or simply because he had to, or die wanting her.

Lexi thrashed beneath him, and he wasn't sure why until he tilted back his head to get a better look at her face. And the answer slammed through him like some kind of cannonball, shot straight into him.

Need. She was wild with need.

And he couldn't seem to get enough of it. Of her.

The part of him that trusted no one, and her least of all, didn't trust this reaction either.

But the rest of him—especially the hardest part of him—didn't care.

Because she tasted like magic and he had given up on magic long, long time ago.

Because her hands tangled in his hair and tugged his face to hers, and he didn't have it in him to question that.

All Atlas knew was that he wanted more. Needed more.

As if, after surviving things that no man should be forced to bear, it would be little Lexi Haring who took him out. It would be this one shockingly pretty woman who would be the end of him. And not because she'd plotted against him, as he believed some if not all of her family had done, but because of this. Her surrender.

The endless, wondrous glory of her surrender.

Continue reading
IMPRISONED BY THE
GREEK'S RING
Caitlin Crews

Available next month
www.millsandboon.co.uk

LET'S TALK

Romance

For exclusive extracts, competitions
and special offers, find us online:

f facebook.com/millsandboon

⬚ @millsandboonuk

🐦 @millsandboon

Or get in touch on 0844 844 1351*

For all the latest titles coming soon, visit
millsandboon.co.uk/nextmonth

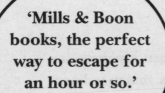